FALKIRK COMMUNITY TRUST

30124 03144654 7

USA ... ...e h...
first book when she was th... ...
people grew up t... ...
doesn't have ... ...get a ... job. A fo... ...kindergarten
teacher and workshop leader, she swapped storytelling
to kids for writing romance, and now she writes romantic
comedies and romantic suspense. Rita lives in Georgia
with her family. She loves to hear from readers, so please
visit her website, ritaherron.com

Carol Ericson is a bestselling, award-winning author of
more than forty books. She has an eerie fascination for
true-crime stories, a love of film noir and a weakness for
reality TV, all of which fuel her imagination to create her
own tales of murder, mayhem and mystery. To find out
more about Carol and her current projects, please visit
her website at carolericson.com, 'where romance flirts
with danger.'

D0674569

Also by Rita Herron

Mysterious Abduction
Left to Die
Protective Order
Suspicious Circumstances
Redemption at Hawk's Landing
Safe at Hawk's Landing
Hideaway at Hawk's Landing
Hostage at Hawk's Landing
Cold Case at Camden Crossing
Cold Case at Carlton's Canyon

Also by Carol Ericson

Evasive Action
Chain of Custody
Unravelling Jane Doe
Buried Secrets
Enemy Infiltration
Undercover Accomplice
Code Conspiracy
Delta Force Defender
Delta Force Daddy
Delta Force Die Hard

Discover more at millsandboon.co.uk

THE SECRET
SHE KEPT

RITA HERRON

THE SETUP

CAROL ERICSON

MIX
Paper from
responsible sources
FSC
www.fsc.org   FSC C007454

This book is produced from independently certified FSC™
paper to ensure responsible forest management.

For more information visit: www.harpercollins.co.uk/green

Printed and bound in Spain
by CPI Barcelona

MILLS & BOON

All rights reserved including the right of reproduction in whole or in part in any form. This edition is published by arrangement with Harlequin Books S.A.

This is a work of fiction. Names, characters, places, locations and incidents are purely fictional and bear no relationship to any real life individuals, living or dead, or to any actual places, business establishments, locations, events or incidents. Any resemblance is entirely coincidental.

This book is sold subject to the condition that it shall not, by way of trade or otherwise, be lent, resold, hired out or otherwise circulated without the prior consent of the publisher in any form of binding or cover other than that in which it is published and without a similar condition including this condition being imposed on the subsequent purchaser.

® and ™ are trademarks owned and used by the trademark owner and/or its licensee. Trademarks marked with ® are registered with the United Kingdom Patent Office and/or the Office for Harmonisation in the Internal Market and in other countries.

First Published in Great Britain 2021
by Mills & Boon, an imprint of HarperCollins*Publishers* Ltd
1 London Bridge Street, London, SE1 9GF

www.harpercollins.co.uk

HarperCollins*Publishers*
1st Floor, Watermarque Building,
Ringsend Road, Dublin 4, Ireland

The Secret She Kept © 2021 Rita B. Herron
The Setup © 2021 Carol Ericson

ISBN: 978-0-263-28328-0

Falkirk Community Trust	
30124 03144654 7	
Askews & Holts	
AF	£6.99
GM	

THE SECRET SHE KEPT

RITA HERRON

To my fabulous editor, Allison, who has been a steadfast supporter over the years! Thanks for helping me publish with Mills & Boon and for always being open to my ideas.

Prologue

They were all to blame.

Anger churned inside him as he stared at the invitation in his hand.

You are cordially invited to the dedication for the new Briar Ridge High School.

Please join us as we dedicate the building to those who were lost in the Briar Ridge High shooting.
Let's celebrate the beginning of a new era!

Kate McKendrick, Principal, Briar Ridge High

He balled his hands into fists. Fifteen years ago, the shooting at the school had torn the town apart. Four students had been killed, along with a teacher. Several others had been injured. Ned Hodgkins, the gunman, had turned the weapon on himself.

His classmates had seemed shocked that Ned would do such a thing. They'd been too busy attending football games, dances, and socializing to notice that Ned had been hurting.

That others had felt left out, too.

He opened the yearbook and cut out photos of all the

classmates who'd wronged Ned. Who'd wronged him. One by one, he carefully spread the pictures on his kitchen table.

They were so popular back then. But they'd been selfish.

He tapped the picture of Kate with his finger. She'd wanted to tear down the old school. To destroy the past. To wipe it away as if it never happened.

She had to pay for that.

So did the others. Each would receive their own message. But he'd start with Kate.

He turned the invitation over and began to write.

Dear Kate,
It was your fault.

He placed the invitation back inside the envelope to send to her. She wanted to forget about the past. To pretend Ned wasn't important.

No one would forget about Ned or what had happened. He wouldn't let them.

Chapter One

Kate McKendrick would never forget the terrible day Ned Hodgins shot up Briar Ridge High School. Sometimes the pain was so unbearable she couldn't breathe.

But she was a survivor. And even though surviving brought guilt, it also inspired her to do something positive for the town where she'd grown up.

Fifteen years had passed now. It was time to move on.

The sound of bus engines roaring to life blended with cheers of students as they left the building. Through her window, she watched the kids high-fiving and gathering by their vehicles to plan where they would go to celebrate.

Summer break was always exciting and meant lazy days at the river, burgers and milkshakes at Frosty's, and swimming at the swimming hole near the falls. Teachers were also anxious for a much-needed vacation from the classroom. Yet this year, the end of the school session marked the beginning of a new era.

Students and faculty would be in a new school come fall. A facility she'd pushed for as the school principal for over two years.

Not only was this old building crumbling around them, but the creek had overflowed and flooded the school. Inspectors had found mold in the walls and the health department had ruled the place a hazard, prompting the building plans to be expedited.

Truthfully, though, the parents in Briar Ridge didn't consider the school a safe place anyway. The shooting that had shattered the town still haunted residents like a black plague.

Mixed emotions filled Kate as the noise outside died down. Inside, the school felt suddenly empty. Cold. Almost eerie.

She left her office, walked into the hall and studied the memorial featuring the students who'd been lost in the shooting. Photographs of the victims hung on the wall. So many lives lost and destroyed that day. So senseless.

But the most personal loss for Kate was her mother, Elaine—a teacher at the time. Forty-five years old. Dead too soon.

She'd taken a bullet to save her students.

Kate blinked back tears. At the time, her mother's dark brown hair hadn't grayed yet, and her smile lit up the room. Every time Kate walked by her mother's English Lit classroom, she could see her mother at the chalkboard, hear her voice as she encouraged students to write their own stories.

Grief clogged her throat as memories taunted her. Her mother dancing around the kitchen at home as she helped Kate and her two best friends, Macy Stark and Brynn Gaines, stir up a batch of chocolate-chip cookies when they were little. Her mother making silly faces as they decorated Christmas stockings, made clothespin reindeer and glittery ornaments. Her mother's off-key singing as she belted out show tunes in the shower.

But the bad memories of the shooting bombarded her, obliterating the sweetness.

Kate could still hear the screams of the terrified kids when Ned Hodgkins unleashed his rage on his classmates with that .38 Special. Athletic Riggs Benford dropping to the floor as a bullet pierced his leg. Mickey Lawson's howl of pain as Ned shot him in the face. Ned turning the gun toward her and Macy. Her mother stepping between them...

Then she was falling, blood gushing from her chest where the bullet pierced her heart....

Reeling with shock, Kate fell to her knees by her mother's side, pressed her hands to her mother's chest and tried to stop the bleeding. Panicked students raced out the door and jumped through windows to escape. Ned barreled down the hallway, shooting wildly.

"Hang in there, Mama," Kate cried.

Tears blurred her mother's eyes, the unconditional love she gave to everyone shining through the pain. She squeezed Kate's hand. "Help the others, honey."

Kate shook her head. She couldn't leave her mother.

But her mother cupped Kate's face in her shaky hands. Hands that had tended to Kate's booboos and comforted her when she was sick or upset. "I love you, Kate. Go. The other kids need you."

What could she do? She was weak, unarmed, couldn't take down a shooter. But the sound of another gunshot bled through the shock immobilizing her. Then more gunfire and screams.

Her mother squeezed her hand again. "Be strong, Kate. Make something good come of this."

Choking back a sob, she ripped off her jacket, folded it and pressed it to her mother's chest. How could anything good come of this horrible, senseless violence?

"Hold on, Mom. Please... I love you."

Just as her mother told her to do, Kate ran to help the injured. Two students were carrying another guy toward the exit. A freshman was huddled in the corner, rocking herself back and forth. Kate helped her up and ushered

her into the chem lab to hide. Rushing back to the hall,
she searched for her friends Brynn and Macy, but didn't
see them. Kids bumped into her as they ran for the doors.
Another freshman had fallen in the stampede, and Kate
dragged her to the side then helped her up. As the girl ran
for the exit, Kate moved on down the hall. Cara Winthrop
lay on the floor near the cafeteria, her body still, eyes life-
less. Her boyfriend, Jay Lakewood, held her in his arms,
rocking her and crying.

Finally, a siren wailed outside. Police stormed in. An
ambulance arrived, medics and firefighters hurrying in to
help the wounded.

Kate raced back to check on her mother, but she was
too late.

Her mother looked ghostly white, her eyes staring wide
open in death.

OUTSIDE THE SCHOOL, the sound of car engines bursting to
life and peeling from the parking lot jarred Kate back to
the present. Her breathing was erratic and she was shaking. But she looked out and saw clouds forming in the sky,
casting a grayness over the treetops.

The last of the staff was also leaving.

Tonight, the mayor had called a town meeting to address
recent unrest about the plans for the new school.

When she was a little girl, Briar Ridge had been a sweet,
sleepy little vacation mountain town where tourists flocked
for the apple and pumpkin festivals in the fall and the Dog-
wood Festival in the spring. Located a few miles from Bear
Mountain, winter vacationers came for skiing and tubing
on the mountain.

Bear Mountain still attracted the winter crowd, but people tended to skirt Briar Ridge and each year the festivals

had grown smaller and smaller. Plans for new construction and homes had dwindled in the oppressive atmosphere.

In honor of her mother, Kate wanted to help restore Briar Ridge to its former glory.

Suddenly anxious to leave the deserted building, she ducked into her office to finish her paperwork before she left for the day. She noticed a stack of mail that still needed sorting. One particular envelope caught her eye because it had no postage mark. A stamp of the school logo, a black bear, marked the outside.

Nerves clawed at her as she opened the envelope and removed the invitation to the dedication for the new school. Her staff had mailed them to the entire Briar Ridge alumni.

Someone had crumpled the invitation, then refolded it and stuck it back inside the envelope.

Frowning, she flipped it over and stared at the scrawled writing on the back.

Dear Kate,
It was your fault.

Her hand shook as she searched for a signature. But it was blank.

RIGGS BENFORD STOWED his helmet and bunker gear at the firehouse, muttered goodbye to his captain and headed outside to his pickup.

He climbed into the cab, started the engine and drove toward the cabin he'd built four years ago on the edge of town. The scent of smoke and sweat permeated his skin from the fire at the abandoned chicken houses a few miles north of Briar Ridge. He definitely needed a shower before the town meeting.

The guys at the house had been talking about it all day.

Locals were still divided over supporting the new build or rallying to repair the existing problems at the old school and turn it into a viable building, perhaps a community center. Although that fight had been lost two years ago, they wanted their voices to be heard. Some even badmouthed Kate McKendrick for pushing the project through.

He hoped things didn't get out of control tonight.

An image of Kate with that fiery red hair taunted him. In high school, she'd been quiet and had kept to herself. Not his type at all. And she sure as hell wouldn't have run around with a guy with the bad reputation he had.

She'd changed since high school, though. Instead of allowing the tragedy that had taken her mother to destroy her, the young, awkward girl had become a leader in the community.

In spite of the fact that he didn't share her optimism, Riggs admired her for instigating positive changes.

The town had been mired in despair for over a decade. Not that anyone should forget the tragedy that had shattered lives, families and friendships, and stolen the innocence of children that day. But living in fear had taken its toll.

Once, people in Briar Ridge had been friendly and welcoming. They'd never locked their doors. Kids had ridden their bikes to the malt shop freely. And when school started each fall, students had raced to class in anticipation of attending football games, pep rallies and school dances.

Now, a wariness pervaded the residents and students.

Hell, he understood that wariness. He'd been a senior at the time and had been shot in the leg. He was one of the lucky ones, though. Sure, he'd had surgery and undergone months of physical therapy to walk again, but he'd recovered physically. Still, his soccer career had come to a halt in spite of the PT and he'd had nightmares of the shooting for months afterward.

Other students hadn't fared so well. The mayor's daughter Brynn had been paralyzed from the waist down. Stone Lawson's younger brother Mickey had been blinded. Another guy had PTSD and had turned to drugs. Some who'd lost loved ones had moved away while others couldn't bear to leave the area, as if leaving meant dishonoring the dead.

Even though Kate's mother had died, Kate had stayed in Briar Ridge. Mrs. McKendrick was the best teacher he'd ever had. No one knew he'd had trouble reading. Dyslexia. Kids had teased him when he was young. Called him stupid. Even his old man had when he was drunk, which was most days.

But Kate's mother had recognized his problem and tutored him in private.

She'd also tended his injuries a few times when his old man had beaten the hell out of him. No one knew about that, either. He'd begged her to keep it that way. Still, she'd talked to his mother. Fat lot of good that had done. When she'd tried to reason with his father, he'd turned his fists on her. Said she was nothing but a dumb seamstress. She'd worked at the sewing plant and made quilts to sell on the side. Riggs had thought they were pretty.

His father had said she was worthless.

Then one day she'd had enough and she'd cut and run.

His old man had blamed him for that, too. When Riggs had been shot, his old man had said he was weak. He'd left, too.

Didn't matter. He hadn't wanted him around anyway.

Shaking off the memories, Riggs parked at his house, grabbed his mail and hurried inside. The invitation to the dedication hung on his fridge, a reminder of the meeting tonight, and that alumni were coming to town for a reunion. Guilt for how he'd treated Ned Hodgkins gnawed at him. Ned hadn't fit into the group of jocks he'd hung out with.

They should have been nicer to him, though, but they'd been young and stupid. They'd never considered how adversely their behavior had affected Ned. No one had.

Until it was too late.

They'd been paying for it ever since.

THE WIND WHISTLED shrilly off Bear Mountain, storm clouds casting a gray across the town as Kate veered into the parking lot at the town hall. Some of the older businesses had fallen into disrepair. Awnings and buildings needed painting, as if they, too, felt the weight of the town's burden. Even the town hall needed a facelift.

Trees swayed in the wind, scattering dust and debris; a soda can someone had discarded rolled across the street. Cars and trucks filled the lot, indicating a crowd had showed up for the meeting.

A frisson of nerves slithered through Kate. She hoped the attendees were congenial but braced herself for animosity. The climate over the changes she'd proposed and pushed through had created an avalanche of mixed reactions for months.

Shoulders knotted, she scanned the parking lot in search of trouble. People gathered on the steps to the building, while others hovered beneath the live oaks, hunched in conversation.

The cryptic message she'd received replayed in her mind. She leaned her forehead against her steering wheel and inhaled a calming breath.

It was your fault.

God... She had blamed herself so many times for her mother's death. For Ned going ballistic.

Two days before the shooting, he'd invited her to the school dance. She'd been so engrossed in studying for her SATs that she'd said no without giving it a second thought.

According to Ned's brother Billy, her rejection had tipped him over the edge.

A car honked and she jerked her head up. A red Trans Am veered into the parking lot, tires squealing. Billy Hodgkins threw open the door, unfolded his beefy body from the front of the car, and strode toward the door, pulling at his wooly beard. The scowl on his face sent chills down her spine. Billy and his family had moved away a few months after the shooting to escape the negative publicity and hate in the town.

But she'd never forgotten his accusations.

A gust of wind whipped at her car, and thunder rumbled in the distance. She checked her watch. Time to go inside and face the crowd.

Her mother's last words echoed in her head. *Be strong, Kate. Make something good come of this.*

She couldn't make anything good come of it. But she could try to help people move past the pain and concentrate on the future.

Another gust of wind swirled around her as she slid from her car, and she shoved her hair from her face. Determined to remain positive, she strode up the steps to the town hall and went inside. Voices and chatter rumbled from the main meeting room, and a family passed her as they entered. She took another breath, pasted on a smile and ducked into the room.

The town council members and Amy Turner, the former school counselor and head of the memorial committee, were seated on stage at the front of the room, where a seat awaited her. Amy had been in her midthirties when the shooting occurred. Like many others, she felt responsible for not recognizing the depth of Ned's depression.

She'd also reached out to Kate after her mother's death and had helped her through the grieving process.

Mayor Gaines was addressing the council as she hurried down the side aisle. Chatter and voices reverberated around her. An argument heated up somewhere near the back, and she saw Billy trying to push his way past two other men blocking his entry.

Sheriff Stone Lawson was perched in the rear by one of the doors. His deputy, Murphy Bridges, stood on the opposite side, braced to handle problems if tempers escalated out of control. Stone and Murphy had been classmates and now worked to maintain order in the town.

As Billy entered, he aimed a menacing look toward Kate. Fear fluttered in her belly as she took her seat.

Be strong, Kate.

I'm trying, Mama.

Mayor Gaines called the meeting to order then introduced the council members. "Tonight, we're here to discuss the plans for our new school. As you all know, due to the dilapidated state of the high school and the costly repairs necessary to ensure the safety of our children's health, the town council approved the funding for a new facility a while back and the new building is almost finished."

Disgruntled whispers floated through the room. Kate surveyed the group. The parents of the victims who'd died that day were present, along with family members of the ones injured. Brynn sat in the front row by her mother, her face pale, hands clenched around the arms of her wheelchair.

Kate's heart gave a pang. She missed their friendship. But when she'd dropped by the hospital to see Brynn after the shooting, Mrs. Gaines had warned Kate to stay away from Brynn. She'd tried to visit multiple times those first few months and over the years, but Mrs. Gaines had repeatedly claimed Brynn didn't want to see her.

The woman's animosity only intensified Kate's guilt.

How could Brynn forgive her for causing Ned to shoot up the school and put her in that wheelchair?

Taking deep breaths to control her emotions, she continued to scan the room.

Riggs Benford was seated behind Brynn. His big body exuded sexuality and was a palpable force of strength and energy in the room.

Kate dragged her gaze away from him. She'd always had a crush on him, but Riggs was brooding one minute and a player the next. She'd put him in the off-limits category long ago. A place where he would always stay. The fact that he'd abandoned his teenage girlfriend when she was pregnant disturbed her. But he was a kid at the time and his behavior could be forgiven.

The fact that he'd never taken responsibility for his son couldn't.

Her own father had done the same thing to her. Even though she'd never known him, it hurt to think he hadn't wanted her.

Still, Riggs wasn't all bad. He'd overcome his own injury, one that had ended his hopes of a soccer scholarship, and now he ran into burning buildings to save others.

The mayor gestured to a man seated in the front row, drawing her attention back to the meeting.

"Local builder and developer Carlton Ethridge has worked with us as an architect on the designs. Many of you already know Realtor Ling Wu, who grew up right here in Briar Ridge. Ling helped us secure a nice piece of property that offers room for growth in the future."

Someone made a rude noise. Mayor Gaines tensed. "I'm aware some of you have reservations about tearing down the old school, but please hear Principal McKendrick out. She cares about our community and our children." He tipped his head toward Kate.

She maneuvered her way to the podium, gripped the edge to steady herself, then forced a smile.

"First of all, I appreciate the fact that so many of you came tonight. I understand the town has been divided emotionally over this issue, but I believe a new building will facilitate goodwill and positive changes for all the residents and future visitors."

"You just want to forget what happened," someone shouted.

"That's not true," Kate said. "I was a student at Briar Ridge High myself. My own mother, a teacher at the school, died during the massacre. I can never forget what happened that day, nor do I believe that any of us should." Her voice rose, filled with conviction. "Lives were not only lost, but families and friendships ripped apart. Students suffered emotional trauma as well as physical injuries. None of us will ever be the same."

"That school is a monument to the ones who didn't survive," a woman cried. "My son was one of them."

Kate's heart ached for the woman, Linda Russell. Her sixteen-year-old son Hughie had had dreams of med school. Yet the building was falling apart just as the town was. "I understand that, and we're creating another memorial for the victims and their families at the new building, one I think you'll all be proud of. We plan to reveal the details at the dedication ceremony."

She glanced across the group, that cryptic message haunting her. Had someone in this room sent it?

Chapter Two

"You expect us to forget that our children died," Harold Guthrie bellowed.

In spite of his accusation, sympathy for the man welled inside Kate. Harold's seventeen-year-old daughter Agnes had been Ned's third victim. A bullet had pierced her aorta.

Kate shook her head. "No one here will ever forget that tragedy, Mr. Guthrie. But I believe it's beneficial for today's students to stop living in fear, fear created because our town still dwells on that devastating event." She pressed her hand over her chest. "That tragedy defined us, but we can't let it destroy us."

"Tearing down the school won't wipe out our grief or bring back our children," a man in the back row yelled.

"It won't stop us from being afraid when we send our babies to school," another woman shouted.

"I can't promise we won't have trouble again. No one can," Kate said earnestly. "But rest assured, we're incorporating security measures to make Briar Ridge High as safe as possible."

A tall man Kate didn't recognize stood and aimed a look at Jose Fernandez, one of the refugees who'd attended the school the year of the shooting. "Terrorists get guns past security all the time."

"My son is not a terrorist," Jose's mother said angrily.

Suddenly protests erupted.

Riggs Benford stood and waved his hand. "Kate is right. Being held hostage to fear is not living at all. We can honor those who've fallen with the new building."

The mayor's wife shot up from her seat. "It's easy for you to say that because you survived and can still walk. My daughter is confined to that chair."

"Mother!" Brynn grabbed at her mother's arm in an attempt to force her to sit. Her look of horror made Kate want to comfort her as they'd comforted each other as kids. But she sensed Brynn wouldn't want that now.

The outburst escalated, angry accusations flying through the room over who was to blame for Ned's breakdown.

The cryptic note Kate received earlier was burned into her brain. She attempted to regain control of the meeting, but no one was listening. A heated exchange in the back erupted and one man raised a fist.

Sheriff Lawson rushed to stop a fight from breaking out while Deputy Bridges made an effort to calm others. Kate's pulse pounded and she slowly backed away from the podium. Images of her classmates running and screaming flashed behind her eyes.

Her mother's blood...

The rage, and then the blank look in Ned's eyes, as if he hadn't quite comprehended what he'd done.

The gun turning on her...

Suddenly she couldn't breathe. She'd suffered from panic attacks for months after the shooting. She was on the verge of one now.

Her gaze met Riggs's for a second. Concern darkened his eyes and he stepped forward. Humiliation washed over her. She couldn't have a meltdown in front of him or any of these people.

The room was blurring, lights flickering wildly, colors

fading to black. She pushed past the other town council members and clawed her way to the side door. Instead of heading toward the front entrance where she'd have to deal with the angry crowd, she staggered toward the rear exit.

RIGGS HAD SEEN enough hotheads in his lifetime, and he didn't like the atmosphere in the room. Hell, he'd been worried about protestors, but the situation was quickly escalating to the point of violence.

Sheriff Lawson and his deputy worked to calm the outburst, and Riggs decided to check on Kate. She hadn't deserved to be under attack, not after all she'd suffered and lost.

And certainly not because of her good intentions. He'd heard she'd instigated measures to stop bullying in school and to keep troubled kids from falling through the cracks. Just like her mother, she cared about students.

And God knew, he owed her mother.

As he wove his way to the front door, he spotted classmates he hadn't seen in over a decade. Jay Lakewood, then Duke Eastman. He'd been buddies with them back in the day, but they'd lost touch over the years. He'd heard Jay had joined the military and become a bomb expert. Duke was a Navy SEAL.

Gretta Wright, another former classmate, who currently worked for the local news station, darted toward a group of angry protestors with her microphone. Gretta had started a gossip rag in high school and had made more enemies than friends whenever she threw anyone in her path under the bus for a byline.

He cut a wide berth around her and stepped into the lobby. Jay and Duke strode toward him.

"Hey, man, long time no see," Jay said.

Duke pounded him on the back. "I saw the way you

were looking at Kate. Do you have something going on with her?" he asked with a chuckle.

Riggs snorted. "She barely gives me the time of day when I see her around town."

"Guess it's your reputation as a ladies' man," Jay said with a grin.

Riggs's gut tightened. His old friend was probably right. He had made mistakes, mistakes that had cost him. "That was a long time ago. I'm not the same guy I was in high school."

Duke rubbed a hand over his stomach where his scar from the shooting would have been. "None of us is."

A tense silence fell between them for a minute, the memories returning. Good and bad.

"I'm surprised to see you two here," Riggs said.

Jay shrugged. "Figured it was time I got up the courage to come back."

That admission surprised Riggs. "You work with bombs. I didn't think you were afraid of anything."

Jay flexed his hands and looked at them, his expression strained. Riggs felt like a heel for his callous remark. Jay had escaped physically unhurt from the school shooting but psychological scars ran deep.

While Riggs had lain writhing in pain, Jay had run to tackle Ned to get his gun. But Ned had grabbed Jay's girl-friend, Cara Winthrop, as a hostage and forced everyone to back off. Then he'd shot Cara five times.

Jay had beaten himself up for years, saying he should have saved Cara.

But no one could have saved her.

"How about we grab a beer and catch up?" Duke suggested.

Riggs hesitated. "Rain check? I need to get going."

They exchanged cell numbers before Riggs hurried through the exit. The scent of impending rain swirled around him as he paused on the steps and scanned the parking lot for Kate's black SUV. He spotted it, but Kate wasn't inside.

Worry knotted his belly. She'd had time to make it to her vehicle by now. Where was she?

Adrenaline pumping through him, he darted down the steps then around the side of the structure. The parking lot was full, several people heading to their cars, some deep in conversation, others ranting about Kate.

The urge to shut them up slammed into him, but he resisted. Violence wasn't the answer.

After he'd recovered from the shooting and worked through his self-pity, he'd made it his life's work to save people, not hurt them.

Worry tightened his muscles as he jogged toward the rear of the building. Kate stood on the back stoop, leaning against the railing. She looked pale, her hands clenching the iron bars as if she needed them to hold her up.

Billy Hodgkins crept up behind Kate, his beady eyes practically disappearing in his face beneath that bushy beard. He looked like a mountain man, wild and dangerous, a predator about to pounce on his prey.

Protective instincts surged through Riggs. "Kate?" Riggs rushed toward the stoop.

Billy's head jerked up and he darted back inside the building.

Riggs climbed the bottom step. "Are you okay?"

She seemed dazed, even confused, but slowly shook her head and looked down at him. Something deep and unsettling stirred in Riggs's chest.

He'd seen that frightened look in his mama's eyes just before his daddy unleashed his temper on her. He'd hated it then.

He hated it now.

Not that Kate was fragile. But at the moment, she looked

so vulnerable and frightened, he had the insane urge to pull her into his arms and hold her.

A ridiculous thought. Kate didn't even like him.

Riggs offered his hand to her. "Let me walk you to your car."

She moved down a step, but didn't accept his hand, proving he was right. Even when she was scared, Kate didn't want anything to do with him.

KATE DRAGGED IN AIR, still battling the panic. The moment she heard Billy mutter her name, déjà vu struck her with the force of a blow to her chest.

"What did Billy say to you?" Riggs asked.

Kate bit her lower lip.

"Did he threaten you?" Riggs pressed.

Had Billy threatened her? She hadn't heard exactly what he'd said. Then Riggs had appeared. "I…he mumbled something, but I didn't catch his exact words."

"I don't trust him," Riggs said.

"Neither do I. He has a right to be at the meeting, though," she said in a low voice. "He suffered, too. His family had to live in the shadow of what Ned did."

Riggs muttered an obscenity. "Don't be naïve, Kate. That guy's a bully and always has been."

She shrugged but tensed at his tone. "Maybe. But he lost his brother that day. And everyone in town and at school treated him like he was a killer, too."

Except he'd blamed her. And, unknowingly at the time, she'd played a role in Ned's breakdown.

They reached her SUV and she leaned against the driver's door and looked up at him. Riggs had been popular in high school. As soon as he'd broken up with one girl, a string of others lined up to take her place. As far as she knew, he was still a womanizer. With his good looks and charm, women fell at his feet.

She didn't intend to be one of them.

Still, he'd turned into a town hero. And it was impossible not to notice the smoky hue of his dark brown eyes.

"I figured some people would be emotional about the demolition of the old building," Kate said. "But I didn't expect the bitterness that's surfaced."

"The town has been steeped in grief and anger for years, Kate. It's time someone forced everyone to move on."

Kate sighed. "I just want Briar Ridge to be a happy place again, for it to be like it was when I was little."

Riggs clenched his jaw. "After all that's happened, I can't believe you look at life through rose-colored glasses."

Kate tensed. He had no idea how she struggled with finding the positive. "Better than seeing the bad in everyone."

She reached inside her purse for her keys before she did something stupid like lean into Riggs for support. Her keys jangled as she removed them from her bag.

Riggs's dark gaze searched her face. "Why don't I follow you home?"

The earlier message, then the animosity at the meeting, and seeing Billy again, had shaken her to the core.

Sexy bad boy Riggs Benford was a danger of another kind.

She couldn't interpret his concern for anything more.

"I'm fine, Riggs. Thanks for walking me to my car." She didn't wait for a response. She slid into the driver's seat and waved goodbye, then slowly backed from the parking spot. More than one vehicle gave a rude honk as she passed.

Only a few days until the dedication for the new building. She refused to allow a few disgruntled residents to keep her from implementing her plans.

With the news constantly reporting about mass shootings

in other cities and towns, nerves ran high. Several students this year had visited the counselor because of anxiety issues over attending school. Students deserved to feel safe and happy. Parents deserved it, too.

A momentary tug of longing enveloped her. She didn't have children herself but her biological clock was ticking and sometimes she imagined having a little one of her own. A baby nestled in her arms. A home…

But with the craziness in the world and seeing it firsthand, she was afraid to love and lose again.

Maneuvering her way onto Main Street, she passed the park situated in the heart of town, then the library, hardware store, the ice cream shop, the Mercantile, Pearl's Dine & Pie, Joy's Fabric and Crafts, and the empty lot where the church sold pumpkins in the fall and Christmas trees in November and December.

Headlights behind her nearly blinded her, and she slowed and checked the rearview mirror. She couldn't make out the car or tell if it was following her. But it was too close for comfort.

Irritated, she pulled over in front of Briar Ridge Inn. For a moment, the car slowed beside her, and she felt eyes piercing her. She didn't recognize the dark sedan, but it was a common make and model. With dozens of visitors in town, it could even be a rental.

Finally, the car moved on. She breathed a sigh of relief then veered back onto the road. She'd almost reached her street when she smelled smoke. A second later, the scent of gas assaulted her.

Pulse clamoring, she checked the rearview mirror. Smoke seeped from the rear near the gas tank. Panic seized her. She jerked the SUV to the side of the road, threw it in Park and jumped out.

Just as her feet hit the graveled shoulder, her car burst into flames.

Chapter Three

Riggs had no idea why he was so anxious about Kate. But he despised seeing any woman attacked, physically or verbally. And some of the locals had practically assaulted her at the meeting.

Billy Hodgkins especially worried him.

Kate might believe the Hodgkins family had gotten an unfair shake, but Billy had always been trouble. Unlike his weaker brother Ned, Billy used his muscles and foul mouth to intimidate.

He'd heard Billy was a mean drunk, too. What if he showed up at Kate's?

She's not your responsibility. She doesn't even like you.

Still, he didn't turn around. He'd just stop by to see that she'd made it home safely.

An image of Kate in front of that podium taunted him, her glossy auburn hair shimmering over her shoulders, her delicate little chin jutted up as she pleaded her cause.

In high school, she'd been quiet, shy, bookish. Some kids had called her Kate the Brainiac. Other horny idiots had made crude comments about her big boobs and curves, which had made her blush. They'd wanted in her pants.

Like any red-blooded teenage boy, he'd fantasized about having sex with her, too. But Kate wasn't the type to sleep around. Somewhere deep inside, the crude comments had irked him. They'd felt…wrong.

Kate was a nice girl, the kind who deserved better than being groped in the back seat of a car.

She'd also avoided him like he was on fire. Obviously, she'd heard the rumors about him knocking up Cassidy Fulton. He had dated Cassidy. A couple of times.

Then he'd learned she was just using him. But he'd never told anyone that part. He'd been too embarrassed, had too much pride, so he'd let everyone think they were an item.

When she'd turned up pregnant a couple of months before the shooting, everyone assumed the kid was his. Hell, he'd thought it was, too. Three months after he was injured, when he was mired deep in self-pity and depression and needed something to live for, he'd insisted on a paternity test. Said if the baby was his, he'd take responsibility and marry Cassidy. But she'd laughed in his face. Told him she'd never marry a cripple.

Then the paternity test proved he wasn't the father. She'd never shared the baby daddy's name, though.

Struggling with physical therapy and the sting of her cruel comment, he hadn't bothered to correct the rumor. Worse, Gretta Wright had spread the news that he'd abandoned Cassidy and her child.

At the time, he'd shrugged it off. Had been ticked off at life and hadn't given a damn what anyone thought about him.

But he was older now and not as shallow. The shooting had changed him. Had literally altered the course of his life.

Not just because he'd taken a bullet. In the chaos of the bloody massacre, he'd felt helpless.

As he'd watched first responders rush to save lives, he'd

been awed by their courage. Later, while he lay in bed after surgery, feeling angry and hopeless, one of the firefighters had visited him at the hospital.

That day, Riggs decided he wanted to be like him. Fire-fighting required skill, physical fitness, as well as mental strength. So, he'd worked his butt off in PT to get back into shape.

Thunder rumbled, storm clouds moving in. He maneuvered a curve then turned onto the street leading to Kate's house. Smoke caught his eye. Thick plumes floated upward into the darkness. Then flames.

Pulse hammering, he pressed the accelerator and sped up. He raced around another curve, made the turn and spotted the source of the fire.

Kate's black SUV.

Fear shot through him as he swerved to the side of the road to park and dialed 9-1-1.

Was Kate inside that vehicle?

COLD FEAR ATE at Kate as she stared at the flames shooting into the sky. Red, yellow, orange...

Fire crackled and popped. Glass shattered. Heat seared her. Smoke billowed so thick she could barely breathe.

If she'd waited a few seconds longer to get out, she would have been trapped in her car.

Trembling, she reached inside her purse for her phone to call for help.

"Kate!"

A man's voice jarred her, and she spotted Riggs jogging toward her.

Firelight from the flames lit his rugged face as he approached. "Are you all right?"

She nodded numbly.

He gently took her face in his hands as if examining her. "Are you hurt?"

Smoke caught in her throat and she coughed. "No," she said in a ragged whisper.

"What happened?"

"I was driving home and suddenly smelled smoke, so I pulled over." Her legs felt weak, but she stiffened her spine in an attempt to hold herself upright.

Riggs gently rubbed her arms. "Let's move away from the fire." He coaxed her beneath a nearby tree. "Help is on the way."

She leaned against a boulder on the embankment and he knelt beside her, calming her with soft reassurances. Seconds later, a siren wailed, lights twirling against the inky sky.

"Have you had car trouble lately?" Riggs asked.

"No, that's what makes this so odd. I don't understand why it just burst into flames."

Considering the temperament of the meeting and the animosity toward Kate, suspicions snaked through Riggs.

The wail of sirens grew closer. The firetruck from his own firehouse careened up, the sheriff's squad car on its tail.

The fire engine screeched to a stop and his team jumped from the truck, geared up and ready to work. His buddy Brian spotted him and threw up a hand.

Riggs squeezed Kate's shoulder. "Are you sure you're all right?"

"Yes," Kate said, although the warble to her voice indicated she was anything but okay.

"Stay here. I'll be right back." Riggs rushed over to his friend, who was already pulling a hose from the truck.

"What happened?" Brian asked. "Where's the driver?"

Riggs relayed his conversation with Kate and described

the climate at the meeting. "This fire might not be accidental, so look for anything suspicious."

Brian's brow lifted. "You think someone tried to kill
Kate?"

Riggs shrugged. "I hope not, but we can't rule it out yet."

Concern flared in his buddy's eyes, and he gave a quick
nod. "On it." Brian hurried to join his team.

The sheriff parked and climbed out, his rugged face a
scowl as he assessed the situation. Although Riggs had
played soccer and Stone football, they'd been friends in
school. When Stone's father had passed, Stone had been a
no-brainer for sheriff.

A woman emerged from the front seat of Stone's car,
her body rigid, face in the shadows.

Riggs's pulse jumped with recognition. Macy Stark. She,
Kate and Brynn Gaines were as different as night and day.
But as teenagers, they'd been inseparable. He'd been sur-
prised Macy had left town shortly after the shooting.

Had the women stayed in touch?

Stone strode toward Riggs, expression intense. "Where's
Kate?"

Riggs pointed to the tree, his gut clenching. She sat
hunched against that rock, her arms wrapped around her
legs as if she was trying to hold herself together. He expected Macy to race over to Kate, but she remained rooted
by Stone's car, eyes assessing, serious, calm but questioning.

"Does she need a doctor?" Stone asked.

"I don't think so. She's just shaken." Heat from the blaze
made sweat break out on Riggs's neck.

Or maybe it was fear that Kate's car fire wasn't an
accident.

KATE SILENTLY REMINDED herself she was safe. She'd lost
her car, but she had insurance. Her SUV could be replaced.

At least no one had been hurt.

For months after the shooting, she'd struggled with survivor's guilt. But losing her mother and seeing classmates die had also taught her to prioritize. A human life, *any* human life, was more valuable than material possessions.

Her breath quickened. Macy was standing by the sheriff's car.

A pang of longing swelled inside Kate. At age seven, she, Macy and Brynn had spit on their hands, rubbed them together and declared themselves spit sisters. For years they'd cried, laughed, and shared secrets together. She'd thought they'd always be friends.

But that was before the shooting.

Kate's shoulders tensed as her gaze met Macy's. Her former best friend had kept her distance at the town meeting. She hadn't voiced an opinion one way or the other about the old school being demolished.

What was she doing here now?

Macy pivoted to look at the fire, and Kate noticed her left arm was in a sling. Macy had been athletic and talked about running track in college and then becoming a coach.

Instead, she'd joined the FBI. Had she been injured on the job?

With a quick glance at Kate, Macy joined the sheriff and Riggs.

Kate fought anger. How could the girl she'd once loved like a sister return to town and ignore her? Macy had deserted her when Kate had needed her most.

Memories of tea parties, sleepovers and playing dress-up in Brynn's mother's ball gowns flooded Kate. The girls had shopped for dresses for their school dances together never missed a birthday celebration, and had dreamed about their weddings.

She'd heard Macy had married Trey Cushing after col

lege. Kate hadn't been invited to the wedding. And Trey seemed an odd fit for Macy, but Kate had never gotten the chance to ask her how they'd wound up together.

A wave of sadness washed over Kate. She and Macy had first bonded when they were five. Kate had heard a noise in the yard by her window and thought it was a sick cat. She and her mother ran outside and found Macy hovering by the bushes, scared and sobbing. Macy's mother had locked her out of the house. Another time, Kate recalled, Macy's mother had left her at the park alone.

Both times, Kate's mother had comforted Macy and welcomed her into their house. Once, when she'd driven Macy home, they'd found Macy's mother having an "episode," at least, that was what Macy called it. Later, they'd learned Mrs. Stark was bipolar and had gone off her meds. From then on, Kate and her mother had become Macy's safe haven.

Yet at Kate's mother's funeral, Macy had stood on the edge of the service and stared blankly, as if she hadn't grown up in Kate's house. Brynn had still been in the hospital and had needed Macy, too.

But Macy had abandoned them both.

Kate felt even more alone now because of it.

Finally, Macy looked back at her and, for a moment, her eyes filled with some emotion Kate couldn't define. Regret? Longing?

Blame?

It was your fault.

Whoever sent that message knew Kate's rejection had sent him over the edge.

Ned's brother had known. And he'd told Macy and Brynn.

Did her best friends blame her for the shooting? Was

that the reason Macy had left town? And the reason she'd finally come back?

When she looked at Kate, did she see their classmates falling to their deaths?

RIGGS KEPT HIS suspicions about the car fire to himself as he drove Kate home. No need to alarm her until it was confirmed the fire was intentional.

She'd been through enough tonight. The sheer fact that she was riding in the truck with him proved how shaken up she was.

He parked in front of her Craftsman bungalow and cut the engine. Her street was in a quiet little neighborhood where mamas and daddies strolled their babies down the sidewalk and joggers ran with their dogs.

An image of Kate smiling as she sipped sweet iced tea on the front porch gave him a pang in his chest. He wished to hell she'd grace him with that smile. At least once.

Instead she was polite. But she kept her distance.

Not that he blamed her.

A picture of Kate pushing a baby stroller struck him out of the blue. Dammit, he'd never thought about having a family himself. But lately a seed of longing had sprouted inside him. He'd grown...what? Tired of being a bachelor? Bored with waking up alone?

Hell, he wasn't alone. He had friends. Plenty of women to sleep with, if he was interested. Only lately his interest in one-night stands had dwindled.

The guys at the firehouse were his family. Maybe he'd get a dog.

Kate's soft voice jerked him from his thoughts. "Thanks for the ride, Riggs."

"No problem." He itched to say more, to ask her to invite him in and let him stay with her for a while. Why, he didn't know.

Maybe because she's the one damn woman who's never given you the time of day.

Was he really that big of a jerk?

She reached for the door handle and opened it, and he hurried around to help her out. Dammit, she might not like him, but his job made him wary. What if Billy showed up?

After the shooting, everyone had wondered if Ned'd had an accomplice. Billy had been their prime suspect. What if the publicity about the new school was making Billy nervous and he feared the truth would finally be revealed?

Riggs took Kate's arm as she climbed from his truck, but she tensed and pulled away. "I'm fine, Riggs." He walked silently beside her to the front door.

Her keys jangled as she removed them from her purse, and her hand trembled so badly she dropped them. He hoped to hell the fire had caused her nerves, that she wasn't afraid of *him*.

He might have been a player, but he'd never been rough with a woman. That was his father's MO.

Riggs stooped, snagged the keys and unlocked the door. "Like it or not, I'm going to look around the house."

Fear clouded her face, making him feel like a heel for putting it there. She dropped her purse on the foyer table then crossed the room to the cushy blue sofa in front of the stacked stone fireplace. "I realize some people are angry with me, but surely no one would break into my house."

She was trusting to a fault. Billy was a loose cannon. Riggs refrained from commenting, though, as he walked through her living room and kitchen. The blue and white décor and farmhouse furniture was tasteful and homey, and the scent of lavender filled the room. His own cabin was more rustic and, although the river ran behind the property, he had very little furniture and no photographs or personal touches. It was just a place to sleep.

Kate sank onto the dark blue sofa, picked up an afghan and began to stroke the blanket. Floor-to-ceiling windows flanked both sides of the fireplace, offering a wooded view of her backyard. She must have chosen the house because it was close enough to the school for a short commute, but the house had been built to accommodate a spectacular view of Bear Mountain.

"It'll just take a minute for me to check the windows and doors," he said.

Wariness crossed her face, but she nodded.

He paused in the hallway to study the photos of Kate and her mother. Mrs. McKendrick had been the only reason he'd passed English Lit. Those private tutoring sessions had helped him save face and keep his position on the soccer team.

Ned had shot him only a few feet away from Kate's mother, who'd stepped in front of Ned to save her students. He'd never forget seeing Kate on her hands and knees sobbing over her mother as she'd tried to stop the bleeding. The screams, the bodies falling…the horror. Even through it, Kate had rushed to help others.

She was still trying to do that.

Shaking off the grisly image of the shooting, Riggs checked the guest bedroom window then the master. The room definitely belonged to a woman. A plush lavender comforter covered a large, white ironwork bed, a watercolor of lilacs on the wall above. Candles sat on the nightstand, the lavender scent stronger in here. The bed drew his eyes, eliciting an image of Kate beneath the decadent covers.

What the hell was wrong with him? This lust for Kate was coming out of nowhere.

Angry with himself, he hurriedly checked the windows then the bathrooms and laundry room, searching for a bomb or trigger mechanism that would send her house up in flames like her car.

You're being paranoid, dude.

Although considering the night's events, maybe he wasn't paranoid at all. If that fire was intentional, someone had just tried to kill Kate.

Chapter Four

A storm was brewing outside, the wind howling off Bear Mountain like a lion roaring. Grateful to be inside, Kate filled the kettle with water to heat for tea.

Having Riggs in her house resurrected teenage insecurities she thought she'd finally overcome. Every girl in school had crushed on him. With his thick dark hair, smoky eyes and that dimple in his right cheek, he was a charmer.

And that body. He'd been fit when he'd played soccer, but the man had gained muscle and grown three more inches. He must be at least six-three because he towered over her and made her feel small, which, at five-seven and with her curves, she wasn't.

She'd never been one of the skinny girls who nibbled on rabbit food and wore crop tops to show off her flat belly like Brynn had done. Brynn's beauty-pageant-coordinator mother had pressured Brynn into near starvation to fit into a size two, so Brynn had always snuck in cookies and pizza at Kate's house before she went home.

Kate had never been a size two and never would be. Her mother said she'd bloomed early. She'd developed boobs by age eleven, which had drawn ogles from the hormonal boys who interpreted that to mean she was easy. Her hips had followed, giving her curves and an added ten, fifteen pounds. The unwanted attention had heightened her insecurities about her body.

But after high school, she'd worked hard to overcome a negative self-image and hoped to be a role model to other young girls.

Footsteps jerked Kate back to reality, and she squared her shoulders. With his sexy physique and those smoldering eyes, Riggs could have a woman disrobing for him in seconds. But she silently reminded herself that he was not there for personal reasons. He'd simply given her a ride home. For all she knew, his latest love interest might be waiting on him at home tonight. Waiting in his bed...

"Everything looks clear," Riggs said, although he didn't quite meet her eyes when he looked at her. "Do you have a security system?"

"No. I've thought about it, but I always felt safe here." An odd thing to say considering the town had nearly been destroyed by a mass murder. And if Ned had had an accomplice as Stone Lawson's father had suspected, another killer might be hiding in plain sight in Briar Ridge. He could have been there all along.

The teakettle whistled and she quickly turned off the stove. Her hand trembled as she poured hot water into a mug and dunked a tea bag inside.

"Would you like some tea?" she asked. Lame. Riggs was not the tea-sipping kind of man. She turned to face him, eyebrows raised. "Or something stronger? I have whiskey."

A small grin tugged at the corner of his mouth. "I didn't figure you for a whiskey kind of girl."

Kate blushed. "What kind of girl did you figure me for?"

"Tea," he said with a chuckle.

She couldn't resist a comeback. "I might surprise you." Perspiration beaded on her forehead. Had she just flirted with Riggs? Heaven help her. She must be more shaken than she'd thought.

"I have a feeling you're full of surprises, Kate," he murmured in a voice laced with innuendo.

He flirts with every female he meets. Don't let it go to your head.

Determined not to make a fool out of herself, Kate reached inside her cabinet, removed a bottle of Jack Daniel's, added a shot to her tea and poured a finger into a highball glass for him.

Their hands brushed when she gave him the drink, and a thread of desire rippled through her.

Riggs's gaze locked with hers, tension simmering between them. Had he read her reaction?

Of course, he had. He was experienced with women. Smooth.

She was as smooth as cracked glass.

Thankfully, her brain interceded and overrode her silly fantasies. She might have escaped a burning car tonight, but she'd be playing with fire if she imagined Riggs was interested in her. Well…he might be interested in sex just because he liked women—all women—but it would be nothing more. And she didn't intend to be a notch on his bedpost.

Needing to wrangle her wayward thoughts, she carried her mug to the sofa and sank onto it. Riggs joined her, facing her from the oversize club chair by the fireplace. Somehow, his big body looked comfortable there, like he belonged.

You must have inhaled too much smoke. It's making you light-headed.

"For the record, Kate," Riggs said, his voice gruff, "I think your plans for the school are admirable."

His praise warmed the chill invading her. "Thanks. After

my mother died, I stayed in our house for a long time. But everywhere I looked, I saw her ghost. And her perfume was permanently embedded in the walls."

His look darkened. "I know losing her was difficult. She was an amazing woman, and the best teacher I ever had."

"She was a great mother, too, loving and kind and always so positive. I never want to forget her and her sacrifice," Kate said. "But living in that house without her was just so h...ard. I knew Mom wouldn't want me having a pity party." She ran her finger around the rim of her mug and bit her tongue. For heaven's sake, why was she babbling?

Unable to stop herself, though, she continued. "After I finished my Masters, I talked to Amy. She suggested I sell the house and make a fresh start." Kate blew into her tea, lost in thought for a moment as she remembered her initial reaction to the suggestion. "I balked at the idea at first. It felt like I was betraying my mother. That if I moved from our home, I'd forget her." The same way locals were reacting to tearing down the school.

"What changed your mind?"

"Eventually, I realized she would have wanted me to move on and be happy. So I slowly started cleaning out, and discovered it was cathartic. I kept things that were sentimental and looked around for a place to move. The developer was just building the bungalows on this street. Suddenly the prospect of having my own place where I could put my stamp on it excited me." She gestured around the living area and kitchen. "I brought the good memories with me here and decided to build a future that Mom would be proud of."

"That's the reason you pushed so hard for the new school building," Riggs said quietly.

"It's been years. I thought it was time to move on," Kate

said "New places inspire new beginnings that can lead to a more positive future."

"People just need time." He sipped his whiskey, drawing her gaze to the long column of his throat as he swallowed.

How could a man's throat possibly be sexy?

Oblivious to her ridiculous thoughts, he leaned forward, his gaze pinning her. She barely resisted the urge to squirm. She had no idea why she'd poured out her personal feelings. Except, Riggs was easy to talk to. And tonight had rattled her and resurrected memories from high school.

Another memory sobered her. Riggs and Cassidy Fulton. Cassidy's son's face flashed in her mind. Roy was a gangly kid who didn't make friends easily. And he desperately needed a father.

But Riggs had never owned up to the fact that he was Roy's father, nor had he been a presence in Roy's life. Just like her own father hadn't.

RIGGS BATTLED THE urge to kiss Kate. Her story had touched his heart.

In spite of his bad boy reputation, he did not take advantage of vulnerable, frightened women.

And judging from the way Kate was avoiding eye contact with him, she wouldn't welcome his lips on hers.

That fact stung, but he wrangled in his libido. If he wanted her to think he was a better man than his father or the lowlife everyone thought him to be for abandoning his teenage pregnant girlfriend, he had to prove it.

Act like a gentleman. Keep his hands to himself.

Even if it killed him.

Talk business. "Kate, other than Billy, is there anyone in particular who'd want to hurt you?"

She ran a hand through the long strands of that wavy auburn hair, making his hands itch to touch it.

"Probably half the folks at that meeting tonight. You heard them." She dropped her hand back to her lap. "The truth is I understand their feelings," she said, compassion flickering in her eyes. "Change is difficult. So is forgiveness."

True. "Have you received any threats lately?"

She worried her bottom lip with her teeth. "Not exactly," she said slowly.

He narrowed his eyes. "What do you mean *not exactly*?"

Indecision played across Kate's face before she set her mug on the coffee table and retrieved her purse. She removed an envelope from inside and offered it to him.

He removed the invitation to the dedication ceremony, confused at first. Then he spotted the hand-scrawled message on the back.

It was your fault.

Anger tightened every muscle in Riggs's body. "When did you get this?"

"Today. It was in the mail at school."

The timing was definitely suspicious. She'd received a cryptic message the same day as the town meeting, only hours before her SUV had burst into flames.

He turned the envelope over in his hand and scrutinized it further. "No return address?"

"And no signature."

"Did you see who delivered it?"

"No. The staff had already left so I didn't get a chance to ask them either."

"Someone must have dropped it off in person?"

"Or put it in the mailbox outside the school."

Riggs considered the possibilities. "Meaning it could have been a student or anyone in town."

Kate ran a hand through her hair again. Dammit, he wished she'd quit touching it. The urge to replace her fingers with his own grabbed him once more. To see if her hair was as silky as it looked.

"I guess it could have been a current student, although I can't think of anyone I've had serious trouble with this year," Kate said. "Besides, the message implies whoever sent it blames me for the shooting, which suggests it's a former student or a family member of one."

Riggs tossed back the remainder of his whiskey then leaned forward, hands on his knees. "The shooting wasn't your fault, Kate. Ned was a troubled teenager."

Emotions clouded Kate's face. "But it *was* my fault," she said, her voice quivering.

Riggs didn't believe that for a minute, but obviously Kate did. "Why would you say that?"

Kate dropped her head into her hands and squeezed her eyes closed. She looked so tormented that he wanted to wrap his arms around her and comfort her.

But he clenched his hands by his sides and forced himself not to reach for her.

SHAME FILLED KATE, mingling with the guilt that had dogged her for years. She'd kept quiet about her part in Ned's breakdown. If Riggs knew her secret, he might hate her.

She'd give anything to be able to go back and rewrite time.

"Kate, talk to me."

The tenderness in his voice almost undid her. But she'd held in the truth for so long that it was time to break her silence. "I turned Ned down when he asked me to the school dance," she admitted. "I...didn't think anything about it at the time. I was shy and worried about my Trig exam, and... I rejected him without considering his feelings."

Riggs scrubbed a hand down his face. "Turning a guy

down for a date is no reason for him to go crazy and shoot up the school, Kate. Ned had emotional problems."

"I know. Kids bullied him and teased him, but I didn't do anything about it. Didn't stand up for him."

"You weren't personally responsible for him or anyone else except yourself," Riggs said.

Tears glistened in Kate's eyes. "But Billy said my rejection sent Ned over the edge."

Anger flashed across Riggs's face. "Billy Hodgkins is a bully. Always was. Always will be."

Kate had never liked Billy, either. He'd pick fights with guys and tried to cop a feel with girls when no one was looking.

But he'd lost his brother because of her, and she understood why he hated her.

"When did Billy tell you this?" Riggs asked.

"At Mom's funeral." Kate massaged her temple as the painful memory resurfaced. The day she'd buried her mother was a rainy day. The wind had blown leaves and silk flowers across the cemetery while half the residents and students stood sniffling and crying beneath black umbrellas. Others were at the hospital with their children who'd been injured. Brynn had been undergoing surgery.

And Macy…? She'd needed her friend, but she'd deserted Kate.

"What else did Billy say, Kate?"

"That Ned had a huge crush on me, and it took him weeks to get up his nerve to ask me out. When I blew him off, it broke him."

She swallowed hard. "If I'd agreed to go to the dance with him, maybe he wouldn't have brought that gun to school and murdered our classmates and my mother." She wrung her hands together. Her nails were clipped short to keep her from biting them, but she had a habit of rubbing her fingers together when she was nervous. She was absentmindedly doing that now.

Riggs's hand covered hers, stilling her jittery movements. "Look at me, Kate."

She shook her head. It was difficult enough to face herself in the mirror, much less look at the town hero.

"Kate. Look. At. Me." His firm but tender voice made her glance up, and she swallowed hard.

"School shootings are a complex problem. If you're to blame, then so am I, and every other kid at school who ever ignored Ned. So are the teachers and society and social media," Riggs said firmly.

Amy had said the same thing. Still, Kate wished she'd been nicer to Ned.

Riggs wrapped her hands in his, rubbing them. "If Billy is still bitter and blames you, he might have sent that note to spook you."

Riggs released her hands and stood. "I'll call Stone in the morning and ask him to have a talk with Billy."

Kate stood, although she was reluctant for him to leave. She'd lived alone for years, but the letter of blame and car fire disturbed her, and she suddenly didn't want to be alone.

"Get that security system set up tomorrow," he reminded her.

Emotions welled in her throat. "I will. I also need to call my insurance company about the repairs and arrange for a rental car."

He carried his glass to the kitchen and set it on the counter, then walked to the door. She followed, torn between pushing him out the door and asking him to stay. He filled her doorway with his massive shoulders and big body.

Lord help her, he oozed sex appeal. Afraid he could read her mind, she dragged her gaze away from him and folded her arms across her chest.

"Thanks for driving me home."

"Of course." He paused at the door. "Remember what I said, Kate. The shooting wasn't your fault, so don't let that damn note get to you."

She gave a little nod, although telling herself that and believing it were two different things.

"You need to show it to Stone," Riggs said. "Maybe he can lift some prints from it, or have the handwriting analyzed."

"I'll drop it by his office tomorrow."

"I can do it if you want," Riggs offered. "I want to talk to him about your car anyway." His brow furrowed. "Or maybe I can pick you up, and we can go together. I'll drive you over to pick up that rental car, too."

Kate stiffened. "I don't want to impose on you. You've already done enough."

His eyes flashed with irritation. "I have a couple of days off and don't mind driving you," he said. "I want to make sure you're safe, Kate."

She wanted to ask why he cared. They weren't even friends. But she clamped her mouth shut. Riggs was not only a fireman, he also worked arson investigation.

Maybe he suspected the fire wasn't accidental.

He removed a card from his pocket and laid it on the table by the door. "My phone number—cell and work. Call me if you need anything."

She needed him to stay. To hold her tonight and help her forget that she could have died in that fire.

To help her forget that someone might hate her enough to want her dead.

Get a grip, Kate. You have to stand on your own.

So she said good-night and watched him leave. As his vehicle disappeared down the drive, she locked and bolted the door and walked back to the living room.

Odd, but the big club chair looked empty without Riggs in it.

Silently chastising herself for falling prey to his charm, she rinsed her mug, stowed it and his glass in the dishwasher.

She checked the sliding-glass doors to make sure they were locked then stepped into her bedroom.

The scent of Riggs's masculine aftershave lingered from when he'd searched her house. She wondered what he'd thought about her furnishings.

Stupid. Riggs Benford was not the kind of man who noticed a woman's furniture. He was a player.

And she didn't intend to be played. Even if he was interested—which he was not.

She changed into a tank top and pajama pants, then folded down her thick purple comforter. An image of Riggs stretched out naked on her bed taunted her.

He would look ridiculous against the plush bedding. But her bed would be so much cozier with his sexy body in it.

She punched her pillow. She had to banish those kinds of thoughts. She wanted more than one night with a man.

And Riggs wasn't the commitment type.

A noise outside jarred her and she startled. The wind? Thunder?

Nerves on edge, she hurried to the sliding-glass doors, opened them, then stepped onto her screened porch and looked out into the night. Lighting zigzagged across the tops of the pines and oaks, sharp jolts of light against the jagged ridges of Bear Mountain and the dark, inky night.

Then a movement.

Fear slithered through her. Someone was in the woods behind her house…

Damn. Damn. Damn.

He watched Kate McKendrick through the window of her bedroom with a mixture of hate and disappointment.

She had made it out of the car alive. She should have died.

Then maybe all this talk about tearing down the old school would stop.

He'd lit a joint and taken a drag as he'd watched that firefighter drive away.

Riggs Benford. Arson investigator. Town hero.

He could be a problem. But he couldn't save Kate. Not if she kept moving ahead with the dedication and reunion.

All the classmates who'd left town were coming back now. He'd heard them at the diner, the coffee shop, everywhere he went in town. They were already gathering and reminiscing. Talking about the good old days.

And the bad one. The one that had ripped apart friends and families and put some of them in the ground.

His life was bad enough. That was the *last* thing he needed.

For folks to remember. Then they might figure out who he was.

He'd blow all of them to pieces before he allowed that to happen.

Chapter Five

The next morning, Riggs rubbed his bleary eyes as he poured his second cup of coffee. He'd barely slept all night for worrying about Kate.

He took a long, slow sniff, grateful for the burst of caffeine in the rich scent of the dark roast blend, then carried it to his back deck and studied the sharp angles and slopes of the mountain ridges.

Kate was right. Briar Ridge had once been a hopping, happy town. He'd grown up enjoying hiking, whitewater rafting, and skiing. Before his mother had had enough of his daddy, she'd sewn handmade quilts to sell at the festivals, and canned jams and jellies for the local mercantile. His father had made fun of her, but tourists had loved the homemade goodies. Kids had flocked to the souvenir section that was complete with stuffed bears, T-shirts with images of Bear Mountain, and crystals from the old mines.

Kate wanted to restore that happy atmosphere.

He swallowed hard. God, Kate.

The frightened look on her face as she'd stood watching her SUV erupt into flames had haunted him in his sleep. Then the pain and guilt when she'd confessed about her conversation with Billy Hodgkins at her mother's funeral.

If Billy hurt Kate, he'd… Do what? Kill him?

He'd never thought of himself as a violent man. He *saved* lives.

But…something about Kate had gotten under his skin last night and triggered his protective instincts.

Hell, not a one of his classmates would probably believe that. In high school, Kate hadn't been his type. On the surface, he'd liked to flirt and date around, anything to feed his ego after his old man had beaten him down.

But he'd never thought about being serious. Hadn't really thought he deserved a good girl like Kate.

Kate was…real. Beautiful, but not a made-up doll who focused on her looks or spending three hundred dollars on a pair of designer shoes.

Oh, yeah, he'd dated a woman, more than one, who'd fit that description.

His sexual prowess and the dangerous side of his job drew them like flies to honey. They thought he was exciting, brave, some kind of superhero for running into burning buildings when everyone else was running the other way.

He was no damn hero. He just did what he could to save others because…because he'd watched friends and classmates die and had been helpless to save them.

Sex was one thing.

Commitment was another.

So far, he hadn't found any woman who made him consider the Big C.

But the bookworm girl who'd hidden behind big square glasses fifteen years ago was smart, cared about people, and had stood up to half the town the night before for something she believed in. She wanted to make a difference in the world and fought for it.

She's not interested in you, buddy.

His phone buzzed with a text from Stone.

Should have the report from the mechanic on Kate's car
by nine.

He sent a return text.

Will meet you at ten. Need to talk.

Copy that. My office. Ten o'clock.

Speaking of the devilish woman who'd kept him up all
night, his phone buzzed. Kate.

He punched Connect. "Morning," he said through gritted teeth. Damn. His voice was gravelly from loss of sleep.
Had his greeting sounded like a come-on?

"It's Kate," she said a little stiffly. "I need to set up a time
for the security installation. What time will you be here?"

Ah, yeah. Back to Kate's safety and the reason—excuse—he'd used to see her today. "I told Stone we'd meet
him at his office at ten."

"Okay, I'll be ready." Her breath rattled over the line.
"Or if you have other things to do, I can Uber."

She almost sounded hopeful that he'd retract his offer.
But if Kate was in danger, she didn't need to get in a car
with a stranger. "No. Like I said, it's my day off. Why
don't we grab breakfast first?" So he was a glutton for
punishment.

Silence for a second. "Thanks, but I've already eaten. I
just need time to shower and get dressed."

He closed his eyes and fought a groan as she discon-
nected. Images of Kate naked and stepping beneath the
shower water made his body harden. For a brief second,
he imagined her luscious curves and full breasts dotted
with water, her pink lips parted for his tongue to dive inside for a taste.

But the sound of the wind beating at the windowpane jarred him back to reality and he cursed himself. Kate McKendrick did not want him. She never had.

He would simply offer his assistance in keeping her safe because firefighters vowed to protect the public. Nothing more.

Kate was a settle-down type of woman. After all she'd suffered, she deserved some happiness.

And a man who'd fulfill her dreams.

He was not that man.

THE EARLY MORNING sunlight forced Kate to look at herself realistically in the mirror. Dark circles marred the skin beneath her eyes, and her face looked...tired. After she'd seen that movement behind her house the night before, she'd studied the woods and darkness for an hour. But no one had surfaced.

She'd finally reconciled that the shadow belonged to a deer, and she'd crawled into bed.

But she'd lain awake listening for sounds of an intruder half the night.

When she'd finally fallen asleep, she'd been running for her life. Billy Hodgkins was chasing her through the woods with a butcher knife. "You'll pay for killing my brother!" he shouted. "It was all your fault."

She'd woken and realized she was alone. Safe from Billy. In her own bed, not in the woods. She'd tossed and turned for another hour, then finally drifted back to sleep only to dream of Riggs in her bed.

Riggs with his sultry eyes raking over her bare skin. His hands and lips following, stirring desires every place he touched...

She'd bolted awake again, her body humming with need. But the face in the mirror gave her clarity. Hers was not the face of a woman Riggs would be lusting for. Besides, how could she be attracted to a man who flirted with every woman he met? With a man who'd abandoned his child?

Granted, Riggs had been seventeen when he'd gotten Cassidy pregnant, but his son lived in the same town and attended Briar Ridge High, and Riggs had nothing to do with him.

Focusing on that thought sobered her and she moved away from the mirror. She phoned her insurance agent and then the rental car company and arranged to pick up a red Ford Escape by noon.

A knock sounded, and through the front window she spotted Riggs's black truck in her drive. She grabbed her purse and rushed to the door, deciding she didn't need Riggs invading her space this morning. His scent and image in that club chair was torture enough.

When she opened the door, he stood towering in front of her, his big masculine body exuding sexuality. Morning sunlight fought through the dark clouds outside, highlighting the caramel streaking his thick dark hair and bronzed skin. His dimple appeared as he greeted her with one of his killer smiles.

"Morning, Kate."

"Hi." She dragged her gaze from his face, which was a mistake because her height put her at his shoulders, forcing her to look at muscles straining the confines of a black T-shirt emblazoned with the logo for the Briar Ridge fire department on the front. A silver-studded belt buckle circled his waist where a tight pair of jeans hugged his muscular hips and thighs.

Dear Lord, the man was built. His forearms looked like tree trunks. He must lift weights…

Could he lift her?

Heat crept up her neck at the unbidden thought and she inhaled sharply to calm her raging hormones.

"Are you ready?" he asked.

She didn't trust her voice to speak, so she simply nodded, stepped onto the porch and locked the door.

"Did you arrange for the security system installation?" he asked as they settled in his truck.

"Yes, they're coming this afternoon."

There, small talk was good.

Except she couldn't think of anything else to say.

He cut his eyes toward her as he started the engine. "Did you sleep okay?"

No, I dreamed of Billy chasing me and then you in my bed. "Not great," she admitted.

"Sorry." Riggs backed from the drive and turned onto the road. An awkward silence fell between them as he drove toward town. Fanny's Five & Dime store looked just like it had years ago, except now the merchandise consisted of dollar items and it had been renamed accordingly. The Cut and Dye was hustling with business as usual, and mothers and fathers were already strolling babies to the park. Other early morning joggers and walkers occupied the running trail, and the parking lot for the breakfast spot, The Bear Claw, was full.

Five minutes later, they reached the sheriff's office, a two-story, rustic brick building with a wrought-iron railing. Riggs parked and rushed around the front of the truck to open her door. Polite.

Kate climbed out before he reached the passenger side.

He quirked a thick dark brow as if in challenge. "Next time I'll get the door."

Next time? "In case you haven't noticed, Riggs, I'm not some delicate little flower." *Like the women you date.*

A tiny smile tugged at his lips. "Just using my manners."

Her heart fluttered. Of course he was. It didn't mean anything personal. And, for heaven's sake, why had she drawn attention to her size?

He raked his eyes over her, making her body tingle from his perusal. Unnerved, she rushed up the steps to escape further comment.

They reached the door to the building at the same time, and Riggs wrapped his long fingers around the door handle. "Now, Kate, I'm going to open the door for you, so say 'thank you.'"

She expected to see laughter in his expression, but his smoky eyes were locked on her face. Serious. Waiting. Challenging her.

"Thank you." She bit out the word then practically jogged inside when he opened it. Irritation at herself needled her. Good grief, she wasn't usually rude to people. But Riggs elicited feelings and thoughts she didn't know how to handle.

The receptionist, Bobbie Jean, a middle-aged woman with a short perm, smiled a greeting as they entered. Stone glanced up from a front desk when they entered, one hand gripping the phone. When he saw them, he ended the call, stood and circled the desk, and offered them a coffee.

Nerves bunched Kate's stomach, so she declined. Riggs muttered a comment about needing all the caffeine he could get and accepted a cup.

Stone spoke to his receptionist. "We'll be in my office if you need me."

Bobbie Jean gave a nod, and Kate and Riggs followed Stone through a swinging door down a hallway. A sign to the left read *Holding Cell*. Two rooms labeled Interrogation Rooms 1 and 2 respectively were opposite it. Beyond those, they stepped into a small private office. A photograph of Stone's father, the former sheriff, hung over the desk with a commendation he'd received from the mayor for his quick response to the school shooting.

Kate sank into a metal chair, noting more pictures of his father hanging on the wall behind the desk. The resemblance between Stone and his father was strong although Stone held a seriousness to his eyes that hadn't been there before the shooting.

The sheriff had visited her after the massacre, but she'd been too traumatized and grief stricken to help. He'd questioned everyone in town, though, determined to find out if Ned had an accomplice.

Unfortunately everyone was either in shock or wasn't talking. And no answer ever came.

Stone and Riggs were about the same height, only Stone's hair was a little shaggy and unkempt, and his eyes hazel. He was handsome, but much more serious than Riggs had ever been. She was surprised Stone was still single, but his brother had been blinded in the shooting, and Stone seemed married to the job. When he'd become sheriff, he'd vowed to one day find out if Ned had acted alone. Once he did, that person would pay.

"I talked to the mechanic about your car," Stone said.

Kate twisted her hands together. "And?"

"Someone cut your gas line, which caused a leak," Stone said.

Kate's pulse hammered. Her gas line had been cut… Intentionally. Not an accident.

Dear God. Someone *had* tried to kill her.

ANGER SHOT THROUGH RIGGS. He'd had a bad feeling about that fire.

Kate's breath rushed out. "I know some people are upset about the new school, but I can't imagine anyone in town trying to kill me because of it."

Riggs squeezed her shoulder. "Tell him about Billy."

Kate clenched her purse strap. "It was a long time ago. I don't want to cast stones at an innocent person."

"Tell him," Riggs said through gritted teeth.

"Please," Stone said quietly. "No matter how insignificant you might think something is, it could be helpful."

Kate forced a neutral tone as she described her confrontation with Billy at her mother's funeral. Sharing the hurtful words was difficult, but she refused to fall apart in front of these two strong men. Or to remain a prisoner of the past.

"Kate, he was wrong to blame you, and you know it," Stone said. "My father investigated the Hodgkins family. The parents were…questionable. Billy was as hard on his brother as the rest of the kids at school or worse. His mother said Billy used to play mean tricks on Ned. More than once, he tied Ned to the doghouse out back and forced him to sleep in it when they were gone."

Kate shivered. Riggs hadn't heard that before, either, but it confirmed his opinion of Billy Hodgkins.

"I'm surprised Ned didn't turn the gun on his brother," Riggs muttered.

Stone shrugged. "I guess blood is thicker than water. Ned was troubled and unleashed it on all of us at school instead."

"Some of our classmates did tease him," Kate said. "And I did reject him."

Riggs huffed, unsympathetic. "If I went off and shot up people every time I got rejected, I'd be in prison for life."

Kate's eyes widened, but she didn't comment.

"Have you seen or spoken to Billy lately?" Stone asked.

Kate shook her head. "Not really. After that day, I avoided him."

"We both know he was at the meeting," Stone said.

"He cornered her outside behind the town hall," Riggs interjected.

"Kate?" Stone arched a brow toward her. "Did he threaten you?"

"He mumbled something, but I didn't understand him, then he ran off when he saw Riggs."

Stone drummed his fingers on his desk. "When I asked Billy why he was at the meeting, he said he wanted to talk to you in private, Kate. I told him to calm down, that that wasn't going to happen."

Riggs angled his head toward Kate. "Did you bring the note?"

Stone leaned back in his chair, hands linked behind his head. "What note?"

Kate removed the invitation from her purse and offered it to Stone. "I received this yesterday in the school mail, but I have no idea who sent it."

Stone rocked forward in his chair, took the envelope and examined it, as Riggs had done. "No return address?"

"No, it was in with my mail at school. Anyone could have dropped it in our outside mailbox without being noticed."

"All the publicity about the new school may have triggered traumatic memories for Billy and his family, and he lashed out at you, Kate," Riggs suggested.

"I'll send this to the lab for analysis." Stone put the invitation card back in the envelope and placed it in an evidence bag. "I also had a crime team go over your SUV, Kate. The fire will make it difficult, but hopefully we'll get some forensics from the vehicle."

"Are you going to question Billy?" Riggs asked.

Stone nodded. "As soon as we finish here, I'll look for him. And I'll find out where his parents are. It's possible they may be upset about the publicity." He gestured to the front-page article in the morning paper.

A photograph of Kate at the podium in front of the town appeared above the headline *Principal Kate McKendrick Pushes for Demolition of Infamous Briar Ridge High Where a Tragic Mass Murder Occurred Fifteen Years Ago.*

Kate stared at the cutline. Locals in An Uproar... Did One of Them Threaten Kate McKendrick?

The article also featured photographs of the bloody scene, the rescue workers, then Ned and his family.

Stone grunted. "That damn Gretta Wright likes to keep things stirred up. She was on the morning news with the story."

"If Ned's parents saw the publicity, I'm sure they're upset," Kate said. "They went through hell after the shooting. People practically ran them out of town."

"True, but my dad suspected they were holding something back," Stone said. "Only he never figured out what." He patted his holster. "Meanwhile, Kate, I'll assign a deputy to guard you twenty-four-seven."

Kate shook her head. "That's not necessary, Stone, I'll be fine."

Riggs gritted his teeth. He wasn't surprised Kate declined protection. She was stubborn and independent.

But she was also in danger.

And he'd be damned if he'd sit by and let anyone hurt her.

Chapter Six

The idea of a bodyguard hovering around her day and night made Kate feel claustrophobic. She was a private person. Led a boring life.

All she'd wanted to do was to help others heal the way she was starting to heal.

"Come on," Riggs said. "I'll drive you over to pick up that rental car."

"Thanks. But I'll walk. I need the exercise."

"Kate, you're not walking three miles to pick up a car when I can drive you, especially under the circumstances." Irritation tinged his voice, so she clamped her teeth together and refrained from a retort.

Why was he being so insistent? "Fine. Then you've done your duty, Riggs."

He paused on the front stoop of the sheriff's office, a frown creasing his brows. "I'm sorry you find my company so repulsive."

Kate squeezed her eyes shut for a moment, chastising herself for being rude. "I didn't mean it like that," she said as she looked up at him. "I appreciate your time and concern. But I don't want to be a burden."

A wry laugh rumbled from his chest. "You are not a burden, Kate. Prickly, but not a burden." His voice turned gruff. "And like it or not, I'm going to stick around and make sure no one hurts you."

She gaped at him as if he'd grown a second head. "That's not necessary. I can take care of myself. And I'm sure you have other friends to meet up with."

"No," he said bluntly. "No plans today."

"Good grief, Riggs. Don't you have a girlfriend waiting?"

He shook his head. "Not that I know of."

"That's right, you have *several*," she said, injecting a teasing tone to her voice. Or was it a hint of jealousy? "I'd hate to upset one of them."

He pressed his lips together in a thin line. "I get it. You think I'm a womanizer. But high school was a long damn time ago, Kate. People change."

She stared at him again, as if she didn't know whether to believe him or to call him a liar.

His chest thundered.

"Let's just get the rental car," she finally said. "I have to drop by the school afterward and pick up some year-end paperwork."

"Fine." He squared his shoulders and started down the steps, jaw clenched.

Lord help her. She had the insane sense she'd hurt his feelings.

But why would he be hurt? He might have changed, but he was Riggs Benford, a poster boy for bachelorhood.

And she wanted a real relationship. A husband and kids one day.

Get hold of yourself, Kate. He's simply giving you a ride.

Although old hurts rose to taunt her. Tony, a popular basketball star in school, had taken her to a movie one night. Later, he'd left her on the side of the road. His words had been like a stake in her heart. *Big girls like you need to learn to put out. That's the only way you'll have a boyfriend.*

Worse, he'd lied and bragged to the other guys on the team that she had.

Jerk.

That incident had taught her a lesson. She couldn't trust players. They used you for sex then bragged about it. She didn't intend to be the butt of anyone's joke, not ever again.

So, in college, she'd kept her nose in her books. Earning her education and becoming a teacher had meant everything to her. She'd wanted to honor her mother and be a mentor to kids the same way she had.

They climbed into his pickup and rode in silence to the rental car office. "Thanks, Riggs." She forced a polite smile. "It was very nice of you to give me a lift."

His chiseled jaw tightened even more, emotions glittering in his eyes. "I'll follow you to school and make sure it's safe."

"Thanks, but again, not necessary. A few teachers are there today, packing up, and the custodian is organizing and boxing up furniture to ship to the new facility. Besides, no one is going to try to hurt me at school during the day."

His look suggested he wasn't convinced, but she'd obviously hammered home the fact that she didn't want him around. Except, he wasn't repulsive at all and she liked having him around. That was the problem.

But Kate was a practical kind of girl. No use fantasizing about things she couldn't have.

"Kate." He caught her arm before she could escape. "I'm serious. Be careful. And call me if you need anything."

Kate stared at his wide, blunt fingers for a moment, her skin tingling from his touch.

Afraid Riggs would read her reaction to him, she slid

from the truck and forced herself not to look back as she hurried up to the rental car office.

Her phone buzzed as she entered. Gretta Wright.

Kate hissed between her teeth. She despised the woman. Gretta's high school gossip rag had fed on any juicy tidbit she could dig up on the students.

Her face stung at the memory of the humiliating picture Gretta had posted of Kate in her gym clothes. Gym clothes that were too tight because someone had switched her uniform with a smaller one as a prank. Her gym shorts had ripped when she'd run hurdles on the track.

Riggs and the entire soccer team had been watching. Laughing.

Cheeks flushing from the memory, she ignored the call and finished the paperwork for the rental car, then snagged the keys to the Escape. When she was safe inside, she checked her voice mail.

"Kate, it's Gretta. I'd like to interview you about the meeting last night, and about your accident. I'll meet you or come by your house if you'd rather, whichever you prefer."

Kate deleted the message. She did not intend to share her fears about the car fire with a reporter, especially Gretta Wright.

KATE'S ALOOF MANNER toward him bothered Riggs as he drove back to the police station. Dammit.

Kate was nice to everyone. Except him.

Because she thought he jumped from one woman's bed to another, and that he was a deadbeat dad.

Well, hell, at one time, he'd been a commitaphobe. But that was a long damn time ago. The shooting, his physical therapy, witnessing others' pain…it had changed him. He used to enjoy a hot night between the sheets. He'd disappear out the door as soon as his lover fell asleep and go home to his own bed where no one demanded anything of him.

But lately the fun had turned to boredom. His bachelor ways, waking up at home alone, had become…lonely.

Maybe he had been a jerk to women. But he never would have abandoned his kid. *Never.*

He knew what it was like to have a father who didn't care.

He parked at the sheriff's office and rushed inside, hoping to catch Stone.

His friend clipped his phone on his belt as Riggs entered his private office.

"Forget something?" Stone asked.

"I wanted to talk about Kate."

Stone pivoted in his rolling chair and raised a brow. "What's up with you and her anyway?"

"Nothing." Riggs jammed his hands in his pockets. "But after the climate of the meeting, I'm worried. Did you find Billy?"

Stone tapped his foot. "Not yet. I was just on the phone with Celeste at the inn. Billy isn't on the guest list."

"Then where the hell is he staying?"

Stone shrugged. "Don't know yet. Do you remember who he was friends with back in the day?"

Riggs struggled to recall. He and Billy had run in different circles.

Stone pulled a yearbook from the shelf above his desk. Riggs looked over his shoulder as Stone thumbed through their class roster.

"Woody Mathis," Stone said. "He and Billy were buddies."

"That's right," Riggs said. "Woody was injured in the shooting."

"Yes, he was," Stone said.

"Did Woody have family?" Riggs asked.

"Just his daddy, but he was mean and a gambler. Died a year after Woody was hurt. Heard the house went into foreclosure. Not sure what happened to Woody. Haven't seen him around."

"I heard he got hooked on painkillers," Riggs said.

"Sounds about right." Stone grunted.

"What about the Hodgkins's old house?"

"That's a place to start. There's also the old lodge outside of town."

"It shut down two years ago," Riggs said.

"The very reason it would make a good place to hide if someone didn't want his or her whereabouts known."

True.

"Problem is, Billy isn't the only one upset about tearing down the old school," Stone said. "Any one of the victims or their loved ones could be responsible for that note, and the attempt on Kate's life."

"That's a lot of suspects. How can I help?" Riggs asked.

Stone crossed his arms. "This is police work, Riggs. Let me do my job."

"Two heads are better than one," Riggs argued.

"Don't you need to be at work?" Stone asked.

Riggs shrugged. "I have a couple of days off. You know how our shifts run. Three days on. Three off."

"Right." Stone drummed his fingers on his desk. "My deputy can start looking into the alumni, and Macy Stark is in town for the reunion. She's with the FBI and on leave because of an injury. I thought we could use a fresh pair of eyes and want her to review Dad's reports for anything that might stand out about the case. Maybe she'll find a clue pointing to an accomplice."

Riggs thought back. The school counselor, Amy Turner,

might know. She was serving on the committee with Kate to create the new memorial. "Did Ms. Turner offer insight as to who she thought might have helped Ned?"

"No. According to Dad's notes, she was determined to protect her students' confidence. But I'll talk to her. Maybe after all this time, she'll change her mind."

"What can I do to help?" Riggs asked again.

A smile teased Stone's eyes. "Keep an eye on Kate for a couple of days. Not in an official capacity, of course, but just as a friend."

Kate wouldn't be happy about that. And she obviously didn't consider him a friend.

His gut tightened. He'd do it anyway. Even if he couldn't charm her into liking him, he could keep her safe. If for no other reason than to finally uncover the truth about Ned's possible accomplice.

Stone stood, adjusting his holster. "I'll ask my deputy to check out the Hodgkins's old homestead. I'm going to take a look around that abandoned lodge."

"I'll go with you," Riggs offered.

Stone gestured to the door. "All right. But follow my lead. If Billy is at the lodge and appears to be dangerous, you have to stay in the car."

"Of course." Riggs forced an even keel to his tone. He'd let Stone take the lead.

But if he learned Billy was behind that note or the attempt on Kate's life, he couldn't promise he wouldn't beat the hell out of him before Stone carted him off to jail.

KATE HAD THE eerie sense someone was watching her as she drove from the rental car office toward the high school. Her stomach growled, a reminder she'd lied about eating breakfast because she'd been too nervous about seeing Riggs again to eat.

She pulled into Pearl's Dine & Pie, parked and glanced around at the red-and-white sign lettering above the metal-embossed image of a red thunderbird. Locals and visitors packed the place, enjoying a late breakfast and chatting over coffee and Pearl's famous cobblers. With school out for the summer, a few teens wandered in, still wearing pajamas, to soak up the blueberry pancakes and lattes.

The parking lot at the inn next door also had more cars than she'd seen in a decade. Most probably belonging to former classmates and alumni. Some of whom had been at the meeting the night before.

Any one of them could have sent her that message.

She checked over her shoulder and scanned the parking lot before she slid from the car. Thankfully, Billy wasn't lurking around.

Mrs. Gaines's silver BMW was parked in the lot. Kate made to leave but decided she couldn't run from everyone opposed to the demolition of the old school.

She ached to reconcile with Brynn, too, only guilt held her back. Brynn was paralyzed because Ned had gone ballistic. Maybe there had been other factors, but she'd definitely contributed with her callous rejection.

How could Brynn possibly forgive her when she was confined to a wheelchair?

Mrs. Gaines had never approved of Kate and had wanted Brynn to socialize with the more elite crowd, as if Kate and her mother weren't good enough. After the accident, she'd cut Kate completely off from seeing Brynn.

Brynn had been groomed for Miss Teen Briar Ridge since the age of five, her mother traipsing her through competition after competition across the state. Her mother insisted on perfection and had been critical of Brynn if every hair wasn't in place. She also demanded perfection in herself and her daughter, an exhausting task.

Was she still critical or had she softened with Brynn's injury?

Kate walked up to the entrance. As soon as she opened the door, the heavenly scent of sausage and gravy wafted around her.

Instead of a sweet tooth, Kate liked hearty food—a biscuit with bacon, sausage, or country fried ham. Mrs. Gaines had once commented that Kate ate like a man.

Her own mother had scoffed at the comment and told Kate to eat whatever her body craved. That protein built muscles, and confidence built character.

Silence stretched across the crowded noisy room as she entered. Kate lifted her chin then crossed to the counter. Some patrons offered a tentative smile while others pierced her with angry looks.

As she seated herself on a stool, Pearl pushed a cup of coffee toward her. "Here you go, sweetie. You want the usual?"

"Yes, to go. Thanks."

Pearl patted her hand. "For the record, I believe in what you're doing. It's high time someone shook this town back to life again."

Kate murmured thanks again, rifling through her purse to pay as the silence giving way to whispers. On their way out, three people stopped to say they supported her.

She sipped her coffee, her senses on edge as footsteps sounded behind her. "Kate?"

She froze, bracing herself for the wrath of the mayor's wife as she pivoted. "Hi, Mrs. Gaines." Brynn sat beside her mother, hands clenched around the arms of her chair, worrying her lower lip with her teeth. Her silky blond hair fell across her shoulders in loose waves, and she wore a pale pink blouse that highlighted her perfect ivory skin.

Brynn was the most beautiful girl Kate had ever known and a tender heart who loved animals. Losing her friendship had carved an empty hole in Kate's already shattered heart. Then again, if the school signified a new beginning, maybe she could start over with Brynn.

"Brynn," she said with a hopeful smile, "it's nice to see you."

Mrs. Gaines stepped in front of Brynn. "I've changed my mind. I think building a new school will benefit this town and the people in it."

Kate narrowed her eyes. The edge to the woman's tone and the sudden tightening of Brynn's face suggested Brynn's mother had her own agenda. Appearances were everything to the haughty woman.

"Thank you," Kate said. "I appreciate your support."

Brynn wheeled her chair away from her mother, an indication something was wrong. "Is it true someone sabotaged your car, Kate?" Brynn asked.

Kate's stomach clenched. "That's what the sheriff said."

Fear darkened Brynn's beautiful blue eyes. "Do they know who did it?"

"Not yet. But Stone is investigating."

Mrs. Gaines snapped her fingers. "We have to go, Brynn. Your therapy session, remember?"

A pained look flashed across Brynn's face before she gestured at her chair. "No, Mother, how could I forget when you constantly remind me?"

Disapproval flared in Mrs. Gaines's eyes at Brynn's tone then she threw up a hand, dismissing Kate.

Brynn looked contrite, as if she wanted to say more as she wheeled herself out the door.

Just as Pearl brought Kate's to-go order, Amy Turner

came in. When she spotted Kate, she hurried over to her. Worry filled her green eyes and she looked upset. Before she took a seat, her eyes darted around the diner as if she was nervous.

"Kate, is it true what they said on the news?" Amy whispered. "Did someone threaten you?"

Kate lowered her voice. "Yes. And my car was tampered with. But I don't know who did it yet." Kate shifted. "How did you know about the threat?"

"It's all over town, and I saw Gretta on the news," Amy said. "People are saying it has to do with the shooting."

Kate licked her suddenly dry lips. "Someone doesn't want the past dredged up. Amy, I know you maintain strict student/therapist confidentiality, but the threats rouse suspicion that Ned did have an accomplice. And that that person doesn't want the truth exposed."

Amy's face paled. "I…don't know what to say, Kate. If I'd known Ned had an accomplice, I'd have spoken up."

Kate studied her friend. "Maybe you can think about it, look back at your old files to see if anything sticks out now that you might have missed then."

Amy nodded, but her phone was buzzing in her purse, and she reached for it. "I will." She squeezed Kate's arm, her eyes darkening with worry. "Be careful, Kate. If Ned did have an accomplice and he got off for fifteen years, he's not going to want to go to jail now."

Kate nodded, her stomach in her throat as she snatched her food and headed out to her car.

Chapter Seven

Riggs skimmed the list of classmates staying at the inn while Stone drove, scrutinizing each name as a potential suspect. He tried to place faces with those who'd attended the meeting the night before, but over the years, classmates had aged and changed in appearance.

Stone parked in front of the abandoned lodge, which was set off the road on a scenic ridge near the top of Bear Mountain. The place had once catered to hunters and fishermen in the summers and skiers in the winter.

A rusted black pickup was parked to the side, beneath a sagging carport with a metal roof. The paint on the wood lodge walls was chipped and muddy, the windows cracked, the awning on the front hanging askew as if a storm had ripped it from the roof.

"Stay here," Stone told him. "If Billy's inside, he might be armed."

Riggs grunted. "I'll back you up."

Stone gave him a stern look. "Keep behind me and be a lookout. I don't want you getting shot on my watch."

"Can't say as I'd like that, either," Riggs said with a wry chuckle.

Stone gripped his service revolver as he climbed from the police car.

As Riggs approached the deserted run-down building, he

wished he had a damn gun. But carrying a weapon seemed counterintuitive to his job.

Riggs scanned the front of the building for signs someone was around. A curtain slid to the side in the room on the end. "Last room," he told Stone.

Stone lowered his gun to his side but held it at the ready. Together they strode up to the door, and Stone knocked. "Sheriff Lawson, open up!"

A screeching noise erupted from the rear. Then a window opened and a man crawled through it.

"He's running," Riggs yelled to Stone. "Side window."

Stone signaled Riggs to stay back and then eased toward the right. Riggs inched down the steps and darted behind a live oak flanking the driveway. The man dropped to the ground, hunched like a wild animal about to pounce.

Not Billy. But Billy's old buddy, Woody Mathis. Dressed in tattered clothing and muddy boots, with several days of beard growth on his face, he looked as if he hadn't seen a shower or a hot meal in days. His eyes appeared glassy, glazed over from drug use.

"Stop!" Stone shouted.

Woody hesitated then cursed and aimed his gun at Stone.

"Put it down, Woody," Stone ordered.

"I didn't do anything wrong." Woody darted for the woods behind the lodge. But he must have decided escaping on foot was futile, so he turned and dashed toward the pickup.

Riggs couldn't let him escape. Stone crept forward, gun still braced, but Woody pivoted and fired a shot. His hand unsteady, the bullet hit the dirt at Stone's feet.

Stone threw up a warning hand. "Woody, don't do this."

Woody shouted a curse and reached for the pickup's door handle. He obviously didn't intend to turn himself in.

With Woody focused on Stone, Riggs took advantage,

left the cover of the oak and jumped Woody from behind, knocking his gun to the ground.

An image of Kate's face haunted him as Riggs slammed Woody up against the truck and jerked his arms behind him. "Did you mess with Kate McKendrick's car?"

Stone jogged up to them, pulled his handcuffs from his belt and gestured for Riggs to let him handle the situation.

Instead, Riggs tightened his hold. He wanted answers. "Did you?"

"I told you I didn't do nothing," Woody said in a shaky voice.

"Then why the hell did you run?" Riggs growled.

RIGGS'S REMINDER ABOUT the security system taunted Kate as she parked at the school. She'd felt safe in her new house until that note and the fire. Now, she wondered if she was being stalked. Watched at school and at home.

The redbrick school, built in the fifties, had served the community for decades. Classrooms were held in four different buildings, one breezeway connecting them, another one leading to the gymnasium. At one time, the school had added overflow trailers to the mix because of the increasing population in Briar Ridge, but they had sat empty since the school shooting. So many families had left Briar Ridge because of the trauma and the national publicity had kept others from moving to town.

The plans for the new building were a different layout with everything housed in one building. There was only one main entrance, which would be locked during the day for security reasons. She hoped that would soothe parents' concerns and that the new football field and stands would be a draw.

Two teachers' cars sat in the lot along with the custodian's truck. Although the teachers had worked in advance to clean out their classrooms, clearing the entire building of everything that needed to be moved was a major undertaking. The county superintendent of schools had hired a crew to transfer furniture, kitchen equipment, desks and chairs, bulletin boards and other large items. Kate wished they could afford brand-new furnishings for the new building, but the budget wouldn't allow it.

She slipped into her office and spent a couple of hours cleaning out files, discarding papers and other expendable items. Then she packed some paperwork to take home.

For a moment, nostalgia wrapped her in its sentimental folds like a warm blanket. She ran her hand over the scarred wooden surface of her desk. The oak piece had belonged to her mother when she'd taught at Briar Ridge High. It was so special, Kate couldn't bear to part with it.

After her mother died, Kate had moved the desk to her house. The place where her mother had once sat had served as a constant reminder of her strength, patience and positive attitude while Kate studied for her teaching degree and then her Masters.

The same desk and memories would travel with her during the next phase into the new building.

Another wave of nostalgia washed over Kate as she packed the photographs on the wall in her office. There were several of her mother, staff members and teachers, along pictures of Kate when she was a little girl. An eight-by-ten of her and her mother Kate's freshman year at Briar Ridge, all pigtails, braces and pudgy awkwardness, resurrected a bittersweet memory.

One of the mean girls had teased her about her weight. After school, her mother had taken her to the bookstore, and they'd come home with a bag of magazines. Together they'd looked at photos of women in all sizes, shapes, colors and nationalities, Kate's mother pointing out the beauty in each of the women. That day Kate had learned to love her body image and ignore kids who didn't appreciate people's uniqueness.

Unlike Brynn's mother, Kate's had embraced individuality and taught Kate to look beneath the surface. Her mother had also been one of the first in town to advocate for the immigrants who'd moved to Briar Ridge.

She hadn't deserved to die.

Kate sucked in a pain-filled breath. Sometimes, out of the blue, the grief still swept over her in horrific waves.

Leaning forward, hands on her knees, she inhaled deep breaths to ward off her emotions.

Finally regaining her equilibrium, she pressed a kiss to her fingers and touched her mother's face in the photograph. "You told me to make something good happen. I'm trying, Mama. I want you to know that and to be proud."

The sunlight flickering through the window reminded her of the time, and she checked the parking lot. The teachers' cars were gone, but Jimmy's truck was parked in its spot. He'd worked at the school for over twenty-five years and never failed to do whatever she asked with a smile.

Suddenly the building felt cold and empty. The halls, normally filled with students' and teachers' laughter and chatter, echoed with an eerie quiet.

Anxious to leave, Kate spent another hour downloading files onto her laptop. Just as she finished, a noise startled her. Voices? Footsteps? Students or alumni stopping by for a last look before demolition?

She packed the laptop and other files in her computer bag then headed to the door. Her shoes clicked on the tiled floor as she left her carpeted office and walked across the entryway. The faces of past students swam behind her eyes, their voices echoing in her head. Memories of the first day of school, of pep rallies, debating competitions, science fairs and school dances made the building come alive with hope.

The wind rocked the trees and dark clouds cast a gray fog over the parking lot.

The moment she stepped outdoors, she stopped short, a cold chill ripping through her. The gym, attached to the main building via a breezeway, faced the drive. Across the cement wall in front of her, graffitied in large, blood-red paint:

Leave the Past Alone or Die!

"Is BILLY HODGKINS with you?" Riggs asked Woody as Stone pushed the man toward his police car.

"I ain't got nothing to say," Woody snarled. "I want a lawyer."

Riggs rubbed the back of his neck in frustration while Stone's expression never wavered. But his look indicated he would make Woody talk.

"Anyone else staying in the lodge?" Stone asked.

Woody shrugged, his face pasty white.

"Stay here with him." Stone angled his head so Woody couldn't hear him. "And don't touch him, Riggs. The last thing we need is a lawsuit. A jail cell and a few hours without a drink or whatever drug he's on will likely loosen his tongue."

Riggs gave a slight nod.

After Stone secured Woody in the back seat of his squad car, Stone went to see if he could dig up the bullet casings to send to the lab. Riggs leaned closer to the car window and pinned Woody with an intimidating look.

"Did you come back to town for the reunion?" Riggs asked.

Woody cut his eyes to Riggs. "I ain't never left."

Riggs frowned. He hadn't seen Woody around town, but they didn't exactly hang around in the same circles or frequent the same places. Riggs went to work then home and hung out with the other men in his firehouse. Woody probably frequented the bars and places where he could score drugs.

"Were you at the meeting last night?"

Woody's jaw tightened and he looked down at his lap. Scrapes marred his knuckles and his thumbnail was bloody. Either he worked with his hands or he'd messed with Kate's car.

"How'd your hands get beat up?"

"Construction job," Woody mumbled.

Possibly. "How do you feel about the old school being torn down?"

"I don't give a flip," Woody mumbled. "Ain't got nothin' to do with me."

Riggs made a low sound in his throat. Was Woody spouting off what he thought Riggs wanted to hear or was he telling the truth? "What about Kate McKendrick?"

A snarl curled Woody's lips then he whistled. "She's got a nice rack on her."

Riggs balled his hands into fists to keep from slugging the jerk. "I meant do you support her plans for the new school?"

"I told you I don't care one way or the other. I ain't got kids."

Riggs mulled that statement over. Woody didn't appear to be the political, sentimental or family type. His biggest concern was probably where he'd get his next fix.

"This is no joke, Woody. Did you tamper with Kate's car?"

Woody raised two bushy eyebrows. "You serious? Someone tried to kill her?"

"Did you mess with her car?" Riggs said between clenched teeth.

The sound of Stone's footprints echoed across the gravel. His expression looked worried as he approached. Riggs expected a verbal chastising from Stone for questioning Woody while he was gone.

Woody looked up, fake innocence written on his face as Stone joined them. "I want a lawyer."

Before Riggs could speak, Stone climbed in on the driver's side. "A call just came in. We need to go."

Riggs tensed at Stone's tone then slid into the front passenger side. "What's wrong?"

Stone fired up the engine. "Kate called. Someone painted a threatening message on the school wall."

HE HOVERED IN THE SHADOWS of the wooded area by the school and smiled at the look of fear on Kate McKendrick's face as she studied his message.

She should be afraid.

The witch had stirred up old hurts and secrets no one even knew existed.

Ned Hodgkins had been troubled. A loner. A kid who'd been bullied by his classmates and invisible to the people who should have helped him.

Ned had ruined lives seeking revenge against those who'd wronged him.

He understood the need for revenge.

Only he didn't want the limelight or attention.

He wanted the opposite. To go unnoticed. To fade into the woodwork until he could escape this god-awful town.

But Kate was dredging it all up. Opening painful wounds that would never heal, reminding everyone that Ned might not have acted alone. Raising questions as to Ned's motive and if there were secrets that hadn't yet been exposed.

Of course there were.

There was more to the story than anyone suspected.

Secrets he did not want revealed.

Kate moved closer to study the message on the wall, and adrenaline spiked his blood.

The message was intended as a warning.

He raised the match he held in his hand, struck it and watched the flame burst to life. It sizzled and burned, the hiss of the tiny blaze a balm to his tattered soul. He'd always liked fire, ever since he was a little boy and had hidden in the shadows to watch his mother light her cigarette.

The beauty of the flames eating the matchstick excited him the way nothing else ever had.

If Kate didn't leave the past alone, she'd find out what it was like to feel the heat of the flame against her skin. To watch her precious life go up in flames just like the match between his fingers.

Chapter Eight

The sense that someone was watching her made Kate's skin crawl. She gripped her phone as she scanned the area around the school. Was the person who'd graffitied the wall still here?

Was it the same person who'd tampered with her SUV?

Shivering as she reread the threatening message, she backed toward the school. She'd be safer inside. In her office with the door locked.

A noise from the rear of the building startled her. A metal trash can lid blowing in the wind? Footsteps?

Panic clawed at her and she ran for the building. When she reached the front door, she grabbed it to go inside, but it was locked. She frantically rattled the door then knocked on the glass and rang the security buzzer, hoping Jimmy would hear her.

Through the front glass window, she spotted a shadow hovering near the science lab. "Who's there?" she shouted.

The shadow ducked into the lab, the door closing. Suddenly someone grabbed her from behind. She screamed, jerked away then swung around, prepared to fight for her life.

But Jimmy stood there, looking contrite and worried. The poor man barely weighed a hundred and twenty pounds and his faded jeans and shirt hung on his bony frame. His

graying hair stood out in tufts, his wire-rimmed glasses
sliding down his nose.

"Sorry, Ms. McKendrick, didn't mean to scare you." His
dentures clacked in a nervous rhythm. "I was around back,
carrying out some trash. Heard you shouting and came to
see what all the commotion was about."

Kate's chest rose and fell with her uneven breathing.
Jimmy was almost sixty-five, thin and wiry, and should
retire. But he'd become a landmark at the school, had even
attended high school here himself when he was young.

"I'm sorry," she said. "I…got locked out, and thought
you were in the building."

A siren wailed as the sheriff's squad car raced into the
school drive. Stone and Riggs climbed from the car and
jogged toward her. Both men halted at the sight of the graffiti.

"Pretty bold to do this in daylight." Stone gestured at
Jimmy. "Did you see anything?"

"No, sir," Jimmy said. "I've been cleaning out the cafeteria, then was around back taking trash to the dumpster."

Riggs crossed to Kate, his voice gruff. "Are you okay?"

She nodded. "I saw someone going into the lab."

Stone raised his weapon. "Stay here with Kate," he told
Riggs. "I'll search the building." He got a key from Jimmy.

Riggs ushered Kate and Jimmy beneath a live oak near
Stone's squad car.

"Hey, Kate!"

Kate stilled then angled her head to see who'd called
her name.

Woody Mathis sat rocking himself back and forth in
the back of Stone's squad car. His shifty eyes raked over
her with a leer.

She hadn't seen him in a while, but his shaggy beard
and greasy hair were hard to forget. Over the years, she'd

seen him around town at the store or diner. He'd always been jittery, as if up to no good.

"Ignore him." Riggs situated himself between the car and Kate and urged her a few feet back. "He's high as a kite."

"What did he do?" Kate asked.

"We drove to the old lodge outside of town, looking for Billy. We found Woody instead."

"What happened?" Kate asked.

"Idiot pulled a gun and shot at Stone."

Kate stared at him. "Why would he shoot at Stone?"

Riggs shrugged. "Panicked. Probably had drugs, but he must have flushed them when we knocked on the door."

A shudder rippled through Kate. Woody hadn't been vocal about the school one way or the other. But Ned had shot him years ago, and word was that he suffered from PTSD and had turned to drugs.

Did he blame her for his problems?

RIGGS KEPT HIMSELF between Kate and Woody just in case the bastard somehow broke free of the handcuffs.

A minute later, the front door to the school opened and Stone appeared, tugging a young man with him.

"Isn't that the mayor's son?" Riggs asked.

Kate nodded. "Yeah, Brynn's younger brother. Don was a late-in-life baby."

"You have trouble with him at school?" Riggs asked.

"Some," she murmured. "I had to call him into the office more than once this past year. Two days ago, I received an anonymous tip that he brought a weapon to school. Our security officer and I pulled him from class and accompanied him to search his locker."

Riggs cleared his throat. "Was there a weapon?"

"Yes, a pocketknife, although Don was furious and said

it didn't belong to him." She shivered. "He said I'd be sorry for embarrassing him."

Riggs scratched his head. He'd seen this kid around town, too. He had an attitude, thought he could get away with anything because his daddy was the mayor. He was especially rude to women, as if he had a chip on his shoulder. Twice he'd caught him stealing Minnie Weaver's tips where she waitressed at the Burger Barn.

He'd made the little twerp give it back. But Don had laughed it off and refused to apologize.

"How did the mayor react when he heard about the incident?" Riggs asked.

"He defended Don," Kate admitted with an eye roll. "Said whoever sent in that tip probably put the knife in Don's locker and I had to find the student and expel him or he'd have my job. But I explained that was counterproductive. We set up the anonymous tip system for everyone's safety."

Stone walked toward them, his expression calm, a contrast to Don's sullen face. The punk sported one of those weird haircuts where it was shaved on one side and the other side hung down over one eye. A diamond stud sparkled from one earlobe and his T-shirt bore the name of a heavy metal band whose song lyrics were tinged with violence against women.

Stone gestured to Don. "Found him in the lab like you said, Kate."

"I didn't do anything wrong. I just went in to get my phone," Don snapped. "I left it here the last day of school."

Riggs exchanged a look with Stone then gestured toward the graffiti on the building. "Did you do that, Don?

The kid's eyes twitched as he looked away. "Hell, no, Ms. McKendrick is picking on me."

"Show me your hands," Stone ordered.

Don gave him a surly look but lifted both hands. "See. I'm clean."

Even from where he was standing, Riggs could see the teenager's hands and clothes were paint-free.

"He could have changed clothes and ditched the dirty ones in the trash," Riggs suggested.

Stone gave a grim nod. "Do you know anything about cars?" Stone asked the kid.

Don shrugged "I know how to drive one. See that fire-engine-red Beamer. It's all mine."

Riggs chewed the inside of his cheek. Typical attitude for a spoiled, entitled kid. And why had he parked his car on the corner instead of the parking lot up front?

"In fact, I need to check in with my father," Don said with a cocky smile. "He's taking me golfing for acing my finals."

Riggs wouldn't be surprised if the boy had cheated.

Stone cleared his throat. "You threatened Ms. McKendrick at school because she searched your locker, didn't you?"

Don shot Kate a nasty look. "I was innocent then and I'm innocent now." Defiance radiated from every pore in the kid's body. "Now, can I go? Or should I call my father and ask him to send his lawyer?"

Stone's eyes darkened. "You can go but stay away from the school and from Ms. McKendrick."

The kid mouthed something Riggs couldn't quite understand, although it sounded foul, then sauntered to the street to his Beamer and slid in. A second later, he peeled away.

"He could have washed up in the lab," Riggs pointed out.

Stone gave a little nod. "I'll have the crime team search there, along with the trash cans and dumpster out back."

"Kate, do you think Don would hurt you?" Riggs asked.

Kate sighed. "I really don't know. He despises me, although I'm not sure why. Maybe he overheard his mother talking about me. Mrs. Gaines forbid Brynn from hanging out with me after the shooting."

Riggs rubbed his forehead. Why wouldn't Mrs. Gaines want Kate to see Brynn?

Stone secured his gun in his holster. "If Don bothers you, call me."

The wind picked up, swirling Kate's hair around her face. She absentmindedly tucked a strand of hair behind her ear. "I will."

"Meanwhile, I'll get a crime team out here to process the building. Maybe we can lift some prints from the graffiti wall. I'll also have them search for paint cans and a ladder." Stone hesitated. "Make a list of any and all students you had trouble with this year. If you expelled someone or put them on probation, rank them at the top of the list. If they're related to one of the victims from our class, note that, as well."

Riggs shifted. If a family member of one of the victims had threatened Kate, that meant everyone in town, including the former students returning for the reunion, was suspect.

KATE RUBBED AT her temple where a headache pulsed. She just wanted to go home and forget about today. But she couldn't escape the terrible sensation that someone hated her enough to want her dead.

Before she and Riggs reached her car, a dark green Lexus rolled into the drive. Kate rubbed her fingers together. Good grief. The car belonged to Gretta.

How had she heard about this incident so quickly?

Gretta squealed to a stop and hopped from her car wearing a hot-pink suit with matching acrylic nails. Her ash-blond hair was swept up in a fancy chignon, emeralds glittering from both ears. She spied the graffiti and snapped a few pictures then made a beeline for them.

Stone stepped in front of the squad car to block her from photographing Woody, who was rocking himself back and forth in the back seat. He must be coming down from his high and needed a fix.

Gretta quickly assessed the scene, addressing Kate. "What happened?"

"Someone vandalized the wall," Stone cut in, his voice dry. "How did you find out?"

"I have my sources." Gretta shrugged nonchalantly.

Kate bit back a comment. Gretta was a calculating, cold-hearted woman who'd sacrifice her own mother for a by-line. She'd never revealed how she'd gotten the scoop on students and exposed their secrets. She also hadn't cared who she'd hurt.

Judging from recent incriminating pieces she'd written about a Ponzi scheme involving her own brother, she obviously hadn't changed.

Gretta gestured at the police car. "Have you already made an arrest?"

Stone waved his hand dismissively. "No. I'm bringing Woody in on a separate matter. And I'd better not see a reference to him in the paper. Now, get out of here, Gretta. I have a crime to investigate."

"I have a right to be here, Sheriff. The people in town need to be alerted if there's a criminal loose," Gretta said, then asked Kate, "Did you see who did this?"

Kate shook her head. She didn't intend to feed Gretta any information. No telling how the woman might construe what she said. "No."

"What about your car catching on fire?"

Kate tensed. Was Gretta simply being her nosy self or did she know more than she wanted to say?

She inched closer and touched Kate's arm in a sympathetic gesture. "That must have been terrifying."

Riggs spoke before Kate could. "What do you know about the fire, Gretta?"

Gretta released a dramatic sigh. "Just that it was suspicious. If someone is trying to hurt the school principal or anyone else in town, the residents need to be warned. And maybe the reunion activities should be cancelled."

Kate frowned. What if that was the purpose of the threats?

"As I said, I have no comment at this time," Stone said sharply. "And if you interfere, I'll arrest you."

Gretta released a long-winded sigh. "Seriously, Stone. Let's be honest here. I witnessed the volatile reactions at the town meeting," Gretta said. "And I know someone tampered with Kate's SUV. Do you have any idea who did it?"

Kate's temper surfaced. "No, I don't. Do *you*?"

Gretta's catlike eyes flashed with a warning. "No, but if you don't share information, I'll find out on my own."

Jaw clenched, Stone straightened to his full six-two. "Don't interfere with my investigation, Gretta."

"I'm just doing my job, Sheriff. Like it or not, Kate's campaign to tear down this building and replace it opened old wounds. If there's someone dangerous lurking around, people should be aware so they can protect themselves. Just look what happened with Ned Hodgkins." Gretta aimed an accusatory look toward Kate. "Maybe if we'd been warned he was so depressed that he was dangerous, someone could have stopped him and lives wouldn't have been lost."

Kate's lungs squeezed for air. Gretta was right.

If she'd accepted Ned's invitation to the dance, she might have picked up on his anxiety and depression.

Then *she* could have saved lives. Including her mother's.

Chapter Nine

Riggs clenched his hands by his sides. He'd never, ever, been rough with a woman. But Gretta's cutthroat techniques tempted him to physically shake her.

She'd always been trouble. He hadn't liked her in high school, and he sure as hell didn't like the way she was pushing Kate now. "Come on, Kate. Let's get out of here."

Kate crossed her arms over her chest and gave Gretta a chilly look. "I have nothing to say to you now, Gretta, and I never will."

A spark of admiration for Kate stirred inside Riggs. Kate might have backed away from trouble as a teenager, but she'd stood her ground with Gretta the same way she had with protestors at the meeting.

"Thank you, Stone," Kate said. "I'll get that list to you as soon as possible."

"I'm going to talk to Jimmy," Stone said. "Maybe he saw more than he thought he did."

Kate murmured okay then started to walk away and dismiss Riggs. But Riggs didn't intend to allow her to go home alone so he rushed to catch up with her. What if Billy was waiting?

And if Billy hadn't painted the graffiti, the culprit might have hung around to see Kate's reaction. He also might be stalking Kate.

Gretta was watching them as if she sensed they were keeping something from her, so he lowered his voice to a conspiratorial whisper.

"I rode with Stone," he said. "Do you mind dropping me by the station to pick up my truck? Then I'll follow you home and make sure no one is lurking around."

Her gaze darted back to Gretta as if she expected the woman to pounce again. But Gretta had finally turned her attention back to work and was snapping pictures of the graffiti.

"I suppose I could do that. I owe you one."

Riggs brushed her arm with his fingers. "You don't owe me anything, Kate."

Her bright blue eyes met his, worry and fear mingling with other emotions he couldn't quite define.

She obviously didn't want to spend any more time with him than she had to.

He squashed the hurt that realization triggered. It didn't matter what she thought of him. All that mattered was keeping her safe.

"All right, let's go." She checked her watch. "I'm supposed to meet the security company soon."

Riggs followed her to her rental SUV. Maybe on the drive to the police station, Kate would tell him more about Don Gaines and the reason he harbored such animosity toward her.

KATE FELT GRETTA'S scrutinizing gaze as she'd walked to her car. She shouldn't let the woman bother her, but old scars ran deep.

Darn it, she was trying to move on with her life and make positive changes. Why couldn't she shake the hurt that woman had caused with her juvenile gossip rag?

Quickly starting the engine, she pulled onto the road leading back to town.

She didn't trust Gretta. The woman was a user and didn't care who she walked all over to get her story. More than once she'd lied about classmates to stir up a frenzy and create drama and conflict.

Sure, she'd retracted the story later on, claiming her source had been misinformed. But the damage had been done.

Kate didn't believe the source was the problem, either. Gretta was a thrill-seeking, attention-hungry, manipulative liar. Embellishment was her trademark.

"I admire the way you stood up to Gretta," Riggs murmured.

His approval sent a warm feeling through her. Why, she didn't know. She and Riggs were simply acquaintances.

Although she was grateful for his support over the new school. With his popularity in town, he might sway others to come around.

They reached the police station, and she swerved into the parking spot beside Riggs's pickup then angled her head to study him.

"Why are you being so nice to me?" Kate asked.

Riggs shrugged. "Maybe I'm a nice guy."

Kate laughed softly.

"That's funny?" Hurt tinged his eyes.

"No, it's just that I can't figure you out. Here you are babysitting me on your day off when you could be out having fun with one of your women."

Riggs arched a brow. "One of my *women*?"

A blush crept up Kate's neck. "You know what I mean."

A muscle ticked in his jaw. "You think all I do is screw around, don't you?"

She bit her lip, sensing she'd offended him. "It's not a

criticism. We're not even friends, so what you do on your own time is none of my business."

"Right." Pulse hammering, he reached for the door handle. "Maybe I did screw around in school, and afterward for a while." His voice thickened. "But people change, Kate. *I've* changed."

Riggs Benford had changed? He wasn't a womanizer now?

Seriously?

"I didn't mean to offend you, Riggs."

He squared his shoulders. "I didn't realize you were so judgmental, Kate."

For a moment, Kate simply stared at him. She felt as if she'd been reprimanded.

But he was right. For all her talk about being positive and moving forward, she still saw Riggs as the teenage flirt he'd been in high school.

Yet on some level she knew he had changed. He risked his life to save others. She'd also heard he visited the children's hospital in his uniform to cheer up sick children.

"I really am sorry," Kate said. "I've lived alone a long time, Riggs. I'm not used to answering to anyone."

His eyes turned smoldering. Intense. She hadn't felt this kind of sexual awareness in…she couldn't even remember.

She didn't want to feel it for Riggs.

Still, for a brief second, she couldn't drag her gaze from his. Her body tingled as if his fingers were raking over her just as his eyes were. Heat stirred deep inside her, dormant needs and fantasies simmering beneath the surface.

It had been forever since someone had held her. Kissed her. Loved her.

She missed being touched. Missed the intimacy.

Most of all, she missed having someone to share her thoughts and dreams with.

The one guy she'd dated in college certainly hadn't wanted to talk. And he definitely hadn't wanted a future with her.

She jerked her mind back to reality.

Sexy or not, Riggs had abandoned his child. He might volunteer at the children's hospital, but his own son lived in Briar Ridge and he'd never even acknowledged him.

"We may not have been friends in the past," Riggs said, "but we could start now."

Kate's breath quickened.

Riggs stared at her for a long tense minute, as if hoping she'd say something, but she clamped her teeth over her bottom lip.

A second later, something akin to disappointment flashed in his eyes before he climbed out, strode to his truck and got in.

Tension coiled inside her as she pulled from the parking lot and headed for her house.

But Riggs's words taunted her as she drove.

Yes, they could be friends. But it terrified her that she might want more...

RIGGS FOUGHT ANGER at Kate's reaction as he followed her. Not that he blamed her for her opinion. At one time, he'd welcomed the reputation as a love-'em-and-leave-'em kind of guy. No strings attached, no commitments, no one to tie him down. That had been his motto.

But he had changed, dammit. Had started to want more.

It bothered him that Kate couldn't see deeper than the surface.

That she must believe the rumors about him and Cassidy and that baby. A baby that was now a fifteen-year-old teenager. One who attended Briar Ridge High.

He had no idea what Cassidy had told her son about his

father. He sure as hell didn't think she'd told the boy he was his daddy.

But who really knew what Cassidy would do? She was brash, unpredictable and needy.

On Saturday night, she frequented bars dressed in low-cut tops and miniskirts, hanging on any guy who'd buy her a drink. Sure, she had the same right as a man to put herself out there. But she couldn't handle her liquor and didn't discriminate about who she took home to bed. Rumors surfaced that she traded sex for drugs on occasion. Made him wonder what kind of mother she was to her son.

Roy. That's the name Cassidy had given the boy. He was thin, gangly, and wore dark square-framed glasses. Riggs had seen him at the arcade, totally enthralled in video games. And he was always alone, as if he had no friends.

Not your problem.

Neither was Kate.

But here he was following her to her house like a lovesick puppy, declaring himself her protector when she clearly did not want his protection.

But, dammit, he cared what happened to her.

It's just because she's in danger. You could never be what Kate wants. A husband... Father to her kids... You're too much like your old man.

No...hell no, he wasn't. He'd worked hard not to be like him at all.

His father had been mean and cold and talked with his fists. The best thing his mother ever did was leave him. Riggs just didn't understand why she hadn't taken him with her.

Better to stay single. Unattached. Guard his heart.

Kate parked in her drive, climbed out and hurried up her porch steps. He parked beside her, leaving room for the driver from the security company, and surveying her property as he walked up to her porch.

More dark clouds rumbled above, casting an ominous gray over the mountains and adding a chill to the air. One of Kate's shutters had come loose and flapped against the pale blue siding.

She unlocked the front door and hurried inside just as he stepped onto the welcome mat.

Although he didn't feel welcome at Kate's, and that bugged the hell out of him.

She paused at the door, the dim light painting lines around her heart-shaped face. "Thanks for making sure I got home okay," she said softly. The shutter flapped again, and she startled.

He jammed his hands into his pockets, determined to remain cool. "Sure. If you have a hammer and some nails, I'll repair that shutter."

She looked as if she was going to argue, but the shutter banged again. "Thanks, but I can fix it myself."

God, she was stubborn. "It's no problem, Kate. I'll repair it while the security company installs your system."

She hesitated, and his gut tightened. "Are you afraid of me?" he asked gruffly.

Her eyes widened and she clamped her teeth over her bottom lip.

"You are, aren't you?" His chest throbbed at the thought.

"No," she said quickly. "I'm just nervous about the threats." She shrugged. "Besides, I'm not used to relying on a man to take care of things for me."

He raised a brow at that. "Then you've been hanging out with the wrong men. You deserve someone who'll treat you right, Kate."

Suddenly he wanted to be that man.

Her eyes searched his again, as if she was trying to figure him out. Indecision warred in his mind, but he decided he had to win her trust.

That meant being honest and sharing something he'd never told a damn soul.

"Can I come in a minute?" he asked gruffly. "We should talk."

Wariness darkened her eyes but she stepped aside and gestured for him to enter. "I guess that would be all right."

He entered the foyer, rubbing a hand down his neck. "I know you don't trust me, but I swear I would never hurt you, Kate."

"Then tell me why you're really doing this."

Man, she was direct. He wanted to say because he liked her. But that was putting himself on the line. And judging from her reaction, she didn't want to hear it.

"Because I owe your mother," he admitted.

Her brow furrowed and she folded her arms across her chest. "What do you mean?"

He ground his teeth, struggling for the courage to admit the truth. "Yeah. She was good to me."

"She was good to all her students," Kate said softly.

"I know." He shifted, uncomfortable, but he'd started this and he was going to damn well finish. "I was having trouble in school," he said. "I thought I was going to lose my position on the soccer team, lose my chance at a scholarship. All the rumors about me didn't help."

Cleary, he'd said the wrong thing, because suspicions flared in her eyes.

Damn, she thought he was referring to Cassidy.

KATE ORDERED HERSELF to keep an open mind. Maybe there were two sides to the story about him and Cassidy. Perhaps he'd tried to be a father to the boy and Cassidy had rejected him for some reason.

Although she couldn't imagine anyone rejecting Riggs.

"It's not what you think," he said quickly. "I don't mean trouble as in the law or with a *girl*," he said pointedly. "I had trouble reading. I struggled through classes and got poor grades. But your mother picked up on the source of the problem."

Surprise made her stomach tighten. "You're dyslexic?"

He nodded then cast his head down slightly. "Kids laughed and teased me when I was little. I failed classes. They called me names—stupid, idiot." He blew out a breath. "I thought I was stupid. So did my father, and he never missed a chance to tell me."

Compassion filled Kate as she pictured Riggs as a little boy being laughed at. And angry at his father who should have supported him.

Although she remembered hearing that Riggs's father had been abusive.

The truth dawned on her. Riggs's cocky, tough-guy attitude had been a cover-up so no one would see his pain.

"Oh, Riggs," Kate said gently. "Dyslexia doesn't mean you aren't intelligent. It's a learning disability."

Anguish twisted his face. "I know that. At least, I do now. Your mother tutored me in private and taught me techniques to read so I could pass my classes and stay on the soccer team."

Tenderness for Riggs welled inside Kate. Just like everyone else, she'd only seen the surface side of Riggs. And she'd made judgments based on his appearance and his past when he was just a kid.

Her mother would not be pleased with how she'd been treating him.

He was a man now. They were both different people.

"I'm glad my mother recognized the problem and that she helped you. She'd be proud of the man you've become."

A relieved look settled in Riggs's eyes, making him look so vulnerable that Kate ached to comfort him.

Then a look of masculine desire filled his eyes and her heart fluttered.

"She'd be proud of you, too, Kate," he said softly. "Proud of what you're trying to do for the town."

Forgetting all her reservations, Kate took a step closer, her heart hammering.

She lifted her hand and stroked his jaw, heat stirring inside her as her fingers brushed his coarse beard stubble.

God help her. Riggs was all masculinity and sexual prowess.

She wanted to kiss him so badly, her mouth watered.

Desire flared in his eyes as if he felt the pull between them. But just as he angled his head and moved toward her, the doorbell rang.

Kate started and Riggs growled a curse.

The security company had arrived and saved her from making a fool out of herself.

HE STRUCK THE match and watched the flame flicker to life. Fire had always fascinated him.

The sudden burst of orange and red and yellow. The heat rolling off the fire. The way the flames caught and spread so quickly, feeding on oxygen and eating up everything in its path.

It was a thing of pure beauty.

It could also be deadly.

His pulse jumped as the flame burned bright and tall, leaping and dancing against the darkening sky, consuming the matchstick until it disintegrated in his fingers. Heat scalded the tip of his thumb and he tossed the last of the match to the ground, then sucked his thumb into his mouth to ward off the sting.

The flame started to die in the brush, but a gust of wind resurrected it and embers burst to life in the thick straw and broken tree limbs. He glanced around the wooded area.

It was deserted. No one knew he was there.

No one would.

He should stomp out the fire. But he was mesmerized by the way it started to grow, slowly jumping from one patch of brush to another. Broken pieces of tree limbs and pine straw crackled and popped, the flames rippling through the forest, creating a path of destruction in its wake.

Heat seared his skin as the fire intensified. Flames shot upward and smoke thickened the air, creating a gray fog. Memories surfaced. The first time he'd played with matches.

He'd seen his mama take a man into her bedroom. Heard them grunting and groaning. Saw the chubby man walk out naked, sweat pouring off him as he grabbed another beer and carried it into the bedroom.

He'd wanted to burn down the house that night.

Kill that bastard.

When the man finally staggered out to his truck and roared away, he'd been relieved. Then he'd seen his mama passed out with her bottle.

He'd covered her naked body with a blanket and then snatched her Camels and matches and slipped outside. First, the old metal trash can. He lit the cigarette, inhaled and coughed his head off. He'd dropped it in the can and it had caught the trash. Paper and plastic melted and sizzled. The flames had grown bolder, shooting up from the can.

While his mother had slept off her drunk, he'd gone inside, broken one of the kitchen chairs, carried it to the backyard, and fed it to the flames.

He'd fallen asleep by the firelight, smiling as he'd imagined it spreading to the house and taking his mother with it.

The next day, she'd never even noticed. From then on, fire had become his obsession.

Now he inhaled the pungent odor of burning wood and excitement zinged through him as the flames raced along the forest floor. A patch of fire slithered up a thin pine and lit the sky as the needles caught.

Houses lay nearby, just beyond the hill.

Kate McKendrick's house.

Another smile tugged at his mouth.

Seconds later, a siren wailed in the distance. Someone had seen the smoke and called it in.

Heart hammering, he turned and ran back through the woods to where he could hide and watch the chaos.

Chapter Ten

Riggs gritted his teeth as Kate rushed to answer the door. Dammit, if he hadn't misread the situation, Kate had been about to kiss him.

He could still feel her gentle fingers on his cheek. He wanted to feel them in other places, his bare chest, his back, his hips...

He wanted to return the favor and erase the fear in her eyes with pleasure.

"Yes, please come on in," Kate was saying to the consultant from the security company.

She avoided eye contact with Riggs as she led the uniformed man inside.

Fool. Kate had simply felt sorry for him because of his confession. Nothing more.

Jaw tight, he cleared his throat. "Excuse me, Kate. Where's your toolbox?"

"The garage." Unease flickered in her eyes. Regret?

Tamping down his lust, he strode to the door leading to her garage, leaving her alone to deal with the security consultant.

Her garage was neat and organized. Gardening tools in one section, a bike in the corner, camping gear in another. A wall of shelves housed her toolbox and other supplies.

Living alone had obviously taught Kate to be independent. He wondered why she'd never married and had a family. Kate seemed like she'd have a passel of kids. Did she have a boyfriend hiding in the woodwork?

If so, where was he now?

Disturbed at the possibility, Riggs carried the toolbox and ladder outside and tackled the repair job.

Just as he finished, the scent of smoke assaulted him.

Senses jumping to alert, he climbed higher on the ladder and surveyed Kate's property. Nothing on fire in the yard.

But... God. In the woods behind her house, smoke curled into the sky and flames licked at the trees and brush, burning through the forest as the wind picked up and fueled its path.

At the rate it was going and with the direction of the wind, it would take no time for it to reach the houses in Kate's neighborhood.

Sweat beaded his skin and he snagged his phone and called the fire station. His captain answered on the third ring.

"A fire at Kate McKendrick's house," Riggs said.

"Someone else called it in already. We're on our way," his boss said.

Riggs didn't like how close it was to Kate's. "I'll meet you there."

He ended the call, jumped from the ladder and rushed to tell Kate where he was going. The fire could have started accidentally.

But considering what had happened with Kate's car and the threats she'd received, it could have been meant for Kate.

THE SECURITY CONSULTANT was installing the alarm pad in her bedroom when Kate glanced through the sliders in her den and noticed smoke. The gray cloud swirled above the treetops, weaving through the spiny needles of the pines and spiraling into the dark sky.

A second later, Riggs rushed in, his face a mask of professionalism although his eyes suggested he wasn't as calm as he appeared.

"The woods—"

"I just saw the smoke," Kate said.

"I'm going to meet my unit there. With the wind gusts, we need to contain it fast."

Kate sucked in a breath. Riggs's job meant running into burning buildings on a daily basis, but the thought of him battling that blaze in the woods sent a streak of terror through her.

"Will you be okay here?" Riggs asked.

Kate couldn't believe he was worried about her when he was the one who faced danger every day. "I'll be fine, Riggs. But you need to be careful."

"Always am, Kate. I know what I'm doing."

Of course he did. "That doesn't mean you can't get hurt."

A smile deepened the grooves at the corner of his mouth, replacing that brooding look and showcasing that sexy dimple. He reached out and stroked her arm. "Don't worry. I'll be back."

She said a silent prayer that he would be as he rushed out the door. Nerves on edge, she walked to the sliding-glass doors, opened them and stepped outside. The scent of smoke, burning wood and charred grass wafted toward her, clogging the fresh mountain air.

The wind picked up again, blowing through the trees and pushing the fire her way. She heard the distant sound of a siren wailing, and imagined Riggs's team descending on the blaze, working to protect her and others in the fire's wake.

Riggs had been such a tease in high school, always cracking jokes and flirting. She'd never imagined he had a serious side. Although, after the shooting, he'd been in pain and had to do physical therapy.

You also didn't know he was dyslexic. You just assumed his good looks and cocky attitude meant he was full of himself. But maybe it was an act to cover his insecurities.

No… Riggs didn't have an insecure bone in his body.

Except he had seemed vulnerable when he'd confided about being teased. And one lesson they all should have learned from Ned was not to assume anything, to dig deeper and uncover what was really going on in a person's head, not to judge someone on the sake of appearances.

"Ma'am, I'm finished."

The consultant's voice broke the silence and Kate closed the sliding-glass door.

"Let me show you the ins and outs," he said, eyes darting to the clouds of smoke above the tree line. "I also installed the doorbell camera as you requested."

Relief spilled through Kate. At least she would know if someone tried to break in. "Thank you."

He spent the next half hour explaining the ins and outs of the system and then asked for a security code word.

Kate glanced at the sliding doors again, her heart pounding at the sight of the flames ripping through the woods.

In spite of the fear clawing at her, she chose the word *Hopeful.*

There's always hope for good, her mother used to say.

Kate intended to cling to her mother's mantra as long as she lived.

RIGGS SUITED UP as soon as he made it to the side of the road where the fire trucks were parked. Acres of wooded property and farmland dotted the mountainous area. Tall pines, oaks and evergreens climbed upward, the first signs of summer evident in the wildflowers pushing through the green.

White blossoms from the dogwoods looked like snow as they fluttered to the ground, and birds soared above, returning from their winter trek to the south.

His fellow firefighters were already busy rolling hoses as far as they could reach. A special team had been called to fly above and unleash water on the blaze.

Containment was key for the safety of the residents who lived nearby.

They weren't ordering evacuations yet, but if the blaze spread another mile and the winds gained speed, the houses in Kate's neighborhood would be in serious danger.

So would Kate.

"Do we know cause yet?" he asked Brian who'd arrived first on the scene with Riggs's coworkers.

"Not yet," Brian said. "So far, it's spread about a quarter of a mile through the woods. The volunteer team from the neighboring county is on its way. We need all the manpower we can get."

"Be on the lookout for signs of arson," Riggs said as he strapped on his helmet.

Brian frowned. "You think it was intentional?"

Riggs shrugged. He didn't want to elaborate yet, but they had to consider all scenarios. "It's possible."

Although, if the fire had nothing to do with Kate, and it was arson, it could have been set to cover up a crime. It was one of the most common causes of arson.

With bitterness pervading the town and former classmates returning, who knew what old vendettas might come into play. Stones had been cast after the shooting, friendships shattered, blame tossed around like live grenades.

Riggs and the men dove into their work, attacking the blaze and tracking it through the woods, creating barriers and soaking the grounds in the fire's path. Others worked to dump water on the flames, a second plane joining the first to cover more territory.

He lost track of time as they worked, simply went into autopilot. Sweat beaded his skin and trickled down his neck, the thickening smoke making it imperative to breathe through his mask. Tree limbs cracked and popped, the heat intensifying. He and his coworkers dodged the falling fiery debris as it snapped off with the weight of the water assaulting the flames.

His boots smashed dying embers, twigs and brush soaked by the water, the scent of fire all around him. Riggs worked for a good two hours with his crew before the blaze began to die down and the air became clear enough to see in front of him.

"The fire is contained," the chief said over Riggs's mic. "I repeat, it's contained, but we'll monitor it overnight."

Riggs and Brian traded relieved looks. "Do you have any idea the point of origin?" Riggs asked.

"We have a general idea," Brian murmured.

The chief spoke again. "Sheriff Stone is at the scene. He's calling in deputies to cordon off and guard the area until we can search for forensics and an accelerant."

So far, Riggs hadn't detected the scent of gasoline. But he could be a half mile from point of origin.

"Thanks for the assist," Brian said as they stowed their gear on the truck. "Hope we didn't tear you away from a hot date."

Riggs made a low sound in his throat. He wished to hell he had been on a date with Kate. But she'd probably turn him down if he asked.

Then another disturbing thought struck him. Perhaps the arsonist set the fire to lure Riggs and the police away from her.

Dammit.

He had to get back and check on Kate.

KATE SHOULD HAVE felt safe with the new security system intact, but each time she looked outside at the smoke-filled sky, her heart pounded with fear for Riggs.

Needing to stay busy, she spent over an hour on the paperwork she'd brought home. Stone's request for the list of students she'd had trouble with nagged at her, so she'd powered up her laptop and run a search for students that had required disciplinary action.

First, a group of kids caught smoking pot in the parking lot: a senior girl and two sophomore boys. She'd suspended them for three days, conferenced with their parents, and allowed them to return to school on probation. The teens had been upset, but they were loners and pacifists, free thinkers and nonconformists that'd never exhibited signs of violence.

Next, she looked at minor infractions—skipping school, cheating, pranks, smoking—but again, none of those students would retaliate with such a degree of violence.

She drummed her fingernails on her lap then examined three students caught fighting in the cafeteria. The first, Darius Holbrook, had moved to Tennessee the second semester. His parents claimed kids were bullying their son and he'd fought back in self-defense. Kate had checked out the story and found it was true, so she'd taken action against the bullies and required them to attend counseling.

She hadn't received reports of their fighting since.

The graffiti incident taunted her. Don Gaines had been at the school, where, she also knew, he'd excelled in art class. She searched for reports of him causing trouble or being involved in any incident of violence. He had been caught smoking in the bathrooms and outside the school. The first time, cigarettes, the second time, weed.

She didn't want to believe Brynn's brother would try to scare her by graffitiing that threat on the side of the school.

Still, Don disliked her. Maybe he knew she was the reason Ned had gone ballistic and shot his sister. The entire family had suffered and been traumatized because of Brynn's paralysis. Mrs. Gaines had always doted on Brynn. No doubt the shooting and Brynn's injury had made that worse. She'd always had high expectations for Brynn. How had she handled the disappointment that Brynn wouldn't walk again? Had she given her attention to Don instead and smothered him?

Or had all her attention been focused on Brynn?

Could Don want revenge for the devastation his family suffered because of the shooting?

FLASHLIGHT IN HAND, Riggs searched the ground as he walked back up the hill toward his truck. The brittle brush, ashes and dying embers made it difficult to see, especially in the dark, but at first light when the area cooled, a full crime scene team would be out hunting for forensics.

A piece of clothing, hair, footprints, accelerant—anything they could use to pinpoint whether the fire was accidental or arson.

His boots dug into the earth, now wet from their efforts to douse the flames, and a patch of weeds shifted. He shone the light onto the patch and spotted something small stuck in the burned leaves, almost hidden by a river rock.

Pulse jumping, he knelt and gently raked the weeds aside.

A matchbook.

Pulling gloves from his pocket, surprised it hadn't completely been destroyed in the fire, he carefully lifted and examined it. The matchbook was empty, the edges charred. He wiped away soot and recognized the logo on the front— Smokehouse Barbecue.

Could it have belonged to the person who'd set this fire? Anger hardened his jaw and Riggs secured it in a bag to give to Stone to send to the lab.

The matchbook could mean nothing. People hiked in the woods all the time.

But it could be a lead. If a match from this book had been used to set the fire, and the lab could pull fingerprints, it might lead to the responsible party.

Accidental or not, this fire could have taken lives.

And if it was intentional, and they were dealing with an arsonist, he needed to be stopped before he struck again.

Chapter Eleven

Riggs backtracked to give Stone the matchbook and found Macy Stark standing beside him, looking concerned as she glanced across the charred woods.

"Good work," Stone said. "I'll have the lab run it for forensics."

"What happened with Woody?" Riggs asked.

Stone shrugged. "Guy's a mess and needs rehab. No confession, and no proof that he's done anything. I'm going to have to cut him loose."

Riggs indicated the matchbook. "Is he a smoker?"

Stone's eyebrows drew together in a frown. "Yeah, matter of fact, he begged for a cigarette. But he's still in a holding cell, so he couldn't have started this fire."

Stone nodded. "But Billy could have."

"He's on my list to question," Stone said before being called away by one of his deputies.

Macy cleared her throat. "Do you think someone intentionally set the fire?"

Riggs shrugged. "Considering the threats to Kate and the point of origin being in close proximity to her house, we have to consider that possibility."

Macy rubbed at her arm, drawing attention to the sling. She was taller than Kate, her long black hair wavy, her green eyes as sharp as a cat's. She'd been physically fit in high school, competitive, a good athlete and the fastest sprinter on the track team.

Macy had always seemed intense, almost aloof at times, unlike sweet Kate, or Brynn with her golden-blond hair, fashion sense, and beauty pageant titles who thrived on being in the social limelight.

The three were so different that he'd thought their friendship odd, but something had drawn them together.

So what had torn them apart?

Macy's voice resonated with concern. "How's Kate?"

"Shaken," Riggs answered. "Haven't you seen her since you got to town?"

Macy glanced back at the woods, a distant look in her eyes. "I saw her after her car caught fire, but we haven't talked."

Curiosity got the better of him. "What's going on?"

Her mouth tightened. "Nothing. I just have a lot to do. I came to clear out my mother's house and get it ready to sell."

Riggs dug his hands in his pockets. He'd heard rumors about Macy's mother having psychological problems, that she'd been institutionalized, and didn't know what to say. "Does that mean you'll be in town for a while?"

"Just until after the dedication ceremony and I put the house on the market."

"Stone said he asked you to look over the files about the shooting."

Macy's expression darkened. "He did. Everyone wants to know if Ned acted alone."

Stone walked back toward them, clipping his phone on his belt. "Crime team is on its way here. I'll meet the deputies and hang around until they rope off the area."

"Did they find forensics on the graffiti wall or anything from the trash cans?" Riggs asked.

"Lifted some partials off the wall. We'll compare them to Don's. No discarded paint-stained clothes, though."

"Someone from the firehouse will stay overnight to make sure the blaze doesn't reignite," Riggs said.

The sound of a car engine rumbled and Gretta's Lexus careened onto the side of the road, pulling to a stop behind the sheriff's car.

"I'll check on Kate," Riggs said. "Keep me posted on the lab results."

Stone muttered he would, and Riggs hiked back toward his truck, determined to avoid the pushy reporter who'd fueled the rumors about his relationship with Cassidy. One afternoon she'd hid behind the bleachers and snapped a picture of him and Cassidy arguing. He'd been trying to convince Cassidy to tell him if he was her baby's father, but she'd refused to talk. That photograph had painted him as a hothead and made Cassidy look like a victim.

If Gretta learned about the letter of blame Kate had received or that Kate felt guilty for Ned's actions, she would plaster it all over the paper and make things worse for Kate.

He ordered himself not to care, but he didn't want to see Kate hurt, especially by someone as conniving and unethical as Gretta.

He went still as a disturbing thought struck him. What if Gretta had sent the letter to Kate? Would she stir up trouble in town to enhance her story?

KATE FINISHED THE list for Stone, although she was hesitant to toss accusations at innocent students.

Then again, she couldn't ignore the facts or students' behavior—that was part of her job. If someone had noticed how deeply troubled Ned had been, he could have been helped and lives wouldn't have been lost.

She'd made it a policy to instill programs to prevent

bullying, to open doors for lonely students to find friends, and had always examined the larger picture when a student acted out. Digging into their family lives often revealed the reasons for their misbehavior. Instead of harsh punishment, students needed counseling and love, to be taught coping skills to deal with their problems.

She pulled the yearbook from her senior year and thumbed through it. A photograph of Macy crossing the finish line first when Briar Ridge went to State brought a pang to her heart.

After the win, Macy had celebrated with the track team and been excited over the prospect of running in college. When she'd gone home that night, her mother had locked Macy out of the house again. She'd been enraged that Macy had been at a school meet instead of at home taking care of her.

Macy had run to Kate's in tears, and Kate had stayed up with her half the night, consoling her. Her mother had made them brownies and hot chocolate, and assured Macy that she should be proud of herself.

Kate's heart swelled with love and pride for her mother as another memory surfaced. One much earlier, when she'd first learned Macy's mother had a mental health problem.

When Kate was five years old, her mother had read bedtime stories with her and then tucked her in. Swaddled in kisses and covers, Kate had nestled in for the night....

A noise startled her. She clenched the covers and listened again. A light rain pinged off the roof. The wind was blowing. Thunder clapped.

The screeching came again. Her heart stuttered. That wasn't the storm. It sounded like a cat was crying. In pain. She had to do something. Save it.

Barefoot, she slipped from bed and tiptoed to the back door. But she hated the dark and the lightning zigzagging

across the treetops, making her jump back from the door.
She couldn't go outside alone. What if it was a wild animal
in the backyard instead of a cat?

She ran to the window, pushed the curtain aside and
peered out into the night. The moon was only a sliver to-
night. A few stars glittered, just enough for her to see some-
thing by the back porch near her window. The crying grew
louder.

She ran to her mommy's room and pushed the door
open. "Mommy, I heard something. I think it's a cat out-
side. It might be hurt."

Mommy stood in front of the bathroom mirror rubbing
face cream on her cheeks. "Are you sure it's not just the
storm?"

"No, I heard crying," Kate whispered. "He's hurt and
out there in the rain."

Mommy set the jar of cream on the counter then clasped
Kate's hand and squeezed it, reassuring her with a smile.
She loved her mommy so much. Mommy was always smil-
ing and made everything all right. "Come on, we'll look
together."

Together they rushed to the front door. Mommy paused
and listened. Worry flickered in her eyes. Then she quickly
opened the door and stepped out onto the porch.

More thunder clapped and lightning lit up the sky. Rain
ran from the roof, pounding the ground by the porch and
splattering mud everywhere.

Kate shivered, hanging on to Mommy's leg. Suddenly
the thunder's rumble grew softer, and an eerie silence fell.
A second later, Kate saw the bushes rustling by the steps.

"Over there." Kate pointed to the right side of the porch.

Mommy patted her shoulder. "Stay here, sweetie. "It's
probably a stray cat trying to get out of the rain."

Kate clung to the porch railing as Mommy ran down the

steps. Another streak of lightning flashed, and Kate saw her mommy stoop beside the stairs.

Her heart pounded with fear. What if she was too late to save the cat? Or what if something got Mommy?

A second later, Mommy stood. She wasn't holding a cat, though. It was the little girl next door, Macy. Macy was shivering and shaking as she wrapped her arms around Kate's mommy's neck and sobbed into her chest.

Kate rubbed her eyes to keep from crying, too. Poor Macy, she looked like a drowned rat.

"Come on, let's get you out of the rain," Mommy said.

Macy clung to Mommy as she carried her into the kitchen. "Get me a towel, Kate."

Kate raced to the drawer and grabbed a couple of drying cloths and handed them to her mommy, who wiped at the mud on Macy's knees and hands where she'd crawled beneath the steps for cover from the downpour.

Kate shivered as her mommy soothed Macy. Finally, when Macy stopped sobbing, Mommy lifted Macy's chin and looked at her face.

"Are you hurt anywhere, honey?" Mommy asked.

Macy's chin quivered, but she shook her head.

"What happened?" Mommy asked.

Macy looked down at her soaking clothes and her face turned red.

"It's okay, you can tell me," Mommy said. "Kate and I just want to be your friend." Mommy rubbed Macy's back. "Did you get locked out of the house?"

Macy ducked her head again, her voice a low pained whisper. "Mommy got mad and put me out. She told me I was too much trouble and I could sleep outside with the dogs tonight."

Kate gasped but her mommy kept soothing Macy. "Sweetheart, no little girl should sleep outside, much less in this weather. Is your mommy okay? Was someone else there?"

"No one was there but her," Macy said on another sob. *"She just got mad at me. She does that sometimes when she doesn't want me around. She says I'm tr...ouble."*

Kate barely held back a cry, but her mommy's warning look told her to stay quiet. That this was bad. Real bad.

"Well, you can stay here tonight with me and Kate, right, Kate?"

Kate nodded, her heart hurting. Mommy would never make her go outside in the rain alone, much less sleep outside. Macy didn't have a dog, either. The only one nearby belonged to Big Rob the Butcher at the end of the street. Big Rob and his dog snarled at you if you got near either one of them.

"Let's get you in some dry pajamas." Mommy lifted Macy, and Kate followed her to Kate's bedroom.

"She can wear some of yours, can't she, Kate?"

Kate's favorite pj's had flying unicorns on them, and she'd never shared her clothes before. But Macy looked like she needed some flying unicorns tonight, so she dug them from her drawer and pushed them toward Macy.

"These are the bestest ones," Kate said. *"They always bring me sweet dreams."*

Macy changed in the bathroom, then Mommy brought them both cookies in bed and Kate gave Macy her stuffed puppy to sleep with. Then her mother sang them songs until they both fell asleep.

The next morning, she heard her mommy raise her voice for the first time ever. She had called Macy's mother and they were having a talk.

Later she explained to Kate that Macy's mother was sick and that illness caused her to do things that might hurt Macy. From then on, it was their job to watch over Macy.

A TREE BRANCH scraped the window outside, bringing Kate back to the present. From then on, Kate and Macy had been inseparable. Kate's mother had driven Macy to school and back. They'd taken her to the park with them and to the zoo and to movies. Macy spent the night at her house more than her own.

But Macy rarely talked about that first night, or the other times when her mother had thrown a fit, or why Macy never invited Kate to play at her house.

Kate knew the reason. Her friend didn't have to say the words out loud.

Kate loved her mother even more for taking Macy in with no questions asked.

And then her mother had died and Macy had disappeared from her life, leaving an even bigger hole in Kate's chest.

Kate walked over to the window. Smoke still seeped into the sky. Riggs hadn't hesitated to rush out to help battle the blaze. He could have gotten killed.

Maybe she was wrong about him.

It didn't matter. She'd lost Brynn and Macy and her mother. She couldn't afford to let herself care about someone else.

BY THE TIME Riggs reached Kate's, he'd decided Gretta might be responsible for the letter of blame to Kate. Gretta's father had owned an auto repair shop before he died. She could have learned enough from him to know how to cut a gas line.

He parked, then sent Stone a text relaying his theory. Maybe Stone could get the blasted woman's fingerprints or DNA for comparison in case they lifted some from the matchbook or car. Stone texted a reply that he would consider Riggs's suggestion.

Riggs scanned Kate's property, alert for trouble, as he walked up to the porch. The scent of smoke and burned wood lingered, but he didn't see anyone lurking around.

He wiped soot from his hands onto his pants and rang the doorbell. Seconds later, the sound of footsteps echoed from inside and then the lock turned.

He sucked in a breath as Kate opened the door. Her long hair spilled over her shoulders in sexy waves.

"Are you okay?" she asked in a raspy voice.

"Yeah. Are you?"

She nodded and gestured for him to come inside. Although he'd removed his firefighting equipment, his hair and skin held the smoky scent of where he'd been.

"We extinguished the blaze," he said. "But it burned at least a half mile of woods. Deputies and the fire department will monitor the area tonight to make sure the wind doesn't spark the fire back to life."

Kate rubbed her arms with her hands. "Was anyone hurt?"

"No. Thankfully, we didn't find casualties or anyone trapped or injured."

Kate heaved a sigh of relief. "Thank God. I was worried about you."

He arched a brow, surprised at her admission. "I know what I'm doing, Kate."

A soft smile flickered in her eyes. "Your job is still dangerous."

What was dangerous was the heat simmering between the two of them. He wanted nothing more right now than to pull Kate into his arms and hold her. To wipe that worry off her face with a mind-blowing kiss.

Her gaze locked with his and, for a second, he thought she might welcome that kiss.

Then she turned and walked over to her desk by the

sliding-glass doors leading to her back deck, and he called himself all kinds of a fool.

"I made a list of students for Stone," she said. "Although I don't think any of them is violent enough to try to kill me."

Riggs didn't want to frighten her, but they couldn't bury their heads in the sand. Everyone had done that with Ned. Ignored the signs.

Then it was too late.

"We can't be too careful, Kate. Someone is playing a deadly game and he or she needs to be stopped."

Kate rubbed her arms with her hands to ward off the chill. "I can't believe this is happening."

"I know and I'm sorry. But I found an empty matchbook in the woods. It could have belonged to the person who set the fire."

"Or someone was smoking and accidentally dropped a cigarette or match."

"That's possible. Or they lit the match and intentionally threw it into the weeds to start the fire," Riggs said. "Woody is a smoker but he's still in a cell, so he didn't do it."

Kate shifted uncomfortably and looked back at the envelope on her desk.

"That the list of students?" he asked.

She murmured that it was.

"Any of them smokers?"

Kate sighed again. "Don Gaines. He was caught in the bathroom at school and outside behind the bleachers."

"You notified his folks?"

"Yes. But Don is all talk. He wouldn't have the guts to come after me."

"His sister was paralyzed because of that shooting, Kate. That had to have affected the entire family."

"I know, but—"

"Maybe you could talk to Brynn," he suggested.

Kate ran a hand through her hair, pushing it away from her forehead. "I can't suggest to Brynn that her brother is an arsonist. Besides, she and I haven't been close in years."

"Why is that? I thought you and Macy and Brynn were best friends."

A wave of sadness washed over her face. "We were. But that was a long time ago."

She didn't elaborate and he sensed the subject was closed.

Kate might not believe Don was dangerous. But the kid had an attitude.

And Riggs didn't trust him.

KATE COULD JUST imagine Brynn's reaction if she showed up tossing accusations at her little brother. And the mayor and his wife... Mrs. Gaines hated her already.

"Macy was with Stone at the scene of the fire tonight," Riggs said.

Kate lifted her head. "What was she doing there?"

"Stone asked her to look over his father's files. He hopes she'll find something he missed."

"That makes sense, I guess."

"She asked about you," Riggs said, his gaze scrutinizing her.

Tears blurred Kate's eyes and she blinked to stem them. Earlier, she'd been thinking about Macy and Macy's awful childhood, and how they'd been like sisters when they were young.

"She said she's going to clear out her mother's house and put it on the market while she's here," Riggs said.

Kate's heart squeezed. "I heard her mother was institutionalized."

"What happened between you two?" Riggs asked.

Kate clenched her hands by her sides, annoyed at his persistence. "Everything changed after the shooting. As soon as graduation was over, Macy just moved away." Without even saying goodbye.

Her abandonment had felt like a knife in Kate's gut at the time.

Her phone trilled, saving her from more questions, and she rushed to answer it, although she had no idea who would be calling at this time of night. Maybe someone from the school council about the memorial.

"Hello?"

"Back off, Kate," a deep muffled voice growled, "or next time your fireman boyfriend won't be able to save you."

Cold fear seized Kate as the line went dead.

Chapter Twelve

Riggs narrowed his eyes as Kate hung up the phone. Her face had gone pasty white. "What's wrong, Kate?"

She sank onto her sofa and dropped her head into her hands.

Riggs gritted his teeth, walked over and joined her. She looked so upset that he wanted to take her in his arms and hold her. "Who was on the phone?"

"I don't know." She raked a trembling hand through her hair and looked up at him with a mixture of fear and confusion.

Riggs couldn't resist. He rubbed her back in slow circles to comfort her. "Talk to me, Kate. What exactly did he say?"

"The voice was muffled, so I couldn't tell if it was a man or a woman. But whoever it was said, 'Back off, Kate, or next time your fireman boyfriend won't be able to save you.'"

Riggs went cold inside. He didn't mind being called her boyfriend, but the fact that the caller knew he was there meant he was watching Kate. That he wanted to do more than scare her. And that she'd been the target of that fire.

"Did he say anything else?"

"No." Her chin quivered. "But he must be nearby, watching me."

Riggs muttered a curse as he rushed to the sliders overlooking the back yard. Shoulders rigid, he stepped outside and searched the darkness. Shadows flitted like dark soldiers in the night through the woods as the trees rustled and moved in the wind.

The caller implied he'd set that fire to get to Kate. That meant the same person who'd set it had tampered with her SUV.

Through the faint sliver of moonlight fighting its way through the fog and smoke, he searched the darkness for her stalker, but he didn't see anyone in the yard. Although a pair of binoculars could allow the perp to watch from afar.

Pulse jumping, Riggs raced to the front of the house. Through the window, he scanned the yard and street, searching for movement. A car, a match striking, or a cigarette glowing in the dark.

Kate moved up behind him. "Do you see anyone?"

The hair on the nape of his neck stood on end. "No. But he's out there somewhere." He sensed it.

His hand went to his belt. "I'll call Stone. He can put a trace on your phone. If this bastard calls back, maybe he can catch him and stop this madness."

Kate ran her fingers through her hair, untangling the strands as she sighed.

His heart stuttered with tenderness for her, and he cupped her face in his hands. "Don't worry, Kate. He's not going to get to you."

Her eyes searched his, emotions flaring. "You don't owe my mother, Riggs. She helped you because she cared. That's who she was."

Yes, he did owe her. Other than his own mother, she was the first person who'd believed he wasn't stupid.

Still, he had to be honest with himself. He wasn't just here to repay a debt to Elaine McKendrick. He liked Kate.

Need and desire leaped inside him, and he leaned closer to her. Her breath quickened, a seed of longing in her expressive eyes.

He threaded his fingers through the soft tresses of her hair, hunger consuming him. "I'm not doing this for your mother."

Then he did what he'd been wanting to do forever. He closed his mouth over hers and kissed her.

KATE'S SELF-PROTECTIVE instincts whispered for her to run. That Riggs had the power to break her heart.

You're a fool to let him get close.

But at the moment, she didn't care. Ever since she was fifteen, she'd wondered what it would be like to taste him. To have him look at her the way he just had.

To feel his lips on hers and his arms around her.

Riggs didn't disappoint.

He swept her hair back with his fingers and deepened the kiss, teasing her lips apart with his tongue and delving inside as if he craved her taste just as she did his.

She lifted her hands, tunneled one into his thick hair and pulled him to her. He teased and explored, taking and giving, until she felt her knees go weak.

Then he caught her around her waist and cradled her against his body. His muscles pressed against her soft curves, teasing her with his masculinity. He mumbled her name on a throaty sigh and unbuttoned her blouse as he walked her backward toward the sofa.

Caught up in the moment, Kate clung to him and fell onto the plush cushions. Her head hit the pillow, her breathing ragged, and he caressed her cheek with his thumb again. Then he dipped his head and pressed tender kisses along her throat, lighting a trail of fire though her body.

That need suddenly sent a streak of terror through her

"You're beautiful, Kate," he murmured.

Tears pricked her eyes as another memory surfaced. Another man, her college boyfriend, telling her she was beautiful and then laughing as he'd walked away after he'd screwed her.

She couldn't do this. Give in to this raging need for Riggs.

The passion in his eyes turned into a question. "Kate?"

"Stop," she whispered. "Please."

He searched her face, her eyes. Then he lifted his body from hers, pushed away from the sofa, and walked over to the sliding glass doors.

The sound of the doors opening made her regret her request, but she'd be foolish to ask him to come back.

Kate McKendrick was a practical kind of girl, not a love-struck teenager.

She quickly buttoned her blouse, humiliation climbing her neck as she realized how close she'd come to letting Riggs strip her naked on the couch.

Outside on the deck, he stood with his back to her, looking out into the woods, his body rigid, hands curled around the railing.

Fighting the urge to go to him and beg him to finish what they'd begun, she hurried into her bedroom and shut the door.

Riggs had promised not to let anyone hurt her.

But *he* could hurt her if she let down her defenses again.

RIGGS GRIPPED THE railing so tightly he thought the wood might splinter. What the hell had just happened?

He'd kissed Kate, that was what had happened. He'd kissed her and that kiss had been so damn hot he hadn't been able to stop himself. No, he could have stopped himself—he just hadn't wanted to.

So he'd kept going and one taste of her neck had made him crave more. And then, for God's sake, he'd unbuttoned her blouse, seen that scrap of red lace, and thought he'd die if he didn't have her.

Who knew sweet, tough, levelheaded Kate liked decadent underwear?

Her breasts…they were every bit as luscious-looking as he'd imagined.

And he had fantasized about them. When he was in high school. When he'd seen her around town. In his sleep. After all, he was a red-blooded male.

And she was…exquisite.

You're a bastard, man. Kate was scared and you came onto her.

Of course she'd told him to stop. He'd practically mauled her.

Although, for a brief second, he'd felt passion between them as if it wasn't one-sided. As if Kate wanted him.

He hadn't imagined it, had he?

Forcing himself to take long, deep breaths, he wrangled his libido under control. The wind picked up, stirring the acrid scent of smoke and burned wood, a reminder of the reason he was at Kate's.

And of the phone call.

Dammit, he had to update Stone. Should have alerted him the minute Kate had told him about the threat.

He snagged his phone from his belt and punched Stone's number. "I came back to Kate's after I left the fire," Riggs said. "Where are you?"

"Just left the mayor's house. I stopped by to see if Don Gaines was home."

Riggs's pulse quickened. "Was he?"

"He'd just gotten in," Riggs said. "Mayor didn't like

my questions, but Don smelled like smoke, and had mud on his sneakers."

"Where did he say he'd been?"

"Out with some buddies. I'll call them and verify his story when I return to the station. Mr. Gaines refused to let Don give me a DNA sample or his prints, so I'm requesting a warrant."

"While you're at it, get one for his cell phone."

"What's up?" Stone asked.

Riggs explained about the phone call. "This bastard is stalking her, Stone."

Stone mumbled a curse. "Poor Kate. I bet she's completely unraveled."

Kate unraveled? He was the one coming unraveled. "She was shaken," Riggs admitted. "She gave permission for you to put a trace on her cell in case the caller phones again."

"On it." He hunched his shoulders. "Macy's been reviewing Dad's old files. She plans to connect with our former classmates at the picnic tomorrow. Maybe time has mellowed everyone and, if someone did know something, he or she is ready to talk."

Kate would probably be front and center at the picnic. So might the person threatening her.

He bit back a curse. He wanted her tucked away safe and sound.

In his bed.

Not going to happen, man.

"Maybe Billy will show up," Stone said.

"Maybe." Twigs snapped from somewhere in the distance and a tree branch splintered and sailed to the ground. Riggs craned his neck to search the area again. "He may be lurking nearby." That would be Billy's style.

Stone nodded. "If he's escalating, he might make a mistake and tip his hand in public."

"We can hope."

Stone hung up, then the slider doors squeaked open. Riggs steeled himself against reacting...or reaching for Kate again.

The scent of her lavender bodywash wafted to him, aromatic and feminine in contrast to the thick, cloying, smoky odor.

"Riggs, I—"

"Go to bed, Kate."

Her raspy breath punctuated the air, torturing him. "W-we should talk," she said in a low whisper.

Hell, no. Not with her standing in the fading moonlight with her hair spilling around her shoulders and the image of that red lacy bra fresh in his mind. "There's nothing to talk about. You wanted to stop and we did. You can lock the door if you're afraid of me."

She took a step toward him. "I'm not afraid," Kate breathed.

But she was. Fear glittered in her eyes.

That hurt more than if she'd physically hit him. "I told you I'd protect you, and I will. I'll sleep on the couch and I won't bother you again."

"Riggs—"

"Please, Kate. Go. To. Bed."

His gruff voice must have gotten to her because she turned and disappeared inside the house. A minute later he heard her bedroom door close.

Good, she was out of sight. Safe.

Riggs was the one in danger of losing himself in her sweet body and eyes.

But he needed to stop any fantasies of having Kate. He had to stay focused and protect her.

He'd lost a friend in the shooting and two more in a fire last year. The sound of that warehouse collapsing, trapping two of his partners who'd gone in to save innocents haunted him every night. Tony Almono and Will Elrod, both over six feet and strong as oxen. But not strong enough to survive an inferno or the burning rubble that had covered them in flames and hot gas.

Hell, he used to be fun-loving and cocky. But he'd seen too many good people get killed to forget that death came for everybody at some time.

Kate was too good a person for it to come for her just yet.

KATE WAS AS shaken by the kiss with Riggs as she was the fire. His comment about Macy reviewing the original case files from the shooting investigation played through her head as she readied for bed.

Why had Macy left town without saying goodbye?

Why did you let the distance between you two go on for so long...? You could have tried harder to reach out to her. Harder to get her to forgive you. Harder to keep her in your life.

But Kate had been too embroiled in her own grief to think about anyone except herself.

She punched her pillow in frustration. As a member of the planning committee, Amy had kept a list of all the addresses and phone numbers for the alumni. Kate rose from bed, booted up her computer and searched the list until she found Macy's.

Even if her former best friend didn't want to reconcile, she at least owed her an apology for how she'd acted fifteen years ago. Macy had never known how to reach out for help, and if she'd needed it, would have tried to handle things on her own, just as she had as a kid.

With the new school, Kate hoped for a new beginning. Maybe she needed a new one with Macy.

Still, her hand trembled slightly as she crawled back into bed and pressed Macy's number.

The phone rang four times then her voice mail picked up.

"This is Special Agent Macy Stark. Please leave a message with your number and I'll get back to you as soon as I can."

Kate tensed. What she had to say needed to be said in person, not on a message machine. Macy knew where she lived and could come by, but she hadn't. Maybe she was screening her calls and didn't want to talk.

Biting her lip, she pressed End Call without leaving a message. She'd try again later. Or maybe she'd see Macy at one of the reunion events and they could talk.

But worry knotted her stomach as Kate closed her eyes and memories of the shooting returned to haunt her....

THE BELL HAD RUNG, signaling time to change to third period, when Ned had flown into a rage. Kate and Macy and Brynn had just met at their lockers, chatting about nothing, when the first bullet was fired.

Their lockers were directly across from Kate's mother's classroom. Riggs had just come out, and she and Macy turned to head into English class while Brynn had Trig. But screams erupted as the bullets began to ping off the lockers and victims began to fall.

Kate's mother stepped out and raised a hand to try to convince Ned to put down the gun. Just as she did, Ned waved the gun. Macy froze, her eyes wide with terror, then Kate heard the sound of the gun going off.

Shock immobilized her as she watched Riggs get hit and fall, blood spurting from his leg as he doubled over in pain. Brynn and the others began to run into classrooms, some kids pushing and shoving to get out of the line of fire.

Ned looked straight at Kate then aimed his weapon at Macy. Then it all happened so quickly that Kate forgot the sequence of events. All she remembered was Macy's scream, the sound of the bullet and then her mother collapsing onto the floor, blood soaking her blouse.

Chapter Thirteen

Riggs's taste still lingered on Kate's lips when she stirred from sleep the next morning, thankfully wiping away some of the bitter taste of the memories that had followed her to bed.

Between the shooting, the recent threats, that unsettling moment with Riggs, and knowing he was sleeping on her couch only a few feet away from her bed, she'd tossed and turned for hours. Finally, when she'd drifted to sleep, instead of nightmares of the shooting years ago, the car fire, or the fire in the woods, she'd dreamed of making love with Riggs.

Her body ached from unsated desire.

But she'd made the right choice by pulling away from Riggs. To her, making love meant more than a physical connection. She couldn't get naked with Riggs without involving her heart. And no doubt Riggs would be turned off by a clingy woman.

Resolve set in. Today it was back to business. She had meetings about the plans for the memorial, and she didn't intend to allow anyone to stand in the way.

She hurriedly showered and dressed in a loose skirt and blouse, then went into the kitchen to make coffee.

Riggs had beaten her to the task, though. He'd also used

her guest bath to clean up and was wearing a fresh blue shirt and jeans that hugged his muscular butt and thighs.

A wave of longing washed over her. Lord help her, she had to get a grip.

Lifting her chin, she strode into the kitchen and poured herself a mug of coffee. For a second, she simply inhaled the aroma, allowing it to jump-start her brain. During the school year, she had to be up early and didn't have time to linger over coffee. Although she still worked several weeks during the summer, she made it a point to savor the morning ritual.

Riggs stared out into the woods, as he had been doing the night before when she'd gone to bed. She realized he was on the phone when he lowered it from his ear and clipped it to his belt.

Curious to learn if he had news, she opened the sliders and stepped onto the deck. The temperature seemed warmer today, although a slight breeze stirred the trees and brought the acrid scent of burned leaves, trees and ash. Cloud cover cast shadows across the land, making it look eerie and desolate in the gray light.

Riggs's big body stiffened as he slowly faced her. His dark brows were furrowed into a frown, his jaw tight. He took a long, slow sip of his coffee. His eyes were smoldering—with memories of the night before and…anger? Disappointment?

Kate swallowed hard to make her voice work and attempted to banish the memory of his lips on hers. "Good morning."

A dark intensity radiated from him. "Morning, Kate."

The gruff way he murmured her name made her touch her lips with her fingers. A mistake. Riggs's eyes followed the movement.

Irritated with herself, she sank onto the glider to sip her coffee. "Did you sleep?" she asked.

"Some."

"I'm sorry," Kate said.

"No sweat. Odd hours go with my job. I'm used to it." He leaned his back against the railing. "Stone called about the phone. Looks like the caller used a burner phone. Makes it damn near impossible to trace."

"That figures." Kate glanced out into the woods. Noises and voices broke the early morning serenity of the mountains.

"The crime techs came back at first light to search for forensics," Riggs explained. "Stone said he stopped by the mayor's house last night to get his son's prints for comparison, but Don wasn't home. I have an idea of how to obtain it. Do you keep a record of the students' locker assignments?"

"Yes," Kate said. "But dozens of kids touch the lockers when they're hanging out between classes."

"True. But he's probably the only one who touched the interior space. Maybe we'll get lucky and he left his prints or DNA inside somewhere."

Kate hated to point suspicion toward Brynn's brother. But if he had set that fire, someone could have been hurt, and she couldn't bury her head in the sand.

A HALF HOUR LATER, Riggs followed Kate to the school. Stone had liked his plan for obtaining Don's prints and agreed to meet them. Kate could hand off the list then.

Over a quick breakfast, Riggs had kept the conversation focused on the investigation and avoided discussing the evening before. Kate had made it perfectly clear she didn't want him.

Still, the devil must be punishing him because he'd dreamed about her all night. Crazy dreams of cuddling on

Sunday mornings. Watching the news together. Enjoying long walks and bike rides. Cooking dinner together. Making homemade pasta.

Homemade pasta for cripes' sake. He'd seen Kate's machine on the counter. But he was a meat-and-potatoes man. Dammit.

He parked in front of the school and cursed at the sight of the graffiti on the wall. Vandalizing a building was a crime, but petty compared to arson or attempted murder. Were these crimes being committed by the same person?

The tone of the threats suggested they were.

Stone pulled in just after him. Riggs exited his truck and waited on Stone, giving Kate the space she needed. This was her work: the new school project, her baby.

He wanted to make it happen for her and for the town.

"Are you going to the picnic today?" Stone asked.

There were only a handful of former classmates Riggs gave one iota about seeing. "If Kate goes, I am."

"Thanks for keeping an eye out for her," Stone said.

Hell, he'd do it even if Stone hadn't asked.

Stone scratched his chin as they walked up to the front of the building. "What if there's more to the threats against Kate than just someone being upset about the demolition of the old school?"

"I've been thinking about that, too. If Ned had an accomplice, that person has gotten off scot-free for years." Riggs opened the front door and stepped inside the school. "He or she sure as hell wouldn't want to be exposed now. And with everyone rehashing what happened, it would make an accomplice afraid of being exposed."

"Exactly."

"Did you talk to Ned's parents?"

"I spoke to Mr. Hodgkins. He and his wife are still out of

town. And, no surprise, he's bitter. I think they still blame themselves for what happened, too."

Riggs made a low sound in his throat. "I can understand that."

"He was adamant that he and his wife would never set foot back in Briar Ridge. They support the new building, though, said they wanted the place where their son murdered innocent kids to be wiped off the map."

Who could blame them? "I can't imagine living with the fact that your own child killed his classmates."

"Yeah, another kind of hell."

Hell was right. Riggs had watched Ned gun down another classmate before he'd shot him. Then he'd aimed his gun at Macy and at Kate. He'd never forget the terror on their faces or the screams that echoed up and down the halls. Doors slamming. Students running for their lives. Taking cover anywhere they could. Bashing windows just to jump outside and escape.

Then the gun firing again. He'd stared in helpless shock, blood soaking him, and expected Kate or Macy to fall beside him. But Mrs. McKendrick had stepped in the way and saved their lives.

Then the sirens, Ned running, the police storming in. Crying all around him, terrified screams and rescue workers rushing in to take care of the injured and dead.

"There's Kate," Stone said, pushing away Riggs's thoughts of the painful past.

Kate motioned them over. When Riggs stepped further inside, it struck him how empty the building felt. Bare walls. Furniture and posters and billboards gone. No sounds of teens talking and laughing, or music, or the bell ringing.

Students wouldn't be returning here in the fall or ever again.

Pleasant memories of his own years at Briar Ridge

drifted back. Football rallies, soccer games, homecoming and prom.

His nervous stomach over tests he was afraid he wouldn't pass.

Then that horrible day all over again.

"Here's the list," Kate said, interrupting his thoughts again.

Riggs was glad the building would be gone soon. Maybe one day they'd all begin to forget.

"Honestly, Stone, I can't see any of these kids trying to kill me," Kate said as she handed Stone an envelope. "None of the infractions were serious."

"Maybe, maybe not. But I'll check them out just in case." He paused. "Is Don Gaines on the list?"

Kate shifted from one foot to the other, her fingers stroking the strap of her bag. "Yes. He was caught smoking in the bathroom and outside. But—"

"Just show me his locker," Stone said flatly.

Kate gestured to the hall leading toward the science wing. "I don't want to accuse Don of something unless you have definitive proof," Kate said as they walked. "The Gaines family suffered enough after the shooting."

A muscle twitched in Riggs's jaw. So like Kate to think about helping the kid instead of being angry with him.

"Look at this way, Kate," Stone said calmly. "Lifting his prints may clear him and we can cross him off the suspect list."

Riggs touched Kate's arm. "Besides, if the prints from the locker don't match the one on the matchbook, Don and his family never have to know you did this."

Kate waffled. "I suppose that's true."

Resigned, Kate stopped at a set of lockers near the exit to the breezeway that connected the main building to the gym. Don had been in the science lab—to retrieve his phone, he'd claimed—around the same time the threat had been graffitied on the outside wall. Don's locker was near the exit closest to the gym.

Kate inserted a master key and opened the locker. Stone indicated for her not to touch anything while he yanked on latex gloves to search the interior.

No books. Trash from a candy bar wrapper. Two foil packs of condoms. A nude picture from a porn magazine.

Riggs shook his head, surprised the kid had left the picture behind. Then again, with his money, Don probably had a stash of girly magazines in his room. And internet porn was so easily accessible, he might have a mile-long list of sites he frequented.

Stone bagged each of the items. Just as he lifted the picture, Riggs spotted a matchbook on the bottom of the locker.

A matchbook from Smokehouse Barbecue.

KATE FOLDED HER ARMS. "The matches—"

"Are from the same place as the matchbook I found in the woods last night," Riggs said.

She bit her bottom lip. "That doesn't mean Don set the fire. Anyone could have picked up a book of matches from Smokehouse Barbecue."

"True, but he still shouldn't have matches at school," Stone said. "Hopefully we can lift prints and compare."

Footsteps echoed from down the hall, and Kate checked her watch as Jimmy appeared. His limp seemed more pronounced today and he looked tired, his wiry hair sticking out, the wrinkles around his eyes more prominent, as if he hadn't been sleeping well. "Ms. McKendrick, there's some folks here from the town council, say they're supposed to meet with you. Amy Turner is already in your office."

"Thanks, Jimmy. Tell them I'll be right there." She tilted

her head at the two men. "I have to go. We need to finalize details for the memorial."

"We're right behind you," Riggs said.

Kate headed down the hall, Riggs beside her, Stone on their heels.

"Are you going to the picnic?" Riggs asked.

They stopped in front of the door to her office. "I have to show up. I helped organize these events. I'd hoped a re-union might help mend friendships." She wished she could mend her own with Macy and Brynn. If Don Gaines turned out to be the one threatening her, she would only drive a wedge deeper between her and Brynn.

"I'll swing back by and pick you up after your meet-ing," Riggs offered.

"Thanks, but I'll drive. I have an errand to do on the way."

"I could help."

Kate shook her head. "The memorial is supposed to be a surprise. Besides, I'm just going to the frame shop in town. There will be dozens of people around."

Stone cleared his throat. "I need to drop this stuff at the lab. You coming, Riggs?"

Riggs shrugged. "Yeah."

Kate spotted the mayor entering the building. His gray eyes cut to Stone.

"Sheriff?" Mayor Gaines raised a brow. "What are you doing here?"

Kate tensed, but Stone didn't miss a beat. "We're inves-tigating that graffiti outside. Someone also tampered with Kate's car, so I have to take the threat against her seriously."

"Last night, someone also set a fire in the woods behind her house," Riggs added. "Kate may have been a target."

The mayor coughed. "I'm well aware of the fire." He pierced Stone with a disapproving look, although Stone let it roll off his back. Stone was not into politics—he was known for being fair and out for justice. He also wouldn't let anyone push him around.

"I hope you find out who's doing this," the mayor continued. "Kate is a valuable member of the community."

"Yes, she is," Stone agreed.

"I can assure you my son was not involved." The mayor's cheeks turned ruddy. "I talked to him after you left, Sheriff. I'm not proud of it, but he and his friends were buying weed last night. That's the reason he wasn't home." He made a guttural sound in his throat. "I intend to see that he gets the help he needs."

"That's wise," Kate said, proud of the mayor for owning his son's problem. Many parents lived in denial.

Stone gave the mayor a deadpan look. "I'm not pointing a finger at anyone yet," Stone said. "Just gathering evidence to see where it leads us."

Amy poked her head into the hallway from Kate's office. "I'm here, Kate."

"We should get started on the meeting." Kate gestured toward the mayor. "Are you ready?"

He nodded and followed Amy as she retreated to Kate's office. Riggs caught Kate's arm before she left. "Don't let him intimidate you."

"Don't worry. I don't intend to."

He squeezed her arm. "Call me if you need me."

Nerves gathered in her stomach. She wouldn't call. She couldn't afford to need him. She had to stand on her own, just as she always had.

Two hours later, storm clouds hovered over the park, threatening to ruin the reunion picnic. To Riggs's surprise, though, the inclement weather hadn't deterred the Briar Ridge High graduates from showing up. In fact, some former classmates seemed to be excited over reconnecting with past alumni. Even now, old friends were introducing their families and kids were running and playing on the playground.

Without realizing it, Kate's efforts might already be working its healing magic. Their senior year had been so fraught with tension and grief that perhaps everyone had needed to come back together to prove they'd survived.

Although with the threats against Kate, Riggs's senses were honed. Anyone at the reunion could have information about Ned's accomplice. Hell, the accomplice could be hiding in plain sight.

Billy Hodgkins ranked at the top of his suspect list. He could have helped his brother and was now panicked that his part in the mass shooting might be revealed.

Don Gaines couldn't have been an accomplice fifteen years ago, but he might be traumatized enough by what had happened to his sister to threaten Kate now.

Riggs stood at the edge of the pavilion, scrutinizing the group. Some faces he recognized instantly. Others had changed or were only blips in his memory because they'd run in different circles.

His two friends, Jay Lakewood and Duke Eastman, were talking to Ellie Kane and Vera Long, former cheerleaders. Stone's brother Mickey was sitting on a park bench with Cassidy Fulton.

That was odd. He didn't think the two were friendly. Cassidy certainly wasn't romantically interested in a man with a disability—as she'd stressed when Riggs had been in rehab for his leg.

But…a thought suddenly occurred to him. Cassidy had never revealed the name of her baby's father. What if Mickey was Roy's father? Before the shooting, Mickey had been a wild party guy.

Losing his sight had shattered his dreams of playing football in college, although he seemed to have found his artistic side. Now he played the guitar and sang in a local honky-tonk. From what Riggs had heard, Mickey was talented and was beginning to write his own music.

Cara Winthrop's little sister Evie was in deep conversation with Rae Lynn Porter. Cara had been Ned's third victim; he'd shot her five times.

He didn't remember much about Rae Lynn, except she'd been a Goth girl. She'd lost the dramatic look of the Goth attire now, but her jet-black hair still contrasted sharply with her milky-white skin, and tattoos snaked up and down her arms.

Gretta sauntered through the park, stopping to chat as she worked the crowd. Although, judging from the way classmates cut her out of their conversations, no one trusted her. Hell, how could they forget how sneaky she'd been? How she'd blurted out personal secrets to the entire school?

A van pulled up and parked, and he recognized Brynn's vehicle, which had been adapted to accommodate her wheelchair. A driver got out, went around to the side, opened the door, retrieved Brynn's chair and helped her into it.

Riggs made himself look away and not stare. He *was* one of the lucky ones. PT had restored his ability to walk so he hadn't been left permanently disabled. Mrs. Gaines, he knew, had always been overbearing and smothering. He couldn't imagine what Brynn's life was like under her roof.

The wind picked up, hurling leaves across the park. Another car sounded, and Kate drove up in her rental SUV. Just as she got out, Billy Hodgkins jumped from a red sports car and cornered her by the Escape. Billy looked upset, his hands swinging wildly, his hair stringy and matted with sweat.

Anger knotted Riggs's stomach and he sprinted toward them.

Chapter Fourteen

Kate pressed herself against the car as Billy Hodgkins lurched at her.

Behind them in the park, former classmates and alumni were mingling and socializing, enjoying refreshments and music. Her heart gave a pang at the sight of the babies and children.

Right now, though, they seemed a million miles away.

"We need to talk." The dark scowl on Billy's face reminded her of the day he'd cornered her at the cemetery.

She tried to maneuver past him, but he trapped her against the car by planting both hands on the hood. The back of her thighs hit the front bumper.

The instructor in the self-defense class she'd taken in college emphasized not to show fear. Or to look vulnerable. To emit an air of self-confidence.

Lifting her chin in a show of bravado, she braced herself for a physical attack.

"Kate, listen to me," he said in a deep voice.

"Move out of my way, Billy." Kate used both hands to push him away and he stumbled backward. But before she made it two feet, he grabbed her arm.

She gave a pointed look to where his fingers held her a little too tightly and then spoke through clenched teeth. "Let go of me."

"You keep running from me and won't listen." Billy's voice took on a shrill edge. "You have to hear me out."

"She doesn't have to do anything," Riggs's deep voice boomed with authority as he walked up behind Billy. "And if you know what's good for you, Billy, you'll take your hands off of the lady like she asked."

A strand of Billy's shaggy hair fell across one eye, adding to his sinister look. "Back off, Riggs. This is none of your business. It's between me and Kate."

Riggs slapped a hand on Billy's shoulder and dug his fingers into the man's skin. "I'm making it my business. Now step away from Kate."

"Kate, listen," Billy cried. "I just need five minutes."

"Back. Away." A threat underlay Riggs's commanding tone.

A shiver rippled through Kate at the menacing look in Billy's eyes. But he released her arm, raised his hands in a surrender gesture and stepped back.

"What's going on?" This time Stone appeared, hands on his hips as he traced his fingers over his gun.

"I just wanted to talk to Kate," Billy barked. "But Benford jumped on me like a mad dog."

Riggs crossed his arms and spread his feet, an intimidating stance. "If you have anything to say to Kate, you can say it in front of us."

"Forget it." Billy cursed and started to walk away.

Stone blocked his retreat, his height towering over Billy as he looked down at him.

"What the hell?" Billy said. "I thought this was supposed to be a damn reunion. A chance to get back together with old friends."

"You were never friends with Kate," Riggs snarled.

"Neither were you." Billy hooked a thumb toward Kate.

"Sheriff, Kate organized this shindig. You gonna stop everyone who wants to talk to her?"

"Anyone who's viewed as a threat," Stone said bluntly.

"Wait just a minute," Billy snarled. "Just because my brother did a stupid thing doesn't mean—"

"This is not about your brother, at least not directly," Stone interjected. "It's about the fact that someone has been threatening Kate and sabotaged her car."

Billy's eyes darted from Stone to Kate. "You think that was me?"

"We know you blame Kate for your brother's death," Riggs said in a cold tone. "The publicity for the new school and demolition of the old building must have triggered traumatic memories for you."

"Yeah, hell, it did. People ran my folks out of town. They had to change their names because the press made our lives a nightmare." He pounded his hand over his chest. "Did you know they received hate mail? Death threats? That people threw rocks in their living room and someone set fire to my father's hardware store?"

Kate had been so grief stricken from losing her mother and traumatized from witnessing the bloody massacre of her friends that the world had blurred. She had no idea the pain and suffering Ned's family had endured.

"I'm sorry, Billy," Kate said, sympathy lacing her voice.

Pain wrenched Billy's face.

"My father documented what happened," Stone added. "It must have been hell for your family, Billy. And for you." He paused. "All the more reason you might retaliate against the town now."

Confusion marred Billy's face. He seemed thrown off by their acknowledgment of his family's suffering.

"Kate is working to help the town revive the love we

once shared and to make a better place for our children," Riggs said. "Blaming her is wrong."

"I didn't attack her," Billy snapped.

"Where were you last night?" Stone asked.

Billy's right eye twitched. "None of your business."

Stone tapped his badge. "As a matter of fact, it is. You can either answer my questions here or down at the station."

Billy shifted and yanked up his baggy jeans, which were sliding down over his hips and barrel belly. "I had dinner at a place outside of town."

"What place?" Stone asked.

"Pie in the Sky. It's across from the Lazy Dog Motel."

Stone tilted his head to the side. "Can anyone verify you were there?"

"Waitress," Billy said with a toothy grin.

Stone didn't find humor in it and neither did Riggs.

"Do you ever go to Smokehouse Barbecue?" Stone asked.

Billy shrugged. "A time or two. Most everyone in town does. Why do you want to know about that place?"

"Because someone set fire to the woods behind Kate's house," Stone said. "And we found a pack of matches at the scene."

Billy's face paled. "I see what you're doing." He motioned at the crowd in the park. "Half the people out there are against tearing down the old school, but because it was my brother who shot it up, you're going to railroad me to jail for something I didn't do."

"I'm not railroading anyone," Stone said coldly. "But my job is to protect the citizens in Briar Ridge."

Billy raised his head in a defiant gesture. "You don't have anything on me because there's nothing to get. Now, I'm out of here." He gave them a go-to-hell look then stormed away.

"Let me grab my fingerprint kit," Stone said. "Billy's prints should be on the hood of your car, Kate. We'll see if his match the ones on that matchbook."

"I CAN'T BELIEVE the nerve of that guy," Riggs muttered as Billy roared from the parking lot.

Kate shrugged. "His family suffered. Maybe I should have listened to what he had to say."

Riggs gently turned Kate to look at him. "You don't owe that bastard anything. You did not cause his brother to kill our classmates or your mother, and you certainly don't have to put up with his bullying tactics."

Stone returned with his fingerprint kit, and Riggs gestured at the crowd. People had brought lounge chairs and picnic baskets, and old friends were getting reacquainted, playing Frisbee and football.

"We should mingle," he told Kate.

"Yeah, I guess we should."

Although she didn't sound thrilled at the idea.

How could she be excited or relaxed when the person who'd tried to kill her might be in the crowd?

For the next half hour, they talked to former classmates. Riggs kept his ears and eyes peeled for anyone acting suspiciously. Two girls he'd once dated flirted with him, but they no longer made his pulse jump like they had when he was sixteen.

Not like Kate did now.

He grabbed a bottle of water while Kate chatted with friends from the yearbook staff. Jay approached him with an eyebrow raise.

"Something going on with you and Kate?" Jay asked.

Riggs hesitated, maybe a fraction of a second too long. "I just don't want to see her get hurt."

"Uh-huh."

Riggs shifted and spotted Macy at the far end of the park, deep in conversation with another classmate, Trey Cushing. He'd heard the two of them had married.

"Keep telling yourself that," Jay said. "From what I've seen, you've got it bad for her."

Riggs heaved a weary breath and angled himself toward Jay so no one could overhear the conversation. "Fat lot of good it'll do. She still sees me as the player I used to be. That and the thing with Cassidy…"

"You could correct her, you know."

Riggs shrugged. "Maybe I will. If the subject comes up."

A frown tugged at Jay's mouth. "What's holding you back? I've never known you to be shy around a woman."

Riggs chuckled. "She's different." He rolled his shoulders. "Besides, why are you giving advice? Do you have a significant other I don't know about? Fiancée? Wife?"

Jay's smile faded. "I move around too much with the job."

"Excuses, excuses," Riggs said wryly.

This time Jay was the one who looked sheepish. "Guess we're both chicken when it comes to matters of the heart."

Turning around, they spotted Gretta stalking through a crowd of their classmates. "Speaking of dangerous women, run."

They both laughed, but their laughter died when Brynn Gaines wheeled her way down the hill to join the crowd. Gretta darted up beside her, her camera poised as she photographed Brynn's struggle over the rough patchy ground.

"That stupid witch," Jay said. "I'm going to rescue Brynn."

Jay strode off as if on a mission. He was going to have to hurry. Brynn had paused to reposition her chair, and

Gretta caught up with her. She blocked Brynn's way and seemed relentless in firing questions at her.

Questions that, from Riggs's position, seemed to upset Brynn.

Speaking of trouble, Cassidy Fulton sashayed toward him.

Riggs steeled himself against a reaction. With her dyed-blond hair, low-cut top and shorts up her rear, Cassidy had been a hell-raiser in high school. She'd also used him and then tossed him aside like trash. Her cruel comments about his injury had shattered the remnants of his self-esteem at the time.

"Riggs." Cassidy fluttered her eyelashes at him as if the past didn't exist and he wouldn't remember what she'd done. "I heard you came to the rescue when Kate's car exploded."

"Just doing my job."

"Is someone really trying to kill her?" Cassidy asked.

He narrowed his eyes. "Where did you hear that?"

"Small town, word gets around."

Didn't he know it? "How's your son?"

A tiny seed of irritation flickered in her eyes. "Fine."

"Did his father ever step up?"

Any sign of friendliness fizzled out as quickly as a flame being doused by water.

"My son and his father are none of your business—or anyone else's." With a huff, Cassidy stormed away.

Riggs shrugged off her dismissal. He felt for the boy. Maybe he should reach out.

Kate's face caught his attention across the lawn, and he noticed her watching him, her face set in a deep frown.

He wanted to win her trust, for her to see him as a stand-up guy.

Dammit. But talking to the woman he'd supposedly impregnated and abandoned had just accomplished the opposite.

KATE SILENTLY CHIDED herself for watching Riggs and Cassidy. If Riggs wanted to talk to Cassidy or to sleep with her, he was free to do so.

So why was her heart hammering out of her chest with jealousy?

Riggs had a past with Cassidy. A child.

No one could change that.

When whoever was threatening her was caught and the activities surrounding the reunion and dedication for the new school were over, things would return to normal.

Riggs would resume his life—without her.

Her heart gave a pang.

Voices on the hill echoed loudly. Brynn… She was talking to Gretta. Only, Brynn looked upset.

Kate started up the hill to see if Gretta was harassing Brynn, but Jay approached them and lit into her.

Loud voices to the right made her halt in her tracks.

She pivoted and strained to see what the commotion was about, then spotted Macy standing with Trey Cushing. They were having a heated argument, though she couldn't hear what it was about.

Kate had never liked Trey. He'd been pushy with the girls.

On graduation night, she'd seen Macy and Trey leave together. Another blow—Kate thought she and Brynn and Macy would be celebrating together.

Instead, her friends had gone their separate ways.

The argument intensified and Trey leaned into Macy, his face contorted in rage. Macy shook her head and backed away as if to leave.

But Trey clutched Macy's wrist and yanked her to him.

Kate tensed. Macy was an FBI agent and could take care of herself. Although, as tough as Macy appeared, Kate knew a vulnerable side lay beneath the surface. The side that had led them to become friends when Macy was five and needed help.

A side Macy didn't show to anyone.

Freeing herself from his grasp, Macy planted both hands on Trey's chest and pushed him back. He spit out a string of obscenities.

Wanting to reassure Macy that she still had her back, Kate veered toward them.

"Leave her alone," Kate said sharply.

Trey swung toward her, resentment and rage darkening his already vile expression. "Stay the hell out of our business, Kate."

Riggs's comments about Billy being a bully echoed in her head. Trey was a bully, too. "Trey, why don't you take a walk and calm down?"

Macy cut her eyes toward Kate. "Leave us alone, Kate. I've got this."

Her sharp tone made Kate's stomach clench and drove home the truth of the distance between them.

Suddenly, Kate felt overwhelmed. She was tired of fighting everyone on the school. Tired of being afraid. Tired of…being alone.

Still, she believed wholeheartedly that what she was doing for Briar Ridge was right, and she would see the school project through. Tomorrow.

Today she needed a break.

Battling tears, she rushed to her rental SUV, jumped in and drove straight to her house.

Her phone was ringing as she let herself in and switched off the alarm. Riggs's name appeared on the Caller ID.

She let the phone roll to voice mail, poured herself a glass of wine and was just about to carry it to the back porch when the doorbell rang. Shoulders knotted with nerves, she checked the security camera. Riggs.

He looked worried. Maybe angry. And so sexy that she wanted to fall into his arms.

"Kate, open up." The doorbell rang again, followed by a loud knock. "Kate, please. I have to know you're okay."

She steeled herself against his sex appeal as she opened the door. "I'm fine, Riggs, you didn't have to come."

"Yes, I did. When you left the picnic so abruptly, I was worried something had happened."

He did sound worried, and a little bit angry. "I'm sorry," Kate said. "You were busy, and I was ready to leave." *And I couldn't stand seeing you with Cassidy.*

"Then you should have come and gotten me." Riggs strode past her into the room, his breathing heavy. "I was worried to death."

Kate's heart squeezed. "I'm okay—" Her voice died as something crashed through the sliding-glass doors.

Glass shattered. Then there was a popping sound and smoke began to pour into the room.

Chapter Fifteen

Riggs cursed. "Come on, Kate, we have to get out of here!" He pulled her through the front door onto the porch then down the steps to the lawn.

They ran to a large tree far away from the porch and Riggs shoved his phone into Kate's hands. "Call 9-1-1. I'm going to see if the bomber is still around."

Kate stabbed at the numbers while he scanned the street and front of the property. No one lurking nearby. No stray cars.

He raced around the side of the house toward the back. Whoever'd tossed the pipe bomb had to have been close by. Had to have climbed the steps to get the bomb through those sliders.

Glancing up at the deck, he saw it was empty. Smoke seeped through the broken glass, filling the deck and swirling upward in the wind.

Pivoting, he surveyed the back property. The area beneath the deck. Then the woods. Dammit, nothing.

Leaves rustled and trees swayed in the wind. The scent of burned wood from the forest fire still clung to the air. He walked along the trees lining Kate's property, searching the shadows.

A slight movement to the right. He stood frozen, listening, watching. A minute later, a deer scampered through the brush.

The sound of a car engine rumbled then tires squealed. Whoever had tossed that pipe bomb could have woven through the woods to the street farther down.

Riggs jogged up the incline and crossed the yard. Just as he made it to the road, the tail end of a car disappeared around the corner. He broke into a sprint, straining to get a read on the license plate, but the dark clouds shaded the remaining daylight, and the car was too fast.

The sound of a siren wailed from the opposite direction, then another. Riggs rushed back to check on Kate. A fire engine roared to a stop in the drive, followed by Stone's squad car.

Riggs darted toward the tree and found Kate looking shell-shocked.

"Are you okay?" he asked as he stopped in front of her.

"First the car fire, then the woods and now this." Her eyes glittered with anger and shock. "I want to know who's doing this."

"We'll find out." Riggs squeezed her arm. "Let me talk to Stone and the fire crew." He joined Stone and Brian where Brian was issuing orders as the crew began to tackle the blaze inside.

"What happened?" Stone asked.

"Someone threw a pipe bomb through the sliding-glass doors." Riggs raked a hand through his hair. "Kate and I ran out. I looked around back. Didn't see anyone, but I heard a car down the way, tires squealing. By the time I made it to the road, the car flew around the corner and disappeared."

"We'll contain the fire," Brian assured him as he and another firefighter geared-up, then rushed into the house.

"Did you see what kind of car it was?" Stone asked. "Get a license plate?"

"No." Riggs clenched his hands in frustration. "Dammit, Stone, Kate could have been seriously injured tonight."

"I know. The perp is escalating, getting bolder," Stone commented. "He'll make a mistake and we'll catch him."

Riggs gritted his teeth. But would they catch him before Kate got hurt?

KATE HAD BEEN in shock over her car exploding and irritated at the graffiti, but she was furious someone had had the audacity to attack her at home.

Everything Kate had worked for the last few years had been to honor the town and her mother and the ones who'd died in the shooting. She'd dreamed of nothing more than bringing Briar Ridge back to glory with happy kids, adults, families and tourists, and to diminish the distrust riddling the town.

But someone so opposed to those things was willing to kill her.

"Kate," Stone said in a quiet tone. "Did anyone approach you at the picnic? Someone you perceived as a threat?"

"Just Billy." The scene between Macy and Trey flashed behind her eyes. Then Brynn with Gretta. Altercations that had nothing to do with her. Had they?

The scene between Macy and Trey especially bothered Kate. It hinted at domestic violence. Although, Macy was helping to investigate the shooting. Perhaps she'd uncovered something and had confronted Trey about it.

At one time, Kate would have known. Macy would have shared her fears and details about her relationship. Although she had been withdrawn at times. Hadn't talked about her mother's illness.

Maybe something had happened that Kate didn't know about. What if Macy had trouble in her marriage and needed Kate? Perhaps she was the one who'd let down her friend. She should have reached out.

"I'm going to issue an APB for Billy Hodgkins. It's time he answered some questions." Stone stepped aside to make the call, and Riggs rubbed Kate's shoulder.

"Did you see Don Gaines hanging around anywhere?" Riggs asked.

Kate searched her memory banks. "No. I noticed Gretta arguing with Brynn at the picnic. I don't know what they were talking about, though, but Gretta wouldn't leave Brynn alone."

Riggs shrugged. "I know. Jay ran to her rescue. He always despised Gretta."

He wasn't the only one.

"Gretta stopped by the school the day you found that graffiti. Maybe she was fishing for the reason Don was there."

Kate shifted. "Or maybe Gretta knows something about all this that we don't."

"That could be true," Riggs said. "She sure as hell seems to be in everyone's business just like she was back in the day."

Kate shuddered.

"I want to look at that pipe bomb," Riggs said. "Meanwhile, think, Kate. Did you see anything else that seemed suspicious at the picnic?"

"Nothing about the school, but Trey and Macy were arguing. He got rough with her and grabbed her arm. I told him to back off."

"How did he react?" Riggs asked.

Kate shivered. "He got mad and told me to mind my own business."

Riggs cleared his throat. "Did you hear what they were arguing about?"

"No, and Macy told me she could handle it," Kate said. "But the look in his eyes…it bordered on abusive."

"Macy is FBI," Riggs pointed out. "She seems tough, not the type to be victimized."

Yet Kate knew Macy's secrets. "Even strong women get caught off guard by the men they love," Kate said softly. Especially a seasoned manipulator.

Pain wrenched Riggs's face and Kate realized she'd hit a nerve. She'd forgotten about the gossip that Riggs's father had been abusive to his mother. "I'm sorry, Riggs, I didn't mean to be insensitive."

A muscle ticked in his jaw. "No problem. If Trey deserves it, I'm sure Macy will kick him to the curb, too."

She hoped so. Although, deep down, Macy had insecurities caused by her mother's mental health issues. A vulnerable spot that an abuser might prey on.

Surely her FBI training would have taught her how to overcome being a victim.

Riggs's brow creased. "Trey's father was a hunter, wasn't he? And Trey used to go with him."

"I did hear that," Kate admitted. "His father owned a gun shop outside town."

"Right," Riggs said thoughtfully. "Trey liked to brag about his father's gun collection." Riggs heaved a breath. "Dammit. What if Trey sold Ned that gun he used to commit the shooting?"

Kate paled. "If he did, maybe Macy figured it out and that's why they were arguing."

RIGGS LOWERED HIS VOICE. "We can't jump to conclusions, but it's worth asking Stone about. Macy could have seen something in the old files that aroused her suspicions."

Kate rubbed her fingers together in that nervous gesture he'd come to recognize. "Now I'm really worried about her."

"Don't, Kate. Macy can take care of herself."

She didn't look convinced. "I'm going to talk to Stone," Riggs said.

While he hurried up to the house, Riggs struggled to remember if he'd ever seen Trey talking to Ned in high school. Trey had been cocky and had always had a chip on his shoulder. He'd driven a motorcycle, was on the wrestling team, and possessed a dark, bad boy side that attracted girls.

Trey would never have been friendly with Ned. But Trey's family had guns and Trey was a loose cannon.

A possible scenario played through his mind. Trey could have met up with Ned some place where no one would have seen them. Some place he could have given, or sold, him a gun.

And after the shooting, Trey had kept quiet because he'd realized he was complicit in multiple murders.

The smoke was clearing slightly inside the house, although debris from the pipe bomb littered the wood floor and a charred odor permeated the space.

Brian gestured across the room. "We managed to keep it from spreading to the bedrooms."

That was good, although there would be water and smoke damage.

"I want to look at the bomb," Riggs said.

"Just don't touch anything," Stone said. "There may be prints somewhere in there."

"It's not my first crime scene," Riggs said, annoyed at the reminder.

"Sorry," Stone said. "Habit."

Riggs gave a nod then relayed his conversation with Kate.

"Did Kate hear what Trey and Macy were arguing about?" Stone asked.

Riggs shook his head no. "But Kate said it looked like Trey was getting physical with Macy."

A dark look crossed Stone's face. "I'll talk to her. Maybe she has insight into Trey and the gun."

Riggs thanked him and crossed the room. Shattered glass crunched beneath his boots as he snapped pictures of the debris on the floor and the damage the pipe bomb had caused. Once he had his pictures, Riggs tugged on latex gloves and squatted to examine the bomb materials.

"You say it was thrown through the sliders?" Brian asked.

"Yeah." Riggs pointed to the floor. "It landed here."

Brian squatted beside him, and Riggs noticed a photo of Kate and her mother that had been shattered in the explosion. Her father wasn't present in any of the pictures, reminding him that she'd never mentioned him. He wondered what the story was there.

In the photograph, Kate looked to be about ten and was wearing a pair of small wire-rimmed glasses. She was young and innocent, and held a book in her hand.

He smiled at the image. The bookshelf by her fireplace overflowed with paperbacks—romance, mystery, family stories.

But his smile faded as he turned back to examine the crime scene.

"Looks amateurish," Riggs said. "Whoever did this used match heads and gun powder."

"I agree. Anyone, even a kid, could make one of these," Brian noted. "All you need is the internet."

"And some basic materials you could pick up anywhere," Riggs mumbled.

Stone joined them, his hands on his hips. "My deputy found Billy and is bringing him in. Once the crime team arrives, I'll question him. What are your thoughts on the bomb, Riggs?"

Riggs gestured toward the pipe. "Not sophisticated at all. I know Billy is a suspect, but the amateurish aspects of the bomb and graffiti suggest we might be looking at a teenager." He pointed to the pipe. "This is an exhaust pipe from a car."

"Or someone who doesn't know what they're doing. The bomber could have gotten the pipe at a car repair shop," Stone said.

"Or a junkyard," Riggs added with a shrug.

"Maybe Billy was just desperate," Brian suggested "and he didn't have time to put together something more sophisticated."

Stone scratched his head. "Don Gaines was in the science lab that day someone painted the threat on the wall."

Riggs sucked in a breath. "Yeah, but I still don't understand his motive."

Stone shrugged. "Maybe he just has anger issues. I'll follow up on the fingerprints. If his match the ones on the matchbook we found in his locker, I'll bring him in."

"Have the team see if they can lift prints from the piping material," Riggs said.

If they did, and the prints matched Billy's or Don's, they'd nail the culprit before he hurt anyone.

THE HOUSE WAS going to be damaged. Kate made a mental list to call her insurance company and her general contractor to get an estimate for repairs.

Finally the firemen emerged and began to pack up to leave. Riggs came out a minute later with Stone, his face grim.

"How bad is it?" she asked.

"Not too bad," Riggs said. "Some smoke and water damage, but it was contained to the living room area." He gave her a sympathetic smile. "I'm sorry, Kate."

Kate shrugged. "It's only things," she said. After losing her mother, she could survive anything except losing someone else she loved.

"You can't stay here tonight, Kate," Riggs said. "Go pack an overnight bag and you can arrange for a clean-up crew in the morning."

She wanted to argue, be brave. Insist that she wouldn't let anyone scare her away from her own home.

But as she climbed the porch steps and reached the door, the acrid odor of the explosive hit her. And was a reminder that someone was stalking her.

She'd survived tonight. What if he succeeded the next time?

Stepping into the foyer, Kate's stomach clenched at the mess in her house. Water soaked the wood floor and furniture, and smoke stained the walls and flooring. The kitchen had survived, but the walls would probably need a fresh coat of paint, as well.

Her briefcase holding the plans for the memorial sat on the table by the door, thankfully undamaged. The pictures of her and her mother on the mantel were safe. And so was she. That was all that mattered.

"Careful where you walk," Riggs said. "And don't touch anything in the living room. The crime team needs to process the room for evidence."

"Understood."

She carefully picked her way along the wall to the bedroom. Inside the closet, she retrieved her overnight bag, tossed her toiletries, pajamas and a dress for the dedication ceremony inside, then slipped back through the living room.

Riggs was waiting by the door, a scowl deepening his face. Outside, voices indicated the crime investigators had arrived. She snagged her briefcase and purse, and Riggs took her overnight bag as they stepped through the door.

Stone directed the crime team toward the porch just as she and Riggs reached her rental SUV.

"I'll have them lock up when they're finished," Stone said.

Kate thanked him. "I'll call my contractor and insurance company in the morning."

Riggs opened the rear door and set her bag inside. "Follow me to my house, Kate."

She shrugged. "Thanks, but I'll stay at the inn."

Rigg's jaw hardened. "You'll be safer at my place."

Not when she wanted to crawl into his arms. "I'll be fine at the inn. Most of the alumni are staying there."

Her stomach knotted. There might not be room though, but she had to try. Although one of the guests could be her enemy.

Chapter Sixteen

In spite of Kate's protests, Riggs insisted on following her to the inn to make sure she got settled safely, then walked her inside.

She admired the changes Celeste, the owner, had made on the exterior before she went inside. Last year, when Kate had first broached the local business owners and town council with the idea of inviting all former alumni to the dedication ceremony and combining it with a class reunion, Celeste had jumped on the idea of a renovation to the inn.

Celeste had lived in Briar Ridge for over twenty-five years. She remembered the glory days of sipping sweet iced tea on the porch with neighbors, when locking the doors to your house and car were things other people did, not the friendly trustworthy residents of the small town who loved one another and welcomed strangers into its fold with open arms.

The town had embraced Elaine McKendrick as a single mother. Half the ladies in town had babysat for Kate at some time before she reached school age. The local church had put on fundraisers for needy families, organized Habitat for Humanity projects and each year hosted a charity Christmas party for the hospital.

When Kate was in elementary school, she had helped

her mother decorate and read to the sick children, after which they'd passed out cookies, hot chocolate and presents.

Celeste had allowed families to stay at the inn, either free or at a discount rate, while their children underwent medical treatment.

She'd given the same loving care to restoring the inn by replacing rotting boards, painting the two-story country farmhouse a pale yellow, and adding flowerbeds and crepe myrtles which made the place postcard-pretty. New rocking chairs and porch swings added homey touches to the wraparound porch, and a gazebo and seating areas in the garden gave it even more charm. Purple, pink and white petunias filled one section while sunflowers danced in the breeze in another. She'd even stocked the small pond behind the gardens for guests who wanted to fish.

Judging from the parking lot, the inn was bustling tonight. Still shaken by the pipe bomb, Kate headed to the front desk and greeted Celeste.

"The inn looks beautiful," Kate said. "The rosebushes in front are gorgeous."

Celeste blushed. "I had to have roses," she said. "The garden has several different varieties."

"You've done a wonderful job," Kate said, remembering how much her mother loved roses. "But tonight I had a fire at my house and I'm looking for a room."

"Oh, my gosh." Celeste glanced at Riggs, then back at Kate. "Are you all right, dear?"

Kate faked a smile. How could she be all right when someone wanted her dead? "It was scary, but I'm okay now."

Celeste tapped a pen on the guest registry. "I'm sorry, hon, but I don't have any rooms available this week. The reunion drew so many alumni to town that we're completely booked."

Kate should have expected as much. But what was she going to do? She couldn't go home…"Thanks. I'm glad you're busy and hope you will be from now on."

Celeste fanned her face. "My nephew is so smart, he made a website and posted pictures on Facebook. He even ran Facebook ads, and we're asking folks who stay here to leave online reviews. So far, I have two more weeks filled this month."

"I'm really happy," Kate said. "I hope this week gives you the business boost you need."

The older woman squeezed Kate's hand. "I'm proud of what you're doing," Celeste said. "Shame on those folks at the meeting for giving you a hard time."

Kate thanked her again then stepped away and glanced at Riggs. Her stomach twisted.

"The offer still stands, Kate," Riggs said. "Just follow me to my place. You'll be safe there."

She sighed but didn't have a choice so she nodded.

Woody Mathis staggered through the door, spotted Kate and snarled something ugly beneath his breath. Riggs started toward him, but Kate clutched his arm and moved aside to avoid him. Orson Johnson, who'd lost his arm from the elbow down in the shooting, followed Woody in. Orson was balding, his face pudgy, his expression bitter. In high school, he'd played football, but his family had moved away after the shooting. She'd heard he raised chickens in North Georgia somewhere.

But she hadn't seen him in years. "Hi, Orson," she said. "Welcome back to town."

He shot her a look of resentment. "Only reason I came is to see that damned old building torn down."

"Then you're in favor of the new school?" Kate asked.

Orson shoved his Falcons hat up on his head. "Sure am."

Woody jerked his thumb at Kate. "She ought to be telling

everyone how sorry she is," Woody said, his words over-lapping. "She's the reason Ned pulled the trigger."

Riggs eased Kate behind him. "Kate is not any more re-sponsible than the rest of us who ignored or teased Ned. I don't recall you being friends with him, Woody."

Woody staggered sideways, his shoulder bumping the wall. "Hell, he wasn't in love with me..."

"There was more to Ned's problems than Kate reject-ing him for a date," Riggs snapped. "And, I thought you were in jail."

"Bail," Woody said, slurring the word. "Can't keep a man locked up for something he didn't do."

"You shot at Stone," Riggs pointed out.

Woody chuckled. "That was an accident. My finger slipped."

Kate shifted and wrapped her arms around her waist.

"Come on, Kate, let's go." He tugged on Kate's arm, coaxing her toward the exit.

"That's it, run and hide behind Riggs," Woody taunted.

Kate wanted to scream at him that she wasn't doing that. Except she *was*.

"Go sleep it off," Riggs growled.

Kate pushed open the door and stepped into the fresh air, her lungs straining.

Woody cursed as he gripped the rail to go upstairs, and Orson followed, mumbling something about wishing the whole damn town would burn down.

Riggs heaved a sigh as he joined Kate on the front stoop of the inn. "Woody is a jerk, but he's all mouth and stays drunk most of the time. I don't think he's got the guts to make a bomb and throw it in your house."

"He needs AA," Kate said.

"Yeah, or to be locked up for his own good."

"I didn't realize Orson was so bitter," Kate said, unsettled by his comments.

"Sounds like Woody's been feeding his anger. And that comment about him wanting the town to burn down makes me wonder." Riggs scrubbed a hand through his thick hair. "I'll call Stone once we get to my place, tell him what Woody said and ask him to look into Orson."

They hurried down the steps, and Kate veered toward her vehicle while Riggs climbed into his truck.

A gust of wind whipped through the trees, thunder rumbling. Just as Kate unlocked the door, a car door opened and slammed shut. Nerves on edge, she glanced up to see Trey vault from a black Range Rover and stalk toward her. His broad body was just as intimidating as his sinister expression.

"Trey." Kate gripped her keys in a self-defense move.

Trey curled both beefy hands on her shoulders and squeezed hard. Then he pushed his face into hers, nostrils flared. "What happens between me and my wife is our business, Kate. You may think you own this town, but you'll never tell me what to do, so stay away from me and Macy."

RAGE HEATED RIGGS's blood at the sight of Trey's hands on Kate. He jumped from his truck, crossed the distance in two strides, and yanked Trey away from her.

"Take your hands off of her," Riggs stormed.

Anger radiated from Trey in palpable waves. "I'll do what I damn well please, Benford."

"The hell you will," Riggs growled. "Touch her again, and you'll pay for it."

Trey barked a nasty sound. "Right. Like you're going to beat me up?"

"At least I know how to treat a woman," Riggs

snapped. "Kate and your wife both deserve respect, not to be manhandled."

"You don't know anything about my wife or me." Trey shoved Riggs backward.

Riggs started to retaliate, but Kate grabbed his arm. "Don't," Kate said softly. "You're not like him, Riggs."

Maybe he wasn't. But he sure as hell didn't intend to let the jerk hurt Kate.

"Let's just go," Kate said. "He's not worth it."

Riggs ushered Kate into her SUV. "Start the engine and drive out of the parking lot. I'm right behind you."

"Riggs, please," Kate said.

He squeezed her hand gently. "Go. I'll follow you."

Trey's boots crunched gravel as he stepped toward Riggs.

Riggs held up a warning hand. "I don't want to fight with you, Trey. This town has seen enough trouble. Just stay away from Kate."

Trey heaved a breath. Every muscle in the man's body was wound tight with the urge to fight, as if he was barely holding on to his rage.

Riggs didn't give him time to make a move. He strode to his truck, got in and cranked the engine, keeping his eyes on Trey the entire time. As he drove from the parking lot, he checked his rearview mirror to make sure the bastard hadn't pulled a gun or followed him.

He caught up with Kate as she turned onto the road. Using his hands-free app, he called Stone. When Stone's voice mail responded, Riggs left a message relaying what had happened with Trey, Woody and Orson.

Remembering Kate had never been to his place, he maneuvered around her so she could follow him.

He wanted her safe at home with him tonight.

KATE COULDN'T SHAKE Orson's comments as she followed Riggs around the curvy road. How in the world had she made so many enemies?

She'd hoped the reunion would bring people together. Instead, her plan seemed to be backfiring.

Riggs veered onto a side road leading to a cluster of cabins offering privacy and views of the river and mountains. She parked in the graveled drive behind him, a frisson of nerves dancing along her spine.

She'd never been to his house and coming here tonight seemed...intimate. Made her wish for a real friendship with Riggs. Or more.

Shutting out the foolish thought, she climbed from her vehicle. A summer storm breeze stirred the air, bringing the aromas of honeysuckle and pine, heavenly scents that reminded her why she liked living in the area. Though she enjoyed vacations at the beach, the stunning peaks and ridges of the Blue Ridge Mountains and closeness to nature filled her with a sense of peace and tranquility. This was home.

Although tonight those mountains looked dark and ominous, a reminder that the rolling hills and dense forests offered dozens of places for the person after her to hide.

Stomach knotted with anxiety, she retrieved her purse, overnight bag and briefcase from the back seat. A second later, Riggs grabbed the overnight bag from her and carried it to the house. She'd never been to Riggs's place, having expected him to have a bachelor pad in town. But this rustic cabin with its stunning mountain view looked cozy and welcoming. The sound of the river behind his cabin was musical and reminded her of swimming in the summer as a kid. She imagined Riggs fishing out back or canoeing on a Sunday. The front porch held two rockers that called her name, but she was so exhausted, she bypassed them and followed Riggs inside instead.

As they entered, moonlight glittered off Riggs's dark hair and glowed through the massive windows overlooking the river. The nine-foot ceilings made the open-concept living room and kitchen seem large and airy. A stacked stone fireplace climbed the wall to the ceiling, flanked by built-in bookcases in a rich dark wood. The kitchen cabinets matched, contrasted by white quartz counters. A peninsula added bar seating, the base of the stools made of tree trunks, the seats, a rich brown leather.

The dark leather couch, painting of wild Mustangs, and plaid club chair gave the room a masculine feel. Yet there was something missing here. No personal touches, no family pictures. "It's beautiful," she said.

A sheepish look crossed Riggs's face. "Thanks. I built here for the view, and the seclusion."

"I like the furnishings, and the view is breathtaking," Kate said, although the way the moonlight through window framed Riggs's tall, muscular body was just as breathtaking as the outdoor scenery.

"There are two bedrooms." Riggs gestured toward the right. "A private bath is attached to the guest room. Make yourself at home."

Kate admired the rustic shiplap as he set her bag on the bed. A blue and white quilt in a Dresden pattern adorned the four-poster bed.

She traced her fingers over the intricate pattern. "This is stunning, Riggs. Did your mother make it?"

"She did," he said, a smile lighting his face. "I used to watch her quilt in front of the fireplace at night."

"I saw some of her quilts at the festivals," Kate said. "She was an excellent seamstress and really creative in her designs."

"I hear quilting is a lost art," Riggs said. "But they were

popular with tourists back in the day, and she made enough for us to get by."

That was the most personal thing he'd shared. "I think they'd still be popular if we had tourists coming in." Kate blinked back tears. "I'd like to see the town lively like that again."

Riggs grunted in agreement and then an awkward silence fell between them for a minute and they returned to the living room. Finally, Kate spoke. "Thank you for letting me spend the night."

Riggs walked toward her, a protective gleam in his eyes. "There's no way I'd let you stay alone, not after what happened today."

A shudder coursed up Kate's spine. "The dedication ceremony is tomorrow," Kate said. "Once the publicity dies down, maybe whoever's threatening me will give up and leave town." At least, she prayed that would happen.

"Maybe. But if it's Ned's accomplice, he needs to pay for all the lives he destroyed."

"That's true." Kate rubbed her arms with her hands, noticing the single picture on the bookshelf above the corner desk. A photograph of firefighters in uniform. "Did you become a firefighter because of the shooting?"

Riggs clenched his jaw. "Yeah. Took me a while to get my act together, though," he said, rubbing at his thigh where the bullet had struck him. "I was bitter at first. Angry. I hated being disabled."

Kate swallowed hard. "You lost your scholarship."

He nodded. "That wasn't the worst part, though. For a while, I thought I might not ever be useful."

"Oh, Riggs, I'm so sorry."

"It wasn't your fault, Kate. My injury was nothing compared to what some others went through. At least I survived." He heaved a weary breath. "I even felt guilty about that."

"I know what you mean." Emotions clogged Kate's throat. "But you still had reason to be bitter. Instead, you turned your life around and made something of yourself."

He shrugged as if he didn't deserve her praise. "I hated being helpless that day. I saw you running to help others, and wanted to do the same, but I couldn't get up."

"It was chaotic and I was terrified," Kate admitted. "I didn't want to leave Mom, but she told me to go, to help the others."

An understanding smile crossed Riggs's face. "That sounds like her."

Kate's heart warmed and some of her earlier tension melted away.

"Why a firefighter?" she finally asked.

Riggs cleared his throat. "Because the first responders rushed inside the school that day and were heroes," he said. "Later, once I got past the self-pity, I realized I wanted to be like them. That I never wanted to be helpless again. That's when I got serious about PT."

Kate's heart squeezed. Like many of their classmates, Riggs would be featured on the memorial wall she had planned for the new school. No one would forget that tragedy, but out of it, unsung heroes had been born.

She hoped their stories and the wall would inspire other students to overcome adversity. Amy had collected information on individual students for months to help with the project.

Kate pressed a hand over Riggs's. "The last thing my mother said before she died was for me to make something good come of the shooting that day. It's taken me years to figure out how to do that."

Riggs's eyes darkened. "And you are. You're amazing, Kate."

"So are you, Riggs."

Riggs's breath quickened and he traced a finger along her jaw. The gentle gesture was so erotic and comforting that Kate couldn't resist.

She wanted to forget about today, about the fire and danger, about the town and the reunion. She wanted to forget that her two best friends were no longer speaking to her and she didn't know how to mend their friendships.

Suddenly needy, she licked her suddenly dry lips and stood on tiptoe.

His mouth parted, his chest rose and fell unevenly, and he angled his head toward hers.

Kate closed her eyes and pressed her lips over Riggs's. Need spiraled through her. For the last few days, Riggs had been a pillar of strength.

She didn't want to be afraid anymore.

She wanted his touch, his kiss, his hands on her.

RIGGS ORDERED HIMSELF not to rush Kate, but when her lips met his, rational thought died a sudden death.

Kate tasted like the most potent combination of sweetness and spice. Heat coursed through his blood, need and desire splintered his control, and he pulled her against his body and deepened the kiss. She moaned softly, an invitation for more, and he teased her lips apart with his tongue then dove inside to explore.

She threaded her fingers through his hair and drew him closer. Her breasts pressed against the hard planes of his chest and drove him mad with want.

Being with Kate meant more than a night of sex. He liked Kate. Cared about her.

He hesitated a moment at that thought then realized he'd

never allowed anyone to get close to him. Losing friends and his mother had taught him to protect his heart.

Kate whispered his name and ran her hands over his back, stroking his muscles, and he forgot about protecting himself. He dipped his head and planted kisses along her neck and throat. She moaned softly and tilted her head back, offering him access to the succulent skin between her breasts.

He itched to strip her clothes and take her right there. On the floor. In the doorway. On the couch. Anywhere she'd have him.

No… Kate deserved better.

She clung to him, and he walked them backward to the guest bed, wrapping one arm around her waist while he cupped her breast with his other hand. She felt full and heavy, her nipple puckering against the silk of her blouse.

His body hardened.

He whispered her name then eased the buttons of her blouse apart, this time revealing a thin, lacy black bra that barely contained her plump breasts. They were ripe now, begging for attention.

Riggs teased one nipple with his teeth while he raked his thumb over the other. She sighed again, breathy and needy, and raked her foot up his calf.

Her low moan of pleasure heated his blood, and he thought he might explode. But giving Kate pleasure overrode his need.

He tugged the lace aside, exposing her skin, and sucked in a sharp breath as passion exploded inside him. Kate moaned, and he closed his lips around one turgid peak and tugged it in his mouth. Cupping her rear with his other hand, he suckled her, deep and long, hard and hungrily, before he moved to the other breast and gave it the same loving attention.

"Riggs," Kate whispered.

Her raspy voice made him pause, and he looked up to see her eyes glazed with passion. But something else lurked in the depths of her eyes—fear?

Pulse pounding, he gently tilted her chin up and forced her to look at him. "Kate, do you want me to stop?"

Chapter Seventeen

Stopping made perfect sense. It was the logical, smart thing to do. Keep her distance. Stand on her own.

Except logic floated out the window as Kate searched Riggs's gaze for any sign he was simply using her for sex. Instead, passion and sincerity shone in his smoky eyes.

His protective nature touched her deeply. She'd been alone so long that she'd forgotten what it felt like to have someone care about her.

"Kate?" Riggs's breath rasped out, making him sound almost...vulnerable. Slowly, he lowered his hands from her shoulders. "I understand."

The tenderness in his tone and his willingness to walk away intensified her desire. Ever since she'd lost her mother, she'd been terrified of giving her heart to anyone.

But Riggs already owned it.

She was tired of being afraid. Of running from what she wanted.

Kate caught his arm, her heart on her sleeve. "Don't leave. I...want you, Riggs."

Her heart fluttered at the way his eyes softened when he smiled at her. With a throaty groan, he yanked her into his arms again and claimed her mouth with his. Kate succumbed to the heat burning between them and tugged at his shirt. Seconds later, he pulled it over his head and tossed it to the floor. The sight of his broad chest dusted in a soft mat of dark hair intensified her desire, and she raked her hands over his chest.

Riggs unbuttoned the remaining buttons on her blouse and gently peeled the fabric away. Cool air met her bare skin, yet she felt as if she was on fire.

She slipped her arms out of the sleeves and her shirt hit the floor beside his. His eyes narrowed, raking over her in a hungry look, then he eased her back onto the bed.

Seconds later, clothes flew off and hands and lips touched and teased, evoking erotic sensations that spiraled out of control.

Riggs trailed his lips across her naked breasts, sucking her nipples until liquid heat pooled between her thighs. She arched her back, moaning his name as he licked his way down her stomach, then he pushed her legs apart and dove into her damp heat with his tongue.

Her body quivered with sensations, need building as waves of pleasure rippled through her. He teased and tormented her with his tongue, then lifted her hips to allow him access as he made love to her with his mouth. One flick of his tongue across her sweet spot, then another and another, and she cried out his name as her orgasm rocked through her.

RIGGS'S BLOOD BURNED hot as Kate threw her head back in ecstasy.

He'd given her that pleasure. He didn't want it to end.

He kissed her again, letting her taste her own sweet release, then snatched a condom from his jeans and rolled it on. Kate watched, her eyes darkening, her chest rising and falling erratically. Her breasts begged for attention again, and he stroked her inner thighs as he twisted her nipples between his fingers. She arched into him, gripped his shoulders and whispered his name on a throaty moan, the pull between them growing more intense.

Her excitement magnified his own, and he slipped a finger inside her heat as he tugged one of her nipples between his teeth and suckled her again. Her slick wet chamber clenched around his finger and he added another one, teasing her as he stroked her body.

"Riggs, please," she whispered. "I want you inside me."

She didn't have to ask twice. He wanted to make her his, completely.

He kneed her legs further apart, then sank his hard length inside her with a groan. She gasped for a breath, and he pulled out then thrust into her again, penetrating her. Blinded by need, he repeated the motion, building a rhythm charged with raw desire. She gripped his hips and guided him deeper, their bodies gliding together, the friction building to a crescendo.

Sweat beaded on his skin as he thrust into her again and again. She dug her nails into his back, clinging to him as he rode her hard and fast.

Seconds later, Kate moaned his name as another orgasm splintered through her. He wanted to join her.

Holding her as the sensations built, Riggs gripped her hips, driving himself deeper, over and over, until their bodies shook with pleasure.

One deep thrust, then he pulled out and thrust again, lifting her hips so he could fill her deeper. She raked her nails down his back, the depth of her passion sending him over the edge. His release hit him, hot and mind-numbing.

And sweet. Even sweeter because he knew Kate didn't give herself to any man easily.

Quickly disposing of the condom, he rolled Kate to her side and cradled her in his arms until she fell asleep, sated and curled against him.

KATE WOKE TO the sound of Riggs's soft snoring. For a moment, she lay still, savoring the moment. His big body was so warm and strong that she felt safe and loved in a way she hadn't felt before.

He'd treated her to a pleasure she'd never experienced because his lovemaking had been giving. Her breasts tingled just at the thought of his lips suckling her.

But sunshine poured through the window, a reminder today was the culmination of months of work and planning. The dedication ceremony was scheduled for two o'clock. She needed to make sure everything was on track.

Amy planned to meet her at the site early so they could set up the memorial display together.

Riggs stirred, rolled over and opened his eyes. A smile tilted the corner of his sexy mouth, tempting her to stay in bed and make love to him again.

But today was too important to be late.

"Morning," Riggs murmured.

Kate's heart fluttered. She imagined what it would be like to wake up every day beside this incredible man, and realized she was falling for Riggs.

"I need to shower. I'm meeting Amy at the site," Kate said. "We have to set things up for the ceremony this afternoon."

He drew her to him for a long, slow kiss, and temptation almost won.

But the image of Cassidy and her son Roy taunted her and Kate scanned the room for her shirt or something to cover up with when she got out of bed.

Riggs ran a hand over her bare hip. "You're beautiful Kate. You don't have to hide that body from me."

How had he read her mind?

A blush climbed her neck and she inhaled. "I need to get ready."

"And I need to make love to you again," Riggs said in a low whisper.

Kate stilled, her pulse clamoring as he cupped her breasts in his hands. "Riggs…"

"Yeah, it's me, Kate. Remember how it feels for me to be inside you." He pushed his thick length between her buttocks and stroked her, and pleasure shot through her.

One last time. She just needed him one more time then she could walk away and he could go to Cassidy or his next lover.

That thought hurt, but she banished it as her breasts throbbed beneath his fingers. He seemed to read her mind again, turned her around, lowered his head and tugged one peak into his mouth. Then he trailed his fingers down to her heat. He sucked the other turgid peak while his fingers claimed her, and she clawed at his back as erotic sensations pummeled her.

On the brink of an orgasm, he snagged a condom, rolled it on, rose above her and entered her with one swift thrust. Kate clung to him, parting her legs so he could dive deeper. He groaned, lifted her and she wrapped her legs around his waist as he pumped inside her.

His hips thrust forward, his hard length sinking so deep inside she felt him to the core. A second later, release splintered through her as if a match had been lit inside her and erupted into flames. Riggs captured her groan with his mouth as he kissed her, then he joined her on the ride as he came inside her.

PERSPIRATION BEADED RIGGS'S skin as he held Kate in his arms. When she'd first started to slip from bed, he told himself to let her. But then she'd blushed and looked shy, and he wanted Kate to know how much he wanted her. How much he liked her body.

Hell, he liked everything about Kate.

He trailed a hand over her hip as their orgasms slowly subsided and leaned his head against hers. "Kate—"

"Shh, you don't have to say anything." Kate eased from his arms. "I know how this works."

He tensed at her tone. He disposed of the condom then turned back to her. "What do you mean?"

Kate folded her arms in front of her breasts as if she could hide the glorious mounds. But the image and feel of them were imprinted in his brain forever.

"I mean I have to go." She licked her lips. "And when this situation is cleared up, I won't expect anything."

There she was, treating him like a womanizer again. "I'm not sure I do."

Some emotion he couldn't identify flickered across her face. "I know you like being a bachelor."

"I like being with you," he said.

A tense heartbeat passed. "What about Cassidy?"

His eyes narrowed to slits. "What about her?"

"I saw you with her yesterday," Kate said. "And then there's her son."

Cold anger balled in his chest. "Yes, she has a son. But I'm not interested in Cassidy, Kate. I never have been."

Confusion clouded her eyes then something akin to anger. "But you have a child—"

He reached for his clothes and began yanking them on, his movements abrupt. "You're certain Cassidy's son is mine, aren't you?"

Kate rose and backed toward the bathroom. "That's what I heard and—"

"And you believe it," Riggs said in disgust. "I thought you were above taking gossip at face value, Kate."

She opened her mouth to speak, but he was too furious to listen. Or maybe he was just hurt. He thought he'd proved he was different than her high school image of him.

"Riggs—"

"Go shower, Kate. I'm going to do the same." Without another word, he strode to his room then to his bathroom and slammed the door. He stared at himself in the mirror, furious with himself for letting down his guard.

He was sated from the best lovemaking he'd ever had.

And disappointed that he wanted their lovemaking to mean more.

He'd never felt those emotions after sex before. Had always just walked away, no attachments, no entanglements. No hurt feelings on either side.

He flipped on the water, undressed, then climbed beneath the hot spray and scrubbed his body as if he was as dirty as Kate thought him to be.

But he couldn't scrub away the pain of her words.

Maybe you should have told her the truth.

Maybe.

But Kate had never asked. She'd just believed the worst of him. And that hurt more than anything.

KATE DREADED FACING Riggs after her shower. But she held her head high. Today was important—the day of the dedication ceremony. She had to focus and get through it.

Before she joined Riggs in the kitchen, she arranged for someone to clean up the mess made by the pipe bomb at her house. The repair crew, a local one she'd used before, assured her they'd have it finished by the afternoon. The painting would have to come later, but at least she could stay at home tonight.

Riggs remained silent and brooding as she poured herself a cup of coffee. He was already sipping a cup as he watched the local morning news on TV. First the weather, then a story about Briar Ridge.

"Folks, this is Gretta Wright with a breaking story," Gretta said with a smile. "I'm coming to you from the town of Briar Ridge, most known for the school shooting fifteen years ago. Despite protests from vocal locals, high school principal Kate McKendrick spearheaded efforts to demolish the old school building in light of a newer modern facility.

"But this week, while alumni have swarmed to town for a class reunion and the celebration for the new school, Kate McKendrick has come under fire. Literally. While driving home from a town meeting, her car burst into flames. Police have confirmed that the fire was no accident. Neither was the fire that was set behind Ms. McKendrick's property. Threats to her also include graffiti on the high school and a pipe bomb that was thrown into her house." She paused for emphasis. "An inside source also revealed that Ms. McKendrick received a threatening letter blaming her for the shooter massacring his classmates."

Kate gasped.

"My God, how did she find out about the letter?" Kate pressed a hand over her heart. "The only people I told were you and Stone."

Riggs's jaw hardened. "Good question."

Gretta's voice cut through her thoughts. "If you have any information regarding these crimes or the attempts on Ms. McKendrick's life, please call the local police."

Frustrated, Kate flicked off the TV, poured her coffee in a to-go cup and grabbed her things.

Riggs followed, the silence stretching painfully between them as they went to their separate vehicles.

The reminder of the threat made Kate scan the area as she pulled from the driveway and drove to the building site to meet Amy. Amy hadn't arrived yet, so Kate parked near the construction trailer.

Workers were already inside, probably discussing the plans.

Riggs didn't get out of his pickup. Instead he drove away, a sign he was upset.

It was better this way. Better to stop the insanity before she completely fell in love with the man and he broke her heart.

Heaven help her. She *had* judged him. But how could she not? He hadn't denied that Roy was his child. He hadn't acknowledged him, either. Just like her father had never acknowledged her.

Her mother had tried to smooth over the truth, but it sat there raw and ugly every day of Kate's life. He hadn't wanted her. She'd been a mistake. He couldn't be saddled with a kid. He'd had places to go and things to do and that did not involve a sniveling, needy kid.

Maybe if she'd been a boy, a *son*, he might have loved her. Or maybe not. Maybe he was just weak and selfish and…and why did she care anyway? Why had she spent every birthday and Christmas wishing he'd show up and tell her he'd been wrong, that he really loved her.

Just like Riggs would leave one day. If her own father hadn't loved her, how could Riggs?

Roy Fulton probably felt the same way. He was a loner, had no friends. Kept his head in his computer and on his phone. Seemed sullen and angry. Maybe because he was fatherless, too.

What she didn't understand was that Riggs seemed changed. That he was a good man. He even volunteered at the kids' hospital. It didn't make sense.

While she waited on Amy, she checked her notes on her

phone for details she needed to iron out. Basically everything was set, though.

The mayor should show up at one thirty along with the
town council.

A sedan swerved into the parking lot and Amy emerged,
her arms laden with a box of photos for the memorial.
Grateful not to be alone, Kate hopped from her car and
greeted her, although she kept her eyes peeled in case anyone else was lurking around.

Riggs had promised to protect her, yet he'd left her alone.
That spoke volumes about how much he cared.

RIGGS SHOULDN'T HAVE left Kate alone. But he needed some
time away from her, needed to put distance between them
and regain control of his emotions. Kate made him think
crazy things about the future.

Things he couldn't have. Like her. And a family.

She would be safe, he assured himself. The building
crew was on site, and Amy was supposed to meet her any
minute.

Dammit, how had Gretta learned about the letter Kate
received?

Did she know who'd sent it? Or had Gretta sent the letter to stir up suspicion and interest for a big story?

Kate's comment about Cassidy's son still bothered him,
too. She thought he was a deadbeat dad. A man who'd abandoned his child.

After the way his own old man had disappointed him,
he'd vowed never to have kids. And if he had one, he'd do
his best to be the kind of father he'd wanted.

For some reason, it was important that Kate believe in
him. Trust him. Be the man she deserved. That meant owning up to the truth.

If he knew who Roy's father was, maybe he could convince Kate he was a stand-up guy.

He had to confront Cassidy. After all this time, he needed her to tell him once and for all who'd fathered her baby.

Determined to get to the truth, he sped toward Cassidy's. He had no idea if she'd show up at the celebration today, but she worked at the Cut and Dye, so he went there first.

Several cars were in the lot, more than usual, which made him curious if alumni were primping for tonight's dance. He pulled into a spot and parked, glancing around as he walked up to the entryway.

As he entered, hair dryers buzzed and the scent of hair products in the air hit him, almost smothering. There were four stations, each occupied with a client. Two were white-haired ladies while the other two clients looked to be about his age. He didn't recognize them. More alumni.

All eyes turned his way, whispers and voices echoing around him. Cassidy looked up and shot him a scowl when he motioned that he needed to talk to her. She spoke to her client then hurried over to him and gestured for him to step outside.

Once on the sidewalk, she jammed her hands on her hips, irritated. "What do you want, Riggs?"

"I want to know who Roy's father is," he said bluntly.

Cassidy narrowed her eyes into a scowl. "Why the hell are you asking me this *now*?"

"Because everyone in town thinks I'm his father and that I abandoned him, and I want it to stop."

Surprise flared in her eyes followed by a wariness that seeped through her lips as she pressed them into a tight line. "It's been years, Riggs. No one cares anymore."

"I care," he said. And Kate did. "What did you tell Roy?"

"My son and I are none of your business," she said.

"It's my business if Roy thinks I'm his father and I won't acknowledge him."

She heaved a breath then pushed her dyed-blond hair away from one cheek where the wind had tossed it. "He doesn't even know about you," she said. "Did it ever occur to you that I kept his father's name quiet to protect my son?"

She didn't wait for a response. She turned and stormed back into the salon, leaving Riggs to wonder what exactly she meant.

Why would Roy need protection from his father?

KATE AND AMY spent the next two hours setting up the display. They showcased photographs on a tall blackboard to emulate how impressive it would look in the front hall of the new school.

The other part of the memorial was just as important. Amy had been working diligently for months collecting information on the students who'd survived and their accomplishments. One wall would feature photos with clippings of students who'd gained notoriety in some way, along with quotes and sayings from others about how the shooting had changed the trajectory of their lives.

Another board held copies of the sketch of the new sports fields and football stadium which they'd been promised would be ready by fall.

When she and Amy finished the display, they stood back to admire it. "I hope we have a good response to this," Kate said. "I want it to be inspirational for all the students at Briar Ridge High, past and present."

Amy squeezed Kate's shoulder. "I hope so, too, Kate. It's a wonderful way to honor the students and their loved ones." Amy glanced at her watch. "Hmm, I'm going to run over to the bakery to pick up the cupcakes for the celebration. I saw the news this morning, though. Will you be all right here?"

Kate nodded although, truthfully, nerves clawed at her. "I'm okay. The mayor should be here soon anyway, and the contractor is still at the construction trailer. Go pick up the cupcakes."

Amy looked reluctant to leave, but Kate checked the time and encouraged her to go.

Just as the dust settled from Amy's departure, the contractor exited the trailer, threw his hand up and waved, then jumped in his truck and peeled from the parking lot.

A gust of wind stirred, whistling through the trees as a dark cloud moved above, casting a shadow across the ground.

The hair on the back of Kate's neck prickled. Then the sound of footsteps crunching gravel echoed from behind her.

She swung around to see if another worker was in the trailer, but a cold voice stopped her.

"Don't make any sudden moves or I'll shoot you right here."

A second later, the cold barrel of a gun dug into her back.

HE JAMMED THE GUN into Kate McKendrick's back. He hadn't wanted it to come to this.

But Kate had pushed and pushed. Now everyone in town was talking about the shooting and asking questions about why Ned had done it and who might have helped him. He'd seen that nosy reporter's morning story about someone being after Kate.

She'd suggested the person who'd set the fire in the woods and tampered with Kate's car might be Ned's accomplice.

She had no idea how close she was. And how off base.

He hadn't been an accomplice.

He was part of the reason crazy Ned had turned that gun on the students at school.

Not that they hadn't deserved it. Some of them had.

There were others that hadn't been shot who were to blame, too.

Kate had dredged it all up.

And if that reporter kept poking her nose into everything, soon the truth would be exposed.

"Walk," he ordered as his hand gripped the gun.

He liked fire better than shooting. But he was desperate now and running out of time. He'd get rid of Kate any way he had to.

Then his secrets would be safe.

Chapter Eighteen

Riggs was still agitated when he met Stone at the police station. Macy was there, perched beside a whiteboard where Stone had posted pictures of persons of interest in the threats against Kate.

Another board held photos of the school shooting, along with pictures of the victims and photos with question marks beside them, noting them as possible accomplices.

"I saw Gretta on the news this morning," Stone said as he led him down the hall toward the interrogation rooms. "How's Kate?"

"Fine." But he was so *not* fine. Nope, not at all. "I left her at the new building site. She and Amy are preparing for the groundbreaking ceremony this afternoon.

"Do you know where Gretta got her information?" he asked Stone.

Stone shook his head. "Not a clue. I sure as hell didn't tell anyone about that letter of blame." He led Riggs to a room where he could view his interview with Billy via a computer monitor.

"Thanks, man. I appreciate you letting me observe."

Stone studied him for a minute. "Sure. But stay here. At no point are you allowed in the interrogation room. If he confesses, I want it to stick. And going all postal on him won't help."

Riggs gritted his teeth. "Do I look like I'd go postal?"

Stone smirked. "I don't know, but something's going on with you, and you're not thinking clearly."

Yeah, because a certain sexy woman was messing with his head.

He dropped into the chair in front of the monitor and raised his three fingers in a Boy Scout salute. Although he'd never been a Boy Scout. "Promise not to move."

Stone gave a wry laugh then closed the door. A minute later, he entered the interrogation room. Billy Hodgkins was fidgeting in his chair, toying with something between his fingers, although Riggs couldn't see what the object was.

"So, Billy…" Stone began. "Here we are."

Billy lifted his shoulders in a shrug. "Yeah, I just don't know why."

Stone claimed the chair opposite Billy, folded his arms and scrutinized Billy. "I think you do."

Billy worked his mouth from side to side. "If this is about Kate, I told you I just wanted to talk to her."

"And when she didn't want to talk to you, you got angry?"

Billy looked down at the table as if studying the scarred grooves in the wood.

"So you made a pipe bomb and tossed it into her house to either get her attention," Stone said matter-of-factly, "or to hurt her."

Billy shot up from his seat, his anger palpable. "I did no such thing."

"Sure you did," Stone said in a harsh tone. "You thought you'd scare her into…what? Stopping the old school from being torn down? Admitting she was to blame for the shooting?"

Billy dropped whatever he was rubbing between his fingers and bent to retrieve it. Riggs narrowed his eyes to try to see what it was, but the camera angle was off and he couldn't discern the object.

Stone pointed to the chair. "Sit down or I'll put you in handcuffs."

Billy dropped back into the chair with a curse and twisted his hands together. "You've got the wrong guy."

"Listen, Billy," Stone said, "I know what you said at her mother's funeral. I also have the note where you blamed her."

Billy's head jerked up. "What note?"

"This one." Stone laid the evidence bag on the table. The scribbled message *It was your fault* was clear through the bag.

Billy rocked back in his chair. "I didn't send that."

Riggs shifted, studying Billy's reaction. He seemed genuinely shocked.

"But you blamed Kate—"

"Yeah, I did. At least back then." Billy's frown deepened. "But that was over a decade ago. My life was hell." Pain contorted his face. "Everyone thought *I* helped my brother. Our classmates, people in town, even my own parents asked me if I'd known what he was up to and kept it quiet."

Pain underscored Billy's voice and he pinched the bridge of his nose.

"That must have been difficult," Stone said quietly.

"It sure as hell was," Billy said. "When my folks moved away, they treated me like I was a piranha. Maybe I did tease Ned when he was young, but he had problems no one knew about."

"What kind of problems?" Stone asked bluntly.

Billy pressed his lips together as if he was going to clam up.

"Tell me," Stone said. "It's time for the truth, Billy."

Billy laid his hands on the table, fingers curled into his

palms. "When he was a baby, my daddy dropped him on his head. He didn't mean to, at least that's what I heard Mom say, but Ned must have hit his head hard. The doctor said he had a concussion. Later on, when he started acting all weird and depressed, they thought that head injury had caused his psychiatric problems."

Riggs pulled at his chin. Medical records were hard to obtain, but Stone could find a way to verify that information.

"What happened after you and your folks left Briar Ridge?" Stone asked.

Billy wiped at his eyes again. "They changed their names, tried to start a new life. But eventually folks would realize who they were or recognize them, and we'd move again. All that time, they just grew madder and madder. They couldn't stand to look at me. Then I started drinking." Billy shrugged. "Got a couple of DUIs, was living on the streets. Took odd jobs to get by."

He paused, and a long silence ensued. Finally, Stone muttered, "Go on."

"About a year and a half ago, I got a job at a trucking company, but my drinking almost cost me the work. Boss gave me an ultimatum. Lose the job or go to AA."

He opened his palm and reveled a sobriety chip. "Been sober now a year." He made a clicking sound with his teeth. "Part of the program is to make amends with those you hurt. That's the reason I wanted to talk to Kate. To tell her I'm sorry for blaming her." His voice warbled. "I know it wasn't her fault. Ned was troubled and bullied, but he had issues anyway. My sponsor helped me understand that."

"Do you know if Ned acted alone?" Stone asked.

Billy made a clicking sound with his teeth. "I honestly don't know."

"Did anything odd happen in the days before the shooting? Was Ned hanging out with anyone specific? Someone who might have given him the gun?"

"Not that he talked about, but Ned wasn't a talker."

"Other than Kate, was he upset with anyone else at school?"

Billy looked down at the chip then shook his head. "I never knew what was going on in his head. Two nights before the shooting, he came in acting all rattled. I asked him what was going on, but he wouldn't talk about it. But I had the weirdest vibe that he'd gotten laid." Billy sighed. "When I teased him about it, he went all crazy and ran out of the room. He didn't come back till the middle of the night. My folks were really pissed and grounded him."

"That was two days before the shooting?"

"Yeah, but I never learned what happened to set him off."

Riggs released a slow breath. He'd been certain Billy was trouble, but after hearing his story, he believed him.

Stone shoved a piece of paper in front of Billy. "One more thing. I need a writing sample. Copy the message."

Billy clenched the pen then copied the wording. It didn't take an analysis expert to determine that Billy's handwriting didn't match.

Stone suddenly stood and looked at his phone. "All right, Billy, you're free to go."

Riggs knotted his hands in frustration. If Billy was innocent, who the hell was trying to kill Kate?

KATE FROZE AT the sound of the man's voice. No, not exactly a man. A teenager. A student.

But she didn't understand why he was so upset or why he'd threaten her. "You don't really want to hurt me," she said, struggling to keep her voice calm. "What good will that do?"

"Just move," the teenager ordered.

He shoved her, and Kate stumbled toward the woods, mind racing. Amy would be back soon. And the mayor. Then other people would start arriving. But they might not be here in time.

She had to stall.

He gave her another push. "I said walk."

Kate moved toward the construction trailer, but with every step she was getting closer to her death. She'd faced it once during the shooting and survived.

She had to survive this time.

Riggs had been nothing but kind to her, and protective. He'd used his days off to make sure she was safe.

Yet she'd hurt him. She had to fix that.

She stumbled over a tree stump and fell, her hands digging into the brush. Inhaling a deep breath, she pivoted on the ground and looked up at the boy holding the gun.

"Why are you doing this?"

"You had to stir up the past with this new school celebration."

Kate narrowed her eyes. "I don't understand what that has to do with you. You weren't even around back then. You'll benefit by enjoying a new building."

Anger slashed his expression, his thin face stark with desperation. For a moment, she thought she saw something familiar in his face. Something that reminded her of another teenager she'd once known. Long ago.

One who had terrorized her and the other students at Briar Ridge High.

His menacing look. Eyes filled with desperation. The crazed look of someone out of his mind.

"Please, don't," she said. "Talk to me. Maybe I can help. Tell me why this project upsets you so much."

"Because you stirred up all the gossip and questions again," he said. "All the talk about him had died down. Finally."

Kate struggled to follow his logic. "Talk of Ned?"

He didn't have to answer. She saw it in his eyes. Pain. Shame. Rage.

"Why would talk about Ned Hodgkins bother you?"

"See, you're doing it, just like I thought," he screeched. "Asking about the past." He clenched his jaw and raised the gun.

Kate's breath caught in her throat as he pointed the barrel at her head.

Then he yanked her arm and dragged her toward the trailer. He pushed her inside, and she fell onto the sofa in the front office. His tennis shoes shuffled across the floor as he paced. "You shouldn't have invited everyone to come back to town," he snarled. "Now it's all everyone can talk about, and it's your fault."

Pausing in front of her, he removed a matchbook and struck a match. The mad look in his eyes intensified as he watched the flame burst to life.

For a moment, Kate sat frozen in horror as a panic attack threatened. She couldn't breathe, she was choking, her lungs straining for air.

She did not want to die.

Forcing a deep breath in to ward off the panic, she summoned her courage then lurched up and dove at the boy. With a wild grunt, he slammed the butt of the gun against her head, and she hit the floor on her hands and knees. Stars swam behind her eyes as she struggled to stand, but she was so dizzy she swayed and the world tilted. Then he yanked her by the arm and began to drag her toward the rear of the trailer...

RIGGS MET STONE in the hallway. Before he could speak, though, Stone's phone buzzed.

Stone connected the call. "Yeah. I'm on my way."

His deep frown made Riggs tense. "What's wrong?"

"Nine-one-one from the new building site. Mayor got there and saw smoke."

"What about Kate?"

"I don't know. Let's go." Stone ducked into the room where Macy was still studying the photographs. "Macy, there may be trouble at the new building site. It's Kate."

Macy's eyes widened and she reached for her shoulder bag. "I'm going with you."

The three of them hurried outside to Stone's police car and climbed in. Stone flipped on his siren and peeled from the parking lot.

Fear pulsed through Riggs. Dammit, if he hadn't been so stubborn and had stayed with Kate, she'd be safe.

If anything happened to her, he'd never forgive himself.

Stone's phone buzzed again and he pressed Connect. His deputy's voice echoed over the speakerphone. "Forensics called, Sheriff. The prints on the matchbook are not a match to Billy, Woody or to Don Gaines. Techs did find a partial on Kate's car that matched the one on the matchbook and on the bomb piping."

"So we're dealing with one perp?"

"Looks that way, although we don't have a name yet, which means he doesn't have priors."

Riggs silently cursed as Stone ended the call. "Then we're back to square one."

Sweat beaded on his neck as Stone sped down Main Street and veered onto Briar Ridge Circle. The moment they rounded the corner, Riggs spotted smoke billowing in the air.

"It's the construction trailer," Riggs muttered. "Kate had better not be in there."

Stone swerved up beside the mayor's Cadillac and threw the squad car into Park.

Stone removed his gun from his holster as he ran to the mayor, who was hovered near his car, on his phone. Macy pulled her gun and headed for the edge of the woods to search the area in case the perpetrator had escaped.

"Mayor," Stone said.

"I'll call you back." The mayor pocketed his phone, his face riddled with anxiety. "Fire department's on its way."

Riggs hit the ground running. Smoke seeped from what looked like a crack in the trailer window. He touched the metal door.

It was warm, but not hot. He didn't have much time. A small trailer like this could go up in minutes.

"I'll look for a back door or way in," Stone said as he disappeared around the side of the trailer.

Riggs turned the doorknob, but it was locked. "Kate!" Terrified for her, he shook the door and yanked on it. The metal rattled. Heat seeped through the door. "Kate, are you in there?"

Nothing but the sound of something inside rattling, then fire crackling. Damn, he had to hurry.

He raced over to the window and looked through the shattered glass. Cold fear and rage hit him. Flames danced through the room, but he couldn't see Kate.

She could be on the floor. Or in a damn closet.

"I'm coming, sweetheart," he murmured. He yanked off his shirt, wrapped it around his hand and punched out the rest of the glass. Oxygen fed fire, so every second counted.

He dove through the window, smoke blurring his vision as he rolled across the floor. "I'm here, Kate! Where are you?" he shouted.

He jumped up and ran through the smoky fog, stomping at flames in his path. The fire was spreading, the blaze eating up the carpet and snapping at the curtains.

He raced through the room, darted across burning patches, and searched the closet. Empty.

Where was Kate?

Chapter Nineteen

A sizzling sound echoed from the bathroom of the trailer. Riggs's instincts surged to life. He jumped over a burning chair and yanked open the door. No Kate. Another pipe bomb. This one had nails attached.

Dammit to hell. It was about to go off.

Cursing, he ran back through the main room, shoved open the door and dove outside just as the trailer exploded. The fire engine careened into the parking lot, sirens wailing.

Stone jogged toward him. "Kate?"

"She's not inside," Riggs shouted.

"People are going to be here any minute." Stone scanned the parking lot. "If the perp has her, he probably took her somewhere."

There were no other cars around. Had he driven away with her?

Riggs pushed up from the ground, pulse pounding. "Where? We don't know who the hell we're dealing with."

"We'll find her," Stone said as the fire crew jumped from the truck and began to roll out the hoses.

A noise sounded from the woods to the right. Riggs pivoted to search the trees then stood bone-still and listened. Footsteps. Faint, but he heard them. Then a voice. A cry.

And movement.

If someone had forced Kate into the woods, he didn't want to alert them he was there. Although the siren had done that.

That meant the person who had Kate might be panicked. Desperate.

Panicked, desperate people did stupid things.

He glanced at Stone to get his attention, but he was talking to the mayor. Macy was out there somewhere in the woods. Maybe she'd find Kate.

Riggs crept toward the woods, slipping between the pines and oaks, eyes scanning.

The wind whistled. Brush rustled. A branch snapped off from a tall pine.

The voice again. Low. Shaky. Kate.

He inched pass a cypress, forcing himself to tread quietly, and continued walking until he spotted Kate. He went still, assessing the situation.

Kate threw up her hand as if pleading with her abductor to release her.

A thin, gangly guy in a dark gray hoodie had his back to Riggs, so he couldn't see the face. He had a gun, though, and was wildly waving it around.

"Think about your future," Kate said. "If you kill me, you'll go to prison."

"I—I won't have a future if it gets out who I am," the guy stammered.

"What do you mean who you are?" Kate said.

"Like I'd tell you or anyone else," he ranted. "Then I'd be crucified."

Riggs inched closer, hovering in the shadows.

"Think about your mother," Kate said, compassion in her tone. "How will she feel if you kill me?"

"She doesn't give a damn about me," the teen muttered.

"I doubt that's true," Kate said softly.

"It is," the boy shouted. "I was just some stupid mistake she made. I heard her say she wished she'd never had me. That she hated my father and was glad he was dead."

"Your father is dead?" Kate asked, confusion lacing her tone.

Riggs froze as the boy's face slipped into view. It was Roy Fulton.

Cassidy's son.

The amateur bomb, the fire behind Kate's house. All Roy.

Now he understood why Cassidy had kept Roy's father's identity quiet. She had been protecting her son. Not from his father, but from the stigma of his name and what Ned had done.

The boy paced in front of Kate, waving the gun like a madman. "Yeah, and you stirring up the past made everyone start talking about him again. That means people will start asking questions and they might find out."

"Find out what?" Kate asked.

Riggs slowly eased forward into the clearing. "That you're Ned's son, aren't you, Roy?"

KATE'S HEART POUNDED so hard she could hear the blood roaring in her ears. Roy Fulton was Ned's son? Riggs wasn't his father...

The boy swung around, gun aimed at Riggs, his eyes crazed. Déjà vu struck Kate. Roy had Ned's long, narrow chin, his high forehead. Why hadn't she seen it before?

"That's right!" Roy's hand shook. "And if everyone finds out, my life will be ruined. They'll think I'm just like him."

"You are just like him if you pull that trigger," Riggs said. "Ned killed innocent classmates and his teacher because he was angry. He had emotional problems and suffered a head injury when he was a baby. If you kill Kate or me, you can't use that as an excuse."

Roy's hand trembled as he glanced at Kate then back at Riggs. The gun bobbed up and down.

Compassion filled Kate's voice. "That must have been a shock. When did you find out Ned was your father?"

Roy dragged a hand over his face where tears trickled down his ruddy cheeks. "When Mama got the invitation to this stupid reunion. She was drunk and went on a rant about hating everyone in school. Then she just blurted it all out." Roy's voice cracked. "Said she and her girlfriend had a bet to see who could sleep with the most boys their senior year. Said Ned was the one she needed to win the bet. He was a nerd and awkward and gave in just like she knew he would. Then she laughed at him." Pain underscored Roy's words. "She laughs at me, too. Says I'm a weirdo like him."

"That's not true," Kate said. "You're smart, Roy, and talented on the computer. You can do something with that talent one day."

"Not if people find out I'm *his* son," Roy cried. "They'll hate me and run me out of town like they did Ned's family."

Riggs cleared his throat. "Did Ned know your mother was pregnant with his baby?"

Roy gave a sinister laugh. "She said when word spread she got knocked up, Ned asked her. She laughed and told him no way a weasel like him would be able to father a kid."

Dear God, Kate thought. Her cruel remarks must have crushed Ned.

"How can you be certain you're his son?" Riggs asked.

"She had one of those DNA tests done. I found it in the box she keeps under her bed."

"Oh, Roy, I'm so sorry," Kate said. "That must have hurt so much."

"You deserved better," Riggs said. "A mother who treated you with love and respect."

"Maybe she was protecting you by not telling you about Ned," Kate suggested softly. "She didn't want you to have to live in the shadow of what he'd done as his brother and his parents did."

Roy shot her a caustic stare. "It wasn't about me. She just didn't want anyone to know she'd slept with a loser like him," Roy muttered sarcastically. "Said she was afraid people would think she helped him plan the shooting."

"*Did* she?" Riggs asked.

Roy hesitated, maybe a little too long. "Hell, I don't know," Roy cried. "I mean, she hated some of the other kids, but she hates guns."

"Ned allowed things to destroy him and gave up. But you can rise above your problems and have a future," Kate said gently.

Roy shook his head back and forth. "No, I can't. I've already done too much. Your car and the fires…"

"No one was hurt though, so we'll work something out," Kate said softly. "You can get probation and receive counseling."

"She's right." Riggs held out his hand for the gun. "Don't let people in town remember you as a killer, Roy."

Roy's bony body trembled with emotions as he pushed his glasses up on his nose. Kate recognized the lost, empty, defeated look that suddenly shadowed his eyes.

The same look Ned had had before he'd opened fire.

But instead of shooting her or Riggs, Roy turned the gun on himself.

Macy and Stone both stepped into the clearing, guns raised, eyes on Roy. "Drop the gun," Macy said calmly.

"Roy, no!" Kate cried. "Please don't—"

She didn't get to finish the sentence. Riggs tackled

Roy, sending the boy to the ground as they struggled for the weapon.

Then a gunshot.

Kate froze in horror as blood spilled onto the ground.

RIGGS GRUNTED AND pushed the kid off him. Blood soaked his shirt as well as Roy's.

The teen had been hit in the shoulder and was howling like an injured animal.

Footsteps crunched leaves and dirt as Macy ran toward them and kicked the gun to the side. Stone sprinted up a second later.

Riggs rolled to his knees, ripped the bottom of his T-shirt and pressed it to Roy's shoulder.

"You're going to be okay, kid," Riggs said.

Kate rushed over, her face horrified. "Riggs?"

"He's all right. The bullet pierced his shoulder, not a main artery or his heart."

Kate knelt beside him. "How about you? Are you hurt?"

"I'm good."

Macy approached them, putting her gun back in its holster. "Kate, are you hurt?"

Kate's gaze met Macy's, and the years fell away as she murmured she was okay. They were five years old again, huddled in the dark in her room while a storm brewed. She wanted to go to her and pull her into a hug, but Macy still seemed to be holding back.

"An ambulance is on the way," Stone said.

"It hurts," Roy wailed.

"Just be grateful you're alive and didn't kill anyone," Riggs said, his sympathy for the kid warring with the fear that had nearly immobilized him at the sight of that gun pointed at Kate.

Kate stroked Roy's hair from his forehead. "Medical help is on the way, Roy."

"But I'll go to jail," he whined.

"You might," Stone cut in. "But you'll also get the help you need."

"I'll call your mother," Riggs promised. Maybe this would bring the two of them closer together.

A siren wailed and Stone hurried off to lead the paramedics to their location while he phoned Cassidy and told her to meet her son at the hospital.

Riggs, contemplating what Roy had done, also understood his reasons. The kid needed a father figure, or at least a big brother.

Maybe he'd offer to help get him in a treatment program. He could even mentor the boy, help teach him about being a man.

And Stone would follow up to see if Cassidy had known what Roy had intended.

Brush rattled and voices echoed, indicating the medics were approaching. Other cars sounded as they arrived, and Macy went to ensure there was no more trouble.

After they loaded Roy on the stretcher, one of them checked Kate where Roy had hit her with the gun. Thankfully, she was bruised but didn't need stitches.

Riggs stood, ready to follow Roy to the ambulance, but Kate caught his arm. His shirt was bloody and sweat soaked his skin.

"Thank God, you're all right, Riggs." She searched his face. "I'm so sorry for what I said earlier, for believing those rumors. I know you're not that man. The last few days, I've realized how strong and brave you are."

Footsteps sounded again, the mayor jogging toward them. "People are starting to arrive, Kate!"

Riggs squeezed her hand. "Let's go. You've worked hard for this." And nearly sacrificed her life.

She squeezed his hand. "We'll talk later, Riggs. Please."

He nodded, his throat thickening. Images of the shooting that had changed the town had struck him the moment he'd seen Roy with the gun.

Today, Roy could have taken Kate from him.

He had survived the trauma of nearly losing his leg when Ned had shot him.

He didn't think he'd survive if he'd lost Kate.

KATE WAS STILL trembling from the ordeal with Roy as she walked up to the outdoor stage.

Cars rumbled into the lot and parked, residents and alumni climbing from their vehicles and gathering on the lawn. Amy, shaken when she realized what had happened, had returned and quickly set up the refreshment table.

Kate spotted Brynn near the front of the crowd, her mother hovering by her side. Friends and groups from school had reconnected and hung together. Macy stood by Stone, their heads bent in conversation. But Trey wasn't with her.

Maybe that was a good sign.

Before the mayor started the dedication, Kate scanned the crowd for Riggs. He'd changed shirts and looked so handsome her breath stalled in her chest. His gaze locked with hers, and he gave her a small nod of encouragement.

His approval and support bolstered her confidence, and she joined the mayor at the podium.

"We're delighted to have such a nice turnout today. The town council, along with Kate McKendrick and the committee she spearheaded, have worked tirelessly to bring this event to fruition. First, Kate will say a few words about the memorial, then we'll start the festivities."

He stepped aside and Kate moved in behind the microphone. She welcomed everyone and thanked them for coming. "I'm excited today about the future of Briar Ridge and our young people. As I said before, I believe this new school will energize our students and families and inspire optimism as well as draw new families to the area." Kate swallowed, an image of her mother's face haunting her. Sunshine broke through the clouds. For a brief second, she could have sworn she saw her mother smiling at her, a proud gleam in her eyes.

"To honor those students we lost, we created a memorial for the front wall of the school. It will be the first thing students and visitors see when they enter the new Briar Ridge High. The shadow boxes are filled with photographs and quotes from loved ones and friends honoring the students."

She paused. "Beside the wall of shadow boxes there will be a special section featuring photos of other students and alumni, showcasing their accomplishments. Each of you, each of us, deserves a badge of courage for proving the shooting didn't destroy us. It's my hope that this wall will inspire students to overcome their own tragedies and obstacles to pursue their dreams." Each of the victims who'd lost their life was featured in one section while another held photographs and the stories of survivors. Stone's brother Mickey was there, along with Riggs and Brynn. Even Orson.

She gestured toward the display. "On the other display board, we've included blueprints for the new sports fields and stadium. Please take the time to look at the plans and the memorial." She motioned to the mayor. "Now, Mayor Gaines will officially cut the ribbon then Sheriff Lawson will break ground."

Voices rumbled, followed by applause. Kate's breath quickened, her fears dissipating at the smiles of approval.

She and Amy joined the mayor where a red, blue and white ribbon had been stretched between two white posts.

"Here's to new beginnings in Briar Ridge and at Briar Ridge High School." Mayor Gaines lifted the scissors and cut the ribbon, bringing cheers.

As the applause died down, Kate gestured at the time capsule. "Fifteen years ago, the members of the senior class were asked to write a letter to themselves that described their goals and dreams and where they envisioned they'd be. We're going to open the time capsule now."

Voices echoed through the crowd as Kate asked Stone to do the honors. He and a team had built the metal capsule in one of the metal-and wood-crafting classes their senior year.

Stone pried the lid off the capsule. "Miss Turner is going to hand out the letters while we mingle and have refreshments. I hope everyone enjoys seeing what their younger selves wrote."

Kate accepted hers and stepped aside to read it while Amy passed out the others. Voices and laughter spread, some expressing disappointment over unattained dreams, others laughing about their teenaged wistful thoughts.

Kate studied the words she'd scrawled on the page.

Dear Kate,
By the time you read this, I hope you've accomplished your dreams. You'll be a teacher and help shape lives just as Mom does. Macy and Brynn and you will still be best friends, and you'll share coffee and conversations while your children run and play on the playground and have sleepovers.

Yes, Kate, you won't be a shy, awkward girl anymore. You'll stop lingering in the shadows and stand up for what you believe in. You'll also go after what you want.

Most of all, I hope you're happy, Kate, that you've found the love of your life. I see you with a big house full of children you'll shower with love. And a man who will appreciate your uniqueness.

Kate blinked tears away as she finished reading the message her younger self had written. She had accomplished part of her dreams. She had taught school and was the principal now. She helped shape young lives.

But she, Brynn and Macy weren't close anymore.

She squared her shoulders and vowed to rectify that.

Riggs was standing by the time capsule, reading his own message.

Young Kate had dreamed about marriage and a family and love.

She wanted that now, too.

She just had to have the courage to go after what she wanted.

Chapter Twenty

Riggs had forgotten what he'd written to himself. But he chuckled as he skimmed the note.

He'd had lofty dreams of being a professional athlete, had imagined making the US Olympic team. He'd wanted fame, and women, and planned to travel the world instead of settling down.

He hissed a breath. Back then, he'd been arrogant and innocent, and full of boyish dreams.

He wasn't that boy any longer. He was a man.

His heart tripped in his chest as he looked at Kate. He wanted different things now.

He wanted Kate and all the strings attached.

But there were too many people here to have a private chat. She was walking toward him, though, so he met her halfway. His breath caught as she clasped his hand.

"Are you okay?" he asked.

She nodded. "I feel badly for Roy."

"Everybody makes their choices." Riggs cleared his throat. "Kate, about homecoming?"

She shrugged. "I didn't go in high school."

He pressed her hand to his chest. "Will you be my date tonight?

A soft smile lit her eyes then she murmured yes. He was

tempted to kiss her, but a commotion erupted by a row of cars in the parking lot.

Stone hurried to the scene, and Riggs and Kate arrived just in time to watch Macy slap handcuffs on Trey Cushing.

KATE'S HEART STUTTERED as Stone rushed to Macy's side. "What's going on?"

Macy jerked Trey's arm and forced him to face the crowd. "I found evidence. Trey gave Ned the .38 Special he used in the shooting."

"I didn't know what he'd planned to do," Trey bellowed.

"You're still under arrest as an accomplice to murder," Macy snapped.

Shocked whispers rattled through the alumni as Macy shoved Trey inside the back of Stone's squad car. Stone and Macy then climbed into the front seat and sped away.

Kate sighed in relief. They finally had the answer they'd needed about Ned's accomplice.

Billy approached, his expression contrite. "Kate?"

She tensed, but Riggs gave her arm a squeeze. "Listen to him, Kate. I think you need to hear what he has to say."

Kate took a deep breath, then nodded at Billy. "Okay."

Billy shifted nervously, but finally made eye contact. "Kate, I wanted to apologize to you for what I said, for blaming you for what my brother did."

Kate softened at his sincere tone.

"I was young and stupid, and my parents blamed me so I passed the buck." He lifted a chip that she recognized as an AA chip. "I'm sorry. Really sorry."

The guilt Kate had lived with eased. "Thank you for saying that, Billy."

"I'm trying to do better. Both for me and for Ned."

A smile warmed her heart. "Good for you."

Amy waved at her and motioned to the podium where

Kate was surprised to see Jimmy standing. He looked worn and frail, but he pounded his knuckles on the podium and everyone turned to see what was going on.

"By now," Jimmy said as the crowd hushed, "you all should have received the letters I sent."

Kate gaped at him. Letters?

"I attended the very school you're tearing down, and I've worked there for over two decades. During that time, I've seen good kids and some not so nice ones." His voice shook. "I watched what you all did to Ned, how your ignored and teased him. My classmates did the same thing to me, and I never got over it."

The mayor inched closer to Jimmy, but Jimmy raised a hand. "I ain't here to hurt anybody. But since Kate called this reunion, I thought everyone should be reminded of who was to blame." He pointed his finger across the crowd, one by one. "You and you and you and you…" He pressed his hand to his chest. "And now we've seen another boy arrested today, another boy lost. When is it going to end?"

Tears filled Kate's eyes and she joined Jimmy on the stage. "We're working on it, Jimmy. I promise, we're working on it."

Kate was just finishing dressing for the homecoming dance when her doorbell buzzed. She checked her reflection and smiled at herself in the mirror, although she wished she'd had time to buy a new dress.

Who would have ever guessed that she would finally go to homecoming with handsome Riggs Benford?

The bell buzzed again and she hurried to answer it. Instead of Riggs, Macy and Brynn were at her door. Hope budded in Kate's heart.

Without a wheelchair ramp, Macy had helped Brynn up the porch steps.

Macy's face crumpled and Brynn sniffed. "Can we come in and talk?" Macy asked.

Kate nodded, emotions welling in her throat, and together she and Macy assisted Brynn inside and settled her into a chair. Kate had longed to see her friends for so long that words failed her.

"Brynn called me after we arrested Trey..." Macy began.

Kate narrowed her eyes and looked back and forth between them.

"Kate," Brynn said, "I'm so sorry."

Kate swallowed hard. "What's going on?"

"You weren't the only one who received a letter of blame," Macy said. "Brynn and I both did, and so did some other alumni. That's one reason I came back. To find out who sent it."

Kate rubbed her fingers together. "Jimmy did it. He wanted us all to think about how we treated each other."

"I know." Brynn knotted her hands in her lap. "I deserved it, Kate. It was partly my fault Ned went on that shooting spree."

"No, Brynn, Ned was troubled. He had a head injury from childhood that caused him to have emotional issues."

Brynn's eyes widened. She hadn't known.

"But I spread gossip about him to Gretta." Brynn's voice cracked. "It...it was stupid, but I never thought Ned would go crazy and get a gun." Tears ran down Brynn's cheeks. "Your mother...you lost her because of me..."

"No, she died because of me," Macy said in a pained whisper. "Ned turned the gun on me, but your mother stepped in front of me and took the bullet instead." A sob escaped Macy. "I'm so sorry, Kate. That's why I left town. Your mother was so good to me, she loved me more than my own mother did. I couldn't bear to face you. I figured you'd hate me."

"Oh, God," Kate murmured. "Neither one of you is at fault." She looked at Brynn. "I thought you blamed me for putting you in that wheelchair."

"No," Brynn cried. "I just felt so bad about your mother, and then..."

"And you couldn't walk," Kate said. "I wish it had been me, Brynn, instead of you."

"Oh, Kate, I never thought or wanted that," Brynn said.

Her mother's face stared down at her from the mantel. "You know, Mom wouldn't want us blaming ourselves," Kate said. "She'd want us to be together."

Macy and Brynn both nodded and the three of them fell together in a group hug just like they had when they were little girls.

Nothing would ever tear them apart again.

Chapter Twenty-One

It took Kate an hour to repair her makeup after Macy and Brynn left, but it was worth it. Brynn had even brought her an outfit to wear for the homecoming, a V-necked green satin cocktail dress that hugged her curves in all the right places and sparkly silver heels.

She'd also told them she was moving into a small apartment on her own, that it was time to get out from under her mother's smothering. Kate and Macy promised to be there for her. It was something Kate was looking forward to. Kate entered the homecoming party on Riggs's arm, elated that she and her friends had reconciled.

The clubhouse was filled with alumni, the mood tonight shifting as if the weight of the past had finally been lifted. Maybe forgiveness would bring them all even closer.

"Cassidy insists she didn't know what Ned planned," Stone told her.

"So she lied and triggered his breakdown, but she can't be charged for that," Kate said. "Not any more than the rest of us."

"No, it's time to move on." Riggs pulled her onto the dance floor and they swayed to the soft lull of music. She spotted Stone dancing with Macy, and Jay Eastwood had scooped Brynn up from her wheelchair and was dancing her across the floor with a look of adoration. Maybe they were all three going to find romance now. And complete their dream of being in each other's weddings.

"I've been waiting a long time to do this," Riggs murmured as he swung her around.

Kate threaded her fingers in his hair. "I'm sorry for believing that rumor about you and Cassidy."

Riggs shook his head, regret darkening his eyes. "I should have told you," he murmured, "but my pride got in the way. I wanted you to see me for who I am now, to realize that I never would have abandoned a baby, not even back then."

"I do see that, Riggs," Kate murmured. "I guess I let my own past get in the way."

He gently tucked a strand of her hair behind her ear. "What do you mean?"

"My father left my mom when he found out she was pregnant. I...never knew him. And he never wanted any part of me."

"Oh, God, Kate," Riggs said gruffly. "I'm sorry. I didn't know."

Kate shrugged. "You'd think it wouldn't have affected me, but it did. And then losing Mom. I was afraid to love and lose again."

"I know what you mean," he murmured. "Sometimes our pasts have a way of interfering with our futures," Riggs said. "And not in a good way."

She lifted a hand and pressed it against his cheek. "But other times, in the best ways. The past shaped you into a hero."

"I'm no hero," he said in a self-deprecating tone.

Kate smiled. "You are to me." Her voice cracked. "I don't want to lose you, Riggs."

"Ah, Kate, you've got me as long as you want me," Riggs said in a sexy whisper. "I want to go to bed with you and wake up with you every morning." He brushed his thumb across her cheek. "I want to marry you and have children with you and grow old together."

Tears blurred Kate's eyes and she looped her arms around his neck. "And sit in those rockers on your front porch and watch our children play."

He chuckled. "And cuddle with them under the quilts my mother made."

Emotions crowded Kate's throat. "I would love that."

Then he dragged her into his arms and kissed her.

* * * * *

THE SETUP

CAROL ERICSON

Prologue

Rule number four. The victim should never be someone you know.

He screwed up his face and squinted at the girl curled up in the back seat of his car. He didn't really know Kelsey. Seeing her around, knowing her name—that didn't count, did it? He hadn't known Shelby or Marissa, either. They didn't know *his* name, had barely given him the time of day.

Through the slits of his eyes, he could almost imagine Kelsey smiling at him. That was better than the last look she gave him. He smiled back.

A rustling noise from the trailhead wiped the smile off his face and made his heart pound—not in a good way, not the way it had raced the first time he'd put his hands on Kelsey. He held his breath until he saw the flash of a squirrel's tail as it hopped out of a tree. The animal turned its head in his direction and pierced him with its beady eyes. He stomped his foot in the squirrel's direction, sending the creature up another tree.

He hooked his arms beneath Kelsey's and dragged her out of the car, the heels of her boots hitting the soft ground. He'd place her off the trail but not too far off. Someone needed to discover his handiwork before the animals got to her. Seemed like he'd made that mistake with Shelby. He'd already scoped out this location, had visited it a few times.

His running shoes scuffed through the dry debris that littered the trail as he pulled her deadweight several feet. He stopped and wiped a bead of sweat from his face with his arm. Kelsey was a lot heavier in death, but he'd discovered this with the others. This wasn't his first rodeo. It was his third rodeo. He giggled at his pun.

Another ten feet, and he located his spot—her spot now—and let Kelsey's upper body drop with a huffing sound on the comfy cushion of leaves, twigs and berries beneath the tree, one arm crossing her body. The scent of pine and citrus tingled in his nose, and he inhaled the clean smell. Maybe he should take up hiking. Being out here made him feel good. He glanced at Kelsey—or maybe this was what made him feel good.

Now the annoying work part started. He crouched beside the body and plucked at the sleeve of her shirt to move her arm to her side. He lined up her legs, straight and together, the toes of her boots pointing skyward. He brushed some dirt from the leg of her jeans.

The bruises ringing her throat created an unfortunate purple necklace, but he didn't have a gun, and a knife would've left a mess of blood in his car. He liked blood, but not if he had to get rid of it.

When he'd killed those little animals, the blood didn't matter. Nobody was running around investigating the deaths of possums. He snorted and a wisp of Kelsey's blond hair fluttered against her cheek. With one gloved finger, he flicked the hair back into place.

On her back, with her arms and legs straight, she looked like one of those mannequins in the store—not that he was a poser. He didn't need to pose his victims in grotesque and disrespectful positions, but now

Kelsey looked as perfect and untouchable in death as she'd looked alive.

He twisted his head over his shoulder and peered into the darkness, swallowing against his dry throat. He'd done his research and this part of the park didn't have cameras, but you never knew who could be watching.

He jumped back and surveyed his handiwork, a flicker of lust stirring in his belly. He'd wanted to have sex with her, but he didn't want to leave his DNA. He didn't want to get caught. He had many more dates in mind. Besides, Kelsey was a nice girl. He could go pick up a hooker on Hollywood Boulevard to satisfy his needs, just as he'd done after his dates with Shelby and Marissa.

Two more steps—the most important ones. He pulled a playing card from his back pocket, leaned over Kelsey's body and stuck it between her lips—the queen of hearts. Then he dug into the front pocket of his jeans and withdrew the box cutter. He knelt beside Kelsey and sliced off the pinkie finger of her left hand.

The souvenir.

Chapter One

"Good thing she was already dead when he took her finger." Detective Jake McAllister lifted the victim's wrist and grimaced. He called over his shoulder, "Tire tracks at the trailhead? We know this isn't the kill site."

"Too many to identify just one." His partner, Billy Crouch, impressive in a dark gray tailored suit, purple pocket square and wing tips, strode down the trail to join Jake where he crouched beside the body. "No tire tracks, no cameras. I had one of the officers check with the park rangers."

"No cameras at the other dump site, either. He's being careful." Jake rose to his feet, inhaling the scent of pine from the trees and locking eyes with an ambitious squirrel who'd been busy scurrying up and down the large oak that provided a canopy over the body.

Griffith Park was an oasis of rugged, untamed land in the middle of the urban sprawl of LA. It housed the zoo, the observatory, a concert venue, a carousel, pony rides and acres of wilderness crisscrossed with hiking trails. It had also hosted several dead bodies in its day, including the Hillside Strangler's first victim.

Jake pointed at the card inserted between the victim's lips. "Queen of hearts, missing finger—looks like we have a pattern here."

Billy whistled as he pushed his sunglasses to the end of his nose. "It's The Player all over again."

"Copycat." Jake raised his hand to the crime scene investigators who had just arrived at the park and waved. "The Player was working twenty years ago and abruptly stopped. He's gotta be dead or in prison."

"Maybe he just got paroled." Billy picked an imaginary speck of lint from the arm of his jacket. "He could've been twenty when he was operating before, spent twenty years behind bars for armed robbery, assault, rape. Now he's forty, tanned, ready and rested."

"Could be. They never got his DNA back then. Never left any—just like these two murders."

Billy whipped the handkerchief, which Jake had believed was just for show, out of his front pocket and dashed it across the shiny tip of one of his shoes. "Damn, it's dirty out here."

Jake rolled his eyes. "It's the great outdoors. Most people don't take hikes in Italian suits and shoes."

Shaking his head, Billy clicked his tongue. "Only the shoes are Italian, man. The suit's from England."

"Excuse me, Cool Breeze." Jake bowed to his partner. He'd given Billy the nickname Cool Breeze, and it had stuck. The man knew his fashion, his fine wines and his women.

Jake had warned him about the women because Billy already had a fine woman, Simone, at home. They needed only one divorce in the partnership, and Jake had that covered—not that he had run around on his wife, unless you counted the job as the other woman...and a lot of cops' wives did.

Someone cleared his throat behind him. "Fingerprints?"

Jake jerked his head toward Clive Stewart, their fingerprint guy in Forensics, his shaved head already sporting a sheen. "Yeah, you can check, Clive. He didn't leave the knife or box cutter behind that he used to slice off the finger. You might try the playing card, her neck. You know your job, man. I'll let you and the others do it."

As CSI got to work, Jake shuffled away from the body on the ground and eyed the crunch of people beyond the yellow crime scene tape. Although still morning, the air possessed that quiet, suffocating feel that heralded a heat wave, and the tape hung limply, already conceding defeat.

Jake pulled out his phone. Holding it up, he snapped some pictures of the looky-loos leaning in, hoping to catch a glimpse of…what? What did they hope to see? Did they want to ogle the lifeless body of this poor woman dumped on the ground?

Maybe one of them was already familiar with the position of the victim. Killers had been known to return to the scene of the crime and relive the thrill.

He swung his phone to the right to take a few more pictures from the other side of the trail. As he tipped up his sunglasses and peered into the viewfinder to zero in on his subjects, he swore under his breath.

What the hell was *she* doing here?

Billy stepped into his line of fire. "He wanted someone to discover her quickly. She's not that far off the trail, but no purse or ID, so he doesn't want us to identify her right away."

"You're blocking my view." Jake nudged Billy's shoulder and framed the crowd at the edge of the tape again… but she was gone.

Jake took a few more pictures, and then cranked his head from side to side looking for that unmistakable flash of blond hair, surprised she hadn't ducked under the tape by now to nose around.

"Trying to find the killer?" Billy raised an eyebrow.

"Could be watching right now."

"The Player never did that."

"Not that they know of. Would be interesting to see some photos of those crime scenes from twenty years ago."

"I'm sure that's in our near future." Billy patted the top of his short Afro. "Two murders, same MO, both bodies found in our jurisdiction, copycat of a previous serial killer—I smell a task force."

Jake's phone buzzed in his hand, and he glanced at the text from Captain Castillo. "You're downright clairvoyant, Cool Breeze. Castillo wants everyone in Robbery-Homicide at the station at four o'clock. He wants me there at three thirty."

"Uh-oh. Hope you weren't planning on getting a life for the next several months."

"Getting a life? I have a life." Jake dropped the phone into the pocket of his non-English suit jacket and turned away from the body.

Billy gave a short laugh behind him. "If you say so, J-Mac."

AT 3:28 P.M., JAKE propped up the wall outside Captain Castillo's office in the Northeast Division with one shoulder. Castillo hated tardiness almost as much as he hated the press.

Jake hadn't bothered knocking on the office door because he could hear Castillo's voice on the other side. He'd end the phone call at precisely three thirty and open that door, expecting Jake to be standing right where he was. And if he weren't there? He didn't know. He'd never tempted fate like that. He had to play by certain rules so that he could break others.

The low drone of Castillo's voice stopped, and Jake stood at attention.

The door swung open, framing Castillo, navy suit slightly rumpled, salt-and-pepper hair already escaping from the pomade Castillo slathered on his head. The captain nodded once. "McAllister."

Jake followed the captain into the room, taking the lone chair on the other side of the functional desk, and dove right in. "I'm assuming this is about the two murders."

"It is. We've identified the second victim, Kelsey Lindquist." Castillo shoved a picture of a pretty blonde across his desk. "No connection to Marissa Perez that we can see. They didn't know each other, live in the same neighborhood, work together or in the same industry."

"That's first glance. They're not working girls, so how is he finding them? Marissa did some online dating. Do we have Kelsey's phone?" Jake glanced at the thick file on Castillo's desk. "Looks like Billy's been doing some work while I was in court. How'd you ID the latest victim so quickly?"

"Parents, unfortunately. Kelsey missed work today. Her boyfriend located Kelsey's car in the parking lot of a shopping center this afternoon, purse and phone on the floor of the car. He called the police. The officers took one look at her driver's license and called us."

"Boyfriend?"

"Not a suspect…yet."

"Tough." Jake's gut rolled. If anything ever happened to Fiona, he'd be ready to do murder himself. "Have her parents identified the body?"

"Not yet." Castillo shoved the folder toward Jake. "This is yours now. We're forming a task force, and I want you to lead it for us."

"For us?" Jake drummed his fingers on top of the file. "You expect more bodies in other jurisdictions?"

"You and I both know that's a possibility. He's gotten away with this twice. Do you really think he's going to stop now?"

"The Player did."

"The Player stopped after six." Castillo mopped his brow with a tissue he'd plucked from a box on his desk. "You've already noticed the similarities."

"Copycat."

Castillo shrugged, his suit crumpling even more around his shoulders. He needed Billy's tailor—they all needed Billy's tailor.

"Most likely. Would be rare for The Player to come out of retirement." Castillo steepled his fingers. "I know you're already thinking about The Player's murder book."

"Thinking about the murder book and Quinn. Does he still live in Venice, near the beach?"

"Ned Verona would know for sure. Hit him up after the meeting." Castillo splayed his hands on the desk, thumbs touching. "I'll take everyone through the slide-show of what we have now on both murders. You and Crouch can chime in whenever you feel the urge. Then I'm going to turn the show over to you for an intro to the task force."

Jake slid the file folder from Castillo's desk and tucked it under his arm. Resisting the urge to flip through the pages, he followed the captain into the conference room, already packed with Robbery-Homicide detectives, several uniformed officers and a few civilians.

The lights dimmed, and for the next hour Castillo briefed them on the two murders. Jake picked up where the captain left off, discussing the formation of the task force and how it would operate.

Blinking his eyes as the lights went up, Jake asked, "Any questions?"

Someone yelled from the back of the room. "Are we gonna call this task force The Player 2.0?"

"Not unless you want to send the public into panic mode. Maybe we'll have a contest. Winner gets extra duty." As the officers and detectives peppered him with questions, Jake scanned the room, his gaze tripping over the blonde in the back.

Oh, hell, no. Had Castillo invited her?

She'd noticed his attention and had taken a step back, folding her arms over a snowy-white blouse, a half smile curling her lip, exuding a confidence born of being connected.

Jake rushed through the rest of the questions, and as the meeting adjourned he elbowed his way toward Castillo, who was talking to Lieutenant Alicia Fields. He waited until Alicia took a breath before butting in. "I need to talk to you, Captain."

Alicia held up her finger. "Do you mind, J-Mac? Give me a minute."

Someone tugged on his sleeve and he jerked his head over his shoulder, meeting the amused blue eyes of Kyra Chase, the quack.

"Get used to it, McAllister. I'm part of this task force—whether you like it or not."

Chapter Two

He didn't like it—not at all.

His hazel eyes narrowed and his nostrils flared, as if he'd just gotten juiced up with adrenaline and was debating between fight and flight. As if Jake McAllister would ever flee from conflict. Quite the contrary. He had a reputation for courting it.

Castillo sliced his hand in the air to cut the tension vibrating between her and Jake. "McAllister, you know Kyra Chase, right? She did a great job on Verona's case a few months ago. Put the department in a good light by assisting with the victims in those gang retaliation shootings, got some cooperation from family members we never expected."

"I know *of* her." Jake thrust out his hand in an aggressive gesture. "Detective Jake McAllister, Ms. Chase."

She clasped his hand, and its warmth and strength rattled her even more than the gesture itself…and the fire in those eyes that had just turned green. "You can call me Kyra. Captain Castillo has assigned me to your task force as a liaison between the victims' families and the investigation."

"You won't be doing any profiling of the killer or coddling any suspects we bring in?" He released her hand abruptly.

She tilted her chin in a challenge. She knew her meeting with McAllister would be adversarial—she just didn't realize how much she would enjoy it. "That's not my job and never has been."

"It shouldn't have been your colleague's job, either."

Castillo cleared his throat. "The Lindquists are going to the morgue tomorrow to identify their daughter. I want both of you there…and civil."

Jake rolled his shoulders. "I'm always civil."

Lieutenant Fields, who'd been quiet through the exchange, snorted and patted Kyra's back. "If you want any tips on how to deal with the ogre, let me know."

Kyra let her eyes wander the length of Jake's fit frame. She'd dealt with worse. "I know you're a top-notch detective, and I look forward to working with you."

She could lie with the best of them, but those two statements were nothing but the truth. Of course, she'd be looking forward to working with Jack the Ripper for a chance to get on this task force.

Jake nodded once. "I'll get your number from the captain, so we can organize for tomorrow."

"I'll be ready." She took her leave of Captain Castillo and Lieutenant Fields and strode from the conference room, which had mostly cleared. Although she could feel McAllister's gaze following her, it would be foolish to turn and acknowledge it, acknowledge him.

She didn't like him any more than he liked her, but she'd face a blazing inferno to stay on this case—and that's exactly what Jake McAllister might prove to be. She'd just have to avoid getting burned.

AFTER SITTING IN traffic for two hours, Kyra poured herself a glass of chilled chardonnay and curled up on her couch with a file folder in her lap. Some people settled in with a good book. She preferred files on murder cases.

She took a sip of wine, the crisp, fruity flavor sliding down the back of her throat and creating a warm spot in her belly. Sometimes she needed something stronger to get through this stuff, but a glass of wine on an empty stomach would suffice for tonight.

She flipped open the folder and shuffled through her notes. She didn't have anything official from the LAPD yet, but she'd get her hands on everything despite Jake McAllister. She understood his distaste for her wasn't personal. She didn't even blame him, but he should do a better job of reining in his emotions. If he wanted lessons, she could oblige.

She ran a finger down a page of notes, pausing at each bullet point where her pen had dug a small hole next to a fact she knew about the two murders. The police hadn't yet released certain details about the homicides, but at the task force presentation Castillo and McAllister had confirmed what she'd already heard—the killer had stuck a playing card between the lips of each of his victims and had removed her left pinky finger.

Kyra flicked her thumb against her own pinky finger and clamped down on a shiver that threatened to rampage through her body. She took another sip of wine, savoring it before swallowing.

The task force would probably reveal one of the killer's proclivities and keep the other one close to the vest to weed out the fakes, frauds and wannabes. Twenty years ago, Roger Quinn had disclosed the card, which was how The Player had gotten his name, but the public never knew about the severed fingers.

That didn't mean the information never got out. People talked.

Had this killer heard the stories? Was he anxious to pick up where The Player had left off? There were cold cases in the annals of the LAPD, but not many serial killer cold cases. Usually, murderers got sloppy or arrogant or desperate for the recognition they felt was their due. But not The Player. She had no doubt he was arrogant, though he'd never been sloppy and he'd never contacted the press or the police to crow about his achievements.

She slid the folder from her lap and rose from the couch, holding her wine in front of her. She placed the glass on the kitchen table and ducked into her bedroom. She swung open the door to her walk-in closet, a rarity in these older, rent-controlled apartment buildings in Santa Monica, and shoved aside some blouses hanging on a lower rod, not doing a great job of hiding her safe. She tapped in the code, her mother's birth date, and waited for the green light to flash its welcome.

She pushed aside her passport, birth certificate and the release papers from LA's foster care system and curled her fingers around the soft, worn edges of a manila envelope. The sharp stub of the clasp, long since broken off, scratched her finger as she slid the envelope from the safe.

Leaving the door of the safe open, she backed out of the closet, clutching the packet to her chest. She swung by the kitchen table on her way back to the couch and grabbed her wine.

Tucking one leg beneath her, she slipped the paper clip, which had taken the place of the clasp, from the top of the envelope and plunged a slightly shaky hand inside.

The sheaf of papers waiting for her fit comfortably in her grip, and she brought them into the light. These weren't official documents, but they told the whole story of The Player's killing spree twenty years ago.

Six women. Six severed fingers. No connection between the victims, except for an age range in their twenties and a general appearance of long blond hair. Nothing unusual in that, hardly a pattern. Young women were more apt to be the target of serial killers, and most young women, then and now, wore their hair long.

The two current women didn't even match The Player's victims, as Marissa was a dark-haired Latina.

Kyra flipped over the stack of papers and slapped them down on the coffee table. She didn't need to look at the pictures again.

She rolled her wineglass between her hands and raised it to her lips. She'd better slow down and get some food in her stomach if she hoped to carry out her plan tonight.

She pushed up from the couch, poured the wine into the sink and grabbed a container of leftover pasta from the fridge. She ate it cold, standing up, one bare foot on top of the other.

Then she changed from the slacks and blouse she'd worn to work and pulled on some jeans, a T-shirt and a hoodie. When she finished tying her running shoes, she reached into her satchel and grabbed her .22. It wasn't easy to get a conceal-carry permit these days, but she had connections.

She slung the strap of her purse across her body and secured her gun in the outside pouch. She closed the safe in the closet and locked up the apartment, its location on the first floor making it vulnerable to break-ins by petty thieves and junkies, but they didn't scare her. She'd faced the devil himself—more than once. Then she hopped in her car, which was parked in the carport in the alley, and drove back the way she'd come earlier.

It didn't take two hours this time. Rush-hour traffic

had thinned out, but the freeway still boasted enough cars to keep her speed below fifty most of the way.

She took the turnoff for Griffith Park, leaving the other cars behind. She crawled down a road toward the trailhead where there'd been a mass of vehicles and people this morning. Now she had the place to herself—she hoped.

This morning, she'd headed to the crime scene as soon as she'd heard a hiker had found a body, the second in two weeks, dumped in the rugged area that nestled in the heart of LA. She'd seen McAllister there, large and in charge, and he'd seen her. He'd been taking pictures of the onlookers, hoping to catch a killer with his camera.

She'd been surveying the crowd herself, but nobody stuck out to her. McAllister's pictures could be valuable further into the investigation once they tracked the movements and acquaintances of these women.

It would've been easier for her if Verona had been tagged to lead the task force, but McAllister was the hotshot, despite certain issues with the department. She could wrap Verona around her little finger, and she could handle McAllister, too. She'd had lots of practice getting the jump on men who thought they ruled the world.

She held her breath as she neared the trailhead. She didn't need some patrol officer assigned to protect the crime scene asking her questions. Her late-night visit would surely get back to McAllister, and she didn't need that, either.

As the car slowed to a stop, she huffed out a breath. She had free rein without an audience. The cops and CSI had been working the crime scene since this morning. They must've squeezed it dry. No need to keep anyone away now.

Darkness met her as she scrambled from her car,

her hand firmly on the zippered pouch concealing her weapon. She didn't expect the killer to be active two nights in a row or choose the same dump site, but this guy wasn't the only evil that lurked in the shadows. She had plenty of experience with evil, and the only way to stop it in its tracks was with a well-placed bullet.

The soles of her running shoes crunched the dried-out discards from the foliage that bordered the trail. A slight warm breeze feathered through the trees, sending another few leaves floating to the ground and lifting the ends of her hair. As summer wound down, it ushered in wildfire season and the debris beneath her feet would be its hapless fuel.

She took several steps down the trail, her breathing shallow, her heart hammering in her chest. He must've parked in just about the same place as she did, his feet treading the same path as hers.

The police had noted drag marks on the trail. Of course, he hadn't killed Kelsey here. He'd brought her to this place, left her, dumped her. Kyra's hands curled at her sides as a hot rage thrummed through her veins.

The wind picked up and whispered down the trail. She whispered a response. "Is it you? Have you come back? If you have, I'm not going to let you get away this time. I'll kill you myself."

A twig snapped behind her and she spun around, her hand plunging into her purse for her gun. A hulking figure took shape under the crescent moon, and she aimed her weapon at it—center mass.

"Take one more step, and I'll drop you where you stand."

Chapter Three

He'd recognize that voice anywhere, even though he'd heard it live and in person just a few times and never so…forceful. He believed her, but he had no intention of letting her off the hook so easily.

He raised his hands. "I'm LAPD Detective Jake McAllister. Are you all right?"

A sudden gust of wind carried her sigh down the trail toward him.

"I—it's Kyra Chase. I'm sorry. I'm putting away my weapon."

Lowering his hands, he said, "Is it okay for me to move now?"

"Of course. I didn't realize, I thought you were…"

"The killer coming back to his dump site?" He flicked on the flashlight in his hand and continued down the trail, his shoes scuffing over dirt and pebbles. "He wouldn't do that—at least not so soon after the kill."

When he got within two feet of her, he skimmed the beam over her body, her dark clothing swallowing up the light until it reached her blond hair. "I didn't mean to scare you, but what are you doing here?"

"Probably the same thing you are." She hung on to the strap of her purse, her hand inches from the gun pocket.

"I'm the lead detective on the case, and I'm doing some follow-up investigation."

"Believe it or not, Detective, I have my own prep work that I like to do before meeting a victim's family. I want to have as much information as possible when talking to them. I'm sure you can understand that."

"Sure, I can. Call me Jake." He pointed to her bag. "What kind of piece do you have?"

"M&P 22 Compact." She clutched the bag with one hand as if she expected him to go for it.

"A Smith & Wesson—nice weapon."

"And before you ask, I do have a permit for it." Her chin jutted forward. "Do you want to see it?"

He raised his eyebrows, even though he'd been planning to ask her about the permit—just to mess with her. "The gun or the permit?"

"Either. Both." She widened her stance.

"I'm good. I've seen the M&P 22 before, and I trust you...about that permit."

"I think I've seen enough." She took a step in his direction and stuttered to a stop, her ponytail swinging over her shoulder, when he didn't make a move.

"Really? You've seen enough? Where's your flashlight?"

She dipped her hand into the pocket of her hoodie and held up her cell phone. "Phones have flashlights now. They even take pictures."

The corner of his mouth twitched. "Did you discover anything we missed?"

"That's not why I was here." She sniffed. "I have to get going. The Santa Ana winds are kicking up, and my allergies are already giving me trouble."

He stepped aside, and as she walked past him he joined her, matching her stride.

She whipped her head around without slowing her pace. "Where are you going? You just got here."

"I'm going to walk you back to your car because it's dangerous out in the middle of Griffith Park after dark." He pulled up next to her on the narrow trail, bumping her shoulder.

"You forgot I have a loaded pistol as my companion." She patted her purse.

His arm shot out. He grabbed her bag and yanked it quickly to the side. Not only could she not reach her gun, he had the strap of her purse around her neck.

She sputtered, knocking his arm with the heel of her hand. Not a bad response, but her blow made no impact on the grip he had on her purse.

"Just sayin'." He released the bag, and the heavy gun banged against her hip.

"And I'm just sayin' you're an ass." She repositioned her purse, kept her hand over the gun pouch and quickened her pace.

"Having a weapon is better than not having one, but don't let it give you a false sense of security. Just because you're packing heat doesn't mean you can waltz into any situation you please. Have a little common sense."

He followed her stiff back and swinging ponytail back to the road. It was clear she thought he'd been trying to get under her skin, but her appearance here on her own truly alarmed him. He wasn't going to allow Kyra Chase or any other woman to walk back to her car alone under these circumstances. He didn't mind ruffling her feathers.

She hit her remote and her lights flashed once. "This is me. Thanks for the escort, Officer."

His lips twisted into smile. "My pleasure, and thanks for not shooting me back there. I've got your number."

She stopped, her hand on the car door. "What?"

"Your phone number. I got it from Carlos… Captain Castillo. I'll text you the time for our meeting at the coroner's office downtown."

"Right. See you tomorrow." She slammed her car door, cranked on her engine and made a dusty U-turn in the road.

Jake stared after the red taillights until his eyes watered. What the hell had Kyra Chase been doing out here? And who the hell had she been talking to in the darkness?

THE FOLLOWING DAY, Jake parked his sedan in the parking structure of the USC Medical Center downtown. The old building that housed the coroner's office for the county was attached to the med center. He slid from the car and reached into the back seat for his suit jacket. He'd wait for the comfort of the building's AC before putting it on. The summer in LA had been mild, but September had brought the heat, and the Santa Anas were gusting in the canyons.

He pulled some lip balm from his pocket and swiped it across his dry lips. It couldn't help his dry throat though. Damn, he hated these IDs with the parents. Having Kyra Chase with him might help though he didn't have to like her involvement in any other aspect of the case.

She'd been there that day—the day he'd gone off on Lizbeth Kruger at the station. The day he'd been reprimanded for his behavior. He didn't give a damn—then or now. He'd do it all over again. Even though it hadn't solved anything, hadn't brought back Jacinda, giving Lizbeth a piece of his mind had assuaged his fury. Or at least for that day. His rage had become a living thing inside him, something to tame on some days and something to give vent to on others.

Man, he needed a visit with Fiona.

He strode to the elevator, his suit jacket draped over one arm. He and Kyra planned to meet early near the front door so they could intercept the Lindquists when they arrived for the sad ritual available to the families of homicide victims. Some didn't want or need the last look at their loved one, and in this day of DNA the in-person ID wasn't necessary.

Kyra had to be an old pro at this, although she barely looked older than twenty-five. How'd she manage to look so fresh when hundreds of patients must've poured thousands of sorrows in her ears? Maybe it didn't affect her. Maybe he could learn something from her.

Nah. Therapists were full of it. How do you *feel* about that, Jake? How the hell did they think he felt and how would talking about it change anything?

Not that his old man was a role model, but Jake could understand drowning in the booze. Not the other stuff, but the booze. Hell, he could name ten cops right now who coped that way.

The elevator doors opened and he crossed over to the coroner's office. He slipped into his jacket as he caught sight of Kyra, standing by the door looking cool in her beige skirt and white blouse. She liked white. It made her look…icy.

A smile tugged at his lips as he recalled her clipped tone during their phone conversation earlier today. He'd decided to add the personal touch by calling instead of texting; she hadn't seemed to appreciate his effort.

He'd stung her pride last night when he captured her purse and gun. To be fair, if she were out there on her own and a strange man approached her, she wouldn't let him get that close. Hadn't she drawn down on him when he came traipsing along the trail? Yeah, he'd give her credit for that.

"Good morning." He kept his distance this time, eyeing the leather satchel slung over her shoulder. Did she have her little .22 in there, too?

"Morning." Her blue eyes flicked over him, and he could feel the chill.

He sure hoped she warmed up for victims' families, or she'd be no use to him at all. Verona had sung her praises, but Verona could be wooed by a pretty face and a nice pair of legs. Jake's gaze dropped to the hem of Kyra's knee-length skirt and below. Yep, she had those.

She cleared her throat. "David and Marie should be here any minute. Is the medical examiner ready for us?"

Jake jerked his thumb over his shoulder. "I can check at the desk to make sure."

Jake looked in at the desk where the receptionist assured him the coroner was expecting the Lindquists. The coroner would conduct the autopsy tomorrow. It was always better if the relatives could ID the victim before the autopsy.

As he walked back to Kyra, a middle-aged couple walked through the front doors. Even without an introduction, he knew they were the Lindquists due to their zombie-like appearance. They shuffled into the lobby, the woman with a dazed look on her face and the man drained of all color and life.

Kyra launched forward to greet them, shaking their hands.

By the time Jake joined the group, they seemed like old friends. Kyra turned to him. "Mr. and Mrs. Lindquist, this is Detective Jake McAllister. He's the lead detective on Kelsey's case. Detective McAllister, this is David and Marie Lindquist."

Jake shook David's hand and gave it an extra squeeze just to try to infuse some strength into him. He took a gentler approach with Marie. He cupped her thin hand in both of his. "I'm sorry for your loss."

"C-can we ask you some questions about Kelsey's death?" Marie's gaze darted to her husband's face and back to Jake's.

Did the two of them have a different approach to how they wanted to handle this? He could understand that. It was a strong marriage that survived the murder of a child.

"I'll tell you what I can, Mrs. Lindquist. There's some information we don't release—even to the family. It gives us a better chance of finding her killer."

"That's what we want." David's watery blue irises were barely distinguishable from the whites of his eyes.

Kyra placed a hand on Marie's arm. "Are you ready? You know, you don't have to do this. You're going to provide her dental records, and that should be enough."

Jake slanted a quick glance at Kyra. Although he knew it would be hard on them, he wanted the Lindquists to ID their daughter this way. They'd have her dental records, her DNA, her picture, but the personal identification seemed to bring some reality to the victims' families, and it also opened up the floodgates sometimes where law enforcement could glean some valuable information for the case. As a victims' rights advocate, Kyra should know this. Maybe she cared more about the families' feelings than catching the killer. In his experience, nailing the bad guy brought peace to the families more than any therapy could.

Marie shook her head. "We need to do this. It wouldn't seem right to let Kelsey take this part of her journey alone. Does that make sense?"

David stared at the dull linoleum floor as if nothing in his life made sense anymore.

Kyra slipped an arm around Marie's shoulders. "It makes perfect sense."

With that settled, at least for Marie, they moved toward the elevator. Jake brought up the rear as he herded the group into the car and stabbed the button for the basement.

In a quiet voice, Kyra asked Marie questions about Kelsey on the ride down.

David murmured to Jake, "Kelsey's murder is connected to that other case two weeks ago?"

"We think so, yeah. We're forming a task force." Jake dipped his head to David's. "We'll get the bastard who did this."

When the elevator settled on the floor, Jake smacked his hand against the door, holding it open for everyone. He'd misjudged Kyra. Marie was hanging on to her like a lifeline, probably confiding things to her about Kelsey she hadn't thought of in years.

That proved it. Kyra Chase was just cold toward him.

They stopped at the door to the morgue, and Jake pressed the button on the outside to announce their presence. A coroner's assistant opened the door, and the chill in the room reached out to grab them. It didn't repel Jake, though. It seemed to suck him inside the room.

"Hello, Detective McAllister, Ms. Chase."

Jake's gaze dropped to the attendant's badge. "Sean, this is Mr. and Mrs. Lindquist."

They had stepped inside, and David looked like he could use Kyra's support even more than Marie could. Jake had witnessed a few grown men keel over in this space, and he didn't blame them.

At least Sean had taken Kelsey from the drawer. Her body lay covered with a white sheet. They already knew it was Kelsey from the picture on her driver's license left in her car. Her parents had provided a more recent picture, too.

Would he insist on ID'ing the body at the morgue if it were his daughter? Probably, and then he'd insist on fifteen minutes alone with her killer.

Sean cleared his throat. "Are you ready? I'm just going to show her face."

He flicked back the white sheet, and Marie gave a quick gasp.

Jake's eyes swept across the face of the young woman, all life drained from her body. He blinked, for a minute seeing light brown hair and freckles. "Is this your daughter?"

"Yes, that's Kelsey." Marie's voice rang in the room, loud enough to wake the dead in their drawers.

David sniffed and staggered back, his shoulders rounding. The man was going to fold in on himself if Jake didn't get him out of here.

He clasped David's shoulder. "You can leave, Mr. Lindquist."

"Wait." David shrugged off his hand. "That can't be her. That's not my daughter."

Uh-oh. He'd waited too late to get David out of the room. He was having a full meltdown.

Marie sobbed. "What are you talking about, David? That's her. That's our Kelsey."

"Look at her nose, Marie." David thrust out a shaky finger at his daughter's face. "Where's the diamond in her nose?"

Jake's heart bumped in his chest, and his eyes met Kyra's across the body. "Kelsey had a piercing in her nose?"

"They took it out, right? The coroner took it out." Marie grasped her purse strap with both hands.

Jake nodded at Sean, whose red face matched the color of his hair. "We did remove her jewelry and we have that for you, but we didn't remove any diamond from her nose. I didn't even know there was a piercing there. I mean, later..."

Sean trailed off because he meant later, when they did the autopsy, that would be something they would note.

"We didn't notice it at the crime scene, either, Mr. Lindquist. Could she have not worn it that day?"

"She just got it. She wouldn't take it out so soon. She wore it all the time, right, Marie?"

"She did." Marie's bottom lip quivered. "But that's Kelsey, David, with or without the nose piercing."

Jake took two steps toward the door. "Thank you, Sean. Mr. and Mrs. Lindquist, are you ready?"

David stumbled to the door. He'd been ready to leave the moment he'd walked in.

Jake opened the door, and they filed out. The cool air of the hallway felt like a sauna after the morgue, and the stifling air smelled like a spring meadow in comparison to the room they'd just left.

As they reached the elevator, Jake touched David's back. "Are you all right, Mr. Lindquist?"

"I'm okay. I never wanted to do this in the first place. We knew it was her, Marie." David's anger had given him life and color. As he straightened to his full height, he could almost meet Jake nose to nose. "We didn't need to do this."

They piled into the elevator, and Marie sagged against Kyra. As one partner gained strength, the other seemed to lose it. There was only so much strength to go around, and they had to take turns with it.

Jake replied, more comfortable with David's anger than his grief. "I know that was hard, Mr. Lindquist, but

we did get some valuable information. Kelsey was not
found with a nose stud, so she may have lost it in the
struggle with her killer or..."

Kyra hit the elevator button with her fist. "Or he took it."

Chapter Four

Jake watched through narrowed eyes as Kyra handed her card to Marie and stepped away from the Lindquists' car with a wave. Jake lifted his own hand, his heart still sore at their grief.

Kyra spun around on the toes of her low-heeled pumps like a ballerina and strode toward him like a boss, her blond ponytail bobbing behind her. She positioned herself in front of him, arms folded over her white blouse.

"Are you going to order another search of the dump site for Kelsey's nose stud?"

"Of course, but as you noticed last night while you were tromping all over the area, the tape is gone and if the diamond was there it might be ground into the dirt by now. We'll also comb her car for it. If there was a struggle outside or inside her car, it might turn up in the vehicle. She was most likely taken at her car, as her purse and phone were still there."

"And if he took it as a trophy?"

Jake scratched his chin. "Definitely would be unusual for a serial killer to claim two trophies—the finger and the nose stud. Not unheard-of, I guess."

"What about Marissa? Was she missing any jewelry?" Kyra hunched her shoulders as if she'd gotten a sudden chill despite the dry heat blanketing them.

Jake loosened his shirt collar. "Not that we know of. Have you talked to Marissa's family, yet?"

"As they're out of state, I haven't contacted them. I plan to meet with her friends, if they request it."

"We'll check with her friends in LA about the jewelry." A bead of sweat crept down Jake's neck and found a path beneath his shirt, looped tight by his tie. How did Kyra manage to look so cool in her crisp blouse and light-colored skirt? She'd sloughed off the tan cardigan she'd donned for the AC in the building and the even colder air in the morgue. His own suit felt like a straitjacket, constricting and smothering him.

Kyra's gaze dipped to his chest, as if following the trickle of sweat making its way to his belly. "Santa Ana winds kicking up since yesterday. Hope that doesn't mean the start of fire season."

He must look as miserably hot as he felt. "Hope not. Keep me posted on anything you find out from Marissa's friends or Kelsey's mom. You established quite a rapport with her in such a short period of time."

"You sound surprised." She smoothed one hand across her already-smooth hair, making him feel more rumpled than ever. "That *is* my job."

What she had with Marie was more than a job to her. Why was she trying to brush it off? Jake cocked his head. "I suppose it is."

Her phone buzzed, and she pulled it from the side pocket of her purse, giving it a quick glance. "You, too?"

He stopped struggling out of his jacket for a second. "Me, too, what?"

She aimed her phone at him. "You keep me posted, too."

She sauntered off while Jake stared after her, yanking on the sleeve of his jacket. He opened his mouth and snapped it shut.

He couldn't very well yell at that swinging ponytail that they had different jobs and he didn't have to inform her of anything if he didn't want to, which wasn't quite true as long as she was on the task force.

He finally struggled out of his jacket and stalked to his car. As long as Castillo said so, Kyra would stay on the task force.

Jake would have to accept it, but he didn't have to like it.

An hour later, back at the station, Jake stopped by Billy's desk, picked up the file on Marissa Perez and shuffled through it while Billy finished a phone call with the dry cleaner.

When he hung up, he said, "Did you do the ID with the Lindquists at the morgue?"

"They ID'd their daughter." Jake wiped the back of his hand across his dry mouth. "They said Kelsey's diamond nose stud is missing. That didn't turn up anywhere, did it?"

Billy sat back in his chair and wedged one expensive shoe on the desk. "No, are you thinking a second trophy? That wouldn't jive with The Player's MO."

"Maybe she lost it in the struggle to subdue her. Did Jenkins and Washington have any luck with cameras in the area where Kelsey's car was found, catching a car coming and going?"

"They're going through some footage now." Billy jerked his thumb over his shoulder. "Do you want to send some people over to Griffith Park and do a search for the nose stud? How about the parking lot where her car was found?"

"Let's do both." Jake waved the file still clutched in

his hands in the air. "Nobody mentioned any missing jewelry for Marissa?"

"Not yet." Billy raised his eyebrows. "How'd it go with Kyra Chase, the victims' rights advocate? I heard she met you at the morgue."

"She was there." Jake's mouth tightened. "Have to admit, she was good with the mom, Marie."

Billy whistled through his teeth. "That's high praise from you, brother. Better watch out, she'll want to shrink your head."

"No chance." Jake snorted and smacked Marissa's file on Billy's desk. "I'm going to look at some reports that have come in since yesterday, and then I'm calling Roger Quinn."

"Going old-school for this one, huh?"

"He does know more about The Player than any other detective, including the FBI guys."

"Speaking of which, the fibbies are looking at our case." Billy swirled the leftover coffee in his cup from a new coffee house down the street. Station blend wasn't fine enough for his palate.

"Let 'em. They play ball with us, we'll play ball with them." Jake rapped on Billy's desk. "Let's nail this guy and save the FBI the trouble."

After skimming through the reports on Kelsey's car and surrounding area, Jake placed a call to Kelsey's boy-friend to set up an interview. The guy had an ironclad alibi for the time of Kelsey's abduction and murder, but he'd be able to shed some light on Kelsey's habits, sched-ules, exes—not that Jake believed this was personal, un-less Marissa had the same acquaintances.

Then he pulled an index card from the top drawer of his desk and flicked the corner of it. Castillo had given him Roger Quinn's phone number. Although the retired detective had become even more reclusive than he'd been before the death of his wife a few years ago, if he'd been following the news, he would be expecting Jake's call.

He punched in the number and waited through two rings before voice mail picked up, an impersonal automated message intoning in his ear. At the beep, Jake said, "Detective Quinn, this is Detective Jake McAllister, LAPD Homicide. I'm leading a task force—"

A gruff voice interrupted him on what must've been an answering machine connected to a landline. "I know who you are. You can come by at four o'clock today."

Without waiting for Jake's reply, Quinn rattled off his address in Venice and hung up.

His mouth hanging open, Jake eyed the telephone receiver until the buzz signaled that the old detective had really just hung up on him. The rumors about Quinn were no exaggeration. Jake would have to bring his A game.

Knowing it would take him at least forty-five minutes to traverse the 405 freeway on the cusp of rush hour, Jake stuck his head in Castillo's office at three o'clock. "I got a summons from Quinn for a meeting at four o'clock."

Castillo glanced at the cell phone on his desk. "Better get going then. You should be fine, J-Mac. Quinn doesn't suffer fools…and you're no fool. In fact, you remind me of a younger Quinn. Should be a good lesson—you could be looking into your future."

With those ominous words ringing in his ears, Jake packed up and hit the road in his police-issued black Crown Vic. He'd shed his suit jacket and tossed it into the back seat.

Now, even with the AC blasting, he pulled his tie over his head, threw it into the back with the jacket and rolled up his sleeves. The news on the radio warned of a small brushfire in the canyons of Malibu, but as Jake peered west over his steering wheel, he let out a sigh. The fire department could contain a small fire as long as the winds subsided.

As he cruised off the freeway onto Lincoln, Jake joined the line of traffic crawling along the busy boulevard. He edged from Santa Monica into Venice and buzzed down his window. He preferred fresh air to AC and gulped in the salty breeze from the Pacific.

As he approached Quinn's walk-street on the canals, Jake kept an eye out for a parking place, even an illegal one. Police business afforded certain perks.

Who would've thought someone would get the bright idea of recreating the canals of Venice, Italy, on a Southern California beach? Tobacco tycoon Abbot Kinney had been so taken with that Italian town, he'd replicated it on the shores of California and dubbed it "Venice, America."

While the area surrounding the canals of Venice left a lot to be desired in terms of crime, gangs and homelessness, the walk-streets along the water, graced with arching bridges, provided a well-heeled oasis for the homes lining the canals.

Jake knew enough of Roger Quinn to know the retired detective hadn't purchased a million-dollar home on the canals several years ago on his cop's salary—any more than Jake had purchased his home with his cop's salary. Quinn's wife, Charlotte, had been a best-selling author of crime fiction before she passed, no doubt culling ideas from her husband's storied career as a homicide detective.

Jake left his car parked on a red curb and traipsed down Canal, entering a different world as he turned onto one of the walk-streets. He checked the numbers on the houses and loped over a low bridge to the other side of the water.

A smooth jazz instrumental floated out the open window of Quinn's modest house. Newcomers to the area had replaced many of the beach cottages with modern monstrosities that loomed over the canal. Quinn's house crouched between two of those, daring them to encroach on its space.

Jake parked himself on the porch in front of the red door with a flower box, sporting geraniums to match, and knocked hard. Could the old guy even hear over the noise in there?

The music abruptly ended, and before Jake could absorb the stillness the door swung open. Quinn hung on to the door handle, his body blocking the entrance to his home as he gave Jake the once-over from head to toe.

Damn. Maybe he should've kept his jacket and tie on.

The man had once been as tall as Jake, but age had robbed his bones of their fortitude. His wild gray eyebrows collided over his hawklike nose as he thrust a gnarled hand toward Jake. "Roger Quinn. Everyone calls me Quinn."

What his spine may have lacked in strength, the bones of his large spatulate hands more than made up for. Jake gave as good as he got. Quinn wouldn't be the type of man who'd appreciate coddling because of his age.

"Detective Jake McAllister. You can call me Jake."

One of those eyebrows twitched as if it had a mind of its own. "Not J-Mac?"

"You know how nicknames get around at the department, sir."

"Sir? Just Quinn." He widened the door and stepped away from it, leaving Jake to shut it.

"You like jazz, Jake?" Quinn held up an old album cover with a gleaming sax on it.

"I'm more of a classic rock guy." Jake lifted his shoulders apologetically.

"You can have a look at my collection before you leave." Quinn aimed a sandaled toe at a row of albums on the bottom of a shelf that supported an old turntable setup.

"I'd like that."

"But you didn't come here to talk about an old man's record collection, did you?" Quinn waved Jake toward a love seat as he eased into a recliner that had formed to its owner's body and welcomed him home.

Jake perched on the edge of the love seat. "You've seen the news about the two murders, both bodies dumped in Griffith Park."

"I have." Quinn dropped his chin to his chest. "A playing card between their lips, and their pinky fingers missing."

Jake's pulse jumped. "We didn't release the information about the fingers."

"You wouldn't be here if it weren't for those missing fingers, would you?" Quinn's faded blue eyes sharpened for a second as his nostrils flared. "You think this might be The Player back in action again."

"Do you think that's a possibility, sir… Quinn?" Jake's gaze shifted around the room, searching for the wall of honor that would boast the commendations and plaques and pictures with the various mayors and governors. Instead, he scanned a collection of watercolors that depicted the canals outside Quinn's front door.

"Do I think The Player killed these two young women?" Quinn rubbed a hand, suffering from a slight palsy, across his chin. "That might be the best scenario."

"Sir?" Jake shifted forward in his seat, his knees bumping the rough-hewn coffee table and causing a cup of tea to rattle in its saucer.

Quinn's fingers balled into misshapen fists on his

knees. "It's my shame. I never brought him in. I never caught him. It's not enough for me to imagine him dead and gone. I wanted him to end his reign of terror on my terms, not his."

Jake made an involuntary noise in the back of his throat and clenched his teeth. He felt the old detective's rage flow into him. He bathed in it.

Quinn closed his eyes. "You know."

"You wish it were The Player killing these women, but you don't think it is?" Jake cleared his throat. "Why is that? I don't have them with me, but I can bring the files later if you want to have a look at them. Captain Castillo would be more than happy to hand them over to you if you're interested."

"I don't need to look at the files to know it's not The Player operating again on the streets of LA." Quinn's sparse lashes flew open. "Why would he start up again? I always had the theory that he stopped because of all the advancements in law enforcement—DNA primarily, but CCTV, cell phones... You young guys have it easy."

"What about the theory that he's been locked up all this time?"

"Even more reason for him not to come out of retirement. If he's been in prison for twenty years it's on a felony, and his DNA will be in CODIS now. He's even more at risk today of getting caught than when he was active."

"So, copycat?"

"Most likely."

"I get the playing card, but you guys kept the finger trophies a secret. How would a random copycat know about the fingers?" Jake hunched forward, his forearms on his knees.

"You know how that goes, Jake." Quinn spread his hands. "These things get out, despite our best efforts. You have a task force now, not your first. Cops talk. Their wives talk. The victims' families talk—even when you ask them not to. You can't blame them."

"Anything we should be looking out for?"

"You're asking me? I failed." Quinn picked up the teacup and stared into the brown liquid, looking for answers.

"*That* time, but you never failed before. We still study your cases and methods at the academy."

Quinn laughed, a rusty bark that seemed to startle some birds outside his window. "Are you buttering me up, Jake? I didn't think you were that kind of cop."

Detective Roger Quinn knew what kind of cop he was? "I'm not. I'm stating a fact. If you don't want to help out, that's okay. Hell, if I were in your shoes, I don't know that I'd want to dip my toes back into the muck."

"The muck. That it is."

A knock at the door caused Jake's elbow to slip off his knee, and he cranked his head around. Quinn was supposed to be a recluse. "Do you want me to get that?"

"I can get my own damned door." Quinn used a cane at the side of the chair to push himself up and then left it behind as he took measured steps to the front door.

Jake's body tensed as Quinn opened the door without even asking who was there or looking out the window.

A woman's voice, low and lilting, filtered into the house on a breeze. "Hello, Quinn. I brought food."

As Jake half rose from the love seat, his brain pingponging in different directions, Kyra swept into the room, a plastic bag swinging from her fingers.

He growled. "What the hell are you doing here?"

She tripped to a stop, the bag swaying back and forth. "Oh, it's you."

Chapter Five

Kyra pasted a smile on her face, a pleasant mask to conceal her emotions. She'd done it a million times. Why hadn't Quinn warned her he'd be having a visitor...and *this* visitor in particular?

She shot Quinn a look over her shoulder. She couldn't put her finger to her lips, but she could wink—and she did.

Jake jumped to his feet, his gaze darting between her and Quinn, a flush staining his throat. He couldn't blame that on the heat, not in the cool confines of Quinn's house, a breeze from the water stirring the white curtains at the front window.

"Didn't mean to overreact." Jake coughed. "You surprised me. I didn't realize you knew Detective Quinn."

Quinn erupted into that hacking laugh of his and slammed the door. "Face it, Jake. You thought Kyra had followed you over here to horn in on your territory."

"I was worried you'd think the two of us were trying to ambush you or something." Jake shrugged.

"The hell you were." Quinn patted Kyra on the back and nudged the bag with his knee. "Smells like fish and chips from the pub."

"It is." Kyra lifted the plastic bag. "I didn't know you had company or I would've picked up another order."

"That's okay. I was just leaving. We were finished." Jake skirted around the love seat and planted his shoes on the wood floor in a wide stance.

"No, we weren't. I know you had more questions, and since Kyra's on your task force there's no reason we can't discuss this together." Quinn snatched the bag of food from her hand. "Besides, that place always gives you way more fish and chips than you can eat. We'll share."

Jake narrowed his eyes as they shifted between her and Quinn. He obviously suspected a setup. "How'd you know Kyra was on the task force?"

"I still have my sources, J-Mac." Quinn raised a finger, his lips twitching.

Kyra curled her hand around the loop of the bag. "Oh, no, you don't. Sit down, and I'll get you a plate of food."

"Only if you grab a couple of those IPAs in the fridge."

"Did Dr. Wong okay you for beer?"

"I don't need Dr. Wong's approval to live my life." Quinn relinquished his hold on the plastic bag and sank into his recliner. "Jake can help you."

To her surprise, Jake joined her in Quinn's small kitchen, his large presence dwarfing everything even more. She'd figured two strong, obstinate personalities like Jake's and Quinn's would butt heads; instead, Jake showed a gentle deference to the older man that granted him a few more notches in her estimation of him.

She grabbed three plates from the cupboard as Jake reached into the bag for the containers of food.

He turned from the counter, and she almost plowed into him with the plates. She clutched them to her chest. "It's a little crowded in here."

Jake folded his arms, wedging his fists into his bunching biceps. He'd lost the tie, and a dusting of dark hair peeked from the V of his open shirt collar. "How do you know Detective Quinn?"

Kyra swallowed before loudly clanking the plates on the tile counter that divided the kitchen from the living room. Quinn needed to hear this, too. "Quinn and I go way back. I helped out on one of his cases—just like I'm helping you. Isn't that right, Quinn?"

"That's right." Quinn twisted his head to the side. "One of my cases. Kyra's a sharp cookie, and she's compassionate. She adds a lot of value to a task force like this."

"I saw her in action today with the Lindquists." Jake popped the lid from one of the containers of fish and chips, and the aroma of fresh cod filled the kitchen. "Seems like she's a natural."

Kyra almost dropped the forks. A compliment from Jake McAllister? "I was able to help Marie. David's still in too much shock to take in anything right now."

"Two each?" The tines of Jake's fork hovered over a piece of fish. "I can do with one. I don't want to ruin your dinner party."

"It wasn't a dinner party. Sometimes I show up on Quinn's doorstep bearing food. If he's home and hungry, we'll eat together. If not, I leave it for him." Kyra sealed her lips and dumped some coleslaw on an empty plate. She was giving Jake the impression that she and Quinn had a deeper relationship than a working one. They did, but Jake didn't need to know about it, and Quinn was playing along.

With a frown between his eyebrows, Jake speared a piece of fish and plopped it on the plate next to the coleslaw. "You're a good coworker."

"What's taking you two so long?" Quinn drove his cane into the floor and rose to his feet a little unsteadily.

"A man could starve while you stand in there blabbing. And where's my beer?"

Kyra rolled her eyes at Jake. "Kind of demanding, isn't he?"

"Last time I checked, this was my house and you were the intruders." Quinn bellied up to the counter and rapped his knuckles on it. "Beer, no glass, and make sure you drizzle some of that malt vinegar on my fish."

"Yes, sir." Kyra arranged the last of the coleslaw, split three ways, on the plates and spun toward the fridge to grab the beers. Cranking her head over her shoulder, she asked, "Do you want a beer, Jake?"

"I'll take one, thanks."

She held one bottle out to him. "Twist off the cap and give this one to Quinn so he'll take a seat and get out of our hair."

Jake took off the cap with a crack and shoved the beer across the counter to Quinn. "Take a seat, sir. We'll bring your food out to you."

Quinn grabbed the bottle by the neck and walked back to his chair with a little more spring in his step.

Kyra handed a second bottle to Jake. "I'll take his plate out."

From the to-go cup, she poured a line of vinegar up and down Quinn's fish and spooned some tartar sauce on the plate. "I've got you covered, Quinn."

Two minutes later, they were sitting around Quinn's coffee table, plates of food in their laps and beers in their hands.

"I'm proposing a toast." Quinn raised his bottle. "Let's get the SOB this time."

Jake lowered the bottle from his lips, which were still puckered. "This time? Didn't you just tell me you didn't believe The Player was responsible for these murders?"

Quinn took a long pull from his bottle. When he lowered it, his misty blue eyes had sharpened—either from the booze or the subject matter. "I meant in general. We always want to nail them, and we usually do."

Kyra twirled her fork in the coleslaw. "Don't you agree with Quinn, Jake? At the task force meeting, you didn't seem to put much stock in the theory that The Player had come back online."

"Yeah, I'm leaning that way." Jake picked up a piece of battered fish with his fingers and dredged it in the mound of tartar sauce on his plate. "It's the missing finger that gets me."

"Don't dwell on that, Jake. You and I both know that stuff gets out, whether we want it to or not." Quinn spread out a piece of paper towel on his lap.

"A lot of times it's leaked from law enforcement." Jake picked up his beer and ran a fingernail through the damp label. "Did you ever suspect a cop as The Player?"

Quinn dropped his fork and it pinged against his plate, flicking a strand of cabbage onto their makeshift dining table. "That's quite a charge."

Jake's gaze shifted to Kyra's face, and then he tipped some beer down his throat. "Not one I make lightly, but it must've crossed your mind. Think about it. If this guy stopped the killing twenty years ago because of advances in law enforcement, he must've been well versed in those advances."

"Or he made it his business to know. The Player wasn't a stupid or clumsy man." Quinn dabbed at the rogue shred of cabbage on the coffee table with his finger.

"Maybe our current killer knows about the severed fingers because he knows about The Player's cold cases. He's seen the files, knows the evidence." Jake lifted and dropped his shoulders. "Just a thought."

Kyra tilted her head and curled one leg beneath her, which brought her closer to Jake on the love seat—close enough to see the gold flecks in his eyes that gave them their hazel appearance in the sunlight. She took a deep breath and said, "If this guy is law enforcement, he also knows about CCTV, cell phone tracking, DNA. All of that is not stopping him if, in fact, that knowledge was what halted The Player's killing spree."

"Not all sociopaths are as careful as The Player. We still have serial killers, despite technology. Some may not know we can track their movements through their cell phones, some may not know which bodily fluids contain DNA, some may not be aware of cameras." Quinn waved a French fry at her. "Some don't care."

A little chill zipped up her spine, and Kyra gritted her teeth. None of them cared. They were driven by some evil inside them. They couldn't be human. Too bad their outer appearance didn't reflect their inner demons for everyone to see and avoid.

"Are you all right?" Jake pointed at her untouched food. "You probably didn't come to visit Quinn to talk about this case. Sorry I ruined your dinner."

Kyra glanced at Quinn from beneath her lashes. "Don't worry about me. This is my work, too."

Jake's lips twisted into a smile, and a flash of heat claimed Kyra's body. That bone he'd thrown her before about her rapport with the Lindquists had been designed to get Quinn on his side. Jake needed Quinn. He didn't think he needed her or her skills at all. He had no idea.

"Jake's right. Eat your food." Quinn wiped his napkin across his face. "You never did tell me what brought you over here, Kyra. To what do I owe the pleasure of your company and fish and chips from the King's Head?"

She dug into her food. "Just wanted to make sure you

were taking care of yourself. You know how the air quality aggravates your breathing, and there's a fire near Malibu Canyon."

"Has that been getting worse?" Jake crumpled his napkin and tossed it onto his empty plate. Easing back, he rested his ankle on his knee, extending his arms across the back of the love seat, his hand dipping toward her shoulder, a little too close for comfort. "When I left work, it sounded like the fire department had that under control."

She shook her head. "The winds have been whipping up in the canyons, and the dry brush from the minimal rainfall last winter is fueling the fire. I could smell it when I got out of the car."

"I sat on my deck earlier today reading and didn't notice it." Quinn lifted his hunched shoulders. "But thanks for checking on me."

Jake slid her a glance from the corner of his eye, still wondering at the relationship between her and Quinn. He wasn't LAPD's hotshot detective and first pick for this task force for nothing.

Toying with the last of the fries on her plate, Kyra said, "I knew Charlotte, Quinn's wife. Uh, we got friendly when she needed a therapist's perspective for a certain character."

"I'll have to pick up one of her books. I'm sure your wife must've gotten a lot of ideas from you, sir." Jake hunched forward and lifted his plate. "Are you finished?"

"I am." She stacked her plate on top of Quinn's and handed them both to Jake.

As Jake carried the dishes to the kitchen, Quinn called after him. "Do you want another beer, Jake?"

"I'm good. I have to drive back to my place in Hollywood. Can I get you another?"

Before Quinn could answer in the affirmative, Kyra held up her hand to him. "Think long and hard about that answer."

"You're a tyrant. Are you channeling Charlotte?" Quinn finished the last sip of his beer. "I guess that's a no for me, Jake."

Jake set the dishes in the sink and rinsed them off. "Should I put these in the dishwasher?"

Kyra raised her eyebrows at his domesticity although she'd heard through the grapevine that he was single. As a bachelor, he'd know his way around a kitchen. She just never imagined Jake McAllister doing anything as pedestrian as the dishes—and the past few days, she'd been imagining Jake McAllister doing a lot of things.

"Yes, dishwasher. Are you done with your beer?" Her hand hovered over his bottle.

"Done."

She picked up the bottle and a few mouthfuls sloshed at the bottom. A lot of cops hit the booze to deal with the stress. Jake must have other outlets…or none at all if she were to believe all the stories about him. If you didn't have a way to cope with the anxiety of the job, it had a nasty habit of building up and exploding.

She reached across the table to collect Quinn's empty. The retired detective had had his own issues with alcohol, but Charlotte had straightened him out.

Quinn encircled her wrist with his arthritic fingers and whispered, "Are you all right?"

She gave him a quick nod and rose with all three bottles clutched to her chest. She joined Jake in the kitchen, where she got a prime view of his backside in his work slacks as he bent over the dishwasher, putting the plates in the slots on the bottom rack. When he straightened to his full height, he almost backed into her.

"Oops." She held the bottles over her head. "I was just going to put these in the recycling bin."

"I'll do it. You know what they say about too many cooks in the kitchen?" He reached up to take the bottles from her hands, moving close enough so that they almost stood chest to chest.

She blinked as she kept her hold on the bottles. "We're not cooking."

He jerked back and when she released the beer, one bottle fell to the floor where it bounced once.

"What the hell is going on in there? That kitchen is too small for the two of you to be dancing around. If he wants to help, let him help, Kyra. You don't have to control everything."

Jake cracked a smile for a brief second before he picked up the bottle. "Sounds like Quinn knows you well."

"But you don't." She leveled a finger at him and flounced out of the kitchen on shaky legs. She wasn't mad at Jake, or Quinn, for that matter, but when Jake had smiled—even though it had been at her expense—something flickered in her heart and she wanted to stomp it out before Jake took up any more space in her brain.

She sat on the arm of Quinn's chair, no longer willing to share the love seat with Jake. When he returned to the living room, he snagged his shoulder holster from a table near the door.

"I didn't mean to stay so long and disrupt your visit… and eat your food. I'm going to head out."

"I invited you and you're welcome back anytime." As Quinn struggled out of his chair, Kyra jumped off the arm and cupped his elbow to give him a boost.

"You don't have to get up for me." Jake slung one strap of his holster over one shoulder. "I appreciate the offer.

I think you can provide us with some valuable insight into this case even if it's not The Player back in action."

"I usher you into my house—" Quinn took a step forward, shrugging off Kyra's hand "—I usher you out of my house. Just don't be like this one, showing up unannounced and uninvited to harass me."

Kyra squeezed Quinn's arm. "You wouldn't have it any other way."

"Thanks for the dinner. I'll pay you back or buy you a lunch at the station sometime."

Jake sure knew how to charm a girl.

She tossed back her ponytail. "Save it. I'm good. I just ask that you keep me in the loop. Use my services. I'm no novice at this, and I'm not going to do an end run behind your back."

Jake's eyebrows shot up to a single lock of dark hair that curled onto his forehead.

Did he really think she didn't know why he didn't trust her? She'd been there.

"Yeah, no problem about that sandwich." He reached past her and shook Quinn's hand. "Sir, good to meet you."

When he stepped onto the porch, Kyra slammed the door after him. "What an insufferable…jerk. Did you hear that comment about the sandwich? He'd rather buy me lunch than keep me informed."

"Oh, I don't know. Sounded like he respected you. Sure seemed to be something between the two of you."

"Something between us?" Her mouth dropped open.

"I don't know." Quinn made a beeline for his chair. "Electricity. Excitement. Something like that. You're not immune to his charms."

"Charms?" Kyra blew out a breath as she got Quinn settled in his recliner. "You've been married too long if you think that man is charming."

Quinn's laugh exploded from his chest in a short burst. "Okay, now sit down and tell me what you really think about these murders. You're sure you're doing all right?"

"I'm fine, fascinated, really." She took the side of the love seat that Jake had occupied earlier, and his scent enveloped her—a spicy smell from his deodorant or body wash, activated by the heat, and a not unpleasant odor that she could only describe as pure masculinity.

"Did Jake mention that the second victim was missing some jewelry? It might be a second trophy, in addition to the finger."

"That would be—"

A pounding on the door stopped Quinn in midsentence.

"Quinn, Kyra, it's Jake. I just got some news."

Kyra jumped up, her heart racing, and dashed for the front door. When she swung it open, Jake charged past her, his cell phone in his hand.

"What is it?" Kyra hugged herself, her fingers digging into her arms. "Did they catch him?"

Jake came to an abrupt halt next to Quinn's chair and tapped his cell phone. "Didn't catch him, but he just made a big mistake."

"Someone saw him? He left prints?" Kyra stood at the door, her eyes wide.

"He just called us to give us the location of another body."

Chapter Six

Kyra gasped and brought her hand to her throat. "Another body? That's three now."

Jake took half a step toward her. Likely sensing his movement, Kyra straightened her spine, making it obvious that she didn't play the damsel in distress.

Quinn scratched his chin with the edge of his cane. "Why would he give you this location and not the others? Is it because nobody else found this body?"

"That's part of it. He may have been content to wait, but the fire forced his hand."

Kyra's fingers clawed against the pale skin of her neck. "He's afraid the fire is going to destroy the body and he won't get credit."

"Exactly." Now Jake knew why his first instinct after receiving the call was to return to this room, to these two people who seemed to get it.

"What the hell are you waiting for?" Quinn pounded his cane on the floor. "You two need to get out there."

Kyra brushed past Jake and dropped a kiss on Quinn's cheek. "Take care. We'll keep you posted."

When they stepped outside, Jake's nose twitched at the faint smell of smoke. "The wind must've shifted. I didn't even smell the fire before."

"Should I follow you over?"

"No point in taking two cars. I have my unmarked vehicle parked on the red. I didn't mean to leave it there that long."

"This is LAPD territory—I'm sure they ran your plate. But if you're offering, I'll tag along with you."

When they made it to the car and slid inside, Jake peeled away from the curb and glanced at Kyra. "I interrupted you and Quinn again."

"Believe me, I appreciated the interruption." She gathered her hair in one hand and dragged it over her shoulder. She loosened it from its regular ponytail, and it shimmered in the dark of the car. "I suppose there's a trace going out on the phone as we speak."

"Yeah, but if it's a burner phone, we'll be out of luck." He accelerated onto the freeway, which had shed half the traffic from rush hour.

She tilted her head at him. "When you walked into Quinn's, you said the killer had made a big mistake. If he used an untraceable phone, how is that a problem for him?"

"Because he made contact." Jake flexed his fingers on the steering wheel. "We have his voice, we have his attention. We know he's following the case. It's not much, but it's more than we had before. Quinn will tell you every piece of information helps."

"Can't hurt, anyway." She tapped on the windshield. "You can see the glow to the west. So, he dumped two bodies in the Griffith Park area and one in Malibu Canyon. Do you think this one came before or after Marissa?"

"Probably his first. That's why he dumped Marissa and Kelsey in a more visible area. He realized he concealed his first victim too thoroughly. He must've been climbing the walls waiting for her to be found."

"I wonder if anyone has reported her missing?" Kyra gnawed on her bottom lip.

"We have a lot of missing persons reports come through. Especially here in LA, we don't know if they're really missing or are runaways. Lots of runaways in this city. Lots of people from other places hoping to make it big."

Kyra turned her head and traced her fingers along the glass of her window. "Yeah, city of broken dreams."

After a few minutes of silence, Jake coughed. "Do you live near Quinn in Venice?"

"Close. I live in Santa Monica. That's why I'm able to pop in and see him occasionally."

"So, I'm actually taking you away from your home."

"Where do you live?"

"Hollywood." He kept it short. He didn't want to get into the details of how he lived in the expensive part of Hollywood, in the hills that overlooked the city. He had his street-tough image to protect.

"If it's too much trouble for you to come back this way to drop me off, I can get a rideshare." She finally turned to face him, blinking her eyes rapidly.

He tapped his cheekbone. "Is the smoke bothering you? I can blast the AC."

She sniffed. "The air's fine."

"And I don't mind giving you a lift back to Santa Monica. When there's no traffic, the driving isn't too bad."

"When is there no traffic?" She rolled her eyes. "Just look at it out here. Where are all these people going?"

"I'm sure they all have a story." Jake steered the car off the freeway. "We're probably going to have to show some ID to get close. The firefighters are probably not even allowing residents into the area."

Kyra ducked her head to peer at the orange sky. "Were any structures damaged?"

"Not that I heard, just threatened." Jake slowed down as he hit the twisty roads into the canyon. Gray ash floated through the air and coated his windshield, but he knew better than to smear it across the glass with his wipers.

He squinted at the figure ahead waving his arms. He slipped the badge from his shirt pocket as he powered down the window.

The sheriff's deputy approached the car and bent forward. "What's your business? Residents?"

Jake flashed his badge. "I'm here for the body. Any LAPD on scene, yet?"

"Yeah, couple of patrol officers. They already called the medical examiner's office, but the meat wagon isn't here yet."

Jake grimaced. How did this deputy know whether or not Kyra was a civilian? The cop should watch his lingo, although if Kyra hung out with Quinn she probably knew all about the dark humor.

"Okay, thanks. Let the coroner's van through when it gets here. I'm not sure how much of the crime scene we're going to be able to process with this fire raging." Jake drove on with the deputy's blessing and pulled behind the LAPD squad car parked on the side of the road.

As soon as he cut the engine, Kyra scrambled from the car and stood with her hands on her hips. "I don't know how much you're going to be able to do here with those flames drawing closer."

He strode around to her side of the car and placed his hands on her shoulders. "You need to wait here."

Her body stiffened, and then she ducked out of his

grasp. "I know that. If anyone comes, I'll direct them in. How long do you want to hold off the ME?"

He tilted his head back as a gust of hot wind sent ashes and flecks of cinder swirling around his face. "Not too much longer, or we'll lose the body completely and be running for our own lives. Maybe you should wait in the car."

Jake walked toward the bushes without looking back. He couldn't control Kyra's action. If she wanted to get back in the car, she would. If he hadn't cautioned her against following him to the crime scene, would she have gone with him? Without a doubt.

He almost tripped over the yellow crime scene tape strung between two low bushes. He stepped over it and approached the LAPD officers standing watch over a decaying body, a swath of black hair spread in the dirt.

How did the killer expect anyone to find the body here? Rookie mistake for someone wanting the notice.

He nodded to the officers. "Detective Jake McAllister. Anyone else besides you two?"

"You're the first, sir. We just got orders to book over here and make sure nobody and nothing got to the body."

Snapping on a pair of gloves, Jake crouched beside the young woman and swept a lock of hair from her neck. The mottled color of her skin concealed any strangulation marks; he didn't see any blood or wounds.

Her mouth gaped open but no playing card nestled between her lips. Jake lifted her left hand with its missing finger. The wind must've dislodged the card and carried it away, or an animal got to it.

This looked like a messy first effort. The copycat had improved. Had he made other mistakes with this one? Had he been seen with her? Caught on camera somewhere?

"Damn, we need to get out of here."

Jake sprang to his feet and almost took a swing at Billy. "Why are you creeping around out here looking like a bank robber?"

"Creeping?" Billy tugged on the bandanna covering the lower half of his face. "I called your name, and we both know only white dudes rob banks."

Jake tipped his head toward the body. "Looks like our guy. The card's missing, but so is the finger. I can't tell if it's strangulation, although there are no visible wounds other than animal bites and marks."

Billy rubbed his hands. "And he called us. We have his voice on tape, even if he used an untraceable phone."

Jake scanned the blackened hillside. "Tells us something about him that he'd rather risk a call than lose credit for this body."

"Tells us he's not going to stop." Billy jerked his thumb over his shoulder. "Did someone call the victims' rights lady? She's hanging out by the road."

"I, uh... She came over with me." Jake surveyed the ground around the body.

"My man." Billy punched his shoulder. "What's up with that? I thought she was enemy number one."

"This guy is enemy number one." Jake jabbed his finger toward the young woman on the ground. "Kyra Chase is just an...annoyance."

"A good-looking annoyance. Not your usual type—cool, stuck-up, blonde—but worth the exception."

"C'mon, man. I ran into her at Detective Roger Quinn's house. I was there when I got the call about the body, so it made sense to have her tag along. Probably couldn't have stopped her, anyway."

"She knows Detective Quinn? How?"

"Worked a case with him or something."

"She looks great for her age."

Jake whistled. "Hang on, what's this?"

He took two steps toward a bush trembling in the dry furnace and crouched down. He pinched a card between his fingers and rescued it from some of the spiny branches of the bush.

"Not that there was any doubt, but look what I found?" He held up the playing card to Billy, the queen of spades facing outward.

"Sorry we missed that, Detective."

Jake waved the card at one of the officers. "No worries. You were here to protect the body, not conduct a search."

A firefighter crashed through the bushes and flipped up his mask, his eyes ringed with black soot. "I know it's not the best of circumstances, but you guys are gonna have to get out of here and let the coroner load the body. The winds haven't died down yet, and that fire's going to leap into this area in the next thirty minutes, if not sooner."

Jake tucked the playing card into a plastic baggie. "The coroner's van is here?"

"Yeah, being kept at bay by a bulldog of a woman out there. Is she really with you?"

"She's part of our task force, and I asked her to buy me some time." Jake patted the cell phone in his pocket. "I took pictures and did a search of the area. It has to be good enough."

Jake followed Billy back to the road, which now included a TV van, several more sheriff's deputies and the medical examiner's truck.

His eyes met Kyra's through the glare of the lights and activity, and he dropped his chin to his chest. She nodded back.

He peeled off his glove and shook the coroner's hand.

"Same killer. I want to go back in there with you while you move the body so I can take a look underneath."

The reporter shouted over the noise of the helicopters that were now circling in to dump water. "Is this the same killer of Marissa and Kelsey, Detective? Who found the body? Did the firefighters find the body? Did he leave a playing card this time?"

"No comment." Jake tugged on the coroner's sleeve. "We'd better get going. We have less than thirty minutes to get her."

Jake and Billy searched the area some more as the coroner lifted the woman's dead body and zipped her into a bag. Like the other dump sites, this one was clean—no cigarette butts, no gum wrappers, no footprints, no tire tracks. Time and the coroner would tell if the killer had left any fingerprints or DNA on the body.

They needed to identify this woman as soon as possible to start their investigation. If this was the copycat's first victim, he may have made other mistakes—and Jake planned to pounce on every one of them.

He gave the scene one last look before retreating to the road. Flames had started creeping over the ridge, and they'd be racing down the hillside in a matter of minutes.

When he got clear of the trees and bushes, he returned to a calmer scene. The cops and reporters had heeded the advice of the firefighters and fled the area.

Billy waved at him from the front seat of his car. "I'll check in with you tomorrow morning. Hoping for some good news on that phone."

"Me, too." Jake swiveled his head from side to side, his pulse ratcheting up a few notches.

"Oh, yeah." Billy stuck his head out the window as he made a U-turn. "Kyra told me to tell you she got a ride home."

"A ride? With who?"

"That reporter." Billy's fingers formed a gun. "Watch yourself with that one, brother."

Jake swore as he watched Billy's taillights fade into the rolling smoke. Kyra was friendly with reporters, too? That was a bad sign.

He slid into his own car, his tongue sweeping across his lips. Felt like he'd just smoked a pack of cigarettes without a filter.

At least the drive back to his house in the Hollywood Hills was closer than making the trek back and forth to Santa Monica. He cruised downhill and escaped from the canyon that had turned into a hellhole.

When he reached his house and climbed from the car, he sniffed the air. Despite the smell of Hades and the ominous glow to the west, you'd never know there was a fire raging out of control.

Jake undressed, tossed his soot-flecked pants in the corner and stepped into the shower. He let the lukewarm water stream down his back as he scrubbed the grime of the day from his body. He didn't even have to land in the middle of a wildfire to feel dirty. His job left a coat of filth on his skin almost daily.

After his shower, he pulled on a pair of gym shorts and a white T-shirt. He scooped some rocky road ice cream into a bowl and carried it, along with his laptop, to his couch in the living room. He clicked on the TV and watched footage of the fire in Malibu Canyon—no mention of a body yet.

He spooned a hunk of ice cream into his mouth and let the cold sweetness melt down his scorched throat. When he'd finished half the bowl, he muted the TV and logged in to an LAPD database. It didn't take him long to bring up Detective Roger Quinn's homicide cases. One jumped out at him in glaring red typeface—The Player—six un-solved murders. A cold case, the bane of every detective's existence, the stuff of nightmares.

Jake wasn't interested in looking at that case. He had the files and was prepared to study them in more depth. He scrolled down to Quinn's more recent cases, the ones toward the end of his career, the ones where he must've worked with Kyra.

Quinn had wrapped up his last homicide case a few months before he retired, ten years ago. Billy's words at the fire had been niggling at the corners of his mind on the ride home. Billy had said something about Kyra look-ing great for her age.

Jake didn't know Kyra's age, but she couldn't be older than thirty, could she? Even if she'd worked with Quinn on his last case for the department, that would mean she would've been twenty at the time. What twenty-year-old had a degree in psychology and enough hours under her belt to get assigned to a homicide task force?

He did a quick search of Kyra Chase. One of those people finder sites had her age at twenty-eight, and he discovered she'd gotten a master's degree from Cal State LA in psychology four years ago. That meshed with her age and meant she'd been eighteen years old when Quinn worked his last case for LAPD.

The sweet ice cream on his tongue turned bitter. She'd been lying about how she knew Quinn. Quinn had been lying about how he knew Kyra.

And he was going to find out why.

Chapter Seven

"Thanks for the ride, Megan. I knew you lived in the Marina or I wouldn't have asked." Kyra rubbed at a smudge of ash on her denim skirt.

"No problem, as long as you don't mind the ostentatious ride." Megan Wright patted the dashboard of the news van. "I'm on the job, so I take the van home with me."

"Don't mind a bit. I didn't want to bother the detective for a lift back, and I didn't want to stay in the middle of that inferno any longer than I had to." Kyra took a gulp of water from the bottle Megan had dug out of her cooler in the back. She closed her eyes as it slid down her parched throat.

"Can't give me anything about what McAllister and those cops were doing out there?" Megan flashed her white teeth in her best news reporter smile.

"Wooded area, lead detective on serial killer task force, coroner's van. I'm sure you can figure it out." Kyra put her finger to her lips. "But I'm not giving you anything official."

"You are on the task force, though, aren't you?" Megan scooted forward in her seat, barely able to see over the steering wheel of the big van.

"I am." Kyra tipped the water bottle at Megan. "And

if I'm ever cleared to release any information, you know I'll hit you up first. Now's not the time. We don't want to compromise anything."

"What's he like?"

"Who?" Kyra's heart thumped too loudly in her chest.

"Oh, come on. You know who. J-Mac. He's hot in that brooding kind of way cops have. Just makes you want to get under their skin, and I mean that in every possible way." Megan puckered her lips.

"He's as you would expect—rude, curt, arrogant." Also, gentle and respectful to Quinn and helpful in the kitchen. Kyra lifted her shoulders. "Typical cop."

"Is he married?" Megan lifted one eyebrow in expert fashion.

"No."

"So, you are interested enough to know his marital status."

"Oh, please. I'm around that station a lot. You tend to learn things about people. I think I had heard he's not married."

"Does he have a girlfriend?" Megan lodged the tip of her tongue in the corner of her mouth, as she maneuvered the van around a sharp turn.

Did he? Kyra pressed a hand flat against her stomach. "Does the station realize you don't know how to drive this thing?"

"It's a battering ram, practically indestructible." She squinted at the road. "Tell me where I'm going. Venice is creepy this time of night."

"You can make a U-turn at the end of the block and then pull over to the right. I'm going to stop in to see my friend first."

Megan slapped both hands against the steering wheel.

"You're going to go traipsing around the canals by your-self with a serial killer on the loose?"

"I'm packing heat, girl, I'll be fine. None of the women were from this area or were taken from this area. I have a better chance of tripping over a homeless guy."

"That's no picnic, either." Megan bit her lip as she cranked the wheel for the U-turn. She had to back up and give it another try.

"Neither is being in this van with you." Kyra rapped one knuckle against the window. "Here, here."

Megan rolled to a stop and watched two joggers run past the van. "At least it's not completely deserted."

"It's not deserted at all. It's a warm night. There will be people on the canals, outside their homes. Don't worry about me."

As she reached for the door handle, Megan grabbed her wrist. "You think because you carry that gun, you're invincible. At least text me when you get to your friend's house so I know you made it inside okay."

"I will. Thanks again for the ride and, for heaven's sake, get yourself a pillow to sit on so you can at least see over the steering wheel." Kyra slammed the door and waved to Megan, who stayed idling at the curb until she made it to the bridge that would take her to Quinn's side of the water.

Quinn's neighbors were in their front yard in lawn chairs, drinking beers. Kyra had never officially met them, but she waved anyway and they returned her greeting. Before reaching Quinn's door, she sent a quick text to Megan to assure her she'd reached her destination.

She didn't want Quinn to get out of his chair if he didn't have to so she used her key to open the door and slipped inside his house. The blue light from the TV cast an eerie glow in the dark living room. Quinn often fell asleep in front of the TV.

She tiptoed to his favorite chair, which he'd already abandoned for his bed, and placed her hand against the warm back.

"Kyra, that you? If not, I've got a .45 pointing at the bedroom door."

"Don't shoot." She crept to his bedroom and wedged her shoulder against the doorjamb. "Sorry to show up so late. I thought you might still be up."

"I just hit the sack." He dropped his gun on the nightstand with a clatter. He hadn't been kidding about his .45. "I drank a second beer and it did me in. What did you find out?"

"Not much. McAllister wouldn't let me near the crime scene."

"You can't blame him for that. He's been burned before by a helpful psychologist."

"You *would* stick up for him."

"He's a good cop. Did he tell you anything?"

"We didn't talk, but when he emerged from the bushes I saw it on his face. The call wasn't a hoax. We do have another victim." She folded her arms, shoving her fists under her armpits.

"You didn't talk? You mean he didn't drive you home?" Quinn struggled to sit up against the headboard of his bed.

"Settle down. I took off before he had the chance." She took a step into the room, which still smelled like Charlotte's perfume. "He went back in with the coroner, and the scene was getting too hot to handle—literally. The fire was raging closer and the firefighters advised us to clear out. A friend of mine, a reporter, was there so I asked her for a ride back. She lives in Marina del Rey."

"All right, and you've got your car here." Quinn yawned and tossed back the covers.

"Where do you think you're going?" She loomed over his bed and twitched the blanket back into place.

"I'll walk you out to your car."

"Don't be an idiot. Your neighbors are outside, partying, and you're not the only one who's armed and dangerous." She patted his pillow. "Relax."

As Quinn burrowed his head against the pillow, his tired eyes narrowed to slits. "That gun is not a magic shield."

"I know, but it helps. Get back to sleep." She squeezed his arm under the covers. "We'll talk later."

"You do realize Jake was suspicious about our relationship, don't you?"

She made a half-turn at the bedroom door. "I know that."

"You're going to have to tell him sooner or later, sooner being better. The man has trust issues."

"I know that, too. Let me do this my way, Quinn."

"You always do, Mimi."

Her nose stung as the nickname floated toward her in the dark. She left the bedroom door open, turned off the TV and locked up.

As she stepped onto Quinn's porch, a warm breeze ruffled the ends of her hair and she sniffed the air. The firefighters were still out there doing battle with the forces of nature…and maybe the forces of man.

Had the killer set the fire in the hope that the body would be discovered? To give him an excuse to call it in? She hoisted her purse on her shoulder and huffed out a breath. She'd be giving him credit for the Santa Ana winds if she kept on this path.

He probably wasn't as smart as he thought he was. They never were—except for The Player.

She ground her teeth together and marched toward the bridge. Quinn's neighbors had called it a night. The water lapped against the man-made shores, and the wooden bridge whispered and sighed as she crossed it.

When she reached the other side, she walked at a fast pace toward the street, her head held high, her arms swinging at her sides, her blood pumping. Both Quinn and Megan had her pegged. Ever since she'd gotten her conceal and carry permit, with the help of Quinn, she felt invincible.

Had she been courting danger? She had dismissed that accusation from Quinn. Going about your business didn't count as inviting danger—at least it shouldn't.

A shadowy figure shuffled toward her when she reached the corner, and her hand hovered over the weapon in her purse.

"Spare some change, lady?" The homeless guy peered at her through a curtain of shaggy, sun-bleached hair.

"No, sorry." She marched past him as he called after her.

"God bless you."

Her heart rate returned to normal when she hit the street and a few cars whizzed by. Unlike Jake, she didn't have the perks of a city-issued vehicle and always parked in the public lot when she visited Quinn. The lot still contained several cars. People could be down at the beach or hitting the bars and restaurants on Washington. She was not taking undue risks by walking to her car at night.

The murdered women probably didn't believe they were taking risks, either, but they didn't have a gun—the great equalizer. On the ride home, she checked her rearview mirror often. Just because she had that gun didn't mean she wanted anyone following her to her apartment.

She pulled into her parking spot behind the apartment building and slid out of the car. She held her breath as she walked past the garbage bins and shoved her key into the gate. Management had replaced the swinging wooden door out here with a solid gate with a lock after thieves had targeted several of the units. Hers had escaped, but then she'd secured additional locks on her doors and windows a few years ago.

As she unlocked her front door, the stray cat she occasionally fed rubbed against her ankles. Her neighbors didn't appreciate her efforts on behalf of Spot, but she'd won him a reprieve by convincing them he was keeping the rats away.

"Hope you've been doing your job, Spot. Wait here and I'll give you some milk and food."

He meowed in response, knowing full well his flea-riddled body wasn't welcome inside her apartment.

She'd left a lamp burning earlier, and smacked her purse down on the kitchen table to rustle up some grub for Spot. She shook a little dry cat food into one bowl and filled the other with milk, noticing her full trash can when she threw away the milk carton.

She placed the bowls on the cement outside her front door and returned to the kitchen to grab her trash. When she walked out the door, swinging the plastic bag, Spot flattened his ears against his head.

"Sorry to disturb your dining, Spot." She chuckled. "Dining spot, get it?"

She shoved through the gate, careful not to allow it to clang behind her. The neighbors didn't like that, either. She held open the lid on the dumpster with one hand and swung her trash bag in, letting it fall with a soft squish.

As she turned, something on the ground caught her eye. A piece of trash must've found its way out of the bag. She crouched down and nearly toppled over as the queen of hearts stared back at her from a playing card.

Chapter Eight

Jake's throat felt scratchy from his time in the inferno last night. He'd gargled with mouthwash this morning, which could've been a mistake. He popped his fifth throat lozenge of the day into his mouth and cruised into a conference room being set up for the task force.

Brandon Nguyen, their tech guy, glanced up and tapped on the desk next to him. "This is yours, Detective. Phone and network lines are in, and your computer's already been moved over."

"Thanks, Brandon. Did you account for a few visitors? The body last night was found in LA County Sheriff territory, not our division. Their homicide guys are gonna want to weigh in."

"Captain Castillo already informed me, and we're getting it covered."

"Damn, you're on top of things." Jake crossed the room and hoisted his bag on top of his assigned desk. "Any news on that phone call last night?"

"Our team's on it. We expect something shortly."

Jake pivoted. "Are you telling me that call didn't go right back to a prepaid cell phone?"

"Doesn't look like it, but we'll know for sure within the hour, I'm thinking." Brandon pointed to the desk next to Jake's. "We're putting Detective Crouch's desk next to yours. Is that okay?"

"He has to sit somewhere." Jake winked and pulled up a chair. He flipped open the file from the body last night. No easy ID had been forthcoming. Preliminary info gave them a woman between the ages of eighteen and twenty-five, Caucasian, five foot four inches, approximately 135 pounds, tattoo of a butterfly on her back, no fingerprints on file. He'd assign someone the task of going through missing persons reports to look for a match, if that person could wrestle them away from Billy. Ever since Billy's youngest sister had gone missing, he'd taken a personal interest in the reports.

Other officers had done a search of Kelsey's car and the area around it for her diamond nose stud, and had come up empty so far. Another search of her body's resting place hadn't yielded anything, either.

Had the copycat gotten greedy and taken two souvenirs? It was unusual, though not unheard-of. Better for them, more to tie him to the crimes once they nailed him.

Billy sauntered into the room and perched on the corner of Jake's desk. "How can you work with all this racket going on?"

Jake reached over and tapped the desk next to his. "This is for you, Cool Breeze. I had Brandon over there set you up right next to me so I can keep an eye on you."

"Seems to me you're the one who needs watching. We were interrupted last night, but I was going to tell you that Kyra Chase is too young to have worked with Quinn on a case. That's not how she knows him, so if that's what she told you—" he lifted his shoulders and his tailored shirt barely creased "—she lied. Thought you had your fill of lying women."

"Yeah, I misunderstood. That's not what she told me.

She knew Quinn's wife, the mystery writer, Charlotte Quinn." Jake rubbed his chin, not sure why he'd jumped to Kyra's defense. Maybe it was a mystery he wanted to figure out for himself.

"That makes more sense." Billy rose from the desk and peeled off his suit jacket. "If you continue to hang out with Kyra, see if you can get me an introduction to Megan Wright. Just saw her on the morning news on KTOP and she's fine."

"You're married, Billy." Jake dusted the spot on his desk where his partner had been sitting.

"Technically, but we're separated again. Simone deserves more in a husband, and the kids need more than a part-time dad." Billy's megawatt smile dimmed as he hung his jacket on the back of his chair.

Jake opened his mouth and then snapped it shut. He was in no position to give marital advice. Maybe Billy was right. Simone deserved better than a stressed-out cop using bad behavior to curb his anxiety. Tess sure had.

Brandon bolted from the room, calling over his shoulder. "They got it."

"What's he talking about?" Billy raised his eyebrows.

"The phone call. They traced the phone call." Jake was out of his chair by the time Brandon rushed back into the room, waving a piece of paper.

"I have it, Detective. We got the phone, and it's not a burner."

Jake snapped his fingers. "Let me have it."

Brandon handed the paper to him, and Jake scanned to the pertinent information—the registered owner's name. "Rachel Blackburn?"

Billy leaned over his shoulder. "Could be a wife or a girlfriend."

"This guy hasn't left one fingerprint or one sliver of

DNA. Do you really believe he's going to use his wife's cell phone to call in a tip about a body?" Jake pinged the piece of paper with his fingertip.

"Of course not. Hoping for anything on the guy." Billy let out a long breath, and the edge of the paper fluttered. "He got that phone somehow, didn't he?"

"He sure did, Cool Breeze, and we're gonna find out how." Jake held out his fist for a bump from Brandon. "Hey, thanks to your team, Brandon. We give you something to do and you deliver every time."

The kid puffed out his chest a little. "Anything we can do to help. That's why we're here."

Billy asked, "I suppose you tried calling the number again after last night?"

"Same thing as before." Brandon shook his head. "The phone's dead, doesn't even go to voice mail."

Jake rolled up the paper and tapped Billy on the chest. "We're going to track down this Rachel Blackburn and find out the location of her phone—if she knows."

Fifteen minutes later, Jake had talked to Rachel's mother and gotten Rachel's place of work. Mrs. Blackburn had informed Jake that her daughter lost her phone yesterday. If she wondered why an LAPD detective was interested in her daughter's lost cell phone, she didn't ask.

Billy grabbed his jacket from the back of his chair. "Where does Rachel work?"

"Clothing shop on Melrose." Jake draped his own jacket over his arm and logged out of his computer.

"Right up my alley." Billy laced his fingers and cracked his knuckles.

"A *women's* clothing store."

"It's still on Melrose. Let's go, partner."

As they reached the door, Jake dug into his pocket and

tossed the car keys to Billy. "Start the car and get the AC going. I have to ask Brandon something."

He watched Billy cruise down the hallway and turned back into the room. "Brandon, did Captain Castillo ask you to set up a workstation for Kyra Chase? She's our victims' rights advocate."

"Yeah, he did." Brandon leveled his finger at a desk in the corner. "That's for Ms. Chase."

"Has she been here yet? You know who she is, right?"

"Yeah, I know Kyra. She hasn't been around today, but I'll let her know which desk is hers when she shows up." Brandon's brow furrowed. "Do you want her somewhere else? I could move her station to the other side of the room."

"That's all right. Leave it." Jake stalked from the room. His distrust of therapists had even reached the tech department. He'd gotten a handle on his anger after the incident with Lizbeth Kruger when she'd used him and information about a case to get a lighter sentence for a killer, but if something similar happened with Kyra he didn't know if he could trust all his deep breathing exercises to get him through his rage.

As he stepped into the parking lot, Billy cruised forward in the sedan. Jake got in, tossing his jacket in the back seat.

Billy dialed up the AC and pulled away from the station. "Is Rachel expecting us?"

"Her mom said she'd call the shop and let her know. I guess Mrs. Blackburn thinks the LAPD tracks down all lost cell phones because she didn't seem all that curious."

"Really?" Billy slid him a look from the corner of his eye. "The way you come across sometimes, people are afraid to ask questions."

Jake lifted one corner of his mouth into a smile.

"That's why I bring you along. You're the good cop, and I'm the very, very bad cop."

They battled the traffic into West Hollywood and nabbed a parking space at a meter a block away from Rachel's store.

They walked to the shop, conspicuous in their suits while dodging hipsters with hats and facial piercings. Jake let out a breath when he ducked into the cool, dark shop.

The musky scent tinged with roses and lilacs enveloped him, and he gave himself over to its soothing qualities. Aromatherapy always made more sense to him than talking therapy.

A young woman behind the counter glanced up at their entrance, her heavily lined eyes widening. She held up one finger to them and continued talking to her purple-haired customer at the counter.

"Hey, look at this." Billy elbowed him. "They do nipple piercing here."

"Knock yourself out, brother." Jake leaned past Billy to read the sign. "They also do nose piercing. Maybe we found a connection to this shop."

The young woman with the purple hair left the store, and Rachel came from behind the counter, her black Doc Martens clumping on the wood floor. "Are you the detectives my mom called about?"

"Yes, I'm Detective McAllister and this is Detective Crouch. You're Rachel Blackburn?" Jake stuck out his hand, and she grabbed it, the tattoos on her arm marching from her wrist to her shoulder in a colorful sleeve.

"Yes, sir." She gave his hand a firm, professional squeeze and turned to Billy. "Nice to meet you, although I'm not sure why my missing cell phone is cause for the LAPD to pay me a visit."

At least she had more curiosity than her mother. "Is there someplace we can talk privately?"

"Sure." She cupped her hand around her red-lipsticked mouth. "Gustavo, can you come out front for a bit?"

A beaded curtain in the back of the store clacked and stirred, and a young man with a shock of platinum hair growing out of the top of his head like the feathers of some exotic bird emerged. "What do you need, chica?"

"I need to talk to these two detectives in private. Can you handle the customers while I'm busy?"

"I sure can." Gustavo strutted across the floor. "She didn't do it, officers. I can vouch for her."

Rachel rolled her eyes. "Don't mind him. You can follow me."

She sailed through the beaded curtain and held it open for them. Flinging her arm to the side, she said, "This is where we do our piercings, but everything's sterile."

"We're not from the health department." Billy sat on the chair that looked like it belonged in a dentist's office, and Rachel sat on the chair next to his. Jake remained standing.

"I take it you haven't found your cell phone yet?"

"I haven't. It's dead because it doesn't even roll to my voice mail, and when I texted it from my friend's phone, the message wasn't delivered." She hunched forward, brushing wispy black bangs from her eyes. "Why are you interested in my phone?"

"Whoever stole it or found it used your phone to make a call." Jake loosened his tie. "And we're very interested in the person who made that call."

Rachel nodded. "I get it."

Jake had no doubt she did. Despite her punk rock appearance, Rachel struck him as conscientious. "So, if you have any idea where you lost the phone, your last usage, if anyone seemed interested in your phone—that's going to help us find that person."

Billy crossed his ankle over his knee. "We're also getting your phone records, so knowing your last text or call before the phone went missing might help you pinpoint that time."

"I can tell you, it was somewhere on Melrose." She gripped the arms of the chair. "I worked yesterday, almost all day. I got coffee, I got lunch, I stopped in another clothing store where my friend works."

"All on Melrose." Jake had dipped into his pocket for his notebook. He liked taking notes the old-fashioned way, and a lot of people didn't want to be recorded.

"Yes, I can tell you which stores I entered. I must've lost it at one of those places because I had it when I came into work, and I noticed it missing when I left work around three o'clock in the afternoon. I never use my phone at work, so I suppose someone could've stolen it from my bag here." She circled her finger in the air. "As you probably already know, there are a lot of cameras in this area."

Jake and Billy exchanged a look. Rachel was practically doing their job for them.

"Can you tell us the names of the stores and the times?" Jake's pen hovered over his notepad.

"Uncommon Grounds at ten o'clock when I got in." She raised her eyes to the ceiling. "Eat A Pita at around noon for lunch, and another stop at Uncommon Grounds for a frap to get through the rest of my workday, and a quick stop at Jenny's, where my friend works."

"Did you use your phone to make any purchases?"

"No, just my debit card."

Jake tapped his pen against his notebook. "That's really helpful, Rachel. We can scan the CCTV footage near those places, around those times, and see if we can spot anyone in your vicinity."

"Glad I could help. My mom's upset with me because she thinks I was careless with my phone, which my parents pay for, but I've never lost my phone before. I think someone definitely stole it, turned it off so it couldn't be tracked from the time he stole it, and then turned it back on to make the...call. Can you tell me what the call was about?"

"No, I'm sorry. We can't." Billy fished in his pocket and handed her his card as he struggled out of the piercing chair. "Give us a call if you find the phone, or if anything else out of the ordinary happens."

"Out of the ordinary?" The corner of her eye twitched. "Is this person dangerous?"

"I don't think you're in any danger, Rachel." Jake added his card to Billy's. "One more thing. You do nose piercings here?"

"We do."

"Do you keep records?"

"My boss wouldn't have it any other way." She pushed to her feet and pulled back her shoulders. "What do you need?"

Jake shoved his notebook into his pocket. "If we gave you a time period and a name, could your records tell us if that person got her nose pierced here?"

"I'm sure we could." She dove through the curtain, sending the beads into a frenzy. "Gustavo, I need to look up piercings from..." She twisted her head over her shoulder.

Jake responded. "About two weeks ago, a nose piercing."

"Check the credit card receipts, chica. It's all there." Gustavo folded his hands with his black-painted fingernails on the counter. "Has she been giving you the third degree?"

"I'm afraid it was the other way around." Jake cocked his head. "What do you mean? Rachel's been really helpful."

Gustavo lifted his narrow shoulders and spread his hands. "Rachel wants to be a cop."

"You do?" Jake studied Rachel behind the counter, rummaging through a drawer.

A color the same hue as her lipstick rushed into her cheeks. "Maybe eventually. I have one more semester at Santa Monica College where I've been studying criminal justice before I get my AA degree. I'd like to get my BA under my belt before I think about being a cop."

"What about Dispatch?" Jake rubbed his chin. Dispatch could always use calm, professional, smart people. "I think you'd do great there."

"Really?" Her voice squeaked. "That would be like taking calls?"

"Yeah." He tapped his card, which she'd put on the glass counter. "Give me a call if you're interested. Seriously, I could get you an interview."

Rachel's dark eyes sparkled as she returned to her task.

Jake asked, "What if she paid cash?"

"The receipt wouldn't be there for cash. We could print those from the register, but they wouldn't tell you anything." Gustavo flicked his fingers in the air. "Nobody pays cash anymore."

Rachel pulled out a stack of receipts between her long fingernails and waved them back and forth. "Okay, two weeks ago. We're looking at the end of August into September for credit card purchases."

"Do those receipts cover those dates?" Jake held out his hand.

Rachel's fingers curled around the receipts, crumpling them at the edges, before she slapped them into his palm. "Yep. Nose is nose piercing and NP is nipple piercing to distinguish them."

Billy hovered over Jake's shoulder. "Do you get a lot of requests for those nipple piercings?"

"Why? You interested?" Rachel's red lips spread into a wide smile.

Jake smacked Billy on the back. "Yeah, you go in the back with Gustavo while I go through these receipts."

"I'm not asking for me." Billy snatched half the receipts from Jake's hand. "I'll look at these."

Jake plucked out all the receipts for nose piercings, checked the dates and looked at the signatures as the receipt didn't have the cardholder's name printed on it.

His pulse jumped as he squinted at a large *K* and a loopy *L* at the bottom of one of the receipts for a nose piercing.

"Billy, I think I got it. I think she came here to get her nose pierced."

Rachel hoisted half her body over the counter to eye the receipt Jake held in his hand.

When she slid back to her side of the counter, she pressed her hand against her heart. "Oh, my God. That's Kelsey Lindquist, one of the copycat's victims. You mean to tell me a killer has my phone?"

Chapter Nine

"I need a favor." Kyra dangled the plastic bag containing the queen of hearts in front of Clive Stewart, the fingerprint technician.

His gaze followed the swinging bag back and forth, and his mouth hung open. "Where did you get that? I already got the queen of spades from the body last night, and I know the queen of diamonds and the queen of hearts from the other two murders are sealed away."

"That's why it's a favor, Clive. It's off-the-books. Can you just dust it for prints and let me know if there are any? If there are, I'll go through the chain of evidence and submit it. I don't want to raise any alarms right now over a simple playing card, especially if it has no prints on it."

He held out his hand and she placed it on his palm, which had surprisingly few lines for a man his age. Clive's hands looked soft, but he was a scholar not a fighter.

Crooking his finger, he said, "Follow me. I can dust it right now while you wait."

"Thank you so much. I owe you one." She followed his stiff back into the lab and clicked the door shut behind them.

A lot of the forensics for LAPD was done at the county, but most of the larger divisions had their own fingerprint techs and other forensic specialists. The lab at the remodeled Northeast Division boasted a blood spatter and ballistics expert, so they didn't have to send out to county for that work.

Clive opened the bag and tipped the card onto a clean piece of paper, faceup. He dipped his brush into a container of black dust, like graphite, and shook off the excess. "You know, playing cards originally came from China, but the suits—the club, spade, diamond and heart—developed from Italian shapes, modified by the Germans and finally simplified by the French."

Kyra compressed her lips, flattening out her smile. Clive's brain contained a wealth of information, most of it trivial. She murmured, "That's fascinating."

"Don't pretend an interest you don't share, Kyra." He shook out the black particles from the brush onto the playing card. "My wife does the same thing, and I can spot disinterest a mile away. I'm used to it."

"I'm sorry. Distracted."

"That's all right." Clive lodged his tongue in the corner of his mouth for the delicate work before him. He'd been at this for as long as she'd been working with the department and probably a lot longer.

He used a pair of tweezers to lift the card and hold it under a light. "Nothing on this side, not even your prints."

"I lifted it off the ground with a pair of tongs from the kitchen and slipped it into that plastic bag. I've been around the block a few times."

"Yes, you have." He flipped the card over so that the queen was no longer staring at her. "You're a therapist. What made you work with the police department?"

She watched as Clive repeated the process with the black powder on the flip side of the playing card. "I—I had a friend who was murdered in college. Her death affected us, affected me, so much I changed my major from pre-nursing to psychology. I did an internship with a therapist who worked with police officers, and my career just kind of took off from there."

"Very impressive." He eyed the card under a magnifying glass and sighed. "I'm afraid there are no prints on this card."

"Okay, that's fine. I'm sure this was just a coincidence. I mean there are lots of decks of cards floating around, aren't there?" She picked up the plastic bag and blew a puff of air into it to open it. "You can drop it back in here. I really appreciate your help, Clive. If there's anything I can do for you, let me know."

"I can't imagine anything, but I'll keep that in mind."

"Lunch, coffee." She drilled her finger into her chest. "I'm your girl."

He slid the card, blackened with fingerprint dust, back into the baggie. "I just ask that you don't spread it around that I'm available to do work under the radar...because I'm usually not."

"I won't." She traced her fingertip across the seam of her lips. "My lips are sealed."

They exited the lab together, and Clive pulled the door tight until he heard the lock click. He nodded in her direction. "See you later."

Clive took off down the hallway, his narrow shoulders set, his head tilted slightly to one side, the light above gleaming off his bald pate.

Clive's ready acquiescence to dust the card for prints surprised her, but he was nearing retirement and seemed a little less buttoned-up than usual.

She careened around the corner and nearly crashed into a solid mass of...man. "Oh, sorry."

Jake placed a hand on her waist to steady her and then

dropped it as his eyebrows lowered. "Slow down. It's not like you're running out to a call or something."

Kyra folded her arms and stuffed the baggie into her purse. "Heard you got a trace on the phone."

"Heard you left with a reporter last night." He propped one broad shoulder against the wall, blocking her escape. Escape? Did she really want to escape Jake's presence? Not once she'd secured the queen of hearts in her purse.

"That's true. Megan Wright. She's my friend. I know you don't have any of those, but they're people you like and associate with and even do things for. You might try one sometime." She shook her finger at him. "I hear they even reduce stress."

The corner of his mouth twitched. "Believe it or not, I actually have a few of those."

"Coworkers and criminals don't count."

He let out a gurgle, which sounded suspiciously like a laugh. "We got some good leads this morning. I wish... Where were you today?"

Had he been about to say he wished she'd been there? Progress. "Leads from the phone call?"

"Yeah, we have security videos to review in about an hour. The stores are sending them over." He glanced over his shoulder. "I think I owe you a lunch. I can fill you in."

"You mean the lunch you promised to drop on my desk in a brown paper bag at the office?"

"Did I mention a brown paper bag?" He pushed off the wall and jingled his car keys. "I mean a real lunch in a real restaurant, away from the station."

"Let's do it. You're going to have to get back here to watch that footage before you prep for the task force meeting. Four o'clock, right?" She took a step past him, and he swung in next to her.

"A lot of updates today but no ID on the victim from

last night." He pushed open the door for her and held it as she walked through.

The man had his odd moments of chivalry. He even opened the door of his Crown Vic for her. He slammed it and circled around to the driver's side. As he got behind the wheel, he asked, "Any preferences?"

"Just no cop hangouts, even if they do give you the discount."

"The last place I want to go with you is a cop hangout." He cranked on the engine and the AC blasted her face.

She nudged the vent in his direction. "You don't want other cops to see you talking to me?"

"Would just prefer an opportunity to talk without getting interrupted every few minutes." He dialed down the air conditioning as he pulled out of the station's parking lot. "Looks like they've got that Malibu fire under control, although it did overtake the body dump site."

"So, the killer's fears were realized, after all. He must be resting easy now that he gets credit for his third victim." She clenched her jaw.

"First victim."

"What?" She jerked her head toward Jake. "What makes you think the woman last night was his first?"

"He made the rookie error of hiding her body too well so that she couldn't be found, or at least not found for several weeks or months. Also, the, um, decomposition of the body. I won't go into that before lunch."

"You don't have to. I get it." Her stomach still gurgled, and she didn't think it was from hunger.

Jake drove just a few blocks from the station and pulled into a strip mall. "There's a good Vietnamese pho place here, and if that doesn't interest you, there's pizza and a taco place."

"Pho sounds good. Not too hot for you on a warm day?"

"As long as the AC's on, I can handle it." He swung his car into a spot in front of a dry cleaner, and Kyra hopped out. When Jake opened the door of the restaurant, a rush of spicy smells made her mouth water.

"Hope you weren't expecting something fancy. You order at the counter and they'll bring your food to your table."

"That's most restaurants I go to." She flipped her ponytail over her shoulder and grabbed a laminated menu to study while they waited for the man in front of them asking a million questions.

After they both ordered, Jake placed their number on a table by the window while she filled up a paper cup with diet soda. Her blood fizzed as much as the soda. She couldn't wait to hear how the case was progressing, and she was getting a preview ahead of the rest of the task force—all for the price of some fish and chips last night, and Quinn vouching for her. All LAPD detectives revered the legendary Roger Quinn. Jake had proved to be no different, and her association with Quinn had given her status in Jake's eyes.

He returned with his own drink from the self-serve fountain machine and pulled out the plastic chair across from her. His large frame dwarfed the chair and the table.

He'd rolled up the sleeves of his light blue dress shirt, and the tail end of some ink crept onto his forearm. It looked like a snake or a tail and she wouldn't mind getting a look at the rest of it, but she averted her gaze to the tip of her straw and sucked down some soda.

"I heard the phone he called from wasn't a burner."

"You get right to the point." He folded his hands on the table; instead of being a prissy gesture as it would be for most men, it only emphasized his strength and masculinity as the veins popped over his corded forearms. "Info has a way of leaking, doesn't it?"

"But you never know if it's true or purely speculation and rumor."

"That particular piece of data is true." As the waitress approached the table to deliver their bowls of steaming pho, Jake moved their cups and silverware to make room.

The server placed the bowls in front of them and put down a silver tray containing little dishes of jalapeño, cilantro, bean sprouts and other ingredients to spice up the soup.

"After you." Jake nudged the tray toward her, and the little dishes trembled.

Using her fork, she added a few more ingredients to her pho, the steam from the bowl already making her sniff. "You haven't led me astray here, have you? I'm not going to take one spoonful of this pho and run screaming for the exit with steam coming from my ears, am I?"

He raised his eyebrows as he dropped a jalapeño into his soup. "For some reason, I thought you were a native Angeleno. Am I wrong? If not and you're like me, you were weaned on spicy food."

She did not want this conversation turning personal. She stirred her soup and slurped a sip from the large spoon. "Perfect."

"Glad you like it. You can always add more chili oil, if you like," he said, which he then proceeded to do.

"If the phone wasn't a burner, whose was it? If it belonged to the copycat, you'd have him in custody by now."

Jake patted his nose with his napkin. "It belongs to Rachel Blackburn, a young community college student who works in a clothing and jewelry shop on Melrose. She lost the phone yesterday—or it was stolen from her."

"Hence the security cam footage for review. You're

going to try to spot the moment someone picked up her phone."

"Exactly. She lost it somewhere on Melrose. She had it when she went into work, and didn't have it when she left work. She'd been to a few businesses along Melrose. We've pulled the video from those places."

"That's a huge lead."

"It gets better." Jake swirled his soda and took a sip, keeping her in suspense. "The shop also does piercings, and guess who got her nose pierced there a few weeks ago?"

Her own drink almost bubbled through her nose as she choked. "Kelsey?"

"That's right."

"One of the victims had her nose pierced at a shop on Melrose a few weeks before her murder, and the killer takes a phone from someone who works at the shop to call in another of his victims. He must live in, work in or frequent that area."

"Yeah, too bad it's so congested, but it's a start."

"It's a great start. You got lucky with that girl, Rachel Blackburn."

"She's a bright kid, interested in law enforcement. I told her to give me a call about a job with Dispatch. I know the sergeant and can put a word in for her."

Kyra dropped her spoon and stared at Jake, open-mouthed.

He jerked his head up and a bean sprout stuck to his chin. "What?"

"First of all—" Kyra tapped her own chin "—you have food on your face. Secondly, I didn't realize you were such a helpful person."

"Thanks." He swiped the bean sprout from his chin with a napkin. "I hate it when you have food on your face or in your teeth and nobody tells you. They just sit back and watch you make a fool of yourself."

She buried her chin in her palm. "That's nice of you to help out Rachel."

"Nice?" The color spiked in his cheeks, although that might be the jalapeño. "Nice had nothing to do with it. We need good people."

Jake didn't want to ruin his rep as a tough guy. She tilted her bowl to spoon up the rest of her pho. "Hopefully, that CCTV footage will reveal the phone thief... and the killer."

"I was thinking you might talk to Rachel. She's freaked out about being close to the copycat and the fact that he used her phone." He jabbed his spoon in her direction. "You do that sort of thing, too, right?"

"That sort of thing? Yes, I do. I'd be happy to talk to Rachel."

"All right then." He checked his cell phone, which had been on the table throughout lunch and buzzing periodically with text messages. "I'm going to get more soda for the road." He tapped his phone. "Just got a text from Billy that the video is queued up and ready for our viewing pleasure."

As she watched him walk to the soda machine, his gait sure and fluid like an athlete's, she felt a twist of disappointment in her belly. She would've liked to have learned a little more about Jake's personal life, his background. He was a Southern California boy, but where did he grow up? What had brought him to police work?

She wanted to learn those things about him, but he was too skilled a detective to allow the flow of information to go one way. And she had no intention of giving him the details of her background.

The secrecy made it hard to date, even harder to date

someone in law enforcement. Of course, she was getting ahead of herself here. Nobody claimed, least of all Jake McAllister, that he was interested in dating her. She considered herself lucky he still didn't have daggers in his eyes when he looked at her.

He placed his cup on the edge of the table. "Do you want me to get you more soda before we leave?"

"Sure." She handed him her cup, and the tips of their fingers met on the damp surface.

Jake snatched the cup away and stalked toward the machine without even asking her what she was drinking.

She called after his back. "Diet, please."

He held up the cup and as he refilled her drink, she slipped her purse from the back of the chair and swung it to hitch over her shoulder.

As she did, it hit the chair, and some of the contents spilled out, including the plastic baggie with the card.

"Sorry." He began to crouch to collect her items.

"That's okay. I've got it." But she didn't have it. Jake had it.

He rose from his crouch, straightening to his full, intimidating height, the bag dangling from his fingertips, the flesh around his mouth white.

Through barely moving lips, he asked, "What the hell is this?"

Chapter Ten

Kyra's blue eyes met his, cool and unflinching chips of ice. "It's a card."

Anger whipped through his body, his veins sizzling with it. He exhaled a long breath through his mouth, which beat banging on the table with his fist. "Thanks, I know *what* it is. You know damned well I'm asking you where it came from and why it was fingerprinted."

"It's a long story, and you need to get back to the station." She tugged on the bag in his hand. "Do I still get a ride back?"

He should just leave her here. She had her phone. She could call up a car.

"I'll give you a ride." But if she thought she was going to retain possession of this card, she'd better think again.

He yanked the baggie from her fingers and stuffed it into his pocket. Then he grabbed his soda, with such a firm grip he almost popped off the lid, and pivoted on his heel.

He could hear the click of her heels following him out of the restaurant as she called out cheerily to the staff behind the counter. "Thank you. Have a great day."

It was as if the hotter his rage burned, the colder she got in response. Did he expect tears? Did he want tears? The tears and recriminations from Tess had made him feel wanted. It was when his ex's feelings turned to dis-interest—and another man—that he knew their marriage was over.

He stalked to the car, and habit compelled him to open the car door for her.

Halfway into the car, she cranked her head to the side. "I'll explain it to you. It's silly, simple."

He stuck his head in the car. "What makes you think I'm gonna believe anything you tell me?"

He slammed the door, shutting out her serene face with the slight curve to her full lips. He'd known women like her before. They sallied through life on their good looks, charming men into doing their bidding. Hell, she must've charmed Clive, of all people, into running a fin-gerprint test on that card.

He dropped onto the driver's seat and punched the ig-nition with his knuckle. He peeled out of the strip mall, the spicy food now burning a hole in his belly.

Kyra cleared her throat. "I found the card."

Jake tightened his jaw and clenched the steering wheel with both hands.

"I found it on the street, in the gutter, outside my apartment building." She shifted in her seat and smoothed her slacks against her thighs. "I didn't think it was a big deal or anything. Just one of those weird coincidences. If you look, it's not a brand-new card, not like the ones with the bodies."

The car jostled as he pulled into the parking lot of the station and Kyra bounced in her seat. He eased off the accelerator.

Turning to her, he threw the car into Park. "If it was no big deal, why hide it from me? I'm leading this task force. If I can't trust actual task force members, I'm in trouble."

She twisted her fingers in her lap, the first sign of agitation. "Look, I felt kind of silly. Why would the killer drop a playing card on my street in Santa Monica, of all places? I saw it and just reacted."

He flexed his fingers on the steering wheel. "And got Clive to run a test on it, on the sly."

She placed her hand on his arm. "Please don't blame Clive or get on his case for this. He's never done it before, and he made it clear he wouldn't do it again."

"What did he find?"

"Nothing." She lifted her shoulders. "There were no prints at all. Just my fevered imagination making connections in my overactive brain."

He brushed his hand against the outside of his pocket, where the plastic crinkled. "Kind of a strange coincidence."

"Just what I thought."

He pulled out the baggie. "Do you want it back?"

"That's okay." She lifted one shoulder. "Keep it, throw it away, whatever."

"All right, then. Um, I'm sorry I may have overreacted back there." He exited the vehicle and waited for Kyra to come around to his side.

"No problem. I get it." She pressed her hand against his back, giving him a little shove. "You have some footage to review."

"If you're not busy, do you want to join us?" He dug his teeth into his bottom lip. He was just trying to make amends for his previous outburst. Maybe she'd see that and decline.

"I would like to join you, thanks."

Did he really think she wouldn't jump at the chance to insert herself further into this investigation? Did he mind? After all, surveying video could be mind-numbing work and the more people on deck, the better.

As they returned to the station, their appearance raised a few eyebrows. Jake put a scowl on his face to ward off any ribbing from his coworkers later. He called out a few names as he marched through the station and held up his finger. "Follow me to the war room."

Brandon and his team had already set up several computers and loaded the footage on them. Before he'd left for lunch, Jake had instructed Brandon to divvy up the video between the different computers so that individual teams would all be reviewing a variety of times and locations.

Standing in the middle of the room, he directed traffic, assigning teams of two to each computer. As they huddled over the monitors, someone tapped him on the shoulder.

He didn't have to turn around to know who it was. The sweet, dusky smell of roses hung around Kyra as if she crushed them against her skin every day.

Twisting his head over his shoulder, he said, "You can hang out with me until Billy gets here."

He took a seat in front of his computer, security footage from Melrose Avenue queued up to start. He taped a picture of Rachel on the monitor next to his. "This is Rachel—black, shoulder-length hair, sleeve of tattoos on her right arm, piercings, about your height, medium frame."

Kyra pulled a chair next to his and settled into it, propping her elbow on the table and balancing her chin on her palm. Her ponytail slipped over her shoulder, the ends of it tickling the keyboard. "What are we looking at now?"

"This is Rachel's afternoon coffee run. By this time, she's already had morning coffee at the same shop, been to work, gone out to lunch and visited her friend in another store. This is her last stop before going back to work." His hand hovered over the mouse. "Ready?"

"Ready." Her nostrils flared slightly and she parted her lips.

Jake clicked the start arrow on the footage, which Brandon's team had queued up about ten minutes before the time Rachel had given them. They watched the busy shop as people ordered their coffee and food at the counter and drifted away to wait for their orders.

The cameras pointed at the registers only, so any other customer interaction they hoped to see would have to be in the background, beyond the people ordering. Another team was studying the footage from outside the store.

They sat still, side by side, Kyra barely breathing. Her proximity overwhelmed his senses, and then her knee touched his pant leg.

Jake rubbed his eyes and brought his face closer to the monitor. About seven minutes in, Kyra jabbed him with her elbow. "Is that Rachel? I see black hair."

"That's Rachel." Jake stalled the video and took screen shots of Rachel's progress through the store. "Too bad she didn't use her phone to buy the coffee."

"She told you that already?"

"Yeah, like I said—" he tapped the side of his head "—she's a sharp girl."

Kyra squinted at the screen. "I'm trying to figure out if I can see her phone in her purse but no luck. I have a pocket on the outside of my bag where I keep my cell. You can see the outline of the phone when you look at my purse."

"Is that on the other side of where you keep your gun?" He raised one eyebrow.

"You're not supposed to be able to see the outline of that."

"I'm a cop. I can spot a purse with a gun pouch a mile away."

She poked him in the leg. "Our girl is up."

Rachel stepped to the counter and ordered from the female barista, exchanging a few words. She swiped her debit card to pay for the purchase, then wandered out of the camera's view, stepping back and to the left to wait for her coffee.

The camera didn't have a clear view of the pickup area. Baristas shoved drinks and little bags of food onto the counter, where impatient, caffeine-deprived hands grabbed them. Jake jabbed a finger at the monitor. "That's Rachel. Notice the tat on her wrist? The nails?"

"We can't see her purse, can't see anyone around her." Kyra slumped in her chair. "I guess I expected to discover someone clearly reaching a hand in her bag and snatching her phone. We can't even tell if she had her cell phone going into Uncommon Grounds."

"We can't—" he swept one arm to the side "—but maybe someone else will pick up something."

As Jake clicked on the timer to run the tape back to see if they'd overlooked something, Billy swept into the war room. He raised one eyebrow when he homed in on Jake's partner and then shrugged.

Clapping his hands, Billy shouted, "How close are you to being done, and has anyone found anything?"

His words were met with a few grumbles and groans and not one eureka.

One cop in the corner raised his hand. "We had Rachel's morning coffee run, and we saw her on the phone. So, she had it then."

"All right. All right." Billy stepped up to a clean whiteboard and made a notation. "Time stamp?"

The officer gave him a time, and Billy ran down the whiteboard with a red marker as others called out their times and findings. With Rachel still in possession of her phone at lunch, Billy circled around to Jake and Kyra. "Which brings us to you two for the coffee break after lunch."

Jake leaned back in his chair, crossing his arms behind his head. "We didn't see anything—no evidence of her phone, no unusual encounters."

"Anyone have footage from the sidewalk of Rachel's return to work? I think that's our last piece since she said she didn't have the phone when she was getting ready to leave for work for the day." Billy swiveled his head from side to side, and the room remained silent.

Jake pushed out of his chair. "Brandon, who had that last part of Rachel's timeline?"

Brandon popped up, red faced, from where he'd been crawling on the floor connecting cables. "We don't have it. It's the same camera from the street where we watched her go in for lunch and then into the coffeehouse, but for some reason there's no footage from later that day."

Jake ran a hand through his hair, the ends of his fingers tingling with frustration. Unlike Kyra, he hadn't expected to see the culprit lifting Rachel's phone, but accurate footage showing a clear timeline would be good.

"I have a question." Kyra wiggled her fingers in the air. "For those of you who saw Rachel with her phone, was she on it or did you see it in her bag or pocket?"

Billy asked around the room, and the teams that had seen her with the phone reported that she had the phone in her hand.

Picking up on Kyra's train of thought, Jake asked, "When Rachel got off the phone, did she put it in her purse? Zip it up so nobody could get to it?"

One of the female officers spoke up. "We saw her texting for several minutes while she was eating lunch outside with her friend. When she was done, she put the phone next to her on the bench. I'd never do that. When I saw her, I thought to myself that was a good way to lose your phone. When she left, she did drop it into her purse, no side pocket or anything like that."

"So, you think she might have left it out at a later time and somebody picked it up." Jake rubbed his chin. "Nobody had to pick her pocket or lift it from her purse if she just left it sitting somewhere."

Billy put a big red arrow pointing at Rachel's lunch and another aimed at her store at three o'clock. "She lost the phone between here and here."

Kyra nudged Jake. "That's us. Can we play it back again?"

"Sure." Jake raised his voice. "Thanks for your hard work, everyone. We'll coordinate with the West Hollywood Sheriff's Station, and do some more canvassing in that area. It has another connection to one of our victims, so it's a hot spot for us. Leave any stills you took with Cool Breeze, and you can take off."

Chairs scraped and empty soda cans hit the recycling bins, and the officers shuffled out of the room.

Billy scribbled a few more words on his whiteboard timeline and pointed the marker at Jake. "Mind if I lean over your shoulders?"

"C'mon over." Jake scooted his chair closer to Kyra's. "I'm glad Kyra was here to help out. I didn't realize you were going to be so late."

"Had some leads on the identity of our Malibu fire victim." Billy clicked his tongue as he pulled up a chair and squeezed next to Jake. "Nothing panned out. That poor woman still doesn't have a name."

"You checked out the missing persons report that looked promising?"

"Chased it down. Showed the sister a picture of our victim, and she failed to make the ID."

"He doesn't seem to be targeting runaways, does he?" Kyra drummed her fingers close to Jake's hand. "Marissa and Kelsey weren't runaways."

Billy lifted one shoulder. "Maybe he's not targeting anyone. He sees an opportunity and takes it. That's why the West Hollywood area is so important. Kelsey got a piercing at Rachel's shop, and Rachel's phone was stolen by the killer, or at least someone connected to the killer."

"I think that was definitely our guy on the phone last night." Jake clicked the mouse. "You ready to put eyeballs on this?"

He'd queued up the video to start seconds before Rachel entered Uncommon Grounds. When the action rolled, Jake poked his finger at the screen. "You can see her arm behind this guy in line."

Three sets of eyes studied Rachel's progress through the line and her turn at the counter.

"Wait," Kyra shouted, and both Jake and Billy jumped. "She has her purse open to get her wallet. That looks like the edge of a phone right there."

As Jake leaned in, he felt Kyra's warm breath on his cheek. "You're right. That's her phone. Good job."

Rachel shoved her card in the chip reader and pulled it out. She tucked the card back into her purse without touching her phone. She stepped out of the camera's view to wait for her drink.

Kyra sighed. "Anything could be happening off camera."

Rachel reached in to grab her drink, and they couldn't even see her purse or her other hand.

Kyra circled an area on the screen that showed Rachel's other arm behind her body. "She could be holding a phone there."

"We can ask her." Jake backed up and snapped a picture of Rachel's open purse with a gleaming corner of her phone visible. "I told you, she's a bright girl. She might remember what happened in the coffee place the moment before or after she picked up her drink—someone bumping into her, some distraction. I'll give her a call when I can."

Billy stood up and stretched. "You canceled the task force meeting today?"

"I figured everyone got a good update in here. I'm going to get on the phone with the Sheriff's Department and let them know we'll be nosing around Melrose."

"And I have a few clients to see later." Kyra shoved back from the desk, linked her fingers and stretched her arms in front of her. "Thanks for allowing me to view the footage."

"You provided some good insight. I don't think I could've made out anything in a woman's purse." Jake felt Billy jab two fingers between his shoulders, and he shrugged him off.

Kyra pushed to her feet and patted her purse. "I left the case for my sunglasses in your car."

"I'll take you down to get them." Jake flicked a finger at the printouts in Billy's hand. "You have everything you need?"

"I sure do."

Jake walked Kyra from the room, and they went down to the parking lot. He unlocked the car, and she ducked inside to retrieve her case.

She held it up over the roof of the car. "Got it."

"Where's your car?"

"I parked it on the street. The lot was crowded, and I didn't want to take up a space."

"I'll walk you out there." He ignored the look she shot him. He knew it was still daylight and they were in front of a police station, but old habits died hard.

"Not necessary, but okay." She retrieved her car keys and jingled them. "No keyless ignition for me yet. My car's ancient."

When they got to the curb where she'd parked her car, Kyra slid forward and slammed her hands against the passenger window.

"Are you all right?" Jake grabbed her arm. Her skin felt clammy beneath his touch.

"I—I'm fine." She twisted away from him and pushed off the car, where her hands had left moist prints on the glass. "I'm so clumsy, I slipped on the curb."

The last thing he'd call Kyra Chase was clumsy. Jake glanced down at the perfectly dry curb without a crack in place. Behind his own sunglasses, he watched her smiling lips tremble.

"You don't seem fine. Did you almost faint or something? Do you want me to get you water?"

"For a little slip?" She clicked the remote on her key fob. "I'm good. Thanks again for including me today."

She stood with her back against the passenger door, her shoulders squared, a bright, fake smile plastered to her face.

"I'll make sure you get to the other side okay." He cupped her elbow and walked her around to the driver's side.

She slid into her car and slammed the door on him. When she started her engine, she buzzed down the window. "Thanks, again."

Jake nodded and hesitated, but Kyra pulled out her phone and bent her head over it, her fingers tapping furiously.

He forced himself to walk away from her car. He couldn't stand there all day looking at her through the window. Raising his hand, he stalked back to the station parking lot. Before he walked into the building, he twisted his head to the side to find Kyra's car still idling at the curb. The white oval through the window looked like her face.

She was still watching him?

When he walked into the station, Jake bolted up three flights of stairs and charged into the lunchroom, which had a view of the street.

As he squinted through the tinted glass, Kyra got out of her car, went around to the passenger side, crouched down and reached beneath the car's chassis.

Jake gritted his teeth. What the hell was she lying about this time?

Chapter Eleven

Kyra clutched the queen of diamonds in her hand and smeared her thumb across the glossy surface to sweep off the particles of dirt clinging to it. Fingerprints didn't concern her this time. He'd left none on the other card, and she couldn't run to Clive with another playing card, anyway.

Could she run to Jake?

She glanced at the white expanse of the station. Would CCTV help to identify who'd dropped the playing card next to her car? If she'd parked in the station's lot, there would've been footage for sure. That would be less likely out here in the street.

She dropped the card onto her console and gripped the steering wheel, resting her forehead on her bunched knuckles. How did the killer know who she was, where she lived, what car she drove? It didn't make sense.

Finding this second card screamed loud and clear that the first card had not been a coincidence. What had Quinn always told her? There are no coincidences in law enforcement.

She had to tell Jake. These cards could lead to the capture of the copycat killer. The task force had precious little to go on right now.

If she told him, she could still keep her other secret.

She could claim she had no idea why someone, possibly this killer, was leaving playing cards for her.

She'd tell Jake…for the sake of the case, for the sake of those victims. She noted the time on the car's clock and shifted into Drive. First she'd see her clients and touch base with Quinn. She hadn't even told him about the first card.

She headed back toward the coast where a gray line of haze sat on the horizon. The Malibu Canyon fire still burned, but the firefighters had contained it, which meant no more nonstop news coverage—until the next wildfire blazed forth. The Santa Ana winds worried the tops of the palm trees and sucked the moisture out of the air, but no new fires had popped up.

When would that body from last night have been discovered had the fire not whipped through the canyon? The copycat may have been more content to wait if it hadn't. He wouldn't have put himself at risk with that phone call.

The copycat had exposed himself in a way The Player never would've done. That meant law enforcement could count on more mistakes from him. Like leaving two playing cards for her? A number of other people could be responsible for that, including a few of the miscreants she'd stumbled across in the foster care system.

By the time she reached her office in Santa Monica, the sun had started dipping into the ocean, its rays filtering through the smoke from the fire to create an orange streak across the sky.

She cruised down Wilshire and pulled into the parking lot of a two-story office building that she and another therapist shared with a realty office, an aesthetician, a pizza place and a hairstylist.

She and her office roomie, as she called Candace,

shared the space, which consisted of a waiting room where they could conduct groups and an inner office for private sessions. They scheduled their clients at different times and used the same space. Saved a lot of money, especially in this area, and Kyra spent a lot of her time at various police stations.

She jogged up the stairs and used her key to unlock the office. She left the door unlocked and retreated to what she and Candace called the treatment room.

A small desk neither of them used huddled in the corner while comfortable chairs with colorful cushions took up the space in the middle of the room.

She knew which chair her next client would take. He always sat in the same one—they all did.

The door clicked in the outer office, and Kyra smoothed back her hair and relaxed the muscles of her face. After the day she'd had, she needed therapy probably more than her clients did. Not that she hadn't already had plenty of it.

The red light above the door flashed, and Kyra answered the call—a cop who, like so many before him, had let the job and alcohol destroy his marriage.

An hour later, Kyra folded her hands in her lap. "We're out of time, Evan."

He sat back in his chair and ran a hand over his close-cropped hair. "That went by fast. It always does."

"I'll see you next time." Kyra rose to her feet and opened the door to the outer office. She accepted all payments online now, which cut out the awkwardness of taking a check or cash after a session.

Evan stopped at the door, close enough for her to smell the faded mint from the chewing gum he used as a substitute for alcohol. "I heard about a third body in this copycat case. I also heard you're on the task force."

She nodded once, hoping to end the conversation before it started.

"How do you like working with J-Mac?" Evan's stocky frame filled the door.

"Excuse me?" Her fingers twisted the handle. She never talked about her personal life with clients. After six months of treatment, Evan should know that rule by now, especially as he'd tried to get too friendly before and she'd put him in his place.

He seemed to flinch at her cold tone. Good.

"Just wondering what the guy was like. Heard he was a great detective but not easy to work with." Evan lifted a square shoulder.

"Yeah, I really wouldn't know. I work with the victims."

"Next time then." Evan thrust out his hand and she shook it.

"Next time." Many clients went in for the hug at the end of a session, but not usually cops. Kyra generally let the clients dictate the level of closeness they needed at the end of an appointment, and guys like Evan preferred the firm handshake to show that they were back in control, even after an emotional hour that sometimes included tears.

When the door to the outside closed, Kyra returned to the office to turn off the lights. During her session with Evan, her next client had canceled, which gave Kyra a chance to get to Quinn's place earlier.

She perched on the edge of the desk and called him.

"What's wrong?"

"There's nothing wrong." The lie sounded thin. "Just a few things I want to run past you. Do you want me to pick up dinner?"

"No need. Rose across the channel dropped off a lasagna. I can't eat the whole thing myself."

"Perfect." She smiled into the phone. "Rose, huh? Didn't she just lose her husband the movie producer last year?"

"She did, but don't get any ideas." He coughed. "And you'd better be prepared to tell me what's wrong when you get here. You're an expert at keeping secrets, but not from me."

"I have no intention of keeping any secrets from you, and I also don't need to worry you over the phone."

She heard a sharp intake of breath. "Do I need to worry?"

"See what I mean?" She hopped off the desk. "Heat up that lasagna. You got stuff for salad?"

"Yes, hurry up."

Kyra ended the call and sucked in her bottom lip. She didn't want Quinn to be concerned about her, but she wanted to bounce this off him before she went to Jake—and she had to go to Jake.

She locked up the office and made the short drive from Santa Monica to Venice—short in distance. The traffic made the journey crawl.

By the time she knocked on Quinn's door, the sun had set and her stomach was grumbling. She reached for the door handle in case Quinn wasn't up to the trek across his living room floor.

He flung it open before she could tell if it was locked or not. He'd slicked back his gray hair and even trimmed his wild eyebrows.

She kissed his worn cheek. "You look nice. Did you make an effort for Rose?"

"Stop." He waved his hand. "Tell me what's going on before you scurry off to the kitchen. The food can wait."

She sniffed the garlic-scented air. "Apparently not."

She followed him to his chair and sat across from him on the love seat. She pulled the queen of diamonds from her purse. "Found this by my car this afternoon, on the ground."

"And put your prints all over it." He snapped his fingers, and she placed the card on his outstretched palm.

"There won't be any prints."

"And how do you know that? People make mistakes." He turned the card over.

"Because that's not the first one I found, and the queen of hearts didn't have prints." She held her breath and watched the lines on his craggy face deepen, a needle of guilt pricking the back of her neck.

"Where and when did you find the other card?"

"On the ground, near the dumpster behind my apartment building—queen of hearts that time." She raised her finger. "I did scoop that one up and had the fingerprint tech at the Northeast Division test it. You remember Clive? He's still there."

"So, you turned it in to McAllister and the task force." He sank back in his chair, tapping the edge of the card on his knee.

"Not exactly."

"Keeping secrets again, Kyra? You don't belong on the task force if you're keeping secrets. That could put someone's life in danger. They need every clue right now, and this is a clue. They both are."

"I know that now after finding the second card." She spread her hands. "I thought the one at my apartment was a coincidence."

"You know what I told you about coincidences in investigations."

She repeated with him. "There are no coincidences in law enforcement."

She brushed a hand across her slacks. "I didn't want to raise any alarms with that first card. Clive didn't find any prints on it and there are no cameras at my place, so I figured it didn't matter."

A spark lit Quinn's faded blue eyes as his gaze drilled into her.

She rose from the love seat and circled around it. "Then when I found the second card, I knew it had meaning. But what? This copycat killer can't know who I am."

"Who says the copycat killer left the cards?"

She linked her hands in front of her and twisted her fingers. "You mean it could be someone else taking advantage of the situation to torture me?"

"Anyone come to mind?" He snapped the card on the coffee table.

Kyra folded her arms and dug her fingers into her biceps. "You're not talking about Matt, are you?"

"Just throwing it out there. He saw the news and thought he'd poke at you. You know he's capable."

"I know Matt is capable of just about anything, but he'd also like nothing more than for me to reach out to him to find out if he's playing tricks." She whipped her head back and forth. "I'm not going to do that."

"And you shouldn't." Quinn prodded the card with his finger. "Where's the other one? You said there were two cards."

"Jake has the other one." She shoved one hand in the pocket of her slacks in a nonchalant pose.

"I thought you said he didn't know about the cards."

"The queen of hearts fell out of my purse when we were at lunch, so I had to tell him about it."

Quinn grimaced with one side of his mouth. "That must've gone over well."

"He wasn't happy, if that's what you mean." Kyra marched into the kitchen. "I don't know about you, but I'm starving and that lasagna smells good."

"He accused you of keeping it from him, being deceptive."

Kyra bent forward and peered at the lasagna heating up on the middle rack, the heat from the oven warming her face. "Of course, he did, but I explained that I brought it in for prints and that I believed it was just a coincidence. I did believe that."

"You don't toy with a man like McAllister. I'm sure you heard about his run-in with that therapist. You must've heard about it. You were working with her."

"Not on that, I wasn't. I never would've tried to get a lighter sentence for that guy. Jake was right to be angry. I was there when it happened." She banged through Quinn's cupboard to retrieve a colander, a large bowl, a knife and a cutting board.

By the time she'd chopped the salad veggies, the oven timer had dinged, signaling the lasagna was heated through. Kyra pulled the dish out of the oven, and Quinn joined her and grabbed a couple of plates from the cupboard.

He said, "I'll set the table."

A few minutes later, they sat across from each other, and Kyra smiled, her eyes misty. "Just like old times."

"The only thing missing is Charlotte." Quinn rested a hand on the empty place mat beside him.

"Charlotte and my bad attitude." Kyra stabbed her fork into her salad.

"Oh, you still have plenty of attitude." Quinn shook his

own fork at her. "When are you going to tell Jake about the second card and why you hid it from him?"

"Soon." She studied a dripping tomato skewered on the end of her fork. "And I'll think of something to tell him—anything but the truth."

"You think you'll get away with that with him?" Quinn's thin lips twisted. "You won't have to tell him the truth because he'll figure it out one of these days... all on his own."

JAKE HUNCHED OVER his computer, his third Diet Coke of the afternoon pumping caffeine through his system. A search of Kyra Chase didn't get him very far. She'd graduated from UCLA with a degree in psychology, and then went to Cal State LA part-time to get her master's in clinical psychology while she worked full-time. Her work ethic and ambition didn't surprise him. Something was driving her, but her background didn't give any hints what that was.

She avoided social media, which was probably a good idea given her line of work. He avoided it, too. He needed suspects tracking him down about as much as Kyra needed clients tracking her down.

He did see where Charlotte Quinn had dedicated one of her books to K.C., her favorite therapist. The connection between Kyra and the Quinns was real, but why had she lied about working with him on a case? And why did Quinn back her up?

Kyra could've lied about that for his benefit, trying to make herself more professionally acceptable in his eyes.

Jake growled to the empty war room. "Nah. That woman doesn't care what you think of her."

He sat back in his chair, rubbed his burning eyes and

tossed back the rest of his drink. Propping his feet onto his desk, he dragged one of The Player files into his lap.

People had started calling this killer The Copycat or The Copycat Player. Despite a few unique touches, he did have The Player's MO down.

Why that killer? Why now? There were many cold cases in LA. Why did he choose that one? Jake refused to believe The Player had come out of retirement, even though he could still be young enough to hunt.

He opened the thick file in his lap and scanned the familiar contents. As scant as it was, most of this stuff—the autopsies and the evidence—was online. Roger Quinn appeared older than his age. Caring for his wife before she died must've taken its toll, but Jake could guarantee The Player took a whole other kind of toll on the old detective.

He flipped toward the back of the file, perusing notes about the victims and their families. He smoothed his hand over a crumpled page with a black, angry scrawl at the bottom. Squinting, he made out the word *Denied.*

His gaze tracked to the top of the page. One of The Player's victims, Jennifer Lake, had left a young daughter behind, no father on the scene. Roger Quinn had gotten involved and had been advocating for this girl to the point where he and his wife wanted to adopt her instead of sending her into LA's foster care system. Ultimately, their request had been rejected.

With his heart pounding in his chest, Jake scrambled through the additional pages in the file, searching for information on Jennifer Lake's daughter. He dropped the file on the floor and dug into the stack on the corner of his desk.

He flipped open the one on Jennifer and stared at the picture of the pretty blonde. It was one of those cheesy modeling photos for an acting portfolio—ruby-red lips, heavily made-up eyes, styled hair. Jennifer had been an aspiring actress and part-time call girl. It had been the latter profession that had gotten her into trouble. She'd been twenty-five years old at the time of her murder, with an eight-year old daughter in tow. That daughter— he skimmed down the page with his finger—was named Marilyn Monroe Lake.

He slumped in his chair. Who the hell named their kid Marilyn Monroe? At least she'd given the kid a nickname.

He thumbed through a few more pages and froze as another photo spilled out of the pile—this one a natural pose of a fresh-faced young woman, her blond hair in a ponytail, her wide aquamarine blue eyes startling in her pale face.

Jake grabbed his bag and slung it over his shoulder. He waved to the guys on the night shift and climbed into his car. The adrenaline in his body weighted his foot on the gas pedal and he sped down the freeway to the coast in record time. He buzzed down his window to gulp in the sea-scented air that caressed his hot face.

Apartments lined the streets in this area of Santa Monica, about two miles up from the beach. Crime came at you here from the transients and the tweakers looking for some quick cash. Jake hugged the side of the street, looking for a gap in the row of cars parked for the night.

He squeezed into a spot and exited his vehicle. The older apartment complexes on this street didn't boast any security except for the lock on your front door. He breezed into the small courtyard, two stories of apartments on either side of him for a total of eight places.

A quick glance at the apartment numbers on the side of the building told him her place occupied the worst possible spot for safety—in the back, near the carport.

As he strode toward the rear of the complex, he cocked his head at the sound of jingling keys. As he rounded the corner to her front door, his leg brushed the spiky fronds of a sago palm. After he moved past it, the frond snapped back into place.

The slight noise was enough. Kyra jerked her head to the side, her hand reaching for her gun pouch, her eyes widening at the sight of him, registering recognition and then suspicion.

Jake stopped several feet from her, planting his wing tips on the cement walkway. "Hello, Mimi."

Chapter Twelve

Kyra dropped her key chain. Despite her weak knees, she did a quick dip to retrieve it. Her brain whirred for several seconds as she gathered herself. She knew it was pointless to deny it, but years of self-preservation kicked in.

She faced him, one side of her mouth quirking into a smile. "You've got the wrong person. I'm Kyra, not Mimi."

"You're Kyra Chase now..." He squared his shoulders as if ready to do battle. "Twenty years ago, you were Marilyn Monroe Lake, a frightened eight-year-old girl who'd just lost her mother to a killer."

"So sad for Marilyn Monroe Lake." Turning her back on him, she shoved her key into the dead bolt and clicked it. What else had he discovered about her? Quinn had been right about J-Mac. She shouldn't have tried to play him.

As she thrust open the door, she felt Jake's presence over her shoulder. And now she couldn't get rid of him.

"Are you going to invite me in to discuss this? Discuss why you lied to me?" He placed his hand flat against the door, holding it wide.

"Do I have a choice?" She floated inside her apartment, dropped the keys into a basket on the low wall that separated her small dining area from the entrance hall and placed her purse next to the basket. "You can close and dead bolt the door behind you."

The door was shut, and the gentleness of it caused her more dread than if he'd slammed it. Would he kick her off the task force? She couldn't allow that to happen. She'd use every favor, every tool in her arsenal, to keep her place on the task force.

She spun around, her fists clenching at her sides. "Why are you snooping into my background? Do you do that for every task force member or just the ones you don't want to work with?"

He clasped a hand on the back of his neck, and for the first time she noticed the weariness in his handsome face, the lines on the sides of his mouth etched deep, the hazel eyes, dark and unfathomable. "Is that what you think? Have I really shown you that I don't want you on the task force? Don't want to work with you? I invited you to survey the video footage with me today. I drove you to the murder scene last night."

She blinked her eyes. And she might've just messed up. She should've listened to Quinn. When had he ever steered her wrong?

"Besides," he sighed, and sank onto her couch, grabbing a throw pillow and dragging it into his lap, "I didn't discover you were Marilyn Lake by looking in your background, although I tried. Your name and ID change are pretty thorough. There is nothing online that links you to that little girl."

"I hired the best to clean my background." She perched on the arm of the chair across from him. "Then how'd you find out and why were you digging into my past?"

"You raised my suspicions. You couldn't have worked with Quinn on any of his cases. He retired before you would've been old enough to work."

"Oh, yeah." She chewed on her bottom lip. She should've had a better story prepared, but she didn't know Jake was going to drop in on Quinn the same night she was bringing him dinner. "That was it? I told you I knew Charlotte, had been her resource for one of her books."

"That wasn't all." He tossed aside the handmade pillow she'd gotten in Guatemala with no apparent regard for the effort required to bring that pillow home. "Today, when I walked you to your car and you stumbled, I watched you from the station as you got out of your car and retrieved something from the gutter."

Kyra felt the blood drain from her face, and she pressed her fingers against her cool cheek. There really was no fooling this man. Of course, she'd planned to tell him about the second card, but she'd had no intention of telling him she'd found it beside her car and had hidden it from him.

"That's what convinced you to look into my past?"

He nodded, his face tight and wary.

For the first time in a long time she felt the burn of regret for her deception, and it wasn't just because she'd been found out. She had the feeling that Jake had endured lies from others, and now she'd become like everyone else in his life.

She didn't want to be like everyone else for him.

Sliding down the arm of the chair to settle onto the cushion, she asked, "You said you didn't find out who I was by looking into my background."

"That's right." He braced one foot against the edge of the coffee table. "I discovered your identity by looking at The Player case file."

Tilting her head, she wrapped her ponytail around her hand. "There are no pictures of me as a child in that file and no indication that I changed my name. Quinn assured me of that."

"That's true, but there is a story about a hardened detective and his wife who were so overcome with pity for a motherless girl that they sought to adopt her and keep her out of the system." He shrugged his broad shoulders.

"You made the connection between that poor, pitiable little girl and me?" She shook her head. "That's some hunch, Detective."

"It was a hunch that didn't bear out when I discovered Jennifer's daughter's name was Marilyn Lake, but then I saw this." He pulled a folded sheet of paper from his pants pocket and shook it out. "Unmistakably you."

Kyra hunched forward and snatched the paper from his hand. Her mother's eyes, so full of hope and optimism, met hers, and the scent of her mother's floral perfume overwhelmed her. Her chest tightened, and her throat closed. The paper floated from her hand as she gasped for breath.

She felt herself tumbling, tumbling through time and fear and sadness. The aching sadness gripped her belly and clawed at the carefully constructed facade that she'd been building for the past ten years since she graduated from high school and changed her name. The wound gaped open and the contents of her pathetic, tortured life began to seep out.

She clutched her midsection and moaned, toppling onto her side. As she began to slide off the couch, into the narrow space between the couch and the coffee table, strong hands pinched her shoulders.

She heard her name from far away… *Mimi, Mimi, it's me and you, Mimi. You're my little good-luck charm.*

"Kyra, Kyra. Are you all right?"

Rough, blunt fingers, not her mother's cool, delicate

ones with the coral polish on the tips, brushed her cheek. The male voice, low and urgent, pierced the fog of her consciousness.

"Kyra, lie back. I'm going to get you some water, or something stronger if I can find it."

He left her, and the haze began to clear from her brain. As Jake knocked around her kitchen, she grabbed the arm of the chair and pulled herself to an upright position.

She smoothed her hand over her hair and dashed the moisture from her cheeks.

By the time Jake made it back to the living room with a glass of water in one hand and a measure of something that looked like apple cider vinegar in the other, her breathing had returned to normal, although her heart still galloped in her chest.

He held up the glass in his right hand. "Water or some really old Scotch?"

"I'll take the water. I'm fine." When she took the glass from his hand, their fingers brushed and she wanted to drop the glass and grab on to his warm, strong hand for dear life.

She gulped back the water. "I'm really okay. It's just that I hadn't seen that photo in a long time. It brought back…memories."

He crouched at her feet and rested a hand on her bouncing knee. "Terrifying, tragic ones. I'm sorry I sprang it on you like that. It's a beautiful picture of your mother. The second I laid eyes on it I knew you were her daughter. You look so much alike, except for the eyes."

Her gaze darted to the picture on the floor. "The eyes? Really? People always used to tell us we had the exact same color of eyes. She assured me that it would be her eyes that would propel her to stardom, just like Liz Taylor's. My mother lived for old Hollywood."

"The color and the shape are almost identical. It's the expression that's different." He pinched the corner of the paper between two fingers. "Hers lack your cynicism, your distrust, your worldliness."

"Maybe if my mother had possessed a little more cynicism and a little less trust, she'd be alive today." Kyra's nose stung and she swiped the back of her hand beneath it. "You must've read about her extracurricular activities. She took the idea of the casting couch a little too far."

"I saw that." Jake squeezed her knee and backed up to the sofa in a crouch. "Was your mother from LA? I noticed she was a young mother. What about your father?"

Kyra pinned her hands between her knees and lifted her shoulders. "My mother was seventeen when she had me. She never told me who my father was. Her small town in Idaho chafed, and she took off for Hollywood when she was twenty."

"Parents, family? Where were they when you were orphaned?"

"I assume they're still in Idaho. They disowned my mother and wanted nothing to do with me at her death. Her murder embarrassed them." She squeezed her knees against her hands until her knuckles dug into her flesh. She had never told anyone this much about her life, except Quinn and Charlotte, and they knew it by heart. She never had to tell them anything.

Tilting her head, she surveyed Jake through her lashes. Now she'd have to kill him.

He raised an eyebrow. "Are you all right now? You looked like you were going to pass out."

"I'm fine." She picked up the piece of paper with her mother's picture and smoothed it out on the coffee table.

Jake cleared his throat. "How come you didn't tell me your mother was one of The Player's victims?"

She raised her eyes from tracing her fingertip around her mother's face. "Nobody knows that."

"Except Quinn." He dragged a hand through his messy, dark locks. "You didn't think it was important information given the nature of this case?"

"Important to me."

"Important to the task force lead? In fact—" he stuffed her Guatemalan pillow behind his lower back "—I would've thought you'd be eager to tell me."

"Eager? Whatever for? It's my deep, dark secret." One of her deep, dark secrets.

"It would've given you cred, another reason why you belonged on the task force."

"The only reason I need for being on that task force is my experience with victims and their families." She took another quick gulp of water, half of it landing in her lap.

"You can't tell me you didn't want on this task force, Kyra. I know you pulled some strings to get assigned, especially because Castillo knows how I feel about working with therapists."

"When I heard the details of the first two killings, it hit me like a ton of bricks. I knew we had a copycat on our hands and, yeah, I wanted to be on the inside." She hardened her jaw and thrust out her chin. "You can understand that."

"I do understand it. Under the same circumstances, you wouldn't be able to drag me away from the investigation." He scratched the sexy stubble on his chin. "I just can't figure out why you didn't tell me your connection to the case. Why hide it?"

She formed a V with two fingers and pointed them at him. "That's why."

He blinked. "What?"

"That look in your eyes—pity, sorrow. The only reason discomfort isn't in the mix is because you're a cop and accustomed to dealing with victims." She drew back her shoulders. "I'm not a victim."

Jake threw up his hands. "Nobody said you were—not in the sense that you can't take care of yourself or that you feel put-upon, but The Player put you in a particular class. You're the daughter of a murder victim. That's not your shame to bear."

"Shame?" She jumped up from the chair and did a quick, agitated trip around the small living room. "I'm not ashamed of my mother or the fact that she was murdered, but I don't want that to inform my entire life."

"And yet here you are."

"Excuse me?"

"Here you are—a therapist, specializing in victims' rights, cops, working on task forces. You're going to tell me your past didn't inform those choices?"

"It did. Of course it did." She jabbed a finger into her chest. "I'm good at what I do. I'm good at what I do because I can empathize like nobody's business. When I tell the daughter of a murder victim that I know how she feels, I ain't lying. When I express sympathy for the loss of someone's daughter, like the Lindquists yesterday, they can hear the truth in my voice, feel it in my touch."

"I agree with everything you say. I've seen you in action." He'd twisted in his seat to follow her progress across the room. One arm lay across the back of the couch, his sleeve rolled up to reveal the tail end of that tattoo. "I'm a cop because my old man was a cop. I have anger management issues because my old man had anger management issues. I have a… We're products of our upbringing and our backgrounds, and having a mother who was the victim of one of the most notorious serial killers in LA is a helluva legacy to carry around."

"Okay, what do you want me to do?" She tapped her chest twice with the palms of her hands and then spread her arms wide. "Shout it from the rooftops? My mother was Jennifer Lake, the third victim of The Player?"

Jake stood up and circled to the back of the couch. Folding his arms, he leaned against it. "You don't have to shout it out to anyone. You should've told me, and I think it would be of interest to the rest of the task force."

Kyra's mouth dropped open and prickles of fear raced across her skin. "I—I couldn't do that. Don't you do that. Don't you dare do that. Don't you dare tell anyone who I am."

Jake straightened up, his muscles coiled, nostrils flaring. "I wouldn't do that, but why? Why in God's name is it so important for you to keep your identity a secret from everyone?"

Kyra glanced over her shoulder at the sliding glass door that led to her little patio and whispered, "Because The Player is still out there…and he knows who I am."

Chapter Thirteen

Jake lunged forward, stopping inches away from Kyra, close enough to see the whiteness around her lips and the corner of her eye twitching. The cool, collected woman who seemed to float just above everyone else was rattled.

He clenched and unclenched his hands. "What does that mean, he knows who you are?"

"He knows his third victim left an eight-year-old daughter behind." She tossed her head, flicking back her thick ponytail. She took a deep breath and swallowed. "And we know he's still out there. He was never caught."

Jake knew backpedaling when he saw and heard it, and Kyra was pumping furiously. "Has The Player ever reached out to you?"

"N-no." She ran her hands over her face. "At least, not that I know of."

"You mean the playing card left by the dumpster out back?"

"That and…" She swept past him, grabbed her purse from the divider where she'd dropped it and plunged her hand inside. "And this one."

She held up a red playing card, and he moved in to get a better look.

He snatched the queen of diamonds from her fingers

and waved it in the air. "Is this what you found by your car today?"

"Yes." She retreated to the kitchen and hung on to the handle of the fridge. "Do you want something to drink? Beer? Water? Juice? Soda?"

The sheet of ice was coming down again, only this time he'd seen the cracks and knew where they were located.

He ignored her offer. "Why would you hide this from me, especially after the first one? There's no coincidence now, is there? Someone left these for you. Do you think it's The Player?"

"I was going to tell you about the second card." She poured herself a glass of orange juice and raised the carton. "Are you sure you don't want some? I don't have AC in this apartment and it's still warm from the Santa Anas, and you look...hot under the collar."

He ground his back teeth together and flicked the corner of the card. "You were going to tell me about the second card but not your connection to The Player."

"That's right." She leveled a gaze at him over the rim of her glass as she took a sip. "But you know that now, too."

He dropped back onto the couch, placing the card on the rough-hewn wood coffee table as if for a game of solitaire. He may as well have been playing solitaire for all the help Kyra was giving him.

"Do you think The Player left these as some kind of reminder or warning?"

"As if I need a reminder." She swirled the orange liquid in her glass. "As a warning? I thought you were convinced that The Player was not responsible for the killing spree we're witnessing now."

He tapped his finger on the card. "I was sure we had

a copycat, but how would a copycat killer know about you? Especially with an identity change, how would some random person find you? In fact, how would The Player know you for Jennifer Lake's daughter?"

"There are a few people out there who know my identity. Quinn suggested it might be one of them."

"You told Quinn about this already?" He supposed he should feel happy that she was confiding in someone. He was sure Quinn was not advising her to keep this from the lead detective on the task force.

She set down her glass and faced him. "I tell Quinn everything."

"Quinn suggested someone other than The Player and The Copycat might be responsible for leaving the cards?"

"Matt Dugan."

"Who's Matt Dugan?"

"When my mom was murdered, I got shunted into the foster care system." Her whole body twitched. "A few of the families took in multiple foster kids for the money. Matt Dugan was one of those kids with a family the same time I was there."

"So, sort of like a foster brother."

Her full lips twisted into a bitter smile. "You could call him that. Like many kids in the system, Matt had issues. He liked starting fires, he liked hurting people and he liked me."

"Did he hurt you?" Talk about hot under the collar. A flash of heat claimed his chest and clawed its way up his throat. How could a system be so broken that it would put a vulnerable girl like Marilyn Lake in a home with disturbed youth?

"A few times before I caught onto him. Then I put him in his place." Her blue eyes flashed with a look he was sure never emanated from her mother's eyes.

Maybe Marilyn Lake hadn't been so vulnerable after all. "This Matt Dugan knows who you are?"

"He kept track of me. He stalked me and found out about my identity change. I suppose I should've made a clean break and moved to another state, but despite everything I never wanted to leave LA."

"Knowing about the current murders and how you might be feeling, is this something Matt would do?"

"Oh, yeah. He's one sick individual. Been in and out of the joint for everything from arson to robbery to domestic violence." She formed her fingers into a gun and pointed at him. "I keep track of him, too."

"Then maybe I need to pay Matt a visit."

"No!" She slammed her glass on the kitchen table. "That's not a good idea. I learned long ago, the best way to handle a stalker is to not handle him at all. He's looking for a reaction—any reaction. That's what fuels him. I never contact him. I don't acknowledge that I'm aware of his existence."

"Okay, okay." He peeled the card from the table. "I'm going to take this with me. I'm assuming there aren't going to be any prints, just like the other card, but you never know."

She strolled toward him from the kitchen and sat on the edge of the coffee table facing him, her nose almost touching his, her long lashes almost brushing his cheek. "Do I have your word you won't tell anyone on the task force who I am, not even Billy Crouch?"

"I won't tell anyone, but you have to promise to keep me in the loop. For God's sake, these cards could've been real clues to stopping this guy. That's what you want, isn't it? To stop this guy?"

"More than anything." She drew back from him and placed a hand over her heart. "I'll let you know if anything else pops up, and just so you know, Quinn never approved of my deception toward you."

"I didn't figure he did. He's not that kind of cop." Jake pushed up from the couch and picked up her water glass and untouched Scotch from the table. He separated himself from her by walking into the kitchen. If she got any closer to him, he'd promise her anything.

He placed the glasses in the sink. "Why didn't the court allow Quinn and Charlotte to adopt you? Why thrust you into the system when they had a couple who wanted you?"

She crossed one leg over the other and clasped her hands around her knee. "Because Quinn was an alcoholic."

Jake turned from the sink and gripped the edge of the counter behind him. "How would they even know that? I mean, a lot of cops are alcoholics. My dad was one of them."

She lifted and dropped her shoulders. "He told them. Quinn is honest…to a fault. He stopped drinking, went to AA, tried to do everything to convince them he and Charlotte would've been good parents. And they would've been. I can't tell you the number of times I ran to them when a foster care situation wasn't working out for me, which happened a lot."

"That's sad. Does he blame himself?"

"Of course he does. Most of all, he blames himself for not catching The Player." She held up the queen of diamonds. "You're taking this, right?"

Was that her way of kicking him out of her place?

"I am." He retrieved her empty juice glass from the kitchen table and added it to the others in the sink, just to buy more time with her. He'd discovered her secret and confronted her with it, and now she wanted him gone.

He'd discovered more than her secret. He'd discovered layers to this woman that he'd never imagined.

She approached him and tucked the card in his shirt pocket, and then patted it. "There you go. I need to get some sleep."

"You're not afraid here by yourself? You said it. The Player is still out there."

"I know that." She reached past him for her purse on the table, unzipped the gun pouch and pulled out her weapon. "That's why I sleep with this by my side every night."

The gleam of the shiny metal piece in her hand matched the gleam in her eye, and something told him she'd rather sleep with that gun right now than any man—especially him.

KYRA SHOVED A box of tissues toward Desiree, who'd shared her story for the first time in the rape survivors support group. Kyra didn't have to say much. The other women and one man in the group had crowded around Desiree at the end of the meeting cooing words of encouragement and petting her.

The petite redhead blossomed under the attention.

Kyra raised her voice above the chatter. "I think we were all so excited to hear Desiree speak, we forgot something."

Tracy, the mother hen of the group, an upper-middle-class homemaker who'd been brutally assaulted and raped by the pool boy, flapped her arms. "Back in the circle, everyone."

People returned to the front of their chairs and joined hands. Tracy started the recitation and they all joined in. "We are not victims. We are survivors. We are not our pain. We rise above it."

Annika, the call girl who'd been beaten and raped by a john, raised her hands and said, "Amen, sistah."

Kyra repeated the amen in her own head. "See you all next week."

Kyra waited while everyone stacked their chairs in the corner. She and Candace held group sessions in the roomier outer office, locking the front door during those sessions. The groups ran themselves, and Kyra had never been more thankful for that than today with Jake's voice mail burning a hole in her phone.

After the last client left the office, Kyra pulled her phone out of the pocket of her sweater. She hesitated before tapping Play for the voice mail. If he was coming at her with more questions, she didn't want to listen. Last night she'd revealed way more than she'd ever intended.

She hit Play and Speaker, and held her breath as Jake's low voice rumbled over her phone. "Hello, Kyra. It's Jake. If you have time today, I'd like you to come with me to Melrose and meet Rachel. I'm heading over to do some follow-up on the video we watched yesterday. I just talked to Rachel, and she's having a hard time with the fact that a killer stole her phone to call in a dead body. I think the shock hit her last night. Let me know."

Kyra released her breath in a long stream. Work, not personal. And she could understand Rachel's uneasiness.

She returned Jake's call, and he answered from his car. "I wasn't sure you were available, so I'm on my way out there now."

"I was leading a group session. I'm heading out the door and can meet you at Rachel's work. Can you give me the address?"

He rattled off the address on Melrose Avenue in West Hollywood, all business now, the pity and even the anger stripped from his voice.

In a sick way, her status as the daughter of one of The Player's victims had given her bona fides in Jake's eyes to belong to the task force. She could've revealed it before to take a seat at the table, but she'd never used her mother's death to further her agenda and didn't intend to start now.

For all the freeways in LA, there was no easy access to West Hollywood from Santa Monica, and she sat in her car on Santa Monica Boulevard anxiously tapping her steering wheel in time to the music on the radio.

Forty-five minutes later, she rolled onto Melrose. Even on weekdays, the crowds surged onto this street, tourists and locals shopping, eating, gawking.

Hunting? Did this area have significance for the killer? Her gaze darted around the street, looking for a parking place—or a killer.

She spotted the store where Rachel worked and, a block down, zeroed in on a car pulling away from the curb across the street. She managed an illegal U-turn in the middle of the street and tucked into the space, careful not to bump the fenders of the high-end cars on either side.

She slid from the car and tugged her skirt down to her knees. She swiped her debit card into the parking meter and added time. The Santa Ana winds had dissipated, and with them the wildfire threat and the dry, suffocating heat, but the sun still beat down on the pavement, sending shimmering waves into the air that seemed to pulse with the traffic.

She strode to the corner to catch the signal because even if the LA County Sheriff's Department hadn't caught her making that U-turn, it didn't mean they wouldn't come down on her for jaywalking.

She joined the hustle and bustle of people as the signal changed and the little green man flashed. When she reached the other side, she noticed Jake's unmarked sedan parked in the red. Didn't the guy ever pay for parking?

She charged toward the store with the blue-and-gold awning and stepped inside. The man at the counter, helping another customer, sang out, "Be right with you."

No sign of Jake, but the low murmurs from the back of the store, behind the shivering beaded curtain, gave him away. She waved to get the clerk's attention, but when he didn't look her way she crept toward the rear and parted the strands of beads with two fingers.

Jake glanced up, a look of relief spreading across his face, as he sat across from a sobbing young woman with tats marching up one arm. Being a cop, he'd surely dealt with upset and traumatized people—it didn't mean he had to like it. The situation with Rachel probably confused him even more, as she'd been a rational human being yesterday. That was yesterday.

"Kyra's here." He gave up his seat and hovered by the chair that looked like it belonged in a dentist's office…or a torture chamber. "I told you she was coming. You can tell her everything you told me…and more."

Kyra took Rachel's trembling hand in both of hers. "Hi, Rachel. I'm Kyra. I just want to tell you, first off, how impressed I was by the help you gave the detectives yesterday. You kept your head, and you gave them valuable information."

Raising her tear-streaked face, black rivulets from her eyeliner trailing down her cheeks, Rachel's voice cracked when she said, "I—I don't know what happened. I felt okay yesterday, a little creeped out but more mad than anything else. Then today when I came into work, it hit me. Some serial killer stole my phone. He saw my contacts, he knows my number, maybe he still has it."

Jake said, "If he does have it, he turned it off. More likely, he won't want to be caught with your phone in his possession so he tossed it."

"If it makes you feel any better, what you're experiencing is totally normal." Kyra patted Rachel's shoulder. "You were mad yesterday, maybe a little shocked. Today you've had time to digest what happened, and it *is* scary. But this guy stole your phone to use it, not to target or terrorize you. He's not interested in that and may not even know or remember who you are."

"You think so?" Rachel hiccupped.

"I do, but all that logic doesn't mean you still can't feel rattled." Kyra glanced around the back room, which obviously functioned as the piercing area. "Do you have a few minutes to talk right now, or do you have to go back to work?"

"I can talk for a few. Gustavo has me covered."

Kyra flicked her fingers at Jake. "Detective McAllister has some canvassing to do in this area."

"Yeah, that's right." Jake coughed and smacked his hand against the back of the chair. "I'm going to be retracing Rachel's steps from the other day if you want to catch up."

"I'll find you." Kyra scooted her chair closer to Rachel, their knees almost touching.

"Detective McAllister?" Rachel dabbed her face with the tissue Kyra handed to her. "Is this going to affect your recommendation for me as a dispatcher?"

"This?" Jake's eyebrows jumped to his hairline. "You mean your reaction to having a close encounter with a serial killer?"

Rachel nodded, shredding the tissue between her black-tipped fingernails.

"Absolutely not. We do like humans working in Dispatch." He winked and plunged through the beaded curtain, leaving it clacking and swaying behind him.

Rachel sat up straight and squared her shoulders. "I like Detective McAllister."

"So do I." Kyra plucked another tissue from the package in her purse and waved it at Rachel. "Now, tell me what you're feeling."

About fifteen minutes later, at the end of their mini-session, Rachel's cheeks were dry and she even managed a laugh. The haunted look in her eyes had disappeared, and a fiery light had replaced it. She'd definitely swung back to anger, and Kyra got a glimpse of the young woman who had so impressed Jake yesterday.

Kyra held out one of her cards between her fingers. "Call me anytime you like. My office is in Santa Monica, but I can meet you anywhere."

"Thank you." Rachel plucked the card from her fingers and dropped it in the front pocket of her polka-dot blouse, tied at the waist. She tugged on her earlobe. "If you want another piercing for your ears, it's on the house."

"Thanks, Rachel." Kyra rose to her feet and smoothed her hands over her skirt. "I'm going to catch up with Detective McAllister. You let him know if you remember anything else, and you let me know if you're starting to feel panicked again."

"The sooner they catch this guy, the better." Rachel rubbed her arms. "Have the police identified that body from the Malibu fire?"

"Not yet."

"So, she's not like the other two, nobody reporting her missing. Nobody noticing her absence." Rachel launched from her seat and swept aside the curtain. "That's sad."

"Not yet. I'm sure law enforcement will get a hit soon."

"You know," Rachel said, aiming her gaze at the window across the store, "there are call girls on this block. They aren't as obvious as the ones on Hollywood Boulevard or Sunset, but they work it here. Maybe she was someone like that."

"Detective McAllister was right. You do have good instincts. I'm sure the task force is looking into all of that." She held out her hand. "You take care and don't hesitate to call me."

Rachel gripped her hand in a professional manner and dipped her chin. "I won't."

Kyra navigated her way through the cluttered store, stepped onto the sidewalk and looked both ways. What were they missing? Kelsey had gotten her nose pierced in this very store, and Rachel's phone had been stolen on this block. What was Marissa's connection to this area?

On her way to Uncommon Grounds, Kyra poked her head in at the pita place, looking for Jake's tall frame. He'd stand out, for his height and also the suit he wore on a warm, sunny Southern California afternoon.

Jake didn't dress to the nines like his partner did, but he had his own style that emphasized a casual masculinity. He didn't try too hard, but his clothes were well made and fit his muscular build to a T.

She puffed out a breath and made a beeline to the coffee place. When had she found the time to make such a detailed study of J-Mac and his sartorial splendor? Was it when he was waving her off crime scenes? Trying to get her kicked off task forces? Or when he was confronting her with truths about her past he'd ferreted out with snooping?

She barged through the front door of the coffee shop and nearly bowled over a woman carrying an Uncommon Grounds cardboard tray with four frothy drinks inserted in it.

"Sorry." Kyra held the door wide for the woman, who scowled at her anyway.

She spied Jake talking to an employee who looked like the manager. Jake was pointing to the corners of the store, probably trying to find more footage.

She waved, and he nodded. Then he shook the manager's hand and loped toward her.

"How's Rachel doing?"

"She's fine. I think the shock from yesterday wore off, and the reality came at her like a freight train today." She tilted her head. "You did a good job reassuring her that the killer didn't have her in his sights. Do you believe that?"

"I do. Taking her phone was a crime of opportunity, which happened somewhere around here." He did a slow pivot to survey the four corners of the room.

Kyra jerked her thumb at the ceiling. "No more cameras with a better view of the store?"

"No. They're mostly geared to the counter to catch any funny business at the register or a robbery." He tipped his chin. "She did point out some regulars, and I wouldn't mind having a chat with a couple of the men who hang out here."

Her gaze tripped from one table to another, hosting mostly single people with their laptops stationed in front of them, stacks of papers, note cards, books and the occasional cup of coffee littering the tables. "What are all these people working on here?"

"My guess." Jake spread his hands. "Scripts, treatments, whatever you call them. This is LA, after all."

She nudged him. "C'mon, don't you think you have one good script in you from your experiences?"

His hazel eyes widened for a split second. "You really don't know, do you?"

"Know what?"

"I'll tell you over coffee." He leveled a finger at the counter. "Let's get a couple of those fancy drinks and sit outside to survey the scene for a while."

"You're on, but it's my treat this time. You got the pho yesterday."

"Was that just yesterday? Seems like a lifetime ago."

"Yeah, my lifetime." She put a hand on his arm as he fell in step with her. "I'll get the drinks. You nab a table."

"I'd rather get a first-hand look at what Rachel saw."

"Good point." They fell in line behind an older couple with matching gray braids down their backs.

Jake tipped his head to hers, his lips close to her ear. "Wanna bet they smoke weed and say things like namaste?"

She flattened her lips to contain the bubble of laughter that threatened to explode. "You shouldn't stereotype."

"Hell, that's part of the job. Isn't that part of your job? Don't you make assumptions about people when you first meet them?"

"Sure, I do, but a lot of times the therapy proves them to be false, and then I'm humbled. Aren't you ever humbled, Detective McAllister?"

"Often." He stepped to the counter and hunched forward to peer at the menu board on the wall.

"What can I get for you today?" The young man behind the counter smiled, which made his cheeks bunch up like apples.

He looked like a fish out of water among the other baristas and even some of the customers, with their piercings and tattoos and alternative hairstyles.

"Ma'am?"

Those apple cheeks flushed an appropriate red, and

Kyra realized she was staring. "I'm sorry, yeah, I'll have a peach iced tea."

"And I'll have an ice coffee, plain. I'll add my own poison."

As the barista rang up the order, Kyra said, "You look like an escapee from another store."

"Ma'am?" A furrow formed between... Jordy's eyes.

"I just mean, you look too—" she leaned in and whispered "—clean-cut for this store."

He laughed. "It's not my regular store. I also work at one of our stores in Studio City."

"Not an aspiring actor, are you?"

"No, ma'am." He handed her a receipt. "Have a nice day."

They shuffled to the side to wait for their order, and Jake poked her in the ribs. "You just did it."

"Did what?"

"You stereotyped Jordy, the barista, because he didn't have tats or piercings. You didn't think he fit in with the West Hollywood crowd."

"And I was right."

"And I'm probably right about the braids."

"I wish spotting a killer was that easy." She sighed.

"Me, too." Jake rested an arm on the counter that lined up against the window with tall stools pulled up to it and USB ports in a row. "Rachel could've waited for her coffee here. She could've even plugged in her phone here to charge while she waited."

"And left it here." Kyra traced one of the ports with the tip of her finger. "Could've happened that way. She picked up her drink and forgot the phone."

"The killer saw it unattended and took his chance."

"This is a busy store." She nodded toward the door.

"One of the street cameras showed just how many people walked in and out of here."

"Could've been any one of them."

A barista called out from the pickup counter. "Order for Kyra."

Jake shouldered his way through the clutch of people waiting for their drinks and grabbed theirs. He handed her the tea and then followed her to the sugar station.

Jake dumped a couple of packets of sugar into his drink, while she opted for the fake stuff.

They wended their way to a table outside, drinks in hand, and sat across from each other in the shade of a Ficus tree, its roots buckling the sidewalk.

Kyra popped the lid off her tea and dumped in the sweetener. She swirled her straw in the amber liquid until all the white crystals disappeared and took one long sip before replacing the lid. "So, what don't I know about you, except just about everything?"

He shook his plastic cup, knocking the ice together. "You don't know that I already wrote a screenplay."

"What? No, you didn't."

"Do you remember the movie on Netflix called *Shots Fired*, starring Tito Valenti?"

"That wrestler?"

"The same. Did you see the movie?"

"I think I missed that one." She sipped her tea and raised her eyebrows. "That was you?"

"I wrote that screenplay and a second one called *Two Shots Fired*." He shrugged. "That one never got made, but they optioned it."

"I'm impressed. Did they pay you well?"

"Well enough to buy a house in the Hollywood Hills, not too far from here, actually."

"Super impressed." Why hadn't she heard that about

him? Probably because she'd never asked. People knew she'd been working with Lizbeth at the time Lizbeth had double-crossed Jake and he'd gone after her in a rage. They probably figured she wouldn't want to hear anything about McAllister—nothing good, anyway. And she hadn't.

She toyed with her straw. "I will be waiting with bated breath for *Two Shots Fired*."

He coughed and wiped his eyes. "Don't wait too long. Tito could be a grandpa by then, all his muscles shriveled and sagging."

Her mouth quirked up on one side, her snappy comeback stalled on her lips as she took in the sight of an attractive young woman on her phone at another table. The woman looked up as a man on his phone approached, but she kept talking, smiling and laughing. When the man reached the table, she ended the call, as did he. They'd obviously been talking to each other.

He leaned forward, kissed her on the cheek and took the chair next to hers, not across, but next to.

"Hey, you." Jake tapped her plastic cup with his finger. "What's so fascinating over there when you have the screenwriter for *Shots Fired* sitting in front of you?"

"I was watching that couple at the table right next to the sidewalk." As Jake shifted his head, she said, "Don't be obvious."

"I'm a detective." He moved his chair, scraping it on the concrete. "Yeah? What about them?"

"Rachel told me that call girls work this block."

"They do."

"We, Rachel and I, were wondering about the woman found at the Malibu fire. You haven't ID'd her yet, right? No missing persons reports match her description?"

"I wouldn't say that. This is LA. It's a vast area and

a lot of people go missing here—some on purpose, just like Marilyn Lake."

Her head snapped back. "Don't say that name in public."

"Sorry." He drew a line across his mouth with his fingertip. "We did consider the idea that the third victim—or she would've been the first victim—was a sex worker, but I don't think he's targeting prostitutes. If he swept her up in his net, it wasn't because he picked her up for business."

"No, but it could've been because she'd been frequenting this area. We already have one of the women tied to Melrose Avenue and the killer himself because of Rachel's phone."

"We'll ID her. Billy will." He took a sip of coffee. "I had the queen of diamonds fingerprinted and—just like her sister, the queen of hearts—it's clean. I also looked at the footage of the street in front of the station, taken yesterday when your car was parked there. A big, fat nothing again. If you had been in the lot, we would've gotten a look at the person who dropped that card next to your car. Couldn't catch anything on the street."

"I can guarantee you, if I'd parked my car in the lot there wouldn't have been any card. Give the guy some credit."

"You're probably right." Jake caught a bead of moisture running down the outside of his cup and smeared it away. He picked up the cup and studied the blue logo on the side. "Uncommon Grounds. I've seen a lot of these popping up."

"I think it started in Portland. There are already a few in Santa Monica and once they get a foothold in Santa Monica and West Hollywood, you know they're going to take off."

He brought the cup closer to his face and traced over the zigzag on the logo that looked like mountains. "I've seen this before."

"Yeah, it's right behind you." She pointed over his shoulder at the same logo painted on the window of the store they'd just left.

"No, I mean I've seen this before." He grabbed the satchel at his feet and hauled it onto the table.

He unzipped it and dragged out a stack of files.

Kyra's heart skipped a beat. "You're not going to look at crime scene photos in the middle of a sidewalk patio, are you?"

"Not quite crime scene, but crime related." He glanced up. "Don't worry, nothing gruesome."

Her leg jiggled up and down, rocking the table. "What is it?"

"The car." He abandoned one file for another. "Pictures of the inside of Marissa's car."

Kyra hopped from her chair to the one next to Jake's and hovered over the open file on the table.

He flipped through the photos quickly until he stopped at one of a red compact. "This is Marissa's car. Just like with Kelsey's car, we found her phone and purse inside. Also, like Kelsey's car, there was no video of what occurred there when she was forced to abandon it."

He thumbed through the next few photos and snatched one from the pile. He stabbed his finger at the picture, and Kyra leaned in closer for a better view.

She jerked up her head. "It's a coffee cup—a coffee cup from Uncommon Grounds."

"You know how we were just discussing connections to this area?" His lids fell over his hazel eyes half-mast, and he seemed to be studying every face coming and going on the sidewalk from beneath them. "Looks like we might be right in the middle of his hunting ground."

Chapter Fourteen

Kyra craned her neck around to look at the coffee place behind them. "You think Marissa got her coffee at this Uncommon Grounds?"

"I know it could've been any of the other stores, but it's interesting, isn't it? Kelsey gets her nose pierced on this street. Rachel has her phone lifted on this street, most likely from Uncommon Grounds, and now Marissa is tied to this same area with an empty coffee cup in her car from the same place. It's a long shot, but we have to start somewhere and this seems like a good place to do that."

"I agree. What next?"

"As long as I'm here and as long as I have Marissa's picture with me, I'm going to ask that manager if she remembers Marissa. They must have their regulars."

"Should I go with you?"

"I'll go in alone." He rapped his knuckles on the table. "Save our spot."

Kyra's face fell just a little. As invaluable as she was to have on this task force, he already had a partner and he still didn't trust Kyra completely.

Jake returned to Uncommon Grounds with Marissa's picture in his pocket. When the manager saw him enter, he waved her over to the corner of the food display.

She stuffed a strand of brown hair beneath her cap. "Something else I can help you with, Detective?"

"You said you had regulars here." He whipped out the picture of Marissa. "Was she one of them?"

The manager gave the picture a hard look. "I don't think so. Pretty girl. Can I keep it?"

"The picture?"

"I want to show the staff. They'd know the regulars more than I would."

"Sure, you can keep it. You have my card. Let me know if anyone recognizes her."

Jake returned to the table outside and dropped into the uncomfortable metal chair. "That was a big nothing. She didn't recognize her, but I let her keep the picture and she's going to show the staff."

"Something might come of it." Kyra checked her phone. "I have an appointment. I'm also going to be talking to Marissa's friends later in a group chat. If anything comes up from that, I'll let you know. I'll definitely ask them about any connections Marissa had to this area."

"Thanks for your help with Rachel, and thanks for the coffee."

"I think you're right about her. She has good instincts and a calm demeanor. She'd work out great on Dispatch."

"I usually am right about people…most people." He stuffed the files back into his bag, wondering how many of them Kyra had gone through while he was inside. "Do you want me to walk you back to your car—in case you find any more cards?"

"I'm parked across the street, and with the number of cameras on this street I doubt I'll find any cards by my car." She stood up and tugged at her slim skirt, which hit just above the knees of her long legs. "I'll be sure to let you know if I do."

"Sure you will." He hitched the satchel over his shoulder and gave her a little salute. "Until next time."

She put on her sunglasses and nodded. Picking up his cup, she asked, "Done? There's a trash can on my way."

"Go for it." He watched her walk away, the sun glinting in the ponytail swaying against her back, which matched the gentle sway of her hips in the pencil skirt.

If Jennifer Lake possessed half the grace of her daughter, it's not surprising she thought she could make it in Hollywood.

Jake turned and strode back to his car on the other side of the street from Kyra's, keeping an eye on her as she walked. He stopped when she reached her car.

She disappeared for a second on the passenger side of the car and then popped up, waving her empty hands.

Grinning, he gave her a thumbs-up and proceeded to his own car. At least she knew he didn't trust her.

That sort of eased his conscience over what he planned to do next.

A FEW HOURS LATER, Jake logged off his laptop and snapped the lid. Matt Dugan had made it easy for Jake to find him because he was a dirtbag with a record a mile long—and he still lived in LA.

Billy swept into the task force headquarters, tossed a balled-up bag into the trash and called out, "Baller."

Jake snapped his fingers in the air. "Hey, baller, any luck tracking down which Uncommon Grounds Marissa's coffee cup came from?"

Billy pulled up a chair and collapsed in it, stretching his legs in front of him. "They don't track those serial numbers like that. Cups and other inventory travel between the stores so even if that cup was delivered to one store, there's nothing that says it stopped there and didn't travel to another store in the area."

"Gotcha." Jake rubbed his eyes. "Still no ID on the Malibu fire victim."

"Nope, and the alibi checked out for Kelsey's boy-friend, not that he was ever a prime candidate." Billy drew in his legs to make room for Jake. "You heading out?"

"Checking on a few leads."

"Mind if I sit these out?" Billy massaged the back of his neck. "I've got a headache coming on."

"Didn't expect you to join me." Jake swung his bag at his desk drawer. "I've got some ibuprofen in there if you need it."

"I've got my own stash. Hey, you're not going to see our task force therapist, are you?"

"No, I told you I saw her earlier when Rachel Black-burn needed some help."

"And did you happen to ask her about her friend, the TV reporter, for me?"

"What are you, in middle school? If you want to ask her out, do it. Do you need her friend to send her a note letting her know you like her?"

"A little introduction to smooth the way never hurt. You need to venture away from your blow-up doll now and then to see how it works in the real world."

A few cops laughed as Jake threw a pen at Billy. He didn't have a blow-up doll, but it had been a while since he'd had a real date. He'd dipped a toe in the online dat-ing scene but had heard too many stories about scams and misrepresentations to be comfortable in that world.

Besides, who wanted to date a guy with trust issues?

Armed with information from Matt Dugan's parole officer about his last known residence, Jake got behind the wheel of his Crown Vic and plugged the address into his GPS.

He knew the area, the shady side of Van Nuys.

The only problem with a sneak attack was that Dugan might not be home, but Jake didn't want to give him a chance to concoct some story—or to contact Kyra.

Once off the freeway, Jake tooled down Van Nuys Boulevard, past the car dealerships, the free clinics, the methadone treatment centers, the churches and the working girls getting a jump on the competition. His GPS directed him to turn left at the next light.

After his turn, he slowed to crawl along the block, stucco apartment buildings in various hues standing rainbow sentry on either side of the street. He spotted Dugan's place, a grimy yellow building going for a Spanish hacienda look that fell short with its chipped stucco, missing red roof tiles and battered arched entry leading to a messy courtyard containing a broken-down barbecue, a few dead potted plants and a unicycle.

He parked and exited the vehicle, staring hard at a clutch of men lounging on the steps of the apartment building next to Dugan's. He grabbed his jacket from the back seat of the car and put it on slowly to give the vatos sizing him up a look at the weapon in his shoulder holster.

As he made his way to the yellow building, the guys meandered away in different directions. Probably parolees holding drugs or weapons or warrants. As he passed beneath the yellow arch, a baby wailed from one of the apartments and a man let loose with a sneeze from another. You'd be hard-pressed to keep anything a secret from your neighbors here.

A quick glance at the dull metal numbers affixed to the right of each front door led Jake upstairs to number twelve. He knocked and stood slightly to the side of the door but in clear view of the peephole. Shuffling sounds came from the other side of the paper-thin door, and Jake's muscles tensed.

"Who is it?" A male voice, ragged from cigarettes and booze, boomed through the open window with the sagging screen to the left of the door.

"You're in luck, Dugan. It's not your parole officer. LAPD Homicide, open the door." Jake banged his fist against it for good measure.

The door swung open, and a big man with a shaved head and a goatee loomed in the space. "Homicide? You bastards haven't framed me for that one, yet."

"The day is young, Dugan. Let me in." Jake didn't wait for the invite and pushed past him, stepping into a cluttered space with the skunky scent of weed hanging over it. He sniffed the air.

"It's legal in homes." Dugan waved at the bong on the coffee table. "And medicinal."

"I don't care about that. Did I say I was Vice?" Jake squinted at the deck of playing cards on the battered coffee table. He *did* care about that.

"Then what do you want, Mr. Homicide?" Dugan folded his pumped-up arms over his chest, and a vein stood out on his neck beneath the tattoo of letters curling into an AB, which proclaimed Dugan a member of the Aryan Brotherhood.

This was the guy stalking Kyra? No wonder she carried a gun.

"Do you know Kyra Chase?"

A smile that didn't have anything do to with happiness spread across Dugan's face, and a knot formed in Jake's gut.

"Why? Is she dead…like her momma?"

A muscle ticked in Jake's jaw, but he matched Dugan

smile for smile. "C'mon, Dugan. You'd know that wasn't true because I hear you keep close tabs on her."

"She wishes, my man. You know them bitches." Dugan stroked his goatee. "They don't never forget their first."

A white-hot rage zipped through Jake's veins. If Dugan had been Kyra's first, it had been by force.

"You obviously know who she is." Jake widened his stance and dug the heels of his shoes into the stained carpet. "Have you been by her place? Her car?"

"Nope. Did she send you here?" Dugan ran his nails along his arm like a junkie looking for a fix. Weed didn't do that.

"No. She doesn't know I'm here." Jake wandered over to the table and swept up the cards.

"Hey, I was playing that game." Dugan took a step forward, and Jake stopped him with a look.

He shuffled the cards in his hands. "You've heard about this serial killer who's copying the MO of the same killer that murdered Kyra's mother, haven't you?"

"I don't pay much attention to that stuff." Dugan's gaze tracked every flick of Jake's fingers as he plucked two cards from the deck.

He held up the two dark queens. "Looks like you haven't been playing with a full deck, Dugan."

He licked his lips. "What do you mean?"

"You're missing the queen of hearts and the queen of diamonds." Jake tossed the deck back onto the table, where it fanned out.

"So what? That's some old deck someone left here." He clenched his ham fists at his sides. "I didn't have nothing to do with no murders."

"Maybe not, but you did have something to do with terrorizing Kyra Chase." Jake rushed the big man and rammed him up against the thin wall, which quaked under their combined weight.

Jake squeezed his hand against the beefy neck, his fingers pinching into the Aryan Brotherhood tattoo. "I'm here to tell you to stop, or you're gonna wind up back in the slammer faster than you can say three strikes. You got that?"

Dugan gurgled in response and Jake took it as a yes. He released Dugan, and he slid down the wall, choking and clawing at his chest.

"And since this is a faulty deck, I'll just take it with me." He gathered the cards and put the stack in his pocket. "Learn to play solitaire on the computer."

Jake strode from the apartment, leaving the door open on Dugan's gasping sounds. The guy deserved worse for tormenting Kyra. At least the killer himself didn't have Kyra in his sights. Why would he? He wouldn't have access to the original case files on The Player and even if he did, you'd have to know what you were looking for to make the connection between Marilyn Lake and Kyra Chase.

Should he tell Kyra he'd paid a visit to Dugan and cleared things up? He yanked open his car door, shrugged out of his jacket and tossed it in the back. She probably wouldn't appreciate his efforts. Instead of the white knight, he'd come across looking like the frog.

He raced back to the station to make his own four-thirty briefing. He wanted to give everyone a heads-up on the Melrose connection between Kelsey, Rachel's phone and Marissa's cup from the coffee place in the same area.

When he walked into the task force war room, his gaze tracked to Kyra chatting with Brandon. She lifted her eyebrows at him, and he nodded her way, a sense of relief flooding his system. He'd spared her from any more random cards showing up on her doorstep. He didn't even need to take the credit for it.

He grabbed a file from his desk and signaled to Brandon to follow him to the briefing room to start the slideshow. When everyone was gathered, Jake presented the Melrose info, calling out the two sheriff's deputies from the West Hollywood division on loan to the task force to help canvass that area. Then he turned the meeting over to Billy for an overview of their efforts in identifying the Malibu fire victim.

Jake wound up the meeting by asking for any new information or clues. One of the detectives who was working closely with the medical examiner's office confirmed that both Marissa and Kelsey had small puncture wounds in their necks, which may have been how the killer had gotten the women away from their cars and into his without much of an apparent struggle. Both toxicology tests were pending. Jake assured everyone once the drug used to subdue the women was identified it would give them another avenue to check.

"This guy is not as clean as he thinks he is." He signaled Brandon to bring up the last slide, which contained pictures of the three murder victims. They had to remember the stakes here. "Anything else?"

From the back of the room, Kyra's hand shot up and uneasiness stirred in his gut, which was reason number eighty-eight why you didn't get involved with anyone from work. "Ms. Chase? You have something to add?"

Her voice, confident and composed, rang out. "I had an extensive conversation with Marissa Perez's friends this afternoon over the phone, and I wanted to bring up the issue of the jewelry and Kelsey's missing nose stud."

She commanded the attention of the room with her cool, professional demeanor, and a little flicker of pride tapped his chest, although he didn't know why or at least didn't want to look at it too closely. "Go ahead."

"Marissa's friends told me she always wore a jade bracelet. I don't know if that was found on her and the friends don't, either, as her belongings are still in evidence. I wanted to know if the jade bracelet was found with Marissa."

Jake turned to his partner. "Billy?"

"I don't remember." Billy pointed a finger at Brandon. "Can you find and bring up the photo of Marissa's possessions?"

Brandon turned off the connection from the computer to the display and began clicking through the electronic files on Marissa's case.

Brandon murmured to nobody in particular. "Got the files. Clothing, jewelry. Here."

He reactivated the display and a photo of jewelry appeared on the screen.

Jake said, "Zoom, please."

The image of the pieces got bigger and contained a pair of hoop earrings, two necklaces—one with a cross, the other with the letter *M*, and three rings.

"I don't see a bracelet. Anyone see a bracelet?" Jake glanced around the room. "So, Marissa wasn't found with a jade bracelet her friends say she wore all the time and Kelsey didn't have her nose stud, which her parents said she'd just gotten. Either those pieces were lost in the struggle, at the dump sites or our boy is taking something other than his victims' fingers for his trophy. To be sure Marissa didn't just leave it at home that day, I'll reach out to her roommate again."

Kyra coughed and Jake jerked his head up. "Anything else, Ms. Chase?"

"Uh, no." She stepped back to her place against the wall.

"Lights." Jake waved an arm in the air. "Thanks, everyone. Good work. We'll get this guy. I can feel it."

The team members who had desks in the war room shuffled back to their seats, the rest left for their own desks or left for the day.

As Jake pulled up a chair to his own desk, Kyra sauntered over and leaned her hip against the corner. "I did have something to add at the end, but I didn't want to announce it."

"Oh?" Jake's pulse ticked up a few notches. He couldn't help it. Excitement and drama seemed to swirl around this woman, and it drew him into her orbit every time.

"Marissa's roommate, Darcy, was on the call today and she invited me over to their place tomorrow—not only to look for the bracelet but to talk with her. She's still pretty upset."

"Can't Darcy just look for the bracelet herself? That's what I was going to ask her to do."

"Darcy is staying with friends right now. She can't go back to the apartment."

"Understood. Thanks for letting me know." His cell phone, sitting on the desk next to his computer, buzzed with an incoming text.

Kyra glanced down at it and then at his face. "Do you need to get that?"

"It's just a text, not a call." He drummed his fingers on the desk. "Is there anything else?"

"No." She picked up his phone and handed it to him, and then pushed away from the desk with her hip.

He looked down at the display and a text from Mike's Bike Shop. He tapped it, and he scanned the message from Matt Dugan.

I left those cards but someone paid me. if you wanna know who and u want the 411 on Mimi, I take cash

KYRA SLIPPED THE set of keys to one of the LAPD detective squad sedans into the pocket of her jacket, which she usually wore in the chilly AC of the station. She caught her breath as one of the guys from the task force swept up behind her to drop off the keys to a squad car.

He smiled and said, "You're a good addition to the task force. Glad to have you on board. Have a nice evening."

"Thanks. You, too." Her fingers curled around the keys so tightly they pinched her fingers.

She had to be ready for Jake's exit. Would he go straight to his meeting with Matt? She hoped so.

Hearing voices from the war room, she ducked into the lunchroom and flattened herself against the wall.

Jake's voice carried down the hallway. "I don't have any plans tonight. Grab some dinner on the way home."

A voice that sounded like Billy's murmured something in reply.

Jake swore. "Dude, if you want to meet Megan Wright, ask Kyra yourself or just call the TV station. When has the lack of an introduction ever fazed you before?"

Kyra pressed her fingers to her lips. Billy wanted to meet Megan? Seemed there was a lot Jake McAllister was keeping from her. A whole helluva lot.

She couldn't try to follow him on foot out to the parking lot. He'd make her in two seconds. She had to believe the noises from the other room meant he was leaving.

Lowering her head and counting the number of tiles on the floor, she scurried from the station and walked quickly to the unmarked cars in the lot. The car she wanted wasn't even locked, so she slid behind the wheel and slumped down. She had no doubt if the LAPD wanted to find out who'd taken one of their unmarked detective cars after the shift change they'd have no problem seeing her on camera, but she'd worry about that later.

She watched the comings and goings over the rim of the steering wheel until she saw Jake's unmistakable stride in the parking lot.

He opened the trunk and loaded his satchel, which contained his laptop, and a couple of boxes of files. Then he climbed into the driver's side and took off.

Kyra started the car and pulled out of the parking lot after him. He wouldn't be expecting one of the other detectives to follow him, but she stayed a few car lengths behind him.

When Jake turned onto a crowded Sunset Boulevard, her stomach knotted. He was going home—and she had his address. Had he already talked to Matt over the phone? No, she'd watched him too closely. After the initial message from Matt, he'd texted a few times and then seemed to settle in to work.

She'd known that the text on Jake's phone had come from Matt. She recognized Mike's Bike Shop as the motorcycle repair place where Matt worked. She couldn't imagine Matt reaching out to a cop. Jake must've contacted Matt first.

So, did she feel sorry about borrowing an LAPD vehicle and following Jake? Not at all. He already knew her car and would've spotted the tail.

She could call Matt and ask him what he was doing, but then she'd be in his debt. And she never, ever wanted to be in Matt Dugan's debt. Besides, she couldn't trust a word out of Matt's mouth. She couldn't trust a word out of Jake's mouth, either.

When he turned off the boulevard and started heading for the hills, she slowed the car. She couldn't follow him to his house in the Hollywood Hills with the winding, narrow roads and spaced-apart housing. He'd see her headlights behind him at every turn.

After the first mile into the hills and as other cars dropped off, Kyra pulled into a turnout that led to a small dog park. She cut her lights and buzzed down the window.

Matt would most likely meet Jake at the bike shop. That's where Matt conducted all his business, and this was business. He wouldn't have Jake at his apartment—too risky with the drugs and weapons and unsavory friends. She pulled up the GPS on her phone. She knew the exact locations of the bike shop and Matt's apartment. She believed in keeping her enemies close, or at least on her radar.

If Jake was driving to Van Nuys, and she believed he was, he'd have to wend his way down the hill again and take Sunset. He'd have to pass this way and she'd see him.

Her stomach rumbled and she regretted not eating something at the station while she waited for Jake to leave. Of course, she could have this all wrong. Maybe Matt had already said all he had to say to Jake over text messaging. Maybe they'd set up their meeting for another night.

But she knew the way Matt's mind worked. If he had info to sell Jake, he'd want to do that right away. She'd have to get to Matt before Jake did. She could convince Matt that Jake wanted to entrap him, to arrest him and send him back inside.

Each time a pair of headlights came winding down the hill, Kyra's heart jumped, until about an hour into her wait when she spotted Jake's sedan. Of course, he'd use his police car. He was technically on police business.

When the red of his taillights disappeared around the

next bend, Kyra pulled out of her hiding place and hurtled down to Sunset.

She saw Jake's car make the left turn. He had to be going to Van Nuys. She'd take the risk. If she couldn't beat Jake to his destination, there was no point in showing up at all.

When she hit the signal at Sunset, she flicked on the light inside the car and squealed around the corner. She'd been in Quinn's car enough times to know how things worked.

She floored it and blared the siren a few times to get around traffic. Jake wouldn't wonder at an unmarked car racing to a call, even if he noticed it. Other cars parted for her as she careened down Sunset, leaving Jake in her dust.

If Mike's wasn't their meeting place, she'd find out soon enough. And if it was, she'd catch Matt by surprise and convince him Jake was up to no good. What *was* Jake up to?

She cranked up her speed on the freeway, slipping into the carpool lane, the red light still revolving in the window of the car. When she got off the freeway, she continued pressing her luck on Van Nuys Boulevard. She'd passed only two patrol cars on her way, and neither one had seemed interested in her pursuit, probably because nothing had come over their radios.

She finally cut off the light and stopped bleeping the siren within about two blocks of Mike's. She'd gotten a good head start on Jake, but she'd have to act quickly.

She spotted the yellow sign with the motorcycle on it and cruised past the closed metal doors of the shop. She knew the owner had a patio in the back of the shop on the alley where bikers gathered sometimes, smoked a little weed and harassed the working girls. Matt's unofficial office. She knew a lot more about her former foster brother than she'd ever let on to him.

She wheeled the big car around the corner and parked it alongside the curb. Before she got out of the car, she hitched her purse across her body with the gun pouch facing out. She scrambled from the car, ignoring a homeless guy and a couple in the shadows, their heads together with their drug dealer.

She stepped into the alley, her nose twitching at the smell of garbage. She still had her work clothes on, and her heels clicked too loudly on the asphalt.

A yellow light spilled onto the white picket fence that marked the patio behind Mike's. As she approached, Kyra called out softly. "Matt? Matt, it's Mimi."

If she had to deal with any of the guys from the shop, she'd try to scare them off too with the promise of an LAPD cop on his way to wreck their little party.

But there was no party. She saw no heads poking above the fence, and she cursed under her breath. She'd been wrong. Jake could be meeting with Matt right now, and Matt could be telling him all kinds of things…about her.

Her ears picked up a slow moan that made the hair on the back of her neck quiver. She flattened her hand against her gun pouch. "Matt?"

When she reached the fence and peered over, she staggered back. Matt Dugan, her nemesis, lay sprawled on the patio, foam bubbling at the side of his mouth and his eyes rolled back in his head. Was he dead?

And then he moaned again.

Chapter Fifteen

Jake rolled down Van Nuys Boulevard just in time to witness the underbelly come alive as the sun sank in a hazy sky.

Dugan had set up their meeting behind his place of work, a motorcycle repair shop that had closed a few hours ago. He'd indicated he conducted all his business from a small patio in the back of the shop. Jake was sure that business could result in several arrests. But he had a different mission.

He parked in front of the business and loped around to the back. A couple veered out of his way by crossing to the other side of the street, the male partner tugging the rim of his baseball cap lower on his face. Maybe they'd just come from doing business with Dugan.

Jake followed the building around the back and spotted an area enclosed by a white picket fence—kind of homey for an alley.

As he peered over the slats, his heart slammed against his chest. The door to the patio stood ajar, sagging on one hinge, and he barreled through it toward the man sprawled on the ground, a woman hovering over him.

Then the woman turned, and Jake almost doubled over from the sock to his belly.

"Kyra, what are you doing here? What's wrong with him?"

Her blue eyes shimmered like waves in a pool. "I think it's a drug overdose. He was conscious when I got here, but he's out now. His pulse is weak. Do you have any Narcan on you?"

"If I were Vice, maybe." He crouched beside her, nudging her away from the fallen man. He placed his fingers against Dugan's neck and rolled him onto his side. "Have you called 911?"

"Not yet. I just found him."

A whisper of…something flitted across the back of his neck.

"C-can you do it? I don't want to have to explain my presence here." She pressed her hand against her heart. "I swear, he was like this when I found him. I'll explain everything to you."

Jake already had his phone out and was calling 911. Before he even started talking to the 911 operator, Kyra scrambled to her feet and fled from the patio and the dying man—her foster brother.

Jake gave his location to the 911 operator and dropped his phone on the ground. He bent his head, putting his face close to Dugan's. "Don't bail on me now, you SOB. Who hired you to plant those cards? Who was it? Give me a name."

Dugan was fading fast and probably couldn't even hear him. He kept trying anyway, grabbing on to Dugan's hand. "Can you hear me? Squeeze my hand for yes."

A breath that sounded like a death knell rattled in Dugan's chest.

"Did the killer pay you to leave the cards?"

Dugan's rough hand lay limply in his own.

Sirens filled the alley and vehicles screeched to a stop, but Jake kept hold of Dugan's hand.

He tried again. "Was it The Player?"

Dugan sputtered, and he convulsively squeezed Jake's hand.

"Drug overdose?" The EMTs swarmed onto the patio, and Jake grabbed the slats of the fence to pull himself up and out of their way.

"Looks like it." Jake flashed his badge. "He's an informant. We had a meeting, and… I found him like this."

Jake stepped over the fence while the EMTs started working on Dugan. An officer from the Van Nuys division intercepted him.

"Do you know this man's identity?"

"Matthew Dugan. He's a parolee. Works in the shop. We had a meeting. He was going to give me some info on a case I'm working—The Copycat Player."

"Oh, damn." The officer shook his head. "I hope you got your information out of him before the dope kicked in."

"I didn't, so I'm hoping like hell those guys can save him, but it doesn't look good. His pulse was weak."

"They'll do what they can." As a small crowd of people gathered in the alley, the cop took some more information from Jake.

Jake stayed until the EMTs loaded Dugan into the ambulance. They hadn't declared him dead yet, no sheet over his head, still connected to an IV.

As the doors closed on Dugan, Jake fished a card from his pocket and handed it to the officer. "Let me know if he comes back like Lazarus. I'd really like to get my info from him."

"Will do."

The clutch of looky-loos began to scatter as Jake made his way back to his car. When he got behind the wheel, he clenched it, along with his jaw. What the hell had just happened?

How had Kyra known about his meeting with Dugan? Had her former foster brother called to warn her? Maybe he threatened to blackmail her, and she came out here to pay up before Jake got there.

How had she paid him? In drugs? What was she doing over his body? Why hadn't she called 911? She must've been waiting a long time for Dugan to exit her life. If he'd been stalking her and could be paid off to terrorize her with those cards, she wouldn't shed any tears over his death. But being happy someone was out of the picture was a far cry from helping him along.

He released the steering wheel and rolled his shoulders. Then he retrieved his cell phone and called Kyra.

It rang once before her husky voice poured into his ear. "Is he alive?"

"He looked like it when they loaded him in the ambulance."

She let out a breath. "He always did have problems with drugs."

"We need to meet. I wanna know what you were doing there."

"I'm waiting for you now."

"Where?"

"In front of your house."

Great. Had he ever given her his address? The woman probably had access to a lot more information than he could dream of. "Wait there. I'm on my way."

He negotiated his way back to the freeway, which was a lot less crowded than on his journey to see Dugan. In less than forty minutes, he was turning off Sunset and snaking his way to his oasis.

He pulled into the drive that led to his house and jammed on his brakes when he saw the unmarked LAPD detective car in front of his place. When Kyra stuck one long leg out of the car, he murmured. "Son of a…"

He slammed his car door and locked it. Couldn't be too careful around her.

"Did you steal that car from the station?"

She glanced behind her as if she'd forgotten how she got here. "Borrowed. I'll return it tonight."

"They'll have you on camera."

She shrugged. "Only if someone's looking for it. Nobody will be looking for it. The detective in Juvenile brings in his own car."

"You know just enough to be dangerous." He stalked past her to his front porch. "How'd you find out where I live?"

Her eyes widened. "You told me."

"I didn't give you my address. There are a lot of homes in the Hollywood Hills."

"Billy told me."

"How'd you…?" He turned at the front door, gripping the door handle. "Never mind."

He pushed open the door and stood aside, gesturing her across the threshold with a sweep of his arm.

The gesture was wasted on her. She stood on the porch, eyes closed, nostrils flared. "It's beautiful here. Peaceful. You don't even feel like you're in the city."

It *was* peaceful. "I call it my oasis."

Her eyelids flew open, and she stepped past him into the entryway. How did she still manage to smell like roses and sunlight after a long day of work, stealing a police vehicle and finding a dying man?

He pointed to the most uncomfortable chair in the house. "Sit and start talking."

She saw through the ruse and sank onto the sofa, the

soft leather whispering beneath her weight. "Can I have something to drink first? I'm parched. Water is okay."

He dropped his bag by the front door and marched into the kitchen. He got her the water and grabbed a bottle of beer for himself, although he had a feeling he needed to be the clearheaded one here.

She took the glass from him with a thanks and downed half of it before he'd even sat down in the chair across from her.

Just like in any interrogation, he didn't want her getting too comfortable. "How did you know about my meeting with Dugan?"

"Did he call you first?" She skimmed her long, delicate fingers along the outside of the glass. "No, he'd never call a cop. You contacted him first. Why?"

He took a gulp of beer to tamp down his anger, knowing full well alcohol was no answer to fury. "That's not how this works. Answer my question."

A little smile lifted the corner of her mouth. "I saw his text on your phone at the station. I recognized the sender—Mike's Bike Shop. I know that's where Matt worked...works. I'd just mentioned Matt to you last night, so I didn't think it was some coincidence. Quinn told me there are no coincidences."

Damn Roger Quinn. Did he realize he'd created a monster?

"I did one better than just contact Dugan—I met the lowlife this afternoon."

A flare of petty pleasure burned in his belly when he saw the smile fall from her lips and her cheeks pale.

"You met with Matt today?"

"I did."

"Why?"

"I wanted to know if he was the one who planted those cards for you."

"And was he?"

"Yes."

She dropped her chin to her chest and tapped the tips of her fingers together. "I see. It doesn't surprise me. So, why the follow-up meeting?"

"When he sent me that text, he promised to tell me who paid him to leave the cards."

Her head jerked up. "Someone paid him to do it?"

"That's what he said in his text." Jake lifted one shoulder. "If he doesn't come out of his overdose, we'll never know."

"Let me guess." She swirled her water in the glass. "He was going to tell you for a price."

"Of course."

"He could've been lying to you."

"Maybe. Hopefully, I'll find out." She opened her mouth and he raised his finger. "My turn. How'd you know the time and place of our meeting? You may have seen the first line or two of that text, but you didn't read the whole thing or the follow-ups."

"That's where the theft of the car comes in." She took a dainty sip of the water as if to counter her confession. "I figured you'd spot me if I followed you in my own car, so I did the deed in a nondescript sedan, one you'd hardly notice even if you were looking for a tail...and you weren't."

He set his bottle on the table next to him harder than he meant to. The crack made her jump. *Good.* "You did not follow me all the way to my house and then to Van Nuys, reaching the bike shop before I did, all without my noticing you."

She folded her hands in her lap on top of her skirt. "I

figured you'd be meeting at Mike's because I know that's where Matt works and does his dirty deeds. I just didn't know the time, and I didn't want to sit on Van Nuys until midnight. I followed you halfway up the hill and waited in a turnout until I saw you come down the hill."

"How'd you beat me to the meeting place?" A prickle of suspicion teased his brain, and he held up his hands. "Wait, stop. I don't want to know."

"I was driving an unmarked LAPD sedan." She cocked one eyebrow. "I'm sure you can figure it out."

"Yeah, that I can figure out, although I can't believe your...nerve." He gripped the neck of his bottle. "What I can't figure out is why. Why did you need to get there before me? Why was it so important for you to talk to Dugan before I did? Or stop him talking to me."

"If Matt's lips are moving, chances are he's lying. I didn't want him to tell you a bunch of lies about me, and he would have."

"Who said he was going to talk about you? He was going to tell me who paid him to plant those cards." He watched her face closely.

Sensing his scrutiny, she raised the glass to her lips to hide the bottom portion of her face. "Matt was obsessed with me. He wouldn't miss a chance to talk about me, spread lies. You don't even know that someone paid him to leave the cards. He'd tell you anything to collect a little dough. He has a problem with drugs—in case you didn't notice."

"Why not just tell me that, then? Why go to all the trouble of stealing a car and following me?"

She widened her eyes. "Maybe if you'd told me you'd contacted him from the beginning. Why did you sneak around behind my back to find Matt?"

Jake jumped up from the chair. He didn't appreciate

being in the hot seat in his own home during what was supposed to be his own interrogation. "I did it for you."

She dropped her lashes over her eyes, closing herself off even more. "Interesting take."

"When you told me you suspected Matt of leaving the cards, I wanted to make sure he stopped. I wanted him to leave you alone."

"Sweet, but I've been handling Matt Dugan most of my life." She leaned back on the couch and wedged her feet against the coffee table. "And you thought you did a good deed because he admitted to playing tricks with the cards, which he may or may not have done."

"Oh, I'm sure he did it."

"Because of your super-awesome detective skills?"

"Because—" he yanked his suit jacket from a stool at the kitchen counter where he'd left it when he came home from work and dipped his hand in the pocket "—I found these at that dump he calls an apartment."

As he spread out the playing cards in his hands, Kyra shot up straight. "He had a deck of cards in his house? So what?"

"A deck of cards that was missing two queens. You wanna guess which ones?"

"That bastard. He *did* do it." Her eyes glittered, and Jake had to wonder who had more to fear in the ongoing skirmish between Matt and Kyra.

"He didn't even admit it to me at the time, but I knew. So, I took the cards. Then he contacted me later to let me know he'd give up the person who paid him to do it... for a price. It could lead to something in this case if he does. If he survives."

"Then I hope he does." She downed the rest of the water and sauntered to the kitchen to put the empty glass in the sink. She pointed to a framed photo on the counter. "Who's that?"

"That's my daughter, Fiona."

Kyra's lips formed an O. "She's cute. I didn't know you had a daughter. Didn't know you had a wife."

"Once upon a time before we got divorced."

Several emotions played across Kyra's face at once, ending with a furrowed brow. "Does your daughter stay with your ex?"

"She does. In Monterey. My ex remarried." He schooled the bitterness from his voice before he continued. "She married one of the partners in her law firm and he relocated up there, so she took Fiona and moved."

"You didn't have any say in it?"

"I approved of it." He tossed back the rest of the beer, but it couldn't douse the bitterness this time. "I was a lousy father, anyway."

"You mean you were a busy father." She planted her hands on the granite counter and hunched forward. "I doubt you were a lousy father any more than Quinn would've been a lousy father."

He met her eyes; the iciness had melted into pools of soothing balm. Was this the way she looked at her clients to assure them they weren't losers who needed some stranger to talk with to sort out their sorry lives?

He grunted. "Why do you care?"

"Maybe I'm just trying to apologize for causing you so much grief tonight even though it would've had the same outcome whether I'd intervened or not. You would've found Matt in the same condition I did."

He scraped the soggy blue foil label from his bottle with his fingernail.

Kyra sucked in a breath. "You're kidding me."

He glanced up from his task. "What?"

"You think I had something to do with Matt's overdose?" Did he?

"Of course not. Did I say that?"

"Sometimes you don't have to say anything at all. If you have super-awesome detective skills, I have super-awesome therapist skills."

He abandoned his project, picked up the bottle and dropped it in the recycling bin, Kyra's eyes following his every move.

"I don't think you killed Matt Dugan."

"You think I delayed calling 911."

He planted himself in front of her and squared his shoulders. "Who could blame you?" Her lashes fluttered and a rose blush stole across her cheeks. The spark hadn't hit her eyes though, so he hadn't stirred her ire. Was she flustered at his closeness?

He could reach for her right now and angle his mouth across hers, plunge his fingers in the silky strands of her hair, free it from the ponytail that kept it and her under tight control.

She blinked several times and stepped back. "I can assure you, I did not delay calling 911. When you arrived, I had just gotten there."

"Then I believe you."

She wiped her palms on her skirt. "I'd better take that car back to the station before someone misses it."

"Good idea."

"You're not going to…?"

"I'm not going to rat you out." He skirted around her to leave the kitchen. "You may not have known about my wife and child, but you do know I'm someone who doesn't always play by the rules, don't you? You'd know that about someone before joining forces with him, wouldn't you?"

"You make me sound…calculating. You know why I wanted on the task force. The fact that I had to work with you worried me until I got to know you better. You're a good cop with good instincts."

"Who doesn't always play by the rules."

She winked. "That's just a bonus."

"I'm going to call the hospital later to check on Matt. Do you want me to keep you posted?"

"Of course. I hope you get what you want out of him." She picked up her purse from the couch cushion. "Thanks for taking charge back there."

Had he taken charge? It seemed as if she'd been in control from the moment she'd seen the text on his phone.

"Be careful driving down the hill. There aren't many lights. And don't do anything stupid with that car."

"Yes, sir." She touched her fingers to her forehead. "Let me know what happens with Matt."

"I will." He moved past her to open the front door, and the air between them hung heavy with expectation. He wanted something more from her. He wanted her to tell him the whole truth. What had Matt been about to reveal about her? Why couldn't she trust him?

A little voice whispered in his ear. *Because you went behind her back to track down Matt Dugan.*

Stepping onto the porch, she lifted her hand. "You have a very cool house, by the way. *Shots Fired* really paid off."

He watched her get into the car and pull out of his driveway. While standing outside, he made a call to the hospital and a nurse told him Dugan was still in a coma. That didn't sound good.

He returned inside and picked up the picture of his daughter. He really wanted to see her right now, but he and Tess had agreed that Fiona didn't need to be here when he was working a big case, especially a task force like this one.

Had he been a good father to Fiona? Probably the best dad move he'd made was giving Tess primary custody and Fiona the chance to be raised in a two-parent home—even if that other parent had cheated with his wife. He couldn't blame Tess for that any more than he could blame Kyra for wishing Dugan would die.

Married life hadn't suited him. But fatherhood? He considered Fiona the best part of his life.

He closed up the house and got ready for bed. When he crawled between the sheets, he put on the TV. Most nights he fell asleep to the blue light that flickered across from him. He couldn't manage any other way.

As he started to drift off, the phone charging on his nightstand rang. For the first time in a long time, something other than work popped into his head when he heard the ringing. Had Kyra made it back okay?

He grabbed the phone, which displayed the number from the station.

"McAllister."

The voice ended all thoughts of Kyra and all thoughts of sleep. "You ready, J-Mac? We have another body."

Chapter Sixteen

Kyra wheeled the LAPD vehicle back into the parking lot of the station. On her way there, she'd picked up a bite to eat and had called the hospital where the ambulance had taken Matt. They wouldn't give her any information over the phone, but Jake hadn't called her yet, either.

Although Matt's death would remove one menace from her life, she didn't wish him dead. She still remembered the scared boy lashing out at anything and everyone when she'd been placed with the same foster parents.

She'd been the one person who could communicate with Matt, talk him off the ledge, but he was already too far gone, too far beyond her help when she'd met him. Matt's mother had been a heroin addict, and a long line of her boyfriends and husbands had beaten and abused Matt.

Kyra pushed through the front doors of the station and swiped the back of her hand across her nose. What kind of chance did a boy like that have in this world? She'd understood him...and he'd understood her. She hoped that Matt survived.

Nodding to the desk sergeant, she said, "I left some things here."

"Go on up. A few people are burning the midnight oil."

Her heart did a backflip. Did that mean Jake was here?

Maybe he couldn't sleep. Maybe he wanted to check up on her to make sure she returned the car. It was not like she could or even wanted to steal it.

Could she have trusted Jake enough to tell him she knew about his meeting with Matt and wanted to be there when she questioned him?

She stabbed the elevator button. Why should she trust him? He didn't trust her. He'd been divorced once and through the ringer with another therapist. It didn't take any special skills or training to understand the guy had trust issues. And so did she. A match made in hell.

Not that she was considering a match with Jake. There'd been a moment tonight when she expected a kiss from him, but she'd backed off. She had a feeling once she started kissing Jake McAllister, there would be no turning back.

She stepped into the task force conference room and blinked at the late-night activity. Her gaze jumped to Jake's empty desk.

Billy called across the room. "You looking for J-Mac? He left a while ago."

"No." She had to stop being so obvious. "I left a few things here. What are you doing here so late?"

Billy slumped in his chair and crossed his hands behind his head. "I'm still trying to ID victim number one. I see her face when I close my eyes."

Billy was a smooth operator, but like Jake, he was a good cop. They did this for the victims, and Billy was doing this for his sister. "None of the working girls around Melrose recognize her?"

"No, and it makes it harder going from a sketch. Her face was in pretty bad shape when we got to her, so we're not showing that around. The sketch artist does a good job, but no hits yet." He rubbed his eyes. Even his typically crisp suit looked wilted.

She took a seat in front of her computer and twisted her head around. "Hey, I heard you're interested in meeting a friend of mine, Megan Wright from KTOP."

Billy's head shot up. "I wouldn't mind an introduction—just to do it right."

"You're not married, are you?"

"Separated." He drew a cross over his heart. "My wife and I aren't living together. We're both free to date."

"Then I'll give Megan your card and put in a good word."

"I appreciate that." The phone on Billy's desk rang and he grabbed it. "Crouch."

Kyra watched his face go hard as he listened to the words on the other end of the line.

"Where? Does J-Mac know?"

Kyra's breath came out in shallow spurts. It had to be another victim.

Billy hung up the phone and steepled his fingers. "The SOB has done it again."

"Another one?" Kyra had wrapped her arms around her body.

"This one dumped in the Ballona Wetlands."

Kyra's arms tightened. "That's...bold. It's not exactly the middle of nowhere like the canyons and trails he's been favoring."

He pushed back from his desk. "I'm heading out there. Do you want to come with me?"

"I'll follow along in my own car, if that's okay. The wetlands are closer to my place—too close."

"I'm leaving now."

"I'll be right behind you."

This time, Kyra left the station to follow an LAPD detective in her own car. She didn't ask Billy if Jake was already at the site. If he wasn't now, he soon would be. Would he be surprised to see her? Irritated?

Forty-five minutes later, she pulled behind Billy's car onto a scene bathed in red-and-white lights. She didn't have to plunge into the trees or hike down a trail. The yellow crime scene tape encircled an area just off the paved walkway through the Ballona Wetlands.

She tugged on Billy's sleeve and pointed to a camera installed on a light post.

He shook his head. "I've already been informed that's broken."

Kyra kicked at a rock, and the long grasses of the wetland tickled her bare legs. She hadn't even gone home yet to change clothes.

Given the hour, the only people shuffling in and out of the area were law enforcement, a few members of the press, including Megan, a few homeless people and a young couple. Had they reported the body?

She knew she wasn't getting close to the crime scene so she sidled up next to Megan. "How'd you hear about this?"

"My guy heard it on the scanner. Young couple called it in. As soon as the Sheriff's Department got here, they knew what they had and reported it to the task force."

"So, she must have the playing card between her lips." Kyra kept her mouth shut about the severed finger. That was not general knowledge.

"And the missing jewelry?" Megan put a finger to her lips. "This is off-the-record, but we've heard reports that the killer is taking jewelry from the victims as a trophy. True or false?"

"That falls under things I can't tell you." Kyra folded

her arms in case Megan thought she could wheedle anything out of her.

"This is his fourth victim, all within two months. He's voracious, isn't he?" Megan looked over her shoulder. "And so close to where I live."

"Are you nervous?" Kyra caressed the outline of her gun. Nerves didn't get to her.

"A little. I mean, these victims are a bit younger than I am, but they're not hookers, are they? They're not runaways. They're young women with jobs and school and regular lives."

"Can I give you a piece of advice that I don't want to see on the evening news?"

"Yes."

"Stay away from Melrose Avenue in West Hollywood."

Megan's eyes popped. "For real? Is that where he's picking them up?"

"He's not picking them up there, but let's just say there are some connections to that area that might mean something."

"I swear I'll keep that hush-hush if you promise to give me what you got when the time comes."

"I do." Kyra caught her breath as Jake emerged from the crime scene, the bright lights highlighting the white T-shirt hugging his large frame.

He'd pulled on the same jeans he'd been wearing earlier for his meeting with Matt. It had been the first time she'd seen him out of his suit. The casual clothes suited him better, more in tune with his blatant masculinity.

Megan elbowed her. "There's a hot guy trying to get your attention."

Kyra had been assessing Jake's body so thoroughly she'd missed his cupped hand gesturing to her.

"Speaking of hot guys, Detective Billy Crouch has you in his sights." She slipped Billy's card from her purse and handed it to Megan. "I told him I'd pass along his number."

"Well, thank *you*."

Kyra started toward Jake, who met her halfway.

Of course, he had to get in the first word. "What are you doing here?"

"I was at the station with Billy when he got the news. He invited me along."

He took her arm and whispered in her ear, "Did you get the car back without incident?"

That was not what she expected from his lips with a dead woman in the wetlands. "I did. Is this for sure another victim?"

"Yes. Queen of clubs this time, severed finger, strangulation, no identification. This isn't a fresh kill." He pressed a hand against his chest. "I'm sorry. What I mean is, she was probably killed last night, not tonight. She's far enough off the path to have been missed. This couple had a dog with them, and he discovered the body."

"But so close to civilization. He's getting brazen." She pointed at the camera. "Billy said it's broken."

"It is." Jake scratched at the scruff on his chin. "The killer didn't do it, though. It's been broken for a while, but he must've known that."

"He's thirsty." Kyra sucked in her bottom lip. "You need to stop him because he's not showing any signs of slowing down."

Jake's mouth twisted up at one side. "I know that. I'm waiting for that one mistake, and then we'll close in on him. They all make mistakes."

"The Player never did."

"He did. Even Quinn will tell you he did. Nobody ever

picked up on that mistake. The world is a different place than it was twenty years ago. Murder investigations are different. We'll get this guy." The coroner arrived, and Jake turned toward the van. "I need to finish this up. Get home safely—in your own car."

"Got it." She hesitated. "Will I see you at Marissa's apartment tomorrow? Remember, I'm meeting her room-mate, and we're having a look at her jewelry."

"I'll be there." He swung around and disappeared into the tall grasses of the wetlands.

Kyra walked back to her car and waved at Megan get-ting into her news van. The drive from the Ballona Wet-lands to Santa Monica took her less than fifteen minutes at this time of night.

She pulled into her parking spot. As she walked past the dumpster, she studied the ground. She saw a plas-tic bag that had probably floated from someone's trash, picked it up and slipped it beneath the lid of the dumpster.

Not that she expected another card, with Matt lying in a hospital bed. If Matt was telling the truth and someone had paid him to leave the cards, that person could just as easily pay someone else to do the deed.

But why?

THE FOLLOWING DAY, Kyra saw two clients in the morning and then drove to Marissa Perez's apartment in Reseda, not far from where her abandoned car was found, to meet her roommate, Darcy Myren. Jake had indicated that he'd be late and to start without him.

She pulled alongside the curb in front of a large apart-ment complex and buzzed the apartment number.

A shaky voice answered the intercom. "Yes?"

"Darcy, this is Kyra Chase. Is this still a good time?" For her answer, Darcy buzzed open the door, and

Kyra stepped into the cool, tiled interior of the apartment building. Neat rows of brass mailboxes lined one wall, facing two elevators.

Kyra went up to the third floor, where Darcy stood at the door of her apartment, waiting for her.

Darcy's dark eyes narrowed. "I thought that cop was coming with you."

"He'll be here later. Is that okay?"

"Yeah, c'mon in." She widened the door for Kyra, and she walked into a place in upheaval.

Kyra raised her eyebrows. "Are you moving?"

"I just can't take it here anymore. I know Marissa wasn't abducted from our place or anything, but it just creeps me out that someone could've been stalking her or watching us."

Kyra's pulse jumped. "Did Marissa ever mention being stalked?"

"No." Darcy placed a hand at her throat. "It's just all too weird. I'm staying with friends now, but I'm moving back in with my parents in Orange County for a while. I can't afford this place on my own, anyway."

"That's probably a good idea. Do you want to talk before Detective McAllister gets here? Then we can look through Marissa's jewelry together."

"Okay." Darcy perched on the edge of a floral couch that had seen better days. "Marissa's sister is coming out from Texas in a few days to pack up her stuff."

"Have you looked through Marissa's things yet?"

"I'm too scared to go into her room."

"I understand." For the next half hour, Kyra allowed Darcy to pour out all her fears and anxieties and paranoia.

By the time the external intercom buzzed, Darcy had cried herself dry.

"Is—is that the detective?"

"Probably. Let him up and go wash your face. I'll meet him."

"Thank you." Darcy dabbed at her wet, swollen eyes. "If I need more help…"

"You can see me again, or I can make a recommendation closer to your parents' place."

Darcy hopped up and answered the intercom, punching the button to allow Jake entrance to the building.

As Darcy retreated to the bathroom, Kyra stood by the door to greet Jake.

He strode down the hallway, his face grim, his muscles tense.

She swallowed and stepped into the hallway. "Everything okay?"

"We identified the victim from last night—Gracie Cho." He shook his head. "Graduated from USC last year."

"Any connection to Melrose yet?"

"Not yet." He pointed to the door. "Everything okay with Darcy?"

"She's very upset. Can't even bring herself to look at Marissa's possessions, but it's a good thing we're here. Marissa's sister is coming out from Texas to pack up her belongings in a few days."

"Then let's get to it."

She let Jake into the apartment just as Darcy was returning with a freshly scrubbed face and a red nose. "Hello."

"Hi, Darcy." He swiveled his head back and forth. "You moving out?"

"Yeah. The landlord's letting me break the lease and everything."

"That's good. Do you want to show us to Marissa's room?"

"This way." She led them down a short hallway and

pushed open a door. "Marissa had the master because she made more money than I did and paid more rent."

Jake poked his head into the neat room. "She worked at an advertising agency in Sherman Oaks, didn't she?"

"Yeah, she did online content for them." Darcy sniffed and pointed to a wooden box on top of a dresser. "She kept her jewelry in there, but like I told Kyra, Marissa always wore that jade bracelet. You won't find it there. He took it."

A chill whispered on the back of Kyra's neck. "Let's make sure."

As Darcy hung by the door, Kyra crossed the room to the small dresser littered with makeup, perfume, ticket stubs and all the other accoutrements of a life well lived by a twentysomething young woman.

Kyra flipped up the lid of the box, and stirred her finger through a jumble of costume jewelry. "I don't see a jade bracelet here. Darcy, can you have a look just to make sure?"

"I suppose." Darcy crept toward the dresser as if she expected someone to jump out at her at any moment. Kyra didn't blame her.

Darcy picked through the tangle of necklaces and bracelets, working some pieces loose and setting them on top of the dresser. "Told you. The bracelet's not here."

"Thanks, Darcy. That's helpful." Jake gestured to the door. "Can we talk a little more? Just a few questions that have come up since we last interviewed you."

Darcy beat both of them to the door and resumed her seat on the edge of the couch, looking ready to take flight. "Is it true that this guy gave her a shot of something before strangling her?"

"We think so. You said Marissa didn't use drugs, right?"

"She barely drank." Darcy clutched the arm of the

sofa with one hand, her multicolored nails digging into the worn fabric. "Why her?"

"Probably no reason at all." Jake sat on the chair across from Darcy, mimicking her pose on the edge of his seat. "Do you know if Marissa had any reason to be in the West Hollywood area, specifically Melrose Avenue?"

"Melrose?" Darcy's dark brows formed a V over her nose. "No. I mean, maybe we shopped there once or twice, but not often. That stuff's expensive down there."

Jake asked, "She didn't know anyone who worked there? Didn't have any reason to be there for business?"

Her head jerked up. "Is he finding women there?"

"We don't know that for sure. Just checking out a few things."

"Darcy…" Kyra shot a glance at Jake to make sure he didn't have any objections to her asking a question. He gave a slight nod. "Do you know that Marissa had an empty coffee cup from Uncommon Grounds in her car when they found it?"

Darcy's gaze darted from her to Jake. "It doesn't surprise me. Marissa drank a lot of coffee. She had some crazy hours and fueled up on caffeine. Do you think the cup belonged to someone else and not her?"

"No, just wondering if she ever went to the Uncommon Grounds on Melrose."

"Not that I know of. She usually got her coffee from fast-food drive-throughs. If she had a cup from Uncommon Grounds, that probably didn't happen too often."

Jake's phone buzzed in his pocket and he snuck a peek. His stoic face betrayed just one telltale sign—a muscle at the corner of his mouth twitched.

He stood up abruptly. "As always, Darcy, if you remember anything else, give us a call and follow up with Kyra if you need help coping."

"Thanks. I think I'll be better once I move out of here."

Kyra stood up beside Jake and felt his body vibrating next to hers. "Are you okay by yourself now?"

"I have a couple of friends coming over to help me move. I'll be fine. Thanks—and I hope you find this guy."

Outside the apartment, Kyra turned to Jake. "What is it?"

"Something important from the task force. Someone may have seen our guy." He held out his phone. "I'll call Billy when I get to the car."

She had no intention of missing out on this message, so she dogged his footsteps to his car. He didn't even blink when she got into the passenger seat beside him.

He placed the call and put the phone on Speaker. Billy picked up on the first ring. "J-Mac, aren't you in Reseda at Marissa's apartment?"

"Just finished up there. Whaddya got?" He cleared his throat. "Kyra's listening."

"Perfect. You may need her for this. Once we released Gracie Cho's name today, the task force got a call from a working girl in Hollywood. Two nights ago, she picked up a john who seemed all hopped up on something. They got down to business and the dude had some kinky requests—nothing she hasn't dealt with before, but he did call her Gracie. She didn't think much about it until she saw the name of the victim today. I think we just might have our first sighting of The Copycat Player."

Chapter Seventeen

Jake slammed his fists against the steering wheel. "He slipped up. The bastard slipped up. Give me her info and we'll get right out there."

Kyra grabbed a pen from the console and an envelope from her purse. As Billy recited the name and location of the witness, Kyra jotted it down.

Jake ended the call and cranked on the engine. "Sounds promising as hell."

"That might explain why the killer didn't rape any of his victims." Kyra's knee bounced up and down.

"Didn't want to leave his DNA, but got his kicks with hookers after the murders to satisfy his sick lust."

She clamped her hands on her knees and curled her fingers into the material of her slacks. "If he did this after murdering Gracie, he probably did it after the other killings."

"Maybe Sunny can introduce us to some of her friends." Jake hightailed it to Hollywood and cruised down Hollywood Boulevard, a little tawdry in the light of day.

Kyra squinted at the signs. "She really wants to meet at a hot dog stand?"

"She's not going to give us her address." Jake jabbed his finger at the windshield. "There it is."

"And not even an illegal parking spot available in front."

"I have other tricks up my sleeve." He wheeled the sedan around and pulled into a parking lot that charged five bucks per half hour. He flashed his badge at the parking attendant, who then waved him behind a couple of cars.

"That's—" he turned off the engine "—how it's done."

They walked the half block to the hot dog stand and staked out a table outside under a pink umbrella. She must've been waiting for them because it didn't take Sunny long to spring up from behind a building, her high heels wobbling on the sidewalk as she sashayed toward them.

She definitely had the walk down, but otherwise she could've passed for the girl next door with her slim figure and Bambi eyes. Must've been how Kyra's own mother marketed herself.

Kyra twisted her fingers in her lap and put on a smile for the woman. She had her reasons for doing what she was doing. Kyra was long past judgment.

Jake, ever the gentleman even in the most questionable of circumstances, stood up at her approach. "Sunny?"

Sunny brushed her long hair from her face, lightly made up for daytime. For all Kyra knew, Sunny could morph into a different persona at night.

"Yeah, I'm Sunny. You Detective McAllister?"

"That's right." He pulled out a plastic chair. "Have a seat."

"Who's she?" Sunny aimed a short pink-tipped fingernail at Kyra.

"She's a victims' rights advocate. She's working with me on the case."

"Good." Sunny dragged the chair back and squirmed

into it. "Because I'm a victim here, right? Dude could've killed me, too."

"Why don't you start from the beginning." Jake pulled out a notebook. "Tell me how you met him, what he said, how he looked. If this seems credible, I'll get you down to the station to meet with a sketch artist."

"Credible? You mean like believable?" Sunny tapped one finger on the table. "This is the real deal."

"So, how did you meet this guy and what time?" Jake held his pen poised over the paper.

"Wait. Can I at least get lunch out of this?"

"Sure." He pocketed his notepad. "What would you like?"

"Get me the Hollywood Dog and a lemonade."

"Kyra?" Jake raised his eyebrows at her.

"Same."

He rose from the table and got in line behind two tourists in shorts, clutching maps to the stars' homes.

Sunny narrowed her brown eyes. "He's fine. Probably doesn't have to pay for it, but sometimes that doesn't matter, you know?"

Kyra nodded.

"You'd be surprised at who comes knocking at my door." Sunny held up her fingers and began ticking off the various professions of men who found themselves in need of her services. She'd just gotten to politicians when Jake returned to the table with three dogs and three drinks.

The Hollywood Dog boasted chili, raw onions and corn chips, and Sunny sank her white teeth into the end of the whole mess.

A few more bites and several napkins later, she got down to business. "Okay, this happened the night before last. I was working my corner when this man approached me for, you know, a good time."

"What time?"

"After midnight. I usually work until two when the bars close."

"What did he look like?"

"Average height. I'm about five foot eight with my heels on, and he was a little taller than me. Average weight, not buff or anything." She eyed Jake's shoulders, her gaze slipping to his strong forearms resting on the table.

"Hair?"

"Longish. Below his ears." Sunny drew a line across her neck. "But shaved up on one side. Brown. Brown eyes. Glasses. No facial hair."

"Did you see a car?"

"He approached me on foot. Wanted the full package, so I took him to one of the motel rooms we use."

Jake hunched forward. "Do you remember which one?"

"Before you get all excited, because I know what you're after, he didn't leave any prints in that room because he was wearing gloves."

Kyra blurted out, "Gloves? It had to be over seventy degrees the other night."

"I know, right?" Sunny spread her hands. "That was the first weirdo thing."

"What were the rest of the weirdo things?" Jake slurped down some of his drink.

"He wanted me to lie still with my hands at my sides. He didn't want me touching him." She shrugged. "Hey, less work for me, right? He also put his hand around my neck. Lotta guys do that."

Kyra had to put down her hot dog and swallow fast as the food turned to ashes in her mouth. That alone should terrify Sunny.

"Then he started calling me Gracie. Gracie this. Gracie that."

Jake glanced at Kyra. "Do you remember what he said to Gracie?"

"Not really. Mumbling pathetic things like, how do you like me now, Gracie? Stuff like that. Like he was getting something over on her." Sunny popped the last of her hot dog in her mouth and brushed her hands together. "Couldn't end fast enough for me. He paid with cash and left. Didn't think about him again until this afternoon when I heard the name of one of those victims of The Copycat Player—Gracie. Freaked me out. I mean it's not a common name, am I right?"

"You're right." Jake slipped Sunny his card. "Can you come to the station to sit down with an artist? We'd like to get this sketch out as soon as possible."

"Really?" Sunny toyed with her rings. "Nobody's gonna know it's me, right?"

Jake raised two fingers. "Complete anonymity."

"Then I'll do it. Can you give me a ride?"

"One more thing." Jake crumpled the waxy yellow paper from his hot dog and lobbed it into a trash can. "You said he didn't leave prints in the room because he wore gloves. Did he leave his... DNA anywhere?"

"His DNA?" Sunny rolled her eyes. "You mean his—"

Jake cut in. "Exactly."

"You know—" Sunny tapped her nails on the plastic table "—now that you mention it, he was my last trick of the night. I always head home after the last one to shower at my own place. I haven't done laundry since then, so the clothes I was wearing that night just might have some of his... DNA."

"Yes!" Jake slammed his fist on the table, rattling the ice in their drinks. "That's what I wanted to hear. Is your place nearby? Can we stop by there on our way to the station?"

"Sure." Sunny dabbed her lips with a napkin and picked up her cup. "You really think this might be the guy?"

"Right now, it's the best we got."

After swinging by Sunny's apartment, where she ran inside and returned to the car with a garbage bag full of clothes, Jake drove on to the station and set Sunny up with a sketch artist. He then had one of the officers on the task force bag Sunny's clothes for a trip to the lab.

When he finally collapsed behind his desk, he raised his eyes to the ceiling. "I have a good feeling about this."

Kyra left her own desk to join him. Maybe Brandon should've put her right next to him instead of across the room. "Do you have other task force members questioning some of the other hookers in the area to see if any of them had similar experiences?"

"They're on it." Jake massaged his temples. "He thought he was being so smart by not sexually assaulting his victims and leaving DNA, but he messed up by mentioning Gracie's name. They always mess up."

"The Player never did." Kyra squeezed the back of her neck.

"He did, Kyra. Somehow, some way, he did mess up. Nobody caught it."

"Quinn would've caught it." Heat rose to her cheeks at the tone of her voice. Quinn didn't need her to defend him.

Jake's hand dropped to her thigh. "Helluva detective, but even he'd tell you he missed something. There is no perfect crime."

Her gaze dropped to his hand, and he snatched it away. "I'm sorry."

"Don't be. You don't have to..." She zipped her lips as Billy entered the room.

He rushed over and high-fived Jake. "I think we got this, my man. Thank the heavens for working girls—I mean that from a law enforcement perspective, of course."

"Of course." Jake snorted. "Sunny's still with the artist and her clothes are being tested as we speak. Rush job on that."

Billy said, "I also sent out a team to look for cameras along Sunny's stretch of turf. Maybe we can get this guy on camera, too. Maybe catch sight of a car."

Kyra scooted Billy's chair away from Jake and stood up. "All yours."

"Didn't mean to chase you off, especially since I got a call from Megan today."

"Oh, good." Kyra shook her finger at Billy. "Treat her right. She's coming out of a bad breakup."

"I treat all the ladies right."

"That's your problem." Jake shoved a file toward Billy. "We're tracking down Gracie's last movements. We don't see a Melrose connection yet, but we're not ruling it out. We're also looking for missing jewelry because Marissa's jade bracelet is definitely gone."

One of the officers from the task force called across the room. "Kyra, can I talk to you a minute?"

She left Jake and Billy, heads bent over the file, and approached the officer. "What do you need?"

"Gracie Cho's parents don't speak English, just Korean. We'd like to get someone to help them out. Can you recommend someone?"

"I think so. Are they here in LA?"

"Yes."

"Let me reach out to my contacts. I'll let you know."

For the next hour before the task force meeting, Kyra stayed on the phone searching for a Korean-speaking therapist or grief counselor. She located one minutes before Jake stood up and announced the meeting.

As they all crowded into the conference room; Kyra stood at the back as she always did. Though the team seemed to accept her, she'd caught a few looks from the other officers as she accompanied Jake through the halls of the station. They couldn't accuse her of currying favor with the boss since their jobs and hers were on different planes, but she and Jake didn't need the gossip.

As Jake started the slides, the first one up contained the sketch based on Sunny's description. As Kyra studied the eyes behind the glasses, she shivered. They looked so mild, yet they had an emptiness about them. She could only guess that they took on a different look when he was hunting his prey. His longish brown hair cut shorter on one side was distinctive, though not distinctive enough for the Hollywood or Melrose crowd—if that's where he hung out. That clean-cut barista at Uncommon Grounds was the exception not the rule in that area.

She shifted her focus to Billy, now doing the talking.

"We didn't find a Melrose connection to Gracie. She lived in Encino and worked in Studio City, but we're not done yet. Still no ID on the woman found at the Malibu fire site, so that hurts us for clues. We're asking Sunny, the hooker who gave us the sketch, to put out the word among her girls to step up if they had an encounter like hers and we just might get DNA from Sunny's unwashed clothing she wore the night of her encounter with the man talking about Gracie. Sorry, no prints, Clive." Billy waved to the fingerprint technician standing in the back with Kyra. "We're in the best shape we've been in yet.

So, keep up the canvassing of the Melrose and Hollywood areas. We need to get him before he kills again."

The meeting adjourned, and Brandon placed a stack of the sketches on a table at the exit. As Kyra wandered out, she grabbed a couple.

Back in the war room, Jake stopped by her desk. "Billy and I are headed out for a few more interviews, and then I have a meeting with Castillo before I knock off. Do you need a ride back to your car? You left it at Marissa's apartment."

"If you're going to Hollywood, that's out of your way. Don't worry. I'll get it."

He leaned in close to her. "I just don't want you stealing another car."

She smiled. "I'll get a rideshare."

"I didn't get a chance to tell you earlier. I called the hospital and Matt's still in a coma. Doesn't look good."

Her bottom lip quivered. "I'm not going to pretend I didn't have problems with him, but he was the closest thing I had to a brother."

"No more cards, though?"

"No."

"He was probably lying about getting paid." Jake rapped his knuckles on her desk. "Thanks for coming out with me today to talk to Sunny. I think it helped having you there. The working girls are always suspicious of cops."

"Happy to help, although you did all the talking."

"Have a good night...and be careful."

"I always am." She was lying, and he knew it.

Kyra worked for another hour, but it was still light when Rachel Blackburn called her.

"I hate to bother you, Kyra, but can you meet me before I head home?"

"Of course. Where?"

"You can just come by the shop. I'm closing at eight."

"That's perfect. I have to pick up my car first. I'll see you around eight."

Kyra gathered her belongings and ordered an app car from her phone. She slung her bag over her shoulder and hurried out to the curb in front of the station.

When her ride pulled behind her car near Marissa's apartment, the sun was beginning to set. The strident oranges and reds produced by the haze from the wildfire had subsided to a creamy vanilla orange Popsicle marking the end of the Indian summer. It felt like the closing of a chapter. Maybe that meant the task force would close in on The Copycat Player.

Kyra paused before she got in her car and gazed at the building across the street. Those young women had probably been full of excitement and big dreams when they moved into that place. Now that chapter had ended, too.

She made it to West Hollywood just about ten minutes past eight and lucked out with a metered parking spot on the street. The Closed sign hung in the window of the shop where Rachel worked, so Kyra cupped her hand over her eyes and peered through the glass.

Rachel, behind the counter, waved and held up a finger.

Kyra waited on the sidewalk like a buoy, interrupting the flow of the pedestrian wave that surged around her.

Rachel stepped outside and locked the door. Turning toward Kyra, she dropped her keys in her purse. "Thanks for coming out. I'm doing okay, but locking up at night always got to me, even before my phone was stolen by a serial killer."

"I can understand that. Do you want to sit somewhere?"

"Uncommon Grounds? They're open until ten."

As they walked through the door of the coffeehouse, Kyra said, "You know, we think your phone was lifted here, maybe when you were waiting for your coffee."

"That could be, and it makes me feel a little better. It means I probably wasn't targeted specifically, just a crime of opportunity."

Kyra's lips twitched.

"What?" Rachel nudged her arm. "Why are you laughing?"

"I'm not laughing. Jake... Detective McAllister was right about you. You've got good instincts." Kyra pulled out her wallet. "It's on me."

When they got to the counter, the clean-cut guy from the other day took their order. Kyra glanced at his name tag. "Still here, huh?"

"Ma'am?" Jordy tilted his head, his dark, rather close-set eyes making him look like a bird.

"Oh, I'm sorry. You probably see hundreds of people all day. I was in the other afternoon and you mentioned you don't always work at this store because you don't look the part. It's the hair."

"Did I?" His brow furrowed. "I'm sorry. I don't remember."

"That's all right. I'd like a peach iced tea and..."

Rachel ordered her frothy concoction and they stepped to the side after Kyra paid for their drinks.

Kyra tapped the counter that lined up against the window. "There are charging stations here and everything. We figured you may have set down your phone or plugged it in and forgotten it."

"I don't know about charging it, but I do have a habit of carrying it in my hand and then putting it down, so it's possible." She sighed. "Anybody could've picked it up in here."

Rachel already knew about Kelsey's connection to Melrose, as she'd had her nose piercing done by Gustavo in the shop, but she didn't know about the Uncommon Grounds coffee cup in Marissa's car. Of course, that cup could've come from a number of Uncommon Grounds sprinkled around the city.

Rachel tugged on Kyra's purse strap. "Can you get the coffees? A table by the window just opened up. I'm going to grab it for us."

Kyra nodded as Rachel spun around to nab the prime table. There seemed to be just as many people using this place as their office during the night as there were during the day.

When her name was called, Kyra picked up both drinks and carried them to the table where Rachel was texting. "New phone?"

"I gave up on ever finding my other phone, and I don't know if I'd want to use it if I did." Rachel hunched her shoulders. "Everything was backed up on the cloud, so I was able to restore all my stuff."

"The wonders of technology." Kyra reached into her bag and pulled out the composite drawing of Sunny's john. She flattened it on the table. "We have a sketch of someone of interest to the case. Have you seen this guy around here?"

Rachel smoothed her hand across the face. "He kind of looks familiar, facially, but I'd remember someone with that hair…even here on Melrose." She picked it up and held it close to her face. "Can I keep this?"

"Of course. I have others. Ask Gustavo." Kyra stirred some sweetener into her tea. "Tell me what's worrying you."

Rachel recited some of her fears and tried to brush

them off. But this hadn't been her first encounter with the seedy side of LA and she'd been feeling rattled.

They chatted for almost an hour until the talk turned toward Rachel's future employment. "I already applied for the dispatcher job, and Detective McAllister said he'd make sure my app gets fast-tracked."

"That's great. Have you followed up with him?"

"No, do you think that's okay?"

"He'd expect it." Kyra tapped her cup. "Do you want another?"

"No, but I am going to hit the ladies' room."

When Rachel left the table, Kyra picked up her cup and swiped her thumb through the moisture on the outside. The blue print circling around the cup listed the locations of Uncommon Grounds in the LA metro area. Her finger traced a line through West Hollywood and trailed to Studio City.

Gracie worked in Studio City. Marissa, who had a cup from Uncommon Grounds in her car, worked in Sherman Oaks, next to Studio City. Kelsey had gotten her nose pierced here on Melrose, steps from Uncommon Grounds, and Rachel most likely had her phone stolen from this shop. Three of the four victims had a connection to areas with Uncommon Grounds. West Hollywood. Studio City.

Kyra plunged her hand into her purse, which was hanging on the back of her chair, and dragged out another composite sketch. Why would a killer with a distinctive hairstyle like this visit a prostitute after one of his crimes? One who wasn't afraid of being caught? That didn't describe The Copycat Player. Did he even realize he'd been saying Gracie's name?

Someone touched Kyra's shoulder, and she jumped and turned her head.

"Sorry." Rachel squeezed her shoulder. "I thought I was the jittery one. I'm going to take off now. Are you ready?"

Kyra covered the sketch with her arm. "Actually, I'm going to hang out and make a few phone calls." She scooted back her chair. "Do you want me to walk you to your car?"

"No, I'm good. There are still a lot of people roaming around, and my car's in a public lot." She bent over and gave Kyra a one-armed hug. "Thanks so much. I'm sorry I'm such a wuss."

"Don't be ridiculous. Call me anytime."

Rachel waved at the door and plunged into the steady stream of people on the sidewalk.

Kyra placed the drawing in front of her again. Maybe he'd worn a disguise for Sunny. The hair. She covered the unique cut with her hand and looked at the face. The glasses. She blotted out the lens on one eye with her fingers.

Then her heart slammed against her chest. She recognized that face. Had just seen it.

Chapter Eighteen

As the meeting with Castillo wound down, Jake checked the time on his phone and saw several missed text messages and phone calls. He squeezed the back of his neck. He hadn't had a good night's sleep in days, but the hard work was paying off. The lab found male DNA on Sunny's underwear, and they'd start running it through CODIS tomorrow. If Sunny's john had been arrested for a felony before, he'd be in the system and they'd have their first real suspect.

Captain Castillo went around the room, but everyone was too eager to get out of there to bring up anything else to discuss on the case. They'd have a whole new ball game tomorrow.

As soon as Castillo adjourned the meeting, almost everyone in the room reached for their phones, which Castillo had demanded be silent for the duration of the meeting.

Jake's stomach demanded food, so he took a quick leave of everyone and headed to his car. He got behind the wheel and listened to his first voice mail.

A sheriff's deputy from the West Hollywood division had talked to a streetwalker who echoed Sunny's account with her weird john. Jake called him back.

"Yates, this is McAllister. What do you have on the hooker? Same guy?"

"Sounds like the same guy. Same night as Kelsey's murder, and she thinks he was saying a name but she doesn't remember if it was Kelsey or not."

"That sounds promising. Will she come in and make a statement?"

"She will, but I'm not sure it's the same guy. I showed her the composite, and she said he looked similar but she can guarantee he didn't have hair like that."

Jake ran a thumb along his jaw. "Different hair?"

"And she thinks her guy had a mustache or some kind of facial hair."

"Give me her contact info, and I'll have her come in for an interview and a session with the sketch artist. If they're the same facially, he might be wearing a disguise. He's being careful."

Jake ended the call and pulled out the sketch. He grabbed a pen from his console and drew in a more normal haircut for the man. The face looked even more familiar than it had when he'd first seen the rendering.

Propping it up on his steering wheel, he went back to his phone and returned a call from Billy.

"Sorry, man. I was in one of Castillo's meetings. You know how that goes."

"Mind-numbing." Billy took a sip of something. "We got a little more info on Gracie's habits. She worked in Studio City. Wasn't known to frequent West Hollywood or Melrose at all. So, that's a blank. Looks like she's missing a ring, which I think we can now deduce is his trophy."

"You're right." Jake drummed his thumbs on the steering wheel. "Coffee?"

"Huh?"

"Any coffee cups in Gracie's car, like Marissa's?"

"I didn't process her car, but I can check on the photos. I did tell you there was no way to tell if Marissa's cup came from the Uncommon Grounds in West Hollywood or some other store, right?"

"Yeah, but I'd like to know about Gracie."

"On it. You still at the station?"

"In my car going through my phone. I'm starving. You wanna get something to eat?"

"I'm meeting up with Megan Wright tonight after she does the ten-o'clock news. Tell me that's not sexy?"

"Watch you don't cozy up too much to the press."

Billy chuckled. "That's exactly what I plan to do, my brother. If you can make an exception for a therapist, I can make one for a reporter."

"Whatever. Text me the info on the contents of the car, if you get it."

"Will do. Go eat."

Jake listened to one more voice mail, this one from Rachel Blackburn.

"Hello, Detective McAllister. I just wanted to know if you saw my application come through for dispatcher. I—I just had coffee with Kyra, and she told me it was okay for me to check with you."

Jake sent Rachel a text, indicating he'd seen her app and flagged it for Personnel.

Then he cranked on the engine with the intent to take Billy's advice, and headed to an all-night diner not too far from his place.

As he sat at the Formica table in a booth to himself, he placed his phone in front of him. He had one more voice mail, which he'd been avoiding. After he ordered some meat loaf, he tapped the final voice mail from the hospital where Matt Dugan lay in a coma.

He listened to the news of Dugan's passing and gulped down some water. Should he tell Kyra now? She'd seemed almost sad about Dugan's condition, but she'd be relieved he wouldn't be around to make her life hell anymore... or to tell her secrets.

Molly, who'd been working at this diner for the past twenty years, placed his food in front of him. "I had the cook get you an extra slice of meat loaf, J-Mac. You look like you could use it."

"Thanks, Molly." He dug into the closest thing he'd had to a home-cooked meal in weeks, savoring every bite until his phone buzzed again.

He glanced at the text from Billy, who must be pouring on the cologne in anticipation of his hot date by now. He wiped his hands on a napkin and tapped his phone.

He read the text aloud to no one. "Coffee cup from Uncommon Grounds in Gracie's car."

Jake's fingertips buzzed as he opened the attachment. He studied the photo of the inside of Gracie's car, which had been left on the street near the house of a friend she was supposed to visit the night she was murdered. The coffee cup sat in the cup holder, a smear of pink lipstick on the lid.

With a pulse throbbing in his temple, Jake dug into the bag he'd brought into the diner with him and stashed on the seat beside him. He pulled out a blank sheet of paper and smacked it down on the tabletop next to his empty plate.

As he'd done many times before, he wrote three names across the top—Marissa, Kelsey and Gracie. They still had no ID on the first victim or a car, but he knew Billy would die trying to give that woman a name. Beneath Marissa's name, he wrote that she had a coffee cup from Uncommon Grounds in her car and worked near Studio

City. Under Kelsey's name, he wrote that she'd frequented Melrose Boulevard where an Uncommon Grounds was located. Now, under Gracie's name he could add that she worked in Studio City and had a cup from Uncommon Grounds in her car.

The coffee place could link all three women, although they couldn't be sure Kelsey went to Uncommon Grounds on Melrose. Same coffeehouse but two different locations—West Hollywood and Studio City. That wasn't much of a link.

He tugged on his ear. How had he known about Uncommon Grounds in Studio City? He scrambled in his bag for the altered sketch of Sunny's client and dragged it out, placing it next to his scribbled chart of the three victims.

His nostrils flared with the shot of adrenaline that rushed through his body. He'd known about Uncommon Grounds in Studio City because a barista in West Hollywood had told him about it.

The barista who'd worked in both places and had an uncanny resemblance to the composite sketch.

"JORDY, RIGHT?" Kyra put on her most understanding therapist smile although her heart was thundering in her chest.

The fresh-faced young man glanced up from wiping the counter, his eyes taking a few seconds to focus on her. "Yes?"

"I was wondering if you could check in the back for more scones." She tapped the glass display case of bakery goods. "It looks like you're out, but I'm hoping you have some left. I'll even take old ones or frozen ones, if you can heat them up."

His features seemed to rearrange themselves on his

face, as if sampling a few expressions until he found the right one—friendly, mild annoyance. "None of our items are frozen. All fresh daily."

"Ah, that's why they're so yummy. Can you please check for me?"

His brown eyes shifted around the mostly empty store, which he'd been prepping for closing. "I suppose I can check."

"That would be great. Thanks."

Jordy stashed his towel beneath the counter and made for the back.

As soon as he disappeared, Kyra dashed to the other end of the counter, the pickup area, and hoisted herself across the counter to grab the cup Jordy had been sipping from for the past ten minutes.

What if he saw his sketch in circulation and took off? She could at least grab a sample of his DNA before that happened. She dropped his cup into her bag, which she'd left gaping open and slithered back to her side of the counter, landing on her tiptoes.

She turned to survey the other customers, all too busy packing up their gear, finishing their conversations and getting that last bit of work in before returning to their homes to notice her actions.

She smoothed back her hair just as Jordy returned from the back empty-handed. "Sorry. We don't have any scones left. Can I get you something else?"

"That's okay. Thanks for checking." She pivoted, clutching her bag against her body and charging for the door. He'd already flipped the sign to Closed.

The nighttime air hit her hot cheeks and she walked toward her car on legs she hadn't realized were trembling. She dipped her fingers into the side pouch of her purse for her keys, sweeping from side to side in the narrow space.

She stopped and zipped open the large compartment of her purse. Her hand clawed through her wallet, makeup bag, a small notebook and a bottle of ibuprofen. She shook the purse, listening for the distinctive jingle of her key chain.

Panic gripped the back of her neck with a cold hand. Had she left them in Uncommon Grounds? She couldn't go back there now. What if Jordy noticed his cup missing behind the counter? He'd link it to her request for scones.

She took a deep breath, her gaze taking in the nightspots on Melrose still open on a weeknight. She could slip into one of the restaurants, call Jake and wait for him there.

He wouldn't be too thrilled with her amateur sleuthing, but he'd be happy to get Jordy's DNA once she told him her suspicions—especially once they got the DNA from Sunny's clothing tomorrow.

Another thought seized her imagination. Jordy could have her keys. He'd been near her and Rachel a few times, mopping the floor and wiping down tables.

She took a deep breath. He wasn't going to steal her car, and he wasn't going to wait for her at her apartment. He didn't know where she lived and wouldn't get it from her registration in the car. Quinn had cautioned her long ago to black out the address on her registration just in case someone did steal her car. With the blacked-out address, the thief wouldn't know where she lived... and neither would Jordy.

Unless he already knew. Had Matt really left those cards at her apartment and car?

She placed a call to Jake and it flipped to voice mail. "Jake, I'm on Melrose, just left Uncommon Grounds. I had some suspicions about that barista who works there and I managed to take something of his, but now I don't

have my keys. Long story. Meet me at The Ripe Tomato.
I think they're open until eleven."

She ended the call and hustled to the corner to wait
for the light to cross the street. When she got to the other
side, she waited for a group of people leaving the restaurant and coming right at her. She stopped and moved
to the side.

As she did so, someone came up behind her. She felt
warm breath on the back of her neck and then a sharp
pinch into her flesh.

Gasping, she spun around—right into the arms of
Jordy.

He grabbed her around the waist and draped an arm
over her shoulder. "Whoa, too much to drink?"

She stumbled against him, inhaling the scent of coffee grounds on his clothing. Why was she thinking about
coffee grounds? She fumbled for her gun pouch with
thick fingers, but Jordy easily removed the purse from
her grasping hands.

"I'll take that. You have something else of mine, too,
don't you? So nice, so friendly. They all pretend to be
nice and friendly." His hand plunged into her open purse
and grabbed the cup.

At least he hadn't noticed the gun tucked in the pouch.
Her tongue felt twice its size as she attempted to form
words being transmitted slowly from her fuzzy brain.

He laughed. "Yeah, she had one too many."

He guided her along the sidewalk, which had turned
into a tunnel.

She could barely focus on her feet tripping over the
pavement, Jordy's arm propping her up, Jordy propelling
her to the same fate as her mother.

"No."

"It's okay. I pumped enough drugs into your system,

you'll hardly notice when the world stops turning for you." He continued to march her along, and she was happy for him to do so, as she could barely feel her legs.

She could still feel the occasional brush of another human and hear voices far off at the end of the tunnel. He didn't have her alone, yet.

Then she heard the jingle of keys, the beep of a horn. His car.

"No." The word screamed in her head, but came out like a whimper.

Jordy mumbled something.

"What?" The word sounded like a wisp of air.

"Rule number four. The victim should never be someone you know. Rule number four. Rule number four."

She put all her efforts into forming words with her mouth and tongue. "You know me, Jordy. I know you."

"None of you know me. You pretend you do. Get muffins, Jordy. Get scones, Jordy. Get decaf, half-whip, low-fat, extra foam, shot on the side, Jordy." He maneuvered her to the passenger side of his car, and she couldn't move her limbs to fight him off, couldn't reach her weapon, couldn't get away.

"Rule number four. Rule number four."

"You're violating rule number four, Jordy."

Had he heard her mumbled words?

He propped her against the car and opened the door. Once he got her in his car, he'd strangle her, dump her body and hook up with a prostitute.

"Rule number four. Rule number four," Jordy sobbed as he grabbed her to shove her into the car.

"Stop, Jordy. It's over. Let her go."

Jordy dropped his hands from her body, and she slid halfway down the car.

Had she imagined Jake's voice in her fog. "Jake?"

Jordy ducked and reached into the car. "Get back. I'll kill her if you don't get back."

"Let her go, Jordy. It's over. I called for backup. More cops than you can imagine are going to be rolling up any second."

The scream of sirens punctuated Jake's words, and Kyra hugged the side of the car to stay upright. It was over. She wasn't going to die like her mother.

Jordy grabbed her around the neck and dragged her backward, a cold blade at her neck. "I said I'd kill her, and I will. It doesn't matter anymore. Nothing matters anymore. I broke rule number four."

Kyra bucked against Jordy's hold, creating a sliver of space between them. In that split second, a blast of gunfire cracked through the air.

Wet droplets sprayed her face as Jordy released his grip on her and crumpled to the ground at her feet. She staggered back, her hand sliding against the blood-splattered car window.

Jake rushed to her side, his weapon drawn, the smell of gunpowder permeating the air. He nudged Jordy's body with his foot, and the unlikely killer rolled onto his back, the knife resting on his outstretched palm.

As several squad cars flooded the area, illuminating the sky with their revolving red-and-blue lights, Jake curled a hand around her waist, burying his face in her hair.

"Kyra! Are you all right? Tell me you're all right." He smoothed a rough hand down her throat.

She swallowed and mumbled, "He drugged me, but I'm fine. He didn't cut me."

Jake must've understood her because he gathered her in his arms and pressed his lips against her temple.

"Thank God, you're safe. I thought I'd lost you. I thought I'd reacted too slowly."

Several cops rushed in, weapons drawn, but Kyra had eyes for only one cop. As she rested her head against his shoulder, she said, "You were just in time."

Epilogue

"Kyra said one beer, Quinn."

The gruff detective snorted. "Just because she solved her first murder case, she thinks she can boss us around."

Kyra placed a bottle of beer in front of Quinn. "If I hadn't gotten ahead of myself and had just left Uncommon Grounds without playing amateur sleuth and called Jake about my suspicions, which he already had, maybe the task force could've arrested Jordy Lee Cannon without fanfare and gotten some answers out of him."

Jake grabbed the plates of fish and chips and brought them to the coffee table. "I don't know what we could've gotten out of him. We know how he met his victims—at Uncommon Grounds in West Hollywood and Studio City. They weren't alarmed when he approached them because they knew him from the coffee place or he looked vaguely familiar to them. He plunged a needle into their necks to disable them, got them in his car where he finished them off by strangulation and then dumped their bodies. He maybe tried to throw us off by mimicking The Player's MO, and he took a piece of jewelry for a trophy—we found all the items in his room at his mother's house."

"But not the fingers." Quinn picked up a fry, considered it and popped it into his mouth.

Jake chewed the inside of his mouth. "Maybe he never wanted the fingers as trophies. He just took them to copy The Player and got rid of them."

"To catching the bad guy." Kyra held up her beer, and Jake and Quinn toasted with her, clinking the necks of their bottles.

She said, "He sure seemed upset about breaking rule number four."

Quinn raised his shaggy eyebrows and Jake said, "We think rule number four was not knowing your victim. Jordy figured he was following rule number four because he didn't really know these women. We wouldn't have been able to find out about Jordy by tracing the victims' friends or family. But he knew he'd broken that rule because he didn't choose random victims. He chose women he knew through Uncommon Grounds."

Kyra shook some vinegar over her fish and chips. "I didn't realize serial killers had sets of rules."

"Of course they do." Quinn glanced at Jake. "Did you find his rules or anything like that when you searched his mother's house?"

"Nope. He must've had them in his head. I wonder what the other rules encompassed."

"Obviously, not leaving prints or DNA. He wore gloves and he didn't sexually assault his victims." Quinn shook his head. "A careful killer...just like The Player."

Kyra hunched her shoulders. "I'm just glad you found Jordy's car so fast when you got to Melrose."

"His manager told me where he parked. When Rachel mentioned that the two of you had met for coffee that night and then you left that message about finding something, I got a sinking feeling in my gut. I'm just glad I got there on time. I'd shoot that guy all over again and damn his interview or any lies he could tell us."

Kyra gave him a look from beneath her lashes that made him glad all over again.

She brushed her fingers together. "At least Billy ID'd the first victim, so we didn't need Jordy's help with that."

"Why did that take so long?" Quinn crunched into a piece of battered fish.

"Shelby Shipton was from out of town. She'd pulled up stakes in Idaho and came out to LA to make a new life and pursue her dreams."

"Sounds like someone else I know." Quinn reached over and grabbed Kyra's hand. "I heard about Matt Dugan's death. Are you okay?"

Kyra shifted her gaze from Quinn to Jake and back to Quinn's face again. "I—I was sorry to hear about Matt. He took a bad road a long time ago, so it's not surprising."

Quinn squeezed Kyra's fingers in his gnarled ones. "He won't bother you anymore."

She sniffed and took a gulp of beer.

Was the sadness feigned? Jake knew all too well you could mourn the loss of someone you didn't like.

They finished their food, and he helped Kyra clean up the kitchen while Quinn watched TV. The old detective had gotten a supreme sense of satisfaction when they caught The Copycat Player—must've been almost as good as solving the original. Almost.

Kyra wiped her hands on a dish towel and snapped him with it. "Do you want to go outside and watch the sunset from the bridge?"

"Sounds good." He called into the living room. "Quinn, you wanna go out with us?"

Quinn waved his hand. "You two go. I'm watching my show. I like to laugh at all the stupid things these detectives do—and the public really believes things work that way."

Kyra poked Jake in the side. "You should watch a great movie called *Shots Fired*, Quinn. True to life."

Jake rolled his eyes. She'd never let him forget that… and he hoped she'd keep on reminding him.

With a last glance at Quinn, Kyra opened the front door and stepped onto the porch.

Jake inhaled the scent of the ocean. "It's pretty out here."

"Not quite like Venice, Italy, but not like LA, either."

When they got to the bridge, they sat down, dangling their legs over the water. Jake slipped an arm around her shoulders, and she leaned into him. They hadn't had a real date yet, but what they'd been through together had brought them closer than a hundred *real* dates could.

He pinched her chin with his fingers and kissed her sweet lips, just a little tart from the lemon. But that was Kyra—sweet and tart.

When he pulled away, she stroked his jaw with her fingertips. "Does this mean you don't hate therapists anymore?"

"Never did." He rubbed her back, which arched like a cat's beneath his touch. "I'm liking *this* therapist a lot right now."

The phone next to him on the wooden bridge buzzed, and he groaned. "The pitfalls of dating a cop. My ex-wife never got used to it."

"I'm not your ex." Kyra swept up the phone and handed it to him. "It's Billy."

"Hey, Billy. You're interrupting my private time."

"I didn't know you had any of that, brother." Billy coughed. "You're gonna want to hear this—or maybe not."

"What is it?" A slow dread thrummed through Jake's veins.

"Body just discovered—card in the mouth and severed little finger."

Jake's gut knotted as he grabbed Kyra's hand.

"What's wrong, Jake?"

"Looks like we have another copycat killer."

* * * * *

COMING SOON!

We really hope you enjoyed reading this book.
If you're looking for more romance, be sure to
head to the shops when new books are
available on

Thursday 1st April

To see which titles are coming soon, please visit
millsandboon.co.uk/nextmonth

MILLS & BOON

LET'S TALK
Romance

For exclusive extracts, competitions
and special offers, find us online:

 facebook.com/millsandboon

 @MillsandBoon

@MillsandBoonUK

Get in touch on 01413 063232

For all the latest titles coming soon, visit
millsandboon.co.uk/nextmonth

WANT EVEN MORE
ROMANCE?
SUBSCRIBE AND SAVE TODAY!

'Mills & Boon books, the perfect way to escape for an hour or so.'

MISS W. DYER

'Excellent service, promptly delivered and very good subscription choices.'

MISS A. PEARSON

'You get fantastic special offers and the chance to get books before they hit the shops.'

MRS V. HALL

Visit millsandboon.co.uk/Subscribe
and save on brand new books.

MILLS & BOON
A ROMANCE FOR EVERY READER

- **FREE** delivery direct to your door

- **EXCLUSIVE** offers every month

- **SAVE** up to 25% on pre-paid subscriptions

SUBSCRIBE AND SAVE

millsandboon.co.uk/Subscribe

MILLS & BOON

THE HEART OF ROMANCE

A ROMANCE FOR EVERY READER

MODERN

Prepare to be swept off your feet by sophisticated, sexy and seductive heroes, in some of the world's most glamourous and romantic locations, where power and passion collide.

HISTORICAL

Escape with historical heroes from time gone by. Whether your passion is for wicked Regency Rakes, muscled Vikings or rugged Highlanders, awaken the romance of the past.

MEDICAL

Set your pulse racing with dedicated, delectable doctors in the high-pressure world of medicine, where emotions run high and passion, comfort and love are the best medicine.

True Love

Celebrate true love with tender stories of heartfelt romance, from the rush of falling in love to the joy a new baby can bring, and a focus on the emotional heart of a relationship.

Desire

Indulge in secrets and scandal, intense drama and plenty of sizzling hot action with powerful and passionate heroes who have it all: wealth, status, good looks…everything but the right woman.

HEROES

Experience all the excitement of a gripping thriller, with an intense romance at its heart. Resourceful, true-to-life women and strong, fearless men face danger and desire - a killer combination!

To see which titles are coming soon, please visit

millsandboon.co.uk/nextmonth

JOIN US ON SOCIAL MEDIA!

Stay up to date with our latest releases, author news and gossip, special offers and discounts, and all the behind-the-scenes action from Mills & Boon...

 millsandboon

 millsandboonuk

 millsandboon

It might just be true love...

GET YOUR ROMANCE FIX!

MILLS & BOON
— *blog* —

Get the latest romance news, exclusive author interviews, story extracts and much more!

blog.millsandboon.co.uk

MILLS & BOON

HISTORICAL

Awaken the romance of the past

Escape with historical heroes from time
gone by. Whether your passion is for
wicked Regency Rakes, muscled Viking
warriors or rugged Highlanders, indulge
your fantasies and awaken the
romance of the past.

Six Historical stories published every month, find them all

millsandboon.co.uk/ Historical

MILLS & BOON
MODERN

Power and Passion

Prepare to be swept off your feet by sophisticated, sexy and seductive heroes, in some of the world's most glamourous and romantic locations, where power and passion collide.

ht Modern stories published every month, find them all at:

millsandboon.co.uk/Modern

MILLS & BOON
DARE

Sexy. Passionate. Bold.

Sensual love stories featuring smart, sassy heroines you'd want as a best friend, and compelling intense heroes who are worthy of them.

Four DARE stories published every month, find them all a

millsandboon.co.uk/DARE

MILLS & BOON
True Love

Romance from the Heart

Celebrate true love with tender stories of
heartfelt romance, from the rush of falling
in love to the joy a new baby can bring,
and a focus on the emotional
heart of a relationship.

ht True Love stories published every month, find them all at:

millsandboon.co.uk/TrueLove

MILLS & BOON
MEDICAL
Pulse-Racing Passion

Set your pulse racing with dedicated, delectable doctors in the high-pressure world of medicine, where emotions run high and passion, comfort and love are the best medicine.

Eight Medical stories published every month, find them all :

millsandboon.co.uk

MILLS & BOON
Desire

Indulge in secrets and scandal, intense drama and plenty of sizzling hot action with powerful and passionate heroes who have it all: wealth, status, good looks… everything but the right woman.

Six Desire stories published every month, find them all at:

millsandboon.co.uk

OUT NOW!

Rules are made to be broken

Available at
millsandboon.co.uk

MILLS & BOON